MEANT
TO BE

Edie Claire

NEW YORK   BOSTON

Cover design and art by George Cornell

Warner Forever is a registered trademark of Warner Books, Inc.

Warner Books

Time Warner Book Group
1271 Avenue of the Americas
New York, NY 10020
Visit our Web site at www.twbookmark.com.

Printed in the United States of America

First Paperback Printing: June 2004

10 9 8 7 6 5 4 3 2 1

For the 1985 staff, counselors, and campers of
Pine Springs Presbyterian Camp
in Jennerstown, Pennsylvania—for the best summer ever

ACKNOWLEDGMENTS

I would like to extend my thanks to the following individuals, whose expert knowledge has helped make this book possible: Dru Quarles, MD, Siri Jeffrey, Scott Robinette, Teresa Huhn, Linda Wilson, and the Webmasters of the Turkeyfoot Valley Area High School. I would also like to thank the Western Pennsylvania Conservancy for their excellent guidebook to the Laurel Mountains and for their tireless efforts to protect that region's magnificent forestland.

MEANT
TO BE

Chapter

~1~

WHEN THE CALL came, I had been thirty years old for all of one day. Yet the lemon cake I had baked was already down to crumbs and a smudge of frosting on the plate. The bottle of champagne that I had fully intended to sip slowly stood empty on my counter, surrounded by the tattered bits of cork I had chipped out of it with a screwdriver. My head ached, and my mind was murky. I was unaccustomed to alcohol in general, cheap champagne in particular. All I knew was that last night, I had felt the need to celebrate.

It had been a long time since I had celebrated much of anything.

The beeping of the phone reverberated painfully through my skull, displacing, albeit temporarily, the relentless ringing of my own words in my ears—resolutions made in the midst of my revelry; resolutions I was, even in the excruciating light of morning, determined to keep.

If it was Todd again, I wasn't going to talk to him. He could beg and he could plead, but I would not let him get to me. I would simply hang up—and if that was rude, so be it. The man was not a part of my life anymore. Period.

I picked up the phone.

"Hello," a woman's voice said politely. She identified herself as an administrator at a hospital I'd never heard of. "Is this Ms. O'Rourke? Meara O'Rourke?"

I confirmed that it was.

"I'm sorry to have to tell you this," she continued, "but we have your mother here as a trauma patient. She was in a car accident several days ago and has only now been able to give us enough information to contact you."

I lifted the receiver away from my ear and stared at it with bleary eyes, as if doing so would somehow result in the woman's words making sense. The effort failed.

"I'm afraid there must be some mistake," I answered, returning the phone to my head and rubbing the opposite, throbbing temple. "My mother passed away over a month ago."

My voice was steady as I said the words, and I was proud of that. My mother's death had not been a surprise; it had come at the end of a protracted illness, as had my father's five years before. In both instances I had functioned as the primary caregiver, the emotional rock. But the reality of my mother's death had hit me far harder than anticipated. I had been an only child; now I was alone. There was no extended family to lean on, no one with whom to share my grief. Only Todd.

What a joke that had turned out to be.

There was a long pause on the line before the woman spoke again. "I'm not sure what to tell you, Ms. O'Rourke. Ms. Sheila Black is a patient here, and she has identified you as her daughter and next of kin. A Mr. Mitchell Black, her husband, was killed in the same accident. We spoke with his family when Ms. Black was admitted, but apparently the couple had only been married a short while. His children were not able to provide any information about her, or we would have contacted you sooner."

The throbbing ceased—replaced with a gnawing coldness in the pit of my stomach.

Sheila. Could it be?

My mind began to replay the image of an afternoon six years before, an afternoon I had resolved to forget.

I had taken only two steps inside the coffee shop before catching sight of the woman I was there to meet. I had known her at once; even a child could see the resemblance. Though her auburn hair was pulled back into a short ponytail, the wavy tendrils that escaped around her face betrayed the same unruly tresses I battled. Her eyes were just as brown, her cheekbones high, her lips full. Her face was only slightly rounder than my own, her nose a tad more prominent. Physically, she appeared fit and around forty, yet something about her countenance implied a greater age. Or perhaps, experience beyond her years.

When her gaze caught mine, her eyes widened. Her wrist faltered, and a liberal dollop of coffee splashed onto the red and white checked tablecloth below.

So, I had thought with a smile. My clumsiness must be inherited.

Meara? the woman asked hopefully, attempting to mop up the coffee with a tiny square of napkin.

Yes, that's me, I had responded, my heart pounding against my breastbone. *And you must be Sheila.*

The voice on the other end of the phone now grew concerned. "Ms. O'Rourke? Are you all right? I'm sorry about the confusion, but we do need to straighten this out. Do you know this woman? Sheila Black?"

My response caught in my throat. Did I know her? No, I did not. I had met her only once. A cup and a half of coffee for me; three for her, plus the spilled one. Two Danishes, neither finished. We had both been far too nervous to eat.

I'm so very glad you could meet me here, she had said, studying my face as if trying to memorize it. I found myself doing likewise. *I'm sure you must have a lot of questions,* she continued, fidgeting with her cutlery.

Questions? Of course I had questions. My parents had been two of the most loving people on earth, but because they had a tendency to panic whenever the subject of my adoption was raised, I learned at an early age to consider the topic taboo. Only after I had finished school and was living on my own did I even contemplate searching for the woman who gave birth to me. Once I made the decision to sign on to a registry, however, I had received a call within days. Yes, the intermediary explained, my biological mother was also registered. And she wanted to meet me.

I trained my mind back on the present. "I'm sorry," I apologized. Then I winced. Ceasing to apologize for anything and everything had been Resolution #2—broken already. "What I mean to say," I corrected, "is that I may know of the woman you're referring to. Was her maiden name Johnson?"

Papers shuffled on the other end of the line. "The only other name I have is Tressler. Are you saying that you are not this woman's daughter, then? Perhaps we misunderstood. She is having some difficulty speaking."

I let out a breath, and my lungs shuddered. "No," I answered. "You probably heard her right. My birth mother's name is Sheila, that much I know." Tears of frustration welled up behind my eyes. I had worked hard to close this particular door, and I didn't want anyone muscling it open again. Particularly Sheila herself.

"I'm sor—" This time I caught myself. I cleared my throat. "I didn't make the connection at first because I haven't seen or heard from her in years. And the truth is, I'm not sure I wish to see or hear from her now."

Another silence passed, after which the woman said, slowly and pointedly, "Ms. Black is in critical condition, Ms. O'Rourke. The doctors are not at all certain that she will recover from her injuries. Her instructions to the nurses were that she wanted to speak to you. I don't know what else I can say."

Guilt swelled within me as the memory of Sheila's sweet, concerned voice badgered my mind. *Is there anything else you want to say?* she had offered. We had talked for forty-five minutes. I thought everything had gone splendidly.

May I contact you again? I had asked. Exuberant, optimistic, naive. She had smiled and written her address and phone number on the back of one of the coffee shop's customer survey cards. I had thrust it in my purse, my heart full of hope for our future relationship. An uncertain one at best, yet for the first time in my life, one not totally out of reach.

I'll call you sometime, I said as we parted.

I'll look forward to it, she had answered.

I had lived in the clouds for weeks afterward . . . until the day I worked up enough nerve to invite her to a home-cooked dinner. Only then did I discover that the number she had given me was that of a pizza delivery outlet, no employee of which had ever heard of a Sheila Johnson. The street address hadn't existed at all.

My hand began to shake as I held the phone. I tried to steady it, but the pain of that moment, once remembered, was difficult to dislodge.

How could she? How could she cut me out of her life not once, but twice—deigning to claim me only in her hour of greatest need?

"I'll leave you to think about it, Ms. O'Rourke," the administrator concluded. "Let me give you directions to the hospital, just in case."

My hand reached for a pen, and with unstable fingers I scratched down the information. We hung up, and I stood for a long time, staring idly at the letters and numbers. Sheila was at a community hospital in Pennsylvania's Laurel Mountains. I was living north of Pittsburgh. It was a two-hour drive, maybe less. Two hours was all that separated us. All that separated me from final closure—or, perhaps, from even greater heartache.

The old Meara would have vacillated—afraid to reopen wounds, afraid to offend. But eventually, she would have decided to go. She would have gone because she felt obligated, because she felt she owed something to the woman who gave her life, no matter what else that woman had—or had not—done for her.

But not the new Meara. The new Meara—as of yesterday—was taking responsibility for her own life and her own happiness.

I would make that same trip to the hospital, yes. But I wouldn't be doing it for Sheila. I would be doing it for me.

Chapter

~2~

"CAN I HELP YOU?"

The bearded young man in the blue cotton uniform could have been anyone from an elevator mechanic to a brain surgeon—his hospital security badge wasn't saying. It identified him only as Ted Inklovich.

I looked at the empty nameplate on the wall outside what I hoped was Sheila's room. After having been told twice by the receptionist in the lobby that the person I was looking for was not listed as a patient, I was finally directed here.

"I was told that Sheila Black would be in this room," I explained courteously. Having spent more than enough time in hospitals the last few years, I was well used to the typical visitor frustrations. It took more than one clueless receptionist to upset me—any unsolicited offer of help was a pleasant surprise. "But as you can see," I explained, "her name isn't listed. And I don't want to intrude on a stranger."

"She's in there all right. Are you a family member?" He smiled at me from an unjaded face that was probably all of twenty. A nursing student, perhaps?

In no mood for an argument over semantics, I nodded my head.

"Then you can go on in. Her name's just not up yet. They brought her down from ICU this morning—she has the room to herself."

I swallowed. Even as I had made the drive, argued with the receptionist, found the room—a part of me hoped that the confrontation might still be avoided. Sheila could have changed her mind. She could have left explicit instructions not to see me. She could have been miraculously cured and walked out of the hospital without looking back.

But none of those things had happened. Here she was. And here I was.

"Do you want to talk to somebody about her condition?" the man offered. "Her nurse's name is Jan. I can ask her to come down."

I smiled. "Yes, that would be wonderful. Thank you."

He returned my smile, and I couldn't help but notice that it came with a certain telltale sparkle of the eyes. Though my first instinct was to drop eye contact, it occurred to me that I was no longer obligated to deflect any and all male attention. Not that Mr. Inklovich would be the least bit interested in me if he knew my true age—but after living with Todd's insecurities, being free to flirt again, however innocently, was a bit of a charge.

"I'll go talk to her nurse," the young man confirmed; then he turned and walked toward the nurses' station.

At his departure my temporarily buoyed spirits plunged once again, and it took no small amount of willpower to face Sheila's door. *She's been moved out of the ICU,* I thought to myself as I forced my fingers to turn the knob. *That must mean she's going to make it.* I pushed the door open just wide enough to admit myself, then slipped inside.

The bed loomed large in the room, tethered by an assortment of tubes and cables to a series of whirring, beeping machines. I approached the bed slowly, my eyes trained on the pale face that lay silently on the pillow, surrounded by a tangled mass of graying auburn curls.

I doubt I would have recognized her. Not only was she six years older, but the accident had taken its toll. One side of her face was bandaged, the other was bruised and swollen. Her eyes were closed, her breathing loud, but steady. She was sleeping.

I stood silently for a moment, trying to draw from her face some understanding of who Sheila Black really was. After our last meeting, I had eventually come to accept that the woman I thought I had met did not exist. The sweet, pleasant woman I thought I was getting to know wouldn't have lied about wanting to contact me again—wouldn't have set me up for such a disappointment. But the real Sheila would—and did. Why?

The battered face held no answers. It showed only a human being as frail and vulnerable as any other. Hurt. Helpless. And with her husband's death—alone. Except, theoretically, for me.

I breathed out slowly, picturing her for a moment as a scared, immature, and pregnant sixteen-year-old. The story she had told me was a predictable one. Her conservative parents had demanded she relinquish the baby. She had not felt as if she had a choice.

The girl's actions I could understand. Those of the forty-year-old woman in the coffee shop, I still could not.

"Hello," a voice behind me announced.

I turned around.

"You must be the daughter," a stout woman in her fifties surmised. "I'm Jan, the head nurse."

Her voice seemed unnecessarily loud, and I greeted her in a whisper, hoping she would follow suit. I had no desire for Sheila to wake up. Not yet.

"She suffered multiple internal injuries," the nurse continued, her volume only slightly reduced. "But she's been holding her own since the surgery. As soon as she came off the ventilator she asked about her husband, and around here we believe in being straightforward with patients, so we told her he was gone, and that her own condition was critical. The next thing she did was ask to see you."

I gazed at Sheila's broken face. Why now? She could have contacted me at any time in the last six years. My number and address had changed several times, but I was always listed in the phone book.

"The surgeon's not at the hospital at the moment," the nurse explained. "But I can give you his office number, or you can come by about seven in the morning and catch him on rounds. In the meantime, administration has some forms they'd like you to fill out."

Any words of response stuck in my throat. None of this seemed real. The woman in the bed was a stranger to me—how could I suddenly be responsible for her? I had nursed my own mother for months, worried over her, prayed over her, turned my own life upside down for her. I had spent countless hours driving back and forth to medical appointments, fetching prescriptions, sleeping upright in hospital chairs, and doggedly defending her interests with an army of doctors, technicians, and insurance bureaucrats.

I had never thought twice about it. At an age when many couples were already grandparents, she and my father had taken me in and adopted me as their own. They had given me a stable, warm, loving home. Taking care of them in illness seemed the least I could do in return.

But the woman in the bed before me was *not* my family. She was not even a friend. Yet the general assumption was that I would take care of her, too. The question was: should I?

It's in your nature to be nurturing, a good friend once told me. *You like taking care of people. It's a wonderful quality, Meara, but you can't let people take advantage of you. No one has any right to make you their doormat.*

Doormat. A painful word. But a tendency I had to force myself to acknowledge when my mother's illness brought problems with Todd to a head. He had been taking advantage of me—of the most basic aspects of my character. And if I had gone through with the wedding, he always would have.

But the wedding was off, thank God. And the free rides were over. Never again would Meara O'Rourke be any man's doormat.

Or for that matter, any woman's.

I turned to face the nurse. "You have to understand something," I explained. "I am this woman's biological daughter, but we have no relationship otherwise. I've only met her once, and I only came today because I was told she wanted to speak with me. I am not prepared to assume any kind of legal responsibility for her—if that's what the hospital needs. I'm sorry, but that's just the way it has to be."

The nurse's face turned stony; and my resolve began to crumble. I had not even gotten through the speech without apologizing. Was I being completely cold? Unfeeling? Maybe the nurse had a right to disapprove. Maybe it was selfish for me to—

"Mandy?"

The hoarse, uneven tone was barely audible, but it cut through the air like a siren. I turned my gaze back to the bed. Sheila's eyes were open, and she was looking right at me.

My body seemed frozen. I said nothing.

"I'll leave you two alone for a while," the nurse answered, her voice once again unnecessarily loud. "If you have any problems," she said to me specifically, "just buzz the desk." She pulled the call-button device from the back of the bed and moved it to the edge of the mattress, within my reach. Then she left the room and closed the door behind her.

My heart thudded rapidly in my chest. I met Sheila's eyes hesitantly, only to be shocked by the fondness in her gaze. Her eyes twinkled with joy, seeming to drink me in. Her mouth attempted to smile, but the swelling around her jaw allowed only the slightest upward crinkling of her lips. Her hand moved haltingly on the mattress, then slid off the edge toward me.

I stared at it dumbly. She wanted to hold my hand. Our previous meeting had been pleasant, but without any physical display of affection. Now she almost seemed to be begging.

Without further thought, I took her hand in both of mine. It was cold. Very cold. Her lips curved a tiny bit more.

"My name is Meara," I corrected, my voice cracking.

Her head nodded ever so slightly. She continued to look at me with eyes that radiated warmth—even love. I squirmed with discomfort. Did she even know who I was? Perhaps her head injuries had made her delusional.

"I heard that you wanted to see me," I continued in a stilted tone. I wished I could release her hand and step back. Nothing about this felt right. I didn't know her; she didn't know me. It was too much.

"Meara." She said the name distinctly, and her eyes assumed a different look. A deliberate, almost pleading look that seemed designed to convince me she knew exactly who I was. She worked her lower jaw for a moment, as if limbering it for her next words. Speaking was obviously painful for her.

She squeezed my hand, and spoke slowly. The words were slurred, but I understood.

"I always loved you, Meara."

My body went rigid. Involuntarily, I began to pull away. But she quickly tightened her grip on my hand, fixing me with soft brown eyes that, so like my own, displayed her emotions like a billboard.

She seemed perfectly sincere.

I averted my eyes, and moistness welled up behind them as I gathered my thoughts. The woman was hurt, perhaps dying. Now was not the time to chastise, or to judge. She had carried me inside her body for nine months—I could certainly stand by her bedside for a few minutes. As of yet, she hadn't asked for more.

Her hand tugged at mine, relenting only when I looked at her. Her expression was changing again. The warmth was still there, but another emotion was taking the forefront: determination. She began to speak, but her voice cracked, and she closed her eyes with pain. When she spoke again her words were slurred and softer, and I had to lean in close to her face to discern them. "I was protecting you," she said firmly, as if making an announcement. "Rosemary died."

She swallowed, and this time the pain made her grimace. Then her whole body stiffened, as if the grimace itself had hurt even more.

I watched helplessly, frustrated at having no idea who or what she was talking about. "Don't talk if it hurts so," I suggested. It was plain to see that Sheila felt what she had to say was important. But the message wasn't getting through, and I couldn't bear to watch her suffer on my account. "We can talk more when you're feeling better," I assured.

Her head shook almost violently on the pillow, and her eyes filled with agitation. I wasn't sure, but it seemed that one of the monitors, beeping steadily before, had increased in speed. My own heart began to race, and I moved my free hand to press the call button.

Sheila was trying to talk again. I shook my head, but her eyes showed desperation, and I leaned in close to her lips once more. "Stay—" she spat out emphatically.

She tried to say more, but seemed to be losing control of her tongue. Within seconds the monitor tone became steady; then a second alarm followed, this one louder and unmistakably ominous.

Before I could decide on further action the door flew open, admitting the head nurse and several others. "Wait outside please," the nurse barked, shoving her way to the bedside. Sheila's grip on my hand had loosened, and I knew, to my horror, that the relaxation wasn't voluntary. I released her and backed away.

Two more people pushed into the room, rolling an equipment cart. One paused to lead me out. "You'll have to wait here," she insisted, depositing me in the hall next to a laundry bin.

I backed myself to the opposite wall of the corridor, then slumped against it. My mother had died peacefully in her sleep, but my father had died much like this. One moment he was attempting to move from the bed to a wheelchair. The next, he was gone.

Gone.

I drew in a breath. Sheila had no right to do this to me. I had seen enough death. I had buried enough parents. This could not happen.

A short woman with a distressed expression hastened down the corridor and into Sheila's room, the tails of her long white lab coat flying behind her. The summoned physician, I was sure. The door closed again.

I'm not certain how long I stood leaning against that wall, wishing I were tall enough to rest more of my weight on the handrail. People came and went from Sheila's room, others strolled past, unaware. Like a computer screen stuck on the hourglass, my mind was in gridlock. I had too many questions. Too many conflicting emotions.

Too much fear.

At some point I realized that a man was standing beside me—quietly, patiently, as if waiting for me to notice him. He appeared to be around sixty, intelligent and well dressed, with an air of authority. I had the impression that he was an attorney, and he proved me right.

"Hello," he said pleasantly, though keeping his tone suitably sedate. His eyes, even as he spoke, flickered occasionally from me to Sheila's door; showing he was not unaware of the situation. "I'm sorry to intrude, but my name is David Falcon. I'm an attorney, and I'm here because I was hoping to speak with a Ms. Meara O'Rourke. Might you be her?"

I didn't have the opportunity to answer. The door to Sheila's room opened, and the woman in the white coat emerged. The head nurse followed at her elbow, then pointed discreetly in my direction. But I didn't need for anyone to tell me the news.

My birth mother was dead.

The door between us had shut again.

Chapter

~3~

"Is there anyone I can call for you, Ms. O'Rourke? You seem quite shaken—I'm sure you shouldn't drive."

I turned toward the man sitting in the lobby chair next to me, thinking that although he must have been somewhere in my vicinity throughout the haze of the last hour, this was the first time I had really looked at him.

No—it was the second.

His kind gray eyes warmed, as if he perceived that he was finally making mental contact. He reached out a hand, and I shook it. "David Falcon," he explained again. "I'm the attorney representing Mitchell Black, who was your biological mother's husband. I'm terribly sorry to have contacted you at such a bad time, and my business can wait. But I hate to leave you here alone under the circumstances. Is there someone I can call for you?"

The man's build was slight, his face and nose both narrow. With his perfectly white hair and gray eyes, he bore more than a passing resemblance to my father, and I found myself wondering if he was Irish.

"That's very kind of you," I answered. "But no, there is no one."

His eyes saddened. I knew that I should appreciate his empathy, but his concern only seemed to widen the hole in my heart.

"That is to say," I explained, "there's no one you need to call for me. My friends are all hours away—I'll be fine."

He considered. "You live in Pittsburgh, isn't that right?"

"North of the city, yes."

"And you plan to drive home tonight?"

I had to smile at his gentle prodding. "I gather you don't think that's wise."

He smiled back. "As I said, you seem quite shaken. Perhaps it would be best if you stayed nearby tonight. Tomorrow there will be—" He hesitated a second. "Arrangements to be made for your mother. And there are several important matters I must discuss with you as well."

I tried to concentrate on what he was saying, but a jumble of similarly legalistic words still swirled in my head like a cyclone. *Regret to inform . . . surgical reconstruction . . . dehiscence . . . cardiac arrest . . . no way to accurately predict . . .* There had been people to talk to, forms to sign. I had consented to have the body sent to the nearest funeral home, wherever that might be. I had no idea how I would pay for another burial.

My parents' protracted illnesses, combined with poor health insurance and even poorer success in the stock market, had wiped out their life savings even before my mother had died. The pending sale of their house would cover their debts, assuming no hitches were encountered on its inspection. But my own savings were scant indeed. Even though I had a coveted job in one of the highest-paying school districts in Pennsylvania, I had not yet paid off my own school loans.

But, I resolved, trying to snap my bleary brain back into focus, the money wasn't important. The fact was that my biological mother was dead, and if she'd had no one to turn to besides me, then my life had unquestionably been the richer of the two. The suddenness of it all had been a shock, yes, but it was time I pulled myself together.

"You're probably right," I said crisply, straightening my back. "It would be foolish for me to drive back tonight, when there is still business to be settled here. Perhaps you could recommend an inexpensive motel?"

He studied me, appearing to be in deep thought. "I know just the place," he said with a smile. "And it won't cost you a thing."

I assumed that he was going to invite me to his own home, which was beyond the call of duty. "Oh, no," I said quickly. "I don't want to put anyone out."

"You won't be putting out a soul," he said, his voice a tad melancholy. He started to say something else, then thought better of it, and sat back in his chair. "I suppose that it might be prudent if we did discuss some of our business now. That is, if you think you're up to it."

I tried not to bristle. The more birthdays stashed under my belt, the more resentful I became of being perceived as a shrinking violet. It still happened frequently. I was petite, with long, curly auburn hair and large, thickly lashed eyes that people couldn't seem to resist comparing with those of furry animals. But my appearance had no relation to my psyche. I was smart, and I was strong. I took care of other people—not the reverse.

"I am most definitely up to anything," I stated. "What is it that we need to discuss?"

His eyes widened slightly, but he proceeded without further comment.

"The situation is this, Ms. O'Rourke. My client, Mitchell Black, was the owner of an estate very near here, on Laurel Ridge. The estate includes close to five hundred acres of forest, as well as the Sheepsworth Inn, a stone mansion built in 1835 that is an historic landmark—and until recently was a thriving bed-and-breakfast. There is also a farmhouse on the property, though I don't believe it's inhabitable at present."

I listened with interest, being a lover of both forests and old things, but I could not fathom the relevance.

"Mr. Black passed away a week ago today, as I suspect the hospital told you. At the time of his death, he was legally married to your biological mother, Sheila Tresswell Black. Because Mr. Black's most recent will had not been updated after his marriage, and because there was no prenuptial agreement in effect, the law dictates that Sheila was entitled to half of his estate. And unless we discover that she had either a will of her own, or another living descendant, her share in that estate will be passed along to you."

I blinked. Sheila's heir? That couldn't be. "But I only met the woman twice," I protested.

The lawyer shook his head. "That doesn't matter. What matters is that Sheila named you as her next of kin. Even though you were adopted, if the facts indicate that you are her only living biological relative, you will be her legal heir."

I sat still a moment, stunned. Hadn't the administrator stated that Sheila had only been married a short while? My mind began to spin again. Black, Tresswell, Johnson. No prenup. How many times had Sheila been married?

She had told me at our last meeting that she was single and had no other children—but it was impossible to know whether to believe her. Had she ever been divorced? Widowed? I tried hard not to assume that she had been some sort of gold digger. But I couldn't help wondering.

"Among Sheila's personal effects," he continued, pointing to the plastic bag that I was—unbeknownst to me—clutching tightly in my hands, "I'm sure you'll find a set of keys. She and Mitchell were living in the back end of the closed bed-and-breakfast; the rooms up front and on the second floor have been sitting empty for a while, but should still be comfortable. Under the circumstances, I'm sure Mitchell would want you to make yourself at home there. I should know," he asserted, the sad smile returning, "I was his friend for many years."

"I'm sorry," I responded sincerely. Mitchell had been dead only a week—I had probably just missed his funeral. Hadn't the administrator mentioned on the phone that he had children, too? "The offer is very kind. Thank you."

The lawyer seemed pleased. "Wonderful. I must tell you, though, that the signs for the inn have been taken down, and it isn't an easy place to get to in the daylight, much less in the dark. So you'd best follow me there. In the morning, I'd like to sit down with you to discuss this in more detail."

I looked into his kind gray eyes again, and believed his concern to be genuine. My swimming brain was in desperate need of some peace and quiet, and an otherwise empty bed-and-breakfast seemed the ideal location. Entering what had been Sheila's home could be unsettling, but given our lack of familiarity, not unbearably so. And perhaps tracing her footsteps, even the last few, could help me to understand her better.

At this point, surely nothing could confuse me more.

The lawyer's Lexus pulled out of the inn's drive, the sound of tires grinding on gravel being replaced with that of a gradually fading engine, then silence. I breathed out a slow sigh, then locked the door behind him.

It was a dark, starless night. The Sheepsworth Inn, being uninhabited, had been devoid of outside illumination as we arrived, and the glimpse of the structure offered by my car's headlamps was sufficient for little more than to confirm that it was a two-story building made of stone.

Mr. Falcon had looked at me oddly when I extracted my overnight bag from my trunk and headed inside. He had said nothing, but I wondered with amusement if he thought I was the sort of woman who routinely woke up in strange places. The truth was far removed. Rather, I was a woman who had spent more than one morning after a supposedly in-and-out hospital visit brushing my teeth with a paper towel. Going prepared had become habit.

As I turned and stood in the foyer, gazing with admiration at the prominent wooden beams of the cathedral ceiling and the splendid curve of the staircase that climbed toward them, I felt profoundly alone. Not in the sense of being frightened, but rather, deeply melancholy. A place like this was meant to be filled with people. Laughing, eating, snoring. Its emptiness now seemed an aberration, much like the hollowness pervading my own body.

My eyes traced the foyer's ornate moldings and finely crafted stair rail—surely grandiose for their time—and most definitely their place. I stretched out a hand toward the newel post, enjoying the cool smoothness of wood polished by over a century's worth of palms.

In doing so, however, I allowed my keys to slip to the floor. Cursing my clumsiness, I bent to retrieve them, and it was upon rising that the sensation struck me. I remembered such a staircase. A very old one, with wooden steps and a runner of carpet tacked down the center. The newel post was high; it seemed as though I had to reach up—rather than down—to grasp it.

I stood up straight again. There was no telling what I was remembering, or even if it was real. I knew that I had not been passed directly from Sheila to my parents; there had been years of foster care and bureaucratic red tape in between. All my life I had been left to wonder about that time—where I had been, whom I had known. My desire to fill in the gaps had at times consumed me, making every inkling of déjà vu, every oddly familiar face, suspect. And when I was anywhere near Somerset, Pennsylvania, the mind games I played with myself escalated.

According to my birth certificate, I had been born only a few miles from here. It was a fact my heart refused to forget, and one that no doubt prompted me, year after year, to return to the area for hiking trips and summer camp. I had only to see the name of the town printed on a road sign, and my pulse would begin to pound. The emotional ride could be exciting at times, but it was always pointless. In my head I knew that I could be remembering any staircase. Or more likely, no staircase at all.

Resolving to keep my mind in the present, I mounted the steps. If Sheila and Mitchell had supposedly lived in the rear of the first floor, I would stick to the second. I did want to look at Sheila's living quarters—at least to the extent that my conscience would allow the snooping. But not tonight. Tonight I wanted only a clean bed and a quiet place to sleep.

The stairs groaned as I walked, and I noted the pronounced dip in each step's center, wood worn thin by thousands of feet. The walls were tastefully papered, the wainscoting well preserved. I stopped when I reached the broad landing, first intrigued by the comfortable bench that offered mid-climb respite, then mesmerized by the wooden cuckoo clock above it.

I stared at the timepiece dumbly for a moment, wondering if my eyes were deceiving me. Perhaps it was molded from some sort of plastic? I stepped forward, daring to touch the feathers of the sparrow that clung to its left side, perched upon the thinnest of branches and posed, worm in mouth, as if just having landed. No, the clock was definitely made of wood. It had been carved by hand, and it was exquisite.

A second sparrow formed the clock's apex: its breast swelled proudly, its beak open to celebrate the day—or perhaps, the accomplishment of its labors. The area of the clock around the cuckoo's door had been fashioned into a nest, its uneven sides heaving with twigs and down. It was not a sanitized, romanticized version of a bird's nest, and it was this imperfection that made it appear so real. The remainder of the clock's body was formed of branch and tree trunk, decorated with finely veined leaves; a circular knot of bark disguised the clock face itself. The cuckoo hole opened out into the nest's base, and I was dying to see if, as I suspected, the stroke of the hour heralded a featherless baby bird.

As I traced my fingertips over the clock's intricate

contours, I couldn't help but think of my true mother. Colleen O'Rourke had dearly loved wood carvings in general, and cuckoo clocks in particular. My father and I had bought her several over the years, but neither of us could ever have hoped to afford one as magnificent as this.

A thought struck me, and my heart skipped a beat. I had seen work like this before—and so had my mother. Amid her collection of magazines regaling the lives of the rich and famous—a fascination she would have been reluctant to confess outside the confines of our home— were several mentions of custom carvings from Herringtons of San Francisco, one of the most prestigious, if not the oldest, fine furniture enterprises in the country. My mother had routinely fantasized about ordering a "custom" carving, joking that she would like a cuckoo clock from which her own head popped out, instructing my father to wake up, take out the trash, and turn off the television for bed.

I leaned in closer, searching the corners and base of the clock for an insignia. I found what I sought on the underside of a leaf that sprang off the right edge, but only by feeling for the indentations first. What was the name I was trying to recall? I had to contort myself to make out the writing in the dim light, but eventually I succeeded.

Ferris Mountain.

My breath caught. The clock had indeed come from Herringtons—it was their signature brand. I backed away a step.

Five hundred undeveloped acres in the mountains was a fabulous legacy, but only people who also had serious capital on hand could afford such a treasure. Had Sheila been that wealthy? Or, more likely, had her husband?

I walked the rest of the way up the staircase, feeling more out of place than I had a moment before. Ostentatious wealth was foreign to me. I had never had money. I likely never would, and that was fine. Getting rich was not on my list of birthday resolutions. Building my own happiness was.

I could see better, however, why Mr. Falcon had wanted me to stay here. He had wanted me to see firsthand what was at stake. Apparently, I stood to inherit one-half of this property not through a well-thought-out testament on the part of the principals, but through an accident of timing. The situation must be a disappointing one for Mitchell's children—a hopelessly awkward one for me.

As I opened the first door in the upstairs hall and switched on the light, my heart fell further. The room was beautiful. A four-poster oak bed with spiraling leaves of ivy towered toward the ceiling, bedecked with a skillfully crocheted spread. Every stick of furniture in the room was wood, most of it handsomely carved. I walked from piece to piece, examining them with awe, but was relieved to note that all of these were antiques. None were from Herringtons.

Perhaps the clock was an extravagant gift, I reasoned, for an innkeeper who obviously appreciated the medium. I walked slowly through the other rooms upstairs, impressed that they had all been kept up so well, despite the inn's closure. Each was unique in decoration and character, many with hand-painted borders or murals. All were lavishly furnished. And though I inspected several other wooden pieces I thought for certain must have been fashioned by the same artist as the cuckoo clock, none bore the famous insignia. Each time I failed to find it, my nerves relaxed.

Sheila and Mitchell weren't filthy rich, I assured myself, not completely understanding why it mattered. All I knew was that I didn't want to fight—didn't want to argue with these unknown heirs of Mitchell's who clearly held all moral, if not legal, rights to his property. These treasures were not mine, and I would not allow myself to pretend that they were.

I had reached the doorway to the room farthest from the staircase, my overnight bag still in hand. Where would I sleep? Had the inn been open, occupied, and alive, the choice might have been a pleasant one to make. But there was something about these rooms that unnerved me. I felt vaguely ill at ease, and watchful. *Surely anyone would feel uncomfortable staying in an inn alone,* I reasoned, but even as I did so, I knew that my discomfort was somehow deeper. More directed.

I opened the door to see a brass bed jutting out into the room, unable to lay flat against any wall because of the slant of the ceilings. Low-backed furniture lined the walls along with dormer windows, built-in bookcases, and cabinets. In the inn's early days, this space had probably been a servant's quarters. One could stand up fully only in the center; a tall man, not even there. In modern times the area might have been redesignated as an attic, but instead, it had been updated with ingenuity, providing a cozy resting place with unique hideaways that any child, and perhaps some short adults, would relish.

Yet the sight of it chilled my blood.

I slammed the door shut in my own face, then stood perfectly still, breathing heavily. What was wrong with me? Was I losing my mind? There was nothing to be frightened of here. Nothing. The inn was empty.

So my heart should slow down.

I remained there, standing in place, until I was convinced that it had. Then I returned with shaky steps to the staircase.

I was hypoglycemic—that was all. I hadn't eaten since lunch. I had suffered a succession of shocks on top of a hangover, and now I was tired. The inn was beautiful, not evil, and to think otherwise could only mean that I had been reading too many gothic novels. Rooms were rooms, beds were beds. Perfectly ordinary people had slept here. Perfectly ordinary people would sleep here again.

Starting with me. Tonight.

Returning downstairs, I walked into the room closest to the front door and shut it behind me. *There.* Nothing wrong with this room, was there?

I looked around. The room was decorated in shades of rose. An ornate iron, queen-sized canopy bed lay between the two large front windows, bathed in eyelet and smelling of floral-scented room freshener. I stepped to the windows and pulled the curtains closed. No, there was nothing wrong with this room. It was feminine, and it was lovely, and I was *going* to get a good night's sleep here.

No matter how loud my instincts screamed otherwise.

Chapter

~4~

"WAKE UP, GOLDILOCKS. The bears are home."

I twisted under the heavy comforter, attempting to focus my bleary eyes. I had not, in fact, gotten a good night's sleep. What I had done was toss and turn until two o'clock in the morning, only then falling into a fitful slumber laced with manic, nonsensical dreams. I was exhausted, I was cranky, and I was sick to death of trying to ward off my stupid, irrational fears.

Which is no doubt why, when I awoke to the sight of a strange man standing in the doorway, I was more annoyed than frightened.

Both my eyes and mind snapped back into clarity. I assessed the intruder.

He was a large man—tall, broad-shouldered, and solid. His full head of hair and smooth, deep voice seemed to indicate he was not much older than I. But given that the hallway was still dim, with only a few streaks of morning light seeping in around my curtains, I could not tell much more. Except that he had no business barging in and waking me up.

"Goldilocks," I retorted irritably, "was a blonde."

He moved forward a half step, coming into the light just enough that I could see his face. The fact that he came no closer assured me that despite his obvious disapproval of my presence, he did not want me to feel threatened. His eyebrows rose slightly at my words; then he offered a glare.

"Who are you?" he demanded. "And why are you here?"

I didn't answer immediately. The old Meara would feel terribly guilty about now, babbling to explain her presence and apologizing for the confusion. But the new, non-doormat Meara was determined to stand her ground. She was also in an uncharacteristically foul mood.

"You answer first," I said simply, sitting up.

The man emitted what could best be described as a growl—appropriately, under the circumstances, reminiscent of a bear. "I," he grumbled, "am the guy who owns this place. *You* are trespassing."

I looked back at him with a stab of guilt despite myself. I had hoped he was merely a caretaker. This could be awkward.

"You must be Mitchell Black's son, then," I stated, pulling back the comforter and slipping out of the opposite side of the bed. The yellow sweats I was wearing were decent, but hardly optimal for meeting a stranger of the opposite sex. "I'm sorry about your father," I said genuinely.

He offered no response. He simply stood there staring at me with displeasure, much like one viewed a fly on the window when no swatter was available.

"If you'll be so kind as to get out of here for two minutes," I proposed, my voice crabby again, "I'll get dressed, and we can have a civilized conversation."

"You have one minute," he snapped back. Then he turned and stomped out of the room.

I was dressed in two minutes, but decided to wait three. I had just put my hand on the doorknob when a phone rang somewhere in the rear of the inn. My birth mother's erstwhile stepson answered it on the first ring, his deep voice carrying easily to my ears as I opened the door and stepped out into the hall.

"David! Why are you calling here?" He made the connection quickly. "You sent this girl over here, didn't you? What gives? Who is she?"

A pause. I had been moving slowly down the hall toward the sound, but stopped as I heard him growling under his breath. "So what if she's Sheila's daughter? She can sleep at the hospital. That woman as good as killed my father, and you know it!"

I took a step back, my limbs suddenly feeling heavy.

"Well, none of that matters now, does it? He's gone. The inn is mine, and I want it empty. So you can tell—"

There was a long period of silence. In its midst, I thought I heard a single, muffled "no," followed by the creaking of a wooden chair.

"He wouldn't do that to me," the voice protested. Its tone had turned serious now—so sober the very air around me seemed to chill with its vibration. "He wouldn't."

Another silence.

"I won't have it, David," he finished, his voice so low now I could barely understand. "This can't happen. You understand me?"

The phone slammed.

Realizing that I had involuntarily flattened myself against the wall of the foyer like a spider, I pulled myself upright. In the next instant, Mitchell's son appeared at the end of the hall, then stomped along it with heavy strides. There wasn't sufficient room for him to pass me politely, so he didn't bother. He brushed by me as if I were a coat-rack, his gaze straight ahead, his broad shoulder forcing me to flatten myself again.

Only after he had opened the door of the inn did he turn around and meet my eyes.

In the full light I could see that his hair was an unusual shade of light brown, perhaps blond as a child. Its bushy locks framed striking eyes of an indeterminate color, while a chiseled jawbone showed several days' progress at a beard. It was a handsome face, or at least it might have been if the jaws in question were not clenched with agitation, the eyes filled with animosity.

But then, I had always been good at ignoring the su-perficial. Physical appearance meant little to me; I prided myself on having a good eye for the soul within. True, when it came to matters of the heart, my lying-SOB-o-meter had thrice failed me. But when my head was in charge, I could often see right through people.

Which is why I was so certain that this man was not as angry as he seemed. What I saw instead, even in that briefest of glances, was a man who had been hurt almost more than he could bear.

A wave of compassion washed over me, and I started to speak. But I wasn't given the chance. He whirled around, stepped outside, and slammed the door behind him.

I stepped forward to follow.

Don't, Meara, a stern voice inside me proclaimed, *he's not your problem. You didn't create this mess, remember? Besides, for all you know, he could be dangerous.*

"Oh, for heaven's sake," I responded irritably, and out loud. "That man is *not* dangerous." I groused at the conflict my resolutions were already causing me, but I did stop walking. The old Meara would not have. The old Meara would have torn out after him, apologized profusely for accidentally inheriting half of his inn, and offered to sign whatever papers were necessary to return the property immediately. Then she probably would have made him hot chocolate.

Not anymore.

The phone rang again, and I leapt at the distraction. I followed the sound through the hall and out into the inn's common room, an attractive, high-ceilinged glass sunroom that enclosed what must have originally been an outdoor courtyard. Its view of the hills beyond, dressed with verdant leaves and bathed in the sun of a clear June morning, was magnificent.

The ringing sound originated from a small office area tucked into a corner of the sunroom near the entrance to the kitchen. I slipped inside, picked up the phone, and said hello.

"Ms. O'Rourke? David Falcon."

"Yes," I responded, trying to sound more cheerful than I felt. "It's me. But if you're calling for Mitchell's son again, I'm afraid he's left."

The lawyer sighed softly. "I'm terribly sorry about this, Ms. O'Rourke," he apologized. "I had no idea that either of Mitchell's children were back in town. I tried to reach them last night just in case, but—" He turned quiet for a moment.

His emotional turmoil was obvious, and it made me uneasy. Not only did the situation with Sheila's inheritance appear more complicated than I knew, but judging from the conversation I had just witnessed, I wasn't the only one in the dark. "I take it Mitchell's son wasn't aware of his father's will," I suggested. "Or rather the lack of an updated one?"

The lawyer cleared his throat. "No, I'm afraid not. Fletcher had no idea—and that was my fault. I knew how hard he was going to take the news, and because of that, I thought it best to hold off until after the funeral. But he disappeared so quickly after the ceremony I didn't have a chance to speak with him. I've been trying to reach him ever since, but he wasn't answering at his home and his cell phone has been off." He exhaled in frustration. "I doubt he's even aware that your mother has passed on—unless you mentioned it, of course."

At the words "your mother," I winced. First at the hospital, now here, the sound of them had begun to grate. I knew that to others the distinction of semantics might seem petty. But for me, to acknowledge anyone other than the woman who raised me as "mother" felt disloyal—and just plain wrong. "If you could refer to her as Sheila, I would appreciate it," I requested. "And no, we didn't discuss anything. But I would," I began, pulling up the desk chair and settling in, "appreciate a more complete explanation of whatever it is I seem to have walked into."

A family portrait, hanging above the desk in a simple brass frame, caught my eye. A middle-aged couple stood close together in front of an aged white frame house; two young people knelt at their feet, wrestling to keep an Old English sheepdog between them. The woman was thin and somewhat pale, but she had a warm face and a merry expression. The man was of average height and build, with wavy hair. He had the sort of soft, gentle features that tag a boy as "baby-faced," but which make a man look both handsome and kind. One arm encircled his wife's waist; the other rested protectively on the shoulder of a slender girl, whose long, dark straight hair and slightly slanted eyes gave her an exotic quality distinct from her parents. The boy's hands were busy with the sheepdog, which had been lunging sideways across the girl's lap as the picture was taken. He was looking at the dog, rather than at the camera, and was laughing heartily. He had the same high cheekbones and light eyes as the man who had just stormed out, but his hair was reddish and his face was thin, shining with a sentiment the mature version had lacked. Happiness.

"I apologize for the awkwardness, Ms. O'Rourke," the lawyer continued. "But I'm afraid the issue of Sheila's marriage and inheritance is rather complex, which is why I hated to burden you with it last night." He cleared his throat once more. "I'll start at the beginning. Mitchell Black lost his first wife a year ago. He was devastated, and so were the children. The bed-and-breakfast fell apart when she became ill—Mitchell had neither the interest nor the ability to keep it going by himself. After she died, he withdrew from everyone and everything, including his friends."

I stared into the man's eyes in the photograph, and felt that I could imagine him. Supportive, helpful, but not a natural leader. He would look for a strong, capable woman, devote his life to her, then quite unintentionally become completely dependent on her.

"As for when and how he met Sheila," the lawyer continued, "I'm afraid that I can't answer that. The fact is, until the hospital notified me about Mitchell's accident, I had no idea he was even seeing anyone, much less that he had remarried."

An uncomfortable lump swelled within my insides. *That woman as good as killed my father,* the son had said. Mere thoughtless, angry words? I could not squelch the term that floated in and out of my consciousness every time my eyes landed on another piece of the inn's fine furniture. *Gold digger.*

"Apparently," the lawyer continued, "the couple eloped to Las Vegas, married, and took a brief honeymoon. They were on their way home from the airport in Pittsburgh when the accident occurred. We might not have known of their marriage at all if the certificate had not been in Sheila's purse. Naturally, I investigated the situation immediately. But the document is perfectly legal."

My stomach had turned to lead. *It's not your fault, Meara,* the rational voice in my head practically screamed. *You are not responsible for your birth mother's character.*

But as I stared again at the portrait, I knew that the heaviness in my gut would not be so easily lifted. A few months ago the smiling, innocent man in the picture had been newly widowed, the sole owner of prime mountain property and an elegant inn. He had probably been a sweet soul. Lonely. Weak-willed. The definition of an easy mark.

What had Sheila done?

"Mr. Falcon," I interrupted, attempting to keep my voice firm. "What did Mitchell's son mean when he said that Sheila had killed his father? Was she driving the car?"

My heart beat so loudly against my chest that I was sure the lawyer could hear it.

"Ms. O'Rourke," he replied gently. "It is a fact that Sheila was driving, yes. And slightly excessive speed was apparently a factor in the severity of the impact. But the authorities have concluded without a doubt that what happened was an accident. The car hit a deer on the road, then swerved into a tree."

My breath let out with a whoosh, but my nerves were far from settled.

"I understand your concerns," the lawyer continued evenly. "And I assure you that at first, I shared them. But I have uncovered some additional information."

Restless, I rose from the desk and began to pace the sunroom, portable phone in hand. As I glanced out across the vista I caught a brief glimpse of a figure emerging into a clearing on the facing hill, then disappearing into the foliage again. It was almost certainly Mitchell's son; he had been wearing jeans and a bright blue shirt, and at no point in the morning, I now recalled, had I heard a car's engine. But if he hadn't driven to the inn, where had he come from? And where was he going now?

"You see," Mr. Falcon stated, his voice slightly uncomfortable, "I took it upon myself to personally contact the individual who performed the marriage ceremony, because I felt obligated to verify that both parties were sober at the time."

I cringed and closed my eyes.

"What I learned was somewhat surprising to me," he continued. "I found the minister a friendly and reasonably intelligent man, who seemed only too willing to attest to the fact that the couple were not only perfectly sober at the time of the ceremony, but that they were, in his self-proclaimed expert opinion, very much in love."

My eyes flew open, and my eyebrows rose.

"So you see, Ms. O'Rourke," he explained. "I now find myself in a bit of a bind. Had Mitchell sought my advice prior to his marriage, I would of course have insisted on a prenuptial agreement. Had he refused that, I would have had him revise his will immediately to ensure that his children would have no difficulty claiming whatever he wished them to inherit. But," he added without bitterness, "it appears that my rather impetuous friend, perhaps genuinely in love again, chose to cut me out of the loop. Taking into account what the officiating minister has said, I cannot, in good conscience, operate under the assumption that Mitchell did *not* want Sheila to share in his estate."

He paused a moment, and I heard without difficulty the words he wasn't saying.

"And yet," I surmised, "it hardly seems likely that Mitchell would be happy to see half his estate go to an illegitimate child of Sheila's that he probably didn't realize existed. Am I right?"

The lawyer was silent a moment, and I could picture him wincing. "Provided that no other relations of Sheila's come forward," he said gently, "you are legally entitled to one-half of Mitchell's estate."

Legally, but not morally?

I sat down again, plunking an elbow onto the desktop and dropping my chin heavily into my palm. Mitchell's children would undoubtedly contest the inheritance, whether or not their father's attorney supported the effort. The situation had the potential for a good deal of ugliness. I couldn't let it come to that.

I opened my mouth to say as much, but the lawyer continued. "My recommendation to you, Ms. O'Rourke, is that you consult an attorney of your own, and the sooner the better."

My head swam. I was supposed to pay for a lawyer now, just to shore up my claim for Sheila's money? Money that I never asked for, much less had any real right to?

Resolution #3: I will actively pursue my own happiness.

The memory of my perhaps ever-so-slightly drunken words rattled loudly in my skull. Had I meant them, or hadn't I? If so, there was no reason I should be so quick to dismiss the possibility of good fortune. How did I know that Mitchell wouldn't have wanted Sheila to share in his wealth—or that she wouldn't have wanted me to? Why should I automatically assume that Mitchell's children were devoted and deserving? For all I knew, they were nothing but spoiled, selfish brats who would squander their father's life savings in a week. Perhaps something good was meant to come out of all this. Perhaps I was the one to make it happen.

Bolstered, I stood up again, carefully avoiding another glance at the portrait. "Perhaps I will get an attorney," I replied.

"Good," the lawyer answered. Yet his voice, far from approving, was almost dispirited.

I tensed with frustration. "Is there anything else you need from me before I head home?" I asked. Though the lawyer was honest enough to follow through with the dictates of the law, his preference that Mitchell's property stay in the family was clear.

"Yes," he responded, "I have some papers you'll want to look over—I'll bring them by whenever you're ready. But also there's—"

His voice trailed off awkwardly; then he regrouped. "I need to tell you that shortly after the accident, Mitchell's daughter, Tia, decided to look around the inn for any identifying information of Sheila's that might be helpful to the hospital in locating her family. The contents of her purse weren't sufficient; apparently the address on her driver's license was out-of-date, and she had no credit or other ID cards."

No credit cards. Fake address. My stomach twisted again.

"Tia came up empty-handed," he continued, "but she did find a fair amount of women's clothing and personal items stored at the inn, which led her to believe that Sheila and Mitchell had been living together before they eloped. If you would be willing to go through Sheila's personal belongings yourself and determine what should be done with them, I'm sure the family would appreciate it."

His last two sentences barely registered as my mind locked on the first. "Mitchell's daughter didn't know about Sheila, either?" I asked, almost in a whisper.

There was silence, and I envisioned the lawyer squirming uncomfortably at his desk. "Apparently, Mitchell chose not to inform either of his children about the relationship. Not that they weren't close," he explained, almost defensively. "There were regular phone calls between them, but Tia is an artist—she flits about the East Coast and only rarely visits the inn. Fletcher lives in California, but ever since Rosemary became ill, he's been back quite often—"

My body stiffened.

Rosemary.

I had not forgotten the words Sheila had spoken with her final breaths. They would be ingrained in my memory forever. "Who is Rosemary?" I asked.

"Rosemary was Mitchell's first wife," he explained. "Fletcher and Tia's mother."

I looked back at the portrait on the wall, and the room seemed to spin. *Rosemary died. Stay—*

Stay where?

I pictured Sheila's eyes again. Determined. Desperate. Then finally—afraid. Was she afraid for herself because she knew she was dying? Or was she was afraid of something else?

"You'll have to excuse me, Mr. Falcon," I said hurriedly, my thoughts racing as I scanned the green hills through the windows of the sunroom. "But there's something I have to do."

Chapter

~5~

I LOCKED THE front door behind me, then skirted the inn's
edge and walked out into the meadow behind. Cupping
my hands around my mouth, I called out the name
Fletcher, then paused to listen for a response. None came.

I walked out farther and looked around. An aged,
white frame house was visible on a small rise to my right,
and though I recognized it from the portrait I'd seen a few
moments before, something about it held an odd fascination for me. I was tempted to take a closer look, but I
knew that if I were to have any prayer of catching up with
Fletcher, I couldn't dawdle now. Turning in the direction
that I had last seen him, I scanned the border of the woods
for some sign of a trailhead and decided to move toward
the lowest point of the clearing, where one opening in the
brush seemed particularly wide. There, a trail did indeed
present itself, and into the forest I went.

Despite my earnestness in wanting to question the
man, hurrying proved difficult. The woods were brilliant.
Fresh young leaves fluttered in a light breeze, sending
shafts of sunlight dappling onto the ground cover below.
The trail was wide and well traveled, winding through

magnificent stands of mature oak, maple, and poplar trees. Clusters of smooth sandstone boulders dotted the hills at irregular intervals, inviting adults to rest and youngsters to climb. And as the trail steepened in its descent to the ravine below, outcroppings of shale began to appear, while narrow rivulets trickled with clear water.

When I reached a wooden footbridge traversing a shallow stream, I had to pause. The streambed was filled with tumbled rocks, creating innumerable tiny, swirling eddies and producing a pleasant splashing sound beyond what seemed possible for such a small volume of water. I felt a sudden impulse to kick off my shoes and wade barefoot amid the stones, but knowledge of the water's chilling temperature stopped me.

I looked up the trail toward the next hill, and still seeing nothing human, called out again, "Fletcher? Fletcher Black?"

There was no response. I felt ridiculous yelling in the midst of such a natural paradise, but I couldn't give up yet. Not when I had no idea when, or if, I would see the man in question again.

I tripped the rest of the way across the bridge and started uphill, noticing soon after that as the grade became steeper, the trail became narrower, traveled by fewer feet.

Wimps, I muttered, motivating myself. I enjoyed hiking, though with my thin leather loafers I was ill-prepared to do battle with a dew-drenched mountainside. Picking out the driest footing possible, I proceeded with determination, and I had not climbed far before finding myself in a small clearing. The same clearing, I was sure, in which I had glimpsed my quarry just a few moments before. Two paths led away—one twisting back down to the ravine, most likely to complete a loop, the other, much narrower trail heading still more steeply upward.

I took a deep breath, grabbed on to a sapling, and commenced climbing. Fletcher had come this way. He must have, or I would have passed him already. Either way, he should surely have heard me shouting by now.

The trail was rough in spots, but despite the dampness now seeping through my shoes, I was enjoying myself. I moved along steadily, finding easy footholds in the plentiful roots and rocks. The cool mountain air felt good in my lungs, and the exercise was exhilarating.

I had been ascending for nearly fifteen minutes when I reached a plateau with another small clearing. I moved to its edge, scouring the visible forest for any signs of movement, then called out again. "Fletcher! If you can hear me, say something! I just want to talk to you!"

I saw nothing, and there was no response. "Blast the man," I muttered out loud. "I *know* he can hear me." Frustrated, I picked up a small stone and threw it out over the ravine. When it fell lamely to the forest floor not twenty feet away from me, I groaned. Sheila had been determined to explain something to me before she died. Now the one person who could clear up that puzzle was ignoring me.

I whirled around, prepared to trek back down the path in failure. I had only spun halfway before a sight so startled me I nearly stumbled.

There, not fifteen feet away, was the man in question. He leaned casually against a giant slab of sandstone, his long legs crossed at the ankle, his arms folded over his chest. He hadn't made a sound. He still didn't.

My face flushed with heat as I realized he must have been watching me. Gearing up my best teacher's voice, I started to reprimand his rudeness, but something in his expression stopped me. The mask of hostility he was wearing might look fierce, but it could not fool Meara O'Rourke. One penetrating glance into those curious eyes of his—bluish-gray one moment, sea-green the next—and I saw the same emotional wound I had sensed at the inn. A pain so deep my own gut reeled with its impact.

His body language, however, was stoic. Both were so different from the carefree, laughing youth in the portrait, I began to wonder if it was indeed his picture I had seen. But as shafts of sunlight broke through the leaves and bounced over his tawny hair, telltale streaks of red confirmed the likeness.

I reminded myself that the man had buried his father just days before, and had only within the last few minutes learned that half his inheritance was gone. It would behoove me to tread lightly.

I smiled politely and stepped forward. "I'm sorry if we got off on the wrong foot," I began, granting myself a freebie on the apology. After all, it was for a good cause. "My name is Meara. Meara O'Rourke. I'm Sheila's biological daughter, but I didn't know her well."

At my last words, he shifted his weight off the rock and stood up straight. "Didn't?" he repeated. His deep voice, though not loud, seemed to echo among the trees.

I nodded. "She died last night."

Now his eyes studied mine. He took a step toward me, and I felt a sudden urge to step back. I wasn't afraid of him, but there was something about him, something about his very presence, that gave me pause. It was probably an inherent bias, I told myself, based on my unfortunate experience with Derrick, my college sweetheart. A bodybuilder and Cary Grant look-alike, Derrick had stolen my heart during freshman orientation and kept it in the palm of his hand right up until we had attended different graduate schools, at which point he dashed it to the ground and stomped on it.

I had been careful from that point on not to be fooled by handsome princes, and this man easily rated five alarms. Still, there was a ruggedness to him that was anything but aristocratic. He exuded a homespun, down-to-earth independence that, princely face or no, was sharply inconsistent with velvet and tights.

Well-fitting jeans, on the other hand, did him justice. Not that I noticed that sort of thing. Ever since Derrick's betrayal, I had been immune.

I stepped back anyway.

At my news, his eyes flickered with what I was certain was compassion, though he seemed determined not to express it. "I'm sorry," he said shortly, keeping his voice deadpan. "I hadn't heard."

My brow furrowed. His distant, brooding demeanor was clearly meant to be off-putting, but the act was wasted on me. I wasn't sure what the man was really like, but I was quite certain that he was not being himself now.

"Thank you," I answered warmly, trying to be optimistic. It was only natural for him to have his guard up where my motives were concerned. But short of childish spite, why wouldn't he be willing to answer a few simple questions?

"I followed you here for a reason," I began, gauging his reaction carefully. "I was hoping you could clear something up for me. Sheila asked to see me after the accident, and I happened to be in her hospital room right before she died. She was trying to tell me something, and it seemed very important to her. But I couldn't understand it, and she wasn't able to finish."

I took a breath. His face remained impassive. "What she said was *'I was protecting you. Rosemary died. Stay—'* I couldn't make out the rest. I was hoping maybe you would know what she meant by that."

I had no idea what sort of response to expect from him, but what I got surprised me. His eyes widened, and his muscles tensed. Worse yet, he stared at me as if I had struck him. When he spoke, his voice was hard and brittle, as if he were expending a great deal of effort to control it. "I never met this Sheila," he answered, "and I have no idea why my father married her. But I do know that she had no business even mentioning my mother's name, and neither do you."

He turned his back on me. "Now I'd appreciate it if you would get off my mountain," he ordered over his shoulder. "If you need a lawyer, get one. But don't be following me around."

The words were harsh—they were meant to be. The fact that he was already heading farther up the trail was a clear sign of my dismissal.

But I would not be dismissed so easily. Something I said had obviously struck a chord with him, and I wanted to know what. "I realize the subject is upsetting," I explained patiently. "But this is important. Sheila was trying to send me some sort of a message. I think she was trying to warn me about something."

He stopped, exhaled gruffly, and turned around. "I have no idea what the woman was talking about," he retorted, "and I don't care. Good-bye."

He presented his broad back once more, then began climbing.

My spirits plummeted. His ignorance seemed sincere.

Sheila's words still badgered my brain. *Rosemary died.* Of course she had died—everyone knew that. Why tell me? Was Sheila attempting to justify her marriage? *I was protecting your interests as well as my own . . . his wife was gone, he was lonely, what was the harm?*

My feet felt cold. Partly because my socks were soaked through, and partly because I sensed that I had stepped into a situation much more complicated than it appeared—and perhaps more unsavory.

I stared after the retreating form that moved nimbly up the hill away from me. The man was reeling with both pain and resentment, and understandably so. He had lost both of his parents within a year, and now he believed that Sheila—and, by extension, I—were stealing something that rightfully belonged to him and his sister.

Perhaps Sheila had. If so, would I?

Of course not. I wanted to tell him he had nothing to fear from me—that I would never feel right profiting personally from my birth mother's death. But I couldn't shake the feeling that my personal gain might not be the only thing at stake—that I owed it to Sheila to at least try to understand the situation before making promises I had no right to make.

I always loved you, Meara.

The words haunted me. I had resolved to be strong, that never again would I let my soft heart make me vulnerable to another person's manipulation.

But despite every way in which Sheila had dropped the ball, despite however shallow or immoral a person she might have been, I knew that I couldn't turn my back on those desperate brown eyes that had—in their last moments of life—looked into mine with such affection.

And if I thought I could, I was kidding myself.

"I *am* sorry about your father, Fletcher," I called out, trying to keep from my voice the sadness that swelled within me. "And I'm not trying to make trouble for you. I don't want to be your enemy."

He paused in mid-climb, and for a moment I thought that he would turn around and say something.

But I was wrong. He continued climbing, and within seconds he was out of sight.

Chapter

~6~

I**T DIDN'T FEEL** right—looking through Sheila's things. No matter how many times I reminded myself that it had to be done and that there was no one else to do it, I still felt as though I were trespassing.

There wasn't much to see: one dresser filled with lingerie and separates, and perhaps half a closet's worth of hung-up clothes. On the closet floor lay two large, battered suitcases, which I assumed were empty until I picked them up. When I realized they were full, a heaviness settled over me.

Had Sheila, in her forty-six years, amassed only enough belongings to fill two suitcases and a couple of garment bags? Or did she have another home somewhere?

My heart beat fast as I dragged one of the suitcases out of the closet and heaved it onto the master suite's exquisite four-poster mahogany bed. The bedroom was no more ornate than the others in the inn, but its bathroom was larger, and it was connected to a small sitting room and walk-in closet. My guess was that the room had once been rented like all the others, but that Mitchell had moved here from the white frame house sometime after Rosemary's death. Like Sheila, the belongings he had carried to the inn were bare bones. If he had been a man of gadgets and tools, he had left them elsewhere.

My hand trembled slightly as I fidgeted with the suitcase's metal latches, though what I was afraid of, I wasn't sure. The lid creaked upward on stiff hinges, and as I gazed at the contents beneath, I breathed a sigh of relief. More clothes. These for colder weather, including a worn leather jacket, wool hat, and gloves. A pair of weatherproof boots. A decorative hand mirror. A plastic snow globe from the Washington Monument.

That was all.

I closed the suitcase again, pushed it aside, then retrieved its mismatched mate. The second was almost as big, but not nearly as heavy. I lifted it onto the bed and opened it hurriedly, anxious to end the process.

On top lay a faded handmade quilt in a Texas Star pattern, well used, but carefully folded. Below it lay a single book: a King James Bible, red, leather-bound, and worn. I lifted the Bible and opened it. The inscription page was blank, dashing my sudden hope of uncovering some of my biological family's history. Yet, as I ran my thumb along the book's outside edge, I noticed that there were gaps among its gold-gilded pages. I slipped a finger into one, and my breath caught as a tiny black-and-white picture fluttered down onto my lap.

I picked it up.

The picture was of a baby. A typical hospital newborn shot—showing only a tiny head with squinting eyes and one clenched fist. The infant, like most babies at that tender age, looked annoyed. Its dark, wavy hair was sparse.

It looked like no one I knew, but then, most newborns didn't. I flipped the photo over.

Amanda Michelle.

I sat motionless for a moment, then turned the picture over again, staring into the tiny eyes. Could it be me?

Yesterday in the hospital, Sheila had called me Mandy. Either the infant in the photo was me or, in her delirium, she had confused me with someone else.

A sister?

My heart leapt, and I worked hard to rein in its exuberance. Having—or finding—siblings had always been one of my deepest longings. As loving as my small family was, I could not deny that I had spent much of my childhood feeling lonely. Not a holiday went by that I hadn't wished for other children to make mischief with, or even for other adults to fill the empty seats at our table. At Thanksgiving the three O'Rourkes had always feasted sensibly on slices of turkey breast or a portion of a ham. And though I never said so to my mother, who had a tendency to take any complaint as a personal failing, I would have traded half my Christmas presents just to see a whole bird on the table—and to engage assorted cousins in a bitter fight over the drumsticks.

The knowledge that I might have biological half siblings somewhere in the world had served as both a constant comfort and tantalizing hope from as early as I was able to understand the concept. I had nursed the prospect silently, like a dirty secret, right up until the day of my first meeting with Sheila, when to my great disappointment I learned that she had never married nor had any other children, and that furthermore, neither my maternal grandparents nor my birth father were still living. My birth father had died in a motorcycle accident only a year after I was born; she was sure I had no paternal half siblings, either.

I had accepted the grim news without question. Now I had to wonder.

Keep your head, Meara. I continued to stare at the baby in the photograph, trying not-so-subconsciously to rule out any likeness to myself. But there was little to go on. I had no idea what I had looked like as a baby; my parents had no photos of me before the age of four.

Amanda Michelle, I repeated to myself. It could have been my birth name. I knew full well that my adoptive parents had named me for my Irish grandmothers, Meara and Kathleen. Sheila could have named me Amanda—then thought of me as Mandy ever after.

It made perfect sense.

My heart fell at the thought, and I chastised myself. Learning that my birth mother had held on to a picture of me should be uplifting, not disappointing. It had been foolish of me to resurrect the sibling dream at all—even for a moment. I was an only child, and I always would be. That was nothing to complain about.

I replaced the baby photo in the Bible and flipped farther along its width. Another gap in the pages appeared, and I opened to it.

A second photograph lay wedged near the Bible's spine. This one was in color, though time and inexpensive printing had distorted its hues to a pinkish purple. I stared at the image as if I were looking at a ghost, my pulse racing. There could be no doubt this time. The child in the picture was me.

Three, maybe four years old, playing in a sprinkler. A two-piece, checked swimsuit spanned my thin frame while my unruly hair, even wet, flung out in all directions like an explosion. My brown eyes sparkled as I mugged for the camera. My cheeks were rosy, my smile bright.

I flipped the photo over in my lap. The back side was blank. Grabbing up the Bible, I pored through its pages roughly, looking for others. The baby picture fell out again, and along with it, one more photograph.

I was around two years old, wearing a dress, white and frilly, with shiny shoes. My hair was shorter, pulled back from my face into two ponderous dog ears. I was standing against an institutional-looking hallway of painted concrete block—perhaps a church. Someone adult-sized had been crouching beside me.

But that someone was gone. A jagged, ugly cut ran along my side, leaving only empty space where my companion should have been.

Who?

My stomach roiled. I gathered the pictures together and stuffed them back into the Bible, then replaced the book in the suitcase. My heart thumped like a jackhammer.

I knew that I had been in the foster care system before my parents adopted me. It was one of the few things they had told me. But how long had I lived with Sheila? After she told me in the coffee shop that I had been relinquished as an infant, I assumed that I had spent the next several years bouncing around in foster homes, waiting for appropriate adoptive parents. But if that were true, Sheila wouldn't have had any pictures of me other than the newborn shot.

She didn't give me up at birth, I thought, confirming a suspicion I had resisted, even when nagged by my common sense. A healthy infant willingly given up for adoption wouldn't require prolonged foster care. Children languished in foster care when their parents were neglectful. Or abusive.

I grabbed both suitcases by the handles and hefted them back into the closet, the leather suddenly seeming hot enough to singe my fingers. I didn't want to touch them. I wanted nothing to do with anything of Sheila's. I started to walk out the door, but didn't make it. Instead I stopped and fell upon the bed, turned my face into the coverlet, and cried.

I could always be counted on to shed tears at touching movies and sad books, but I didn't often cry for myself, and almost never with this much abandon. The events of the last twenty-four hours, however, could not leave me unscathed. I had met my birth mother once again, seen in her face the love I had always wanted to see, then watched her die before my eyes. She had kept pictures of me in her Bible—she had been thinking of me all along. Yet when we met that day at the coffee shop, she had lied to me.

I had probably lived with her, off and on, throughout my early childhood. The person cut from the photograph was likely some foster parent or other—some meaningless nonentity she preferred to pretend didn't exist. She cared enough about me to keep my pictures, but not me. Not as a child. And not as an adult.

She had lied to keep me away from her.

Minutes passed, and just as I was beginning to feel that the worst of my sobs had subsided, I was startled by the sound of approaching footsteps squeaking on the ancient floorboards. I wiped my face on my sleeve and looked up.

An elderly woman, stooped and painfully skinny,

watched me from the doorway. She appeared to be some-where in her seventies, with a heavily wrinkled, age-spotted face and a thin crown of white hair bound up in a net. Her expression was dour, her frown lines permanent. She was clad entirely in polyester except for a ragged cotton apron whose pockets overflowed with aerosol cans and cloths.

"Don't mind me," she insisted in a scratchy voice. "I'm just here to tidy up a bit."

I sat up straight and tried to finish drying my face with the opposite sleeve. The woman walked slowly toward me, then reached into a pocket and produced a large square of cloth, an old cotton diaper turned dust rag. "Try this," she suggested.

I accepted the makeshift handkerchief, then stood up and thanked her. "I'm sorry if I startled you. I'm sure you didn't expect to find a sobbing stranger in the master suite."

The woman stared back at me with dark eyes that were anything but startled. Rather, their piercing gaze suggested she knew everything about me but the color of my underwear. "I expected you all right," she said with a cocky tone that was neither friendly nor hostile. "I'm just glad to see you're not still asleep. Can't stand people who lay around the bed all day."

She tilted her chin, the dark eyes probing me still further. "Your mother was a lazy one."

My pulse quickened slightly, but I was too worn-out from crying to react any more dramatically than that. "It sounds like you knew Sheila better than I did," I answered smoothly. "She didn't raise me. I was adopted."

The woman's already wrinkled face wrinkled further. "You mean that hussy gave you up?" she exclaimed. "A pretty little thing like you?"

I tried to take a deep breath, but the air came in with ragged heaves. The woman didn't mean to be cruel, but reminders of my rejection always struck deep, evoking pain from a wound that would never completely heal. Yes, I had been "given up." It was a fact, and the compliment trailing afterward did nothing to lessen the sting.

I didn't answer, but as the woman took in my reaction her eyes softened. "You were raised by good people, then?"

Her attempt to be comforting, if that's what it was, was so off the mark I had to smile. Clearly, she did not think Sheila had been "good people." At this point, I was not inclined to disagree with her.

"My parents were wonderful," I confirmed. I took another deep breath, studying her. Rough social skills or no, the housekeeper was the only person I had met so far who actually knew Sheila, and no matter how difficult the topic was for me, I needed some answers before I could settle the inheritance issue.

"It's very nice to meet you," I offered, attempting a more proper introduction. "My name is Meara O'Rourke; I assume Mr. Falcon told you I would be staying here last night. I should be leaving very soon, though. I hope I'm not in your way."

Her face didn't smile. "My name's Estelle Harkins. I've been housekeeper here for twenty years, and you're not in *my* way," she answered.

"In that case," I began, my voice still trembling more than I would like, "I was wondering if I could ask you a few questions about Sheila."

Her hawk eyes bore into me, but their expression was not unkind. Their scrutiny was more like that of a mother dog, sniffing an orphan puppy while debating whether to add it to her brood.

"I've got to work," she said finally. "If you want to talk, you can help." She extracted a cloth and can of furniture polish from her apron and extended them. "Damned lot of wood in this place."

I took the cloth and can without hesitation, welcoming the opportunity to keep my hands busy. Estelle walked across the hall to the front bedroom opposite my own, then proceeded to polish each piece of furniture with a devoted intensity. I imitated her actions to the best of my ability, but since I couldn't find a speck of dust anywhere, I felt useless. Several minutes of silence passed before I worked up the nerve to speak.

"What I was wondering," I explained, my hands still dusting, "was how Sheila and Mitchell met. How long they dated. Whether you thought they were really—" I broke off awkwardly. "Or if maybe you suspected—" My voice cut out altogether, and I swallowed hard. I would *not* cry again in front of this woman.

She stopped dusting and stared at me a moment. Then she stepped over and inspected the chest of drawers I had just finished, running a bony finger over its carved trim, squinting at the result. "Waiting a year's the least you can do respectably, you know," she said flatly. "Those two started up long before that. I'd find a brassiere here, a lady razor there. I knew Mitchell had a woman living with him. It was none of my business, and I didn't call him on it. But they were plenty ashamed. Every time I'd show up, she'd take off the other way."

I was breathing far more rapidly than necessary, and I took a moment to remind myself, once again, that I was not responsible for my birth mother's character.

Estelle pulled a plastic bottle from her apron and began polishing a spotless mirror. "After that first time I caught her lazing around the bed, she stopped hiding. But she always seemed nervous, like I was the police. I told her what Mitchell did was on his own conscience, and that he could deal with his children on his own time—I wasn't going to be the one breaking their hearts." Her expression turned regretful. "But then I had no idea Mitchell would be fool enough to marry her, either."

She moved on across the hall to my room, where she began to polish the walnut vanity. Glad that my things were already packed up and out of her way, I set about removing imaginary dust from the bed's iron headboard. "Was it your impression," I asked, willing the conversation to be over soon, "that they were in love?"

Estelle's only answer was a sideways, cynical stare.

I took a slow breath. "But Mitchell did marry her," I reasoned. "He didn't have to. She was already living here."

Estelle stopped dusting. She raised herself to her full height, which appeared uncomfortable for her spine. "Love had nothing to do with it," she said sternly. "Mitchell was lonely; she was a willing, good-looking woman. He was too blind to see that any woman living out of her car—" her voice broke off. When she spoke again, it was with renewed determination. "I've got nothing against you, young lady. And your mother was always nice enough to me, I'll give her that. But this place was Rosemary's more than it was his—it came down through her family. She wanted her children to have it after they were both gone, and that's the way it should be."

We looked at each other in silence, and when she seemed certain that her point had been made, she relaxed her back and bent at the waist again. An acute pain had taken over my midsection, and I felt like doubling over as well. "Do you think that Fletcher—"

She cut me off in a trice. "What do you know about Fletcher?" she asked, her tone suspicious.

"Virtually nothing," I answered, surprised. "He came by the inn this morning—"

"What did he say to you?"

My brow furrowed. "He didn't say anything," I explained, perplexed. "In fact, he couldn't get away from me fast enough."

The wrinkles on one side of the older woman's mouth deepened, pulling her lips into a crooked grin. "Well, that's just as well," she said pointedly. "You take some advice from a woman who's been around a long, long time, and stay away from that one." She leaned in toward me, her hawk eyes glistening. "As far away as you can get."

Chapter

~7~

WHEN THE PHONE rang, I was only too glad to excuse myself from Estelle's company. The caller, David Falcon, informed me that he was on his way over to the inn, and as I had several calls of my own to make before we began our meeting, I left the older woman to her cleaning and remained at the phone. My heart seemed hopelessly heavy now, and my mind still reeled with conjecture. But I delved into the tasks before me with verve, hoping that—as Colleen O'Rourke was always so fond of saying—honest work did soothe the soul.

First I contacted the funeral home, then the papers. Sheila Black would be buried with a simple graveside ceremony three days hence, in a plot relatively near, but by no means beside, those of Mitchell and Rosemary Black. The interment would be preceded by a brief window of visitation. Her obituary, sadly bare-boned, would appear in both Pittsburgh papers as well as the local one, in hopes of dredging up someone—anyone—who might have cared about her. It seemed impossible that a woman nearing fifty would have no one to mourn her passing, yet even as I made the arrangements, I feared I would attend her visitation alone.

My last call was to my answering machine, which I had neglected to check since leaving for the hospital yesterday afternoon. The time that had passed since seemed much longer, and I was relieved when only three beeps followed my recorded message.

"It's me," Todd's thin, irritating voice proclaimed. *"And I'm getting tired of your not returning my calls. It's high time you got over this snit of yours, Meara, because I'm not going to wait around for you forever. Call me."*

I exhaled with a sigh. It had been a month now, and Todd seemed no closer to accepting our breakup than he had when I told him I never wanted to see him again. Of course, I knew that the man had a great deal of talent at ignoring what he didn't wish to happen. He hadn't wished for my mother's funeral to happen, for instance, because on that day, like all Saturdays, he had had other plans. He and his father would relax in front of the big-screen television in their basement, and his mother, before she had been hospitalized, would keep their TV trays replete with sandwiches and cookies. It was a tradition. Since she had become unable, they had depended on me to fill her shoes. And what were the two of them supposed to eat if I was at a funeral?

Resolution #1, I repeated to myself, *I will not allow any man to use me.* With a flourish of my index finger, I hit the code for ERASE and moved on.

"Meara—it's Alex. Call me back as soon as you get this. We've got problems with the inspection. Major *problems."*

I let out a whispered curse. Problems with the inspection? There couldn't be. I was barely getting enough out of the sale of my parents' house as it was. I couldn't afford more repairs. And with the payments for Sheila's funeral coming due—

"Meara—it's Alex again. Where are you? I've got to talk to you TODAY. Why don't you get a cell phone like the rest of the world? Call me!"

I hung up the phone with haste and dialed the number at the end of the message. Alex was a good friend and a competent real estate agent, and if he said there were problems, he meant it.

"Meara!" he exclaimed when I reached him, his familiar tenor a welcome sound, despite the alarm in his voice. "Thank goodness. Where have you been? Listen, I know you're not going to want to hear this, but the inspector found *mold*."

He said the word as if it were a dread disease. "Mold?" I repeated. "What seventy-year-old house doesn't have mold?"

"Not bathroom-shower mold," he corrected. "Mold with a capital *M*. The black stuff. A seller's nightmare. Haven't you heard the hype?"

I had not, but Alex quickly filled me in.

"But my parents lived there for years!" I protested. "And I've been living there too for the last six months. None of us ever had any of those symptoms."

"None of that matters, Meara," he explained patiently.

Alex and I had met during our first year as elementary school teachers; luckily, our friendship had lasted longer than his perseverance in the field. He was a bit goofy, but a kind person, and I could feel the sympathy in his voice. "All that matters is that the inspector found it and the buyer is worried about it. They won't go forward with the sale unless we have it taken care of."

I exhaled. "And that means?"

"An abatement contractor. I've already found a reasonable one, and we need to jump on it. This company is normally booked months ahead—they only have an opening now because another client decided to demolish instead of abate."

Demolish? My head spun. "How much is this going to cost?"

He told me, and my head spun the opposite direction.

"Meara?" he spoke into the silence. "Are you there? Don't faint on me. Please."

"I'm here," I said defensively. "But I don't have that kind of money. The funeral—" I cut myself off. Alex already knew I was paying for one mother's funeral. I wasn't inclined to explain about the other one.

"We'll work it out," he insisted. "There are always ways. But we have to do this now. I really don't think this buyer will wait, and you know we're not loaded with other prospects."

I was silent for a moment, which he took as consent. "There's something else," he continued. "You'll need to vacate the house for at least seventy-two hours, starting Monday. Is that a problem?"

"Three days?" I exclaimed, my voice rising. "Where am I supposed to live? I have to be back here on Sunday—" my voice trailed off. I had no business complaining to Alex. None of this was his fault.

"Meara," he offered, "if you don't want to spend the money on a motel, you can always crash at my place. I've got a brand-new futon in my computer room."

I winced. Alex was a sweetheart, but I had visited his apartment enough to know that his idea of hygiene was a can of Lysol on the back of the toilet.

"Thank you," I said sincerely, "but I don't want to impose. I'll find someplace inexpensive." I took a breath.

"And as for the abatement, I'll figure out a way to pay for it somehow."

"Great," he praised. "And listen—can you possibly make it in here today? I have some papers for you to sign."

A movement in the corner of my eye startled me, and I looked out from behind the desk to see two men standing in the corridor. David Falcon had arrived, and Fletcher Black was with him.

They had probably heard every word I'd just said.

The lawyer nodded at me and raised a hand politely, as if urging me not to rush. Fletcher didn't look at me at all. I told Alex I would be back at his office in Pittsburgh by five, then hung up. It was a promise I intended to keep.

I looked at the document spread in front of me, puzzling over the handwritten scrawl. The language was legalese, or at least an approximation of it, but the papers were dusty and smudged, and the ink looked like it had come from a cheap ballpoint on its last legs. My guess was that Fletcher had prepared the proposal himself—possibly on the dashboard of a car.

"You want to buy me out?" I asked incredulously, trying to catch his eye. I was unsuccessful. He refused to look at me.

He sat leaning back in his chair, his lumberjacking ensemble and casual pose in distinct contrast to David Falcon's formal carriage with crisp suit and tie. Fletcher's jeans were not only tattered, but stained with large patches of reddish brown, and the drying mud on his hiking boots was detaching itself at a steady rate onto the inn's previously spotless floor. His hands were folded in his lap. He didn't speak. He made every effort to exhibit nonchalance.

His every effort was wasted. Little did he know that he was dealing with a schoolteacher, for whom interpreting body language was as instinctive as raising a coffee cup. I noted immediately the tense set of his jaw, the too-rapid rise and fall of his chest, the continual, rhythmic scraping of his boot heel on the rung of his chair. He was tight as a drum. Strained, anxious. Not to mention resentful. And judging by the lack of eye contact, I had a pretty good idea whom he resented.

"I'm perfectly willing to talk with you about this," I said warmly, attempting to thin the tension. "But if you don't mind, I would rather put off any decisions about the inheritance until after Sheila's funeral." My belief that my birth mother hadn't deserved a dime of her husband's money was nearly cemented, but I couldn't ignore the possibility that publication of her obituaries might bring new information to light. What if, despite the house-keeper's not-so-subtle allusions to Sheila's poverty, she had brought some money of her own to the marriage? What if she had another relative or dependent who truly needed it? I had no right to give away anything that might be Sheila's until I knew for sure, no matter how eager I was to wash my hands of it.

I took a breath. "There's no need to rush, is there?"

The men exchanged an awkward glance.

"Well, not—" the lawyer began.

"It's just easier this way," Fletcher interrupted, focusing on a spot above my left shoulder. "You sign that, I write you a check, and you leave."

My eyebrows rose. "I understand this is important to you—"

"This does *not* have to be a big deal," he insisted, his voice rising. "It's just a broken-down inn and some land, okay? But I don't have time for this right now. I need to get back to California. That's why I want everything settled today. Now, how much is it going to take?"

Broken-down inn? I blinked. Did the man have no concept of what he possessed here? The antiques? The Ferris Mountain clock? He had to. "I really don't think—"

I broke off when I realized he was looking at me. His eyes still swam with pain, but now they also blazed with determination—and in them I glimpsed a passion so powerful, so acute, that it startled me into silence.

He averted his eyes again.

"I-I can't name an amount," I said with a stutter, reeling. "I have no idea what property like this is worth."

David Falcon cast another enigmatic glance at his companion, then leaned toward me. "You realize, Ms. O'Rourke, that you have every right to seek an independent appraisal—"

Fletcher glared at him, hard. "There's no need for that," he snapped. "The whole point of offering cash is to end this today." He removed another paper from the top of the lawyer's stack. "Here's what I'm prepared to offer you." He released the paper in the air so that it floated down in front of me. "You'll see it's very generous. I can write the check now."

I looked at the figure circled in red, and my eyes widened. I knew little about real estate, and the value of the inn and its contents was particularly difficult to gauge, but the offer in front of me was more than my best guess for the total.

I stole a glance upward. Our eyes met for only a split second before he turned away, but it was enough for me to catch the same look of intensity. Why was he so desperate to remove me from the picture? Was I sitting on some sort of gold mine?

My mind raced for an explanation. Perhaps he and his sister had a buyer waiting in the wings already—a buyer who wouldn't take kindly to waiting around while they contested my inheritance legally. Neither of them had chosen to live here—they hadn't even stayed in this part of the country. Of course they would want to sell. But who would pay an inflated price for an old stone mansion and some forestland in the mountains? A real estate developer? A mining company?

My stomach lurched. What I had seen of these forests was breathtaking, and an undeveloped tract this large was a rarity. Many of the trees were hundreds of years old. The streams were clear. Wildlife abounded. There was a peace here that I had felt the first moment I stepped out onto the meadow—a peace no one could put a price on.

Was I paving the way for its destruction?

My face flushed with heat. I pushed the paper back roughly across the table. "I'm not signing anything today," I announced with the same underestimate-me-at-your-peril tone I used with my more pugnacious eleven-year-olds. "I won't be making any decisions about the estate until after Sheila's funeral. And that's final."

Silence descended as the two men absorbed my statement. Then David Falcon threw his companion yet another visual message, this one unmistakable.

I told you so.

Fletcher stiffened. He glared back at the lawyer, and a short staring match ensued. "Just ask her what she wants," he ordered.

With a barely audible sigh of exasperation, the lawyer

turned his attention back to me. "Are there any circumstances," he asked politely, "under which you would consider signing over your rights to Sheila's portion of the estate without first seeking the opinion of a qualified attorney?"

Fletcher sprang from his chair with a groan. "Oh, for God's sake, David," he chastised. "Could you possibly make the offer sound a little less idiotic?"

The lawyer eyed him coolly. "As a matter of fact, no."

Fletcher cast the briefest of glances over at me, his expression venomous. Then he turned away. "Well then," he said, his deep voice frosty, "I have nothing else to say."

With that pronouncement, he strode to the French doors and walked out. I rose myself, watching anxiously as he headed across the stone slabs of the patio and out into the meadow. He was moving toward the same trail he had taken earlier in the morning.

I turned to the lawyer. "Where is he going, exactly?" I asked. "That's the second time today he's disappeared into those woods."

I knew that where Mitchell's son spent his time should be of no concern to me. The man was brusque and unfriendly, and I should want no part in his trials and tribulations. But despite my aggravation at his behavior, there was something about him that affected me—that drew me in as forcibly and invisibly as an undertow.

The man had lost both his parents, as had I. But the pain in his eyes, the passion I had seen smoldering beneath, was coming from something deeper. He was grieving his father, yes—but there was more. I was certain now that the Fletcher Black I kept meeting did not really exist. I was seeing some sort of facade, a grand act. The question was why.

"He owns a tract of land adjoining this one," Mr. Falcon explained. "And there's a cabin just over the hill that he likes to stay in when the weather's decent."

I waited for the lawyer to rise and collect his papers, but he remained seated, indicating that we were not yet finished. Reluctantly, I withdrew my eyes from the window and sat back down.

"I should explain, Ms. O'Rourke," he said quietly, "that I represent Mitchell Black's interests, not those of his son. I brought Fletcher over with me this morning only because he told me that he was planning on approaching you on his own. As an old friend of the family, I convinced him that might not be wise."

I had to smile. David Falcon, like my father, seemed chivalrous by nature—a rarity in men my age.

"The situation is this," he continued. "Fletcher and Tia Black are virtually certain to contest Sheila Black's inheritance, and by extension, yours. Whether they are likely to succeed is a matter you'll have to discuss with your own attorney. Regardless of outcome, if the case goes to trial the process will be both lengthy and costly. An out-of-court settlement is a perfectly reasonable option, provided both parties enter into it with competent representation."

I nodded, understanding his point, but my mind was drifting. I could not stop thinking about Fletcher, hiking back over the hill to some ramshackle cabin, smarting over his failure to bamboozle me. What did he really want? If his offer had been sincere, he would have to be wealthy in his own right to make good on it. But if he was, how might he have gotten that way? And why would he buy land adjacent to his family's estate? To increase the investment?

"Fletcher and I need to talk," I announced.

The lawyer tensed. "I don't think that's a good idea, Ms. O'Rourke," he responded. "I can't stress enough—you need to handle this through an attorney."

His voice was intent, and as I considered his words, Estelle's bizarre warning rang with them in my ears. *Stay away from that one.*

I dismissed the notion. The lawyer was only trying to give me good legal advice. Estelle's motives were more obscure, but I was not going to discount my own intuition. The real Fletcher Black was a decent person, and when the time came, I was certain that I could get through to him somehow—that we could settle things without my having to pay an attorney. We would have to, because I couldn't afford one.

David Falcon seemed to be reading my mind. "Fletcher's cabin isn't accessible by car," he reported, "at least not a car like yours. I had to borrow my son-in-law's truck to chase him down this morning, and I nearly got stuck three times. So don't try it. As soon as you hire an attorney, have him or her call me, and I'll put them in touch with Fletcher.

"In the meantime," he continued, his tone paternal, "I have some papers for you to look over." He withdrew a neatly organized folder. "And I wanted to make you aware of this." He extracted an official-looking document from the right pocket and placed it in my hand. "This is Sheila and Mitchell's original marriage certificate, from Nevada. I've acquired copies, but this one was in Sheila's purse at the time of the accident, so I'm returning it to you. You should know that her birth certificate was found in her purse as well. It should still be there."

I stared at the document in my hands, and my heart began to pound. *Sheila Marie Tresswell.* My birth mother's entire name, spelled out. A simple thing, to most people. Yet to an adoptee who had grown up wondering, the mere sight of the words was somehow amazing. Parents: *John and Margaret Tresswell.* My grandparents, whom I would never know. Sheila had told me at the coffee shop that her father had died of a heart attack when she was still a teenager, and that her mother had succumbed to lung cancer only a year later. Birth: *Uniontown, Pennsylvania. January 13, 1953.*

"I did investigate whether her parents were still alive," the lawyer explained gently. "But I'm afraid they've both been deceased for some time now. I could find no evidence of any other living relatives, but I did not do an exhaustive search. If you'd like to find out more, you might consider hiring a private investigator."

His last words were lost to me as my eyes became riveted on a single numeral. "This is wrong," I announced, my heart beating faster still. "Her birth date is wrong."

"Oh?" the lawyer responded without concern. "Well, she wouldn't be the first woman to try to make herself younger on a legal document, I can tell you that."

"No," I insisted, my hands clenching the paper tight. "Not younger. *Older.* This says she was born in 1953. But she wasn't. She couldn't have been. She was only sixteen when she had me, and I was born in 1974."

The lawyer didn't speak for a moment. "Perhaps you should check her birth certificate," he suggested.

I rose with a jerk and retrieved the bag of Sheila's personal effects I had brought from the hospital. I returned to the common room, pulled out a tattered black leather purse, and placed it on the tabletop. A single piece of paper protruded from the flat pocket on the purse's side, and I pulled it out.

Sheila Marie Tresswell. Female infant, born to Margaret Orr Tresswell, age twenty-eight, and John Franklin Tresswell, age thirty-two. In Uniontown, Pennsylvania. *January 13, 1953*.

My hands fell to my sides.

The lawyer remained silent.

"Another lie," I said in a whisper. If I didn't whisper, I would shout, and my parents had never tolerated shouting.

A wave of nausea rolled up in my throat. Sheila hadn't been a frightened teenager when she gave birth to me. She had been twenty-one years old.

Chapter

~8~

I SHIFTED IN the comfortably padded chair, crossed my legs the opposite way, and stole another glance at my watch. Exactly three minutes had passed since the last time I had checked it.

Sheila's coffin, plain but dignified, lay underneath a single spray of flowers—the least expensive fresh ones that had been available. A pair of silk ficus trees, no doubt permanent residents that had been moved from the room's corners to help fill the emptiness, marked either end of the coffin. In an hour and forty-five minutes, only one visitor had strayed into the room. That had been David Falcon, whose dutiful appearance had provided a brief but welcome diversion, despite his gentle scolding over my failure to hire an attorney since our last meeting.

No one had contacted the funeral home in regard to Sheila's obituaries. Nor had anyone called my home number directly, despite the carefully worded plea in all three that asked friends and family members to contact Meara O'Rourke for more information. I hadn't wanted to spell out my relationship to Sheila in print—at some level I feared the disclosure might alienate the very people I was trying to reach. But I had included virtually all the facts I knew about Sheila before her life with Mitchell, with the exception of the surname she had used at the coffee shop, which I strongly suspected was fictitious.

At this point, believing anything she had ever told me seemed naive.

I had had three days now to absorb the information I had learned about Sheila, and to come to grips with the reality of her death. But I was making great progress on neither front. Learning that she had lied to me about her age when I was born had been another slap in the face, and my cheek was still smarting. I had returned to my parents' house in a fog of denial, setting about the grim task of preparing for the abatement with a single-mindedness that precluded introspection. I hadn't wanted to think about Sheila. And for the last seventy-two hours, I had succeeded.

But there was no avoiding the issue now.

I stared at the closed coffin from a safe distance. The funeral director had insisted I view the body privately before the lid was brought down, a task that had stabbed at my very core, releasing a landslide of raw emotions I had hoped to keep contained. Every ounce of evidence in my possession pointed to the same conclusion—that my birth mother had been a drifter and a swindler. An attractive woman physically, yet evidently so unlikable that in a half-century's worth of living she hadn't acquired a single friend to mourn her passing. She had given me up when I was a child, and she had lied to me when I was an adult. There was little in her history to engender my sympathy—certainly nothing that should obligate me to become embroiled in her affairs, much less oversee her burial.

Nothing except my memory of a dying woman lying in a hospital bed, looking at me with love in her eyes.

It shouldn't matter to me. I knew that. Sheila had never known me as a person, and now she never would. Within an hour her body would be in the ground, and by the end of the day her few belongings would be out of the Sheepsworth Inn and on their way to charity. But it wouldn't be over then. Not for me. Her last words would haunt me for the rest of my life.

I always loved you, Meara.

Once upon a time, those same words might have begun to heal the chasm her abandonment had left in my heart. But now, with the incongruity of all I had learned, they brought only more confusion. And more pain.

"Ms. O'Rourke?" Two funeral home employees entered the viewing room from the rear, propping open the double doors as they came. "We're ready to transport your mother to the cemetery now. The minister will meet us there. Are you—expecting anyone else?"

Unsure whether I could answer, I simply shook my head.

It was a beautiful June day. The mountain breeze was cool, but the sun was comfortably warm, sitting high in an azure sky marked only by the thinnest of clouds. The cemetery was a picturesque one, uniformly populated with flat, unostentatious stones. Rolling mounds of grass were punctuated by splashes of color from an abundance of silk wreaths, and in every direction higher hills towered above, verdant with the lush, deciduous forest of the Laurel Mountains.

I had driven to the grave site alone, sparing myself the further expense of a limousine. I watched silently as the coffin was manipulated into position, then breathed a sigh of relief when the designated pastor arrived. Recommended to me by the funeral home, the Presbyterian minister had not known Mitchell personally, much less Sheila, and the information I had shared with him had been scant. Subconsciously, I suppose, I had thought it best she be eulogized by a stranger.

He took in the scene with a compassionate eye, asking directly if I was ready to begin, rather than inquiring over the obvious lack of mourners. He had spoken only a few words when his gaze caught something over my shoulder, and he smiled. "Let's wait another moment," he suggested.

I turned to see a man approaching up the hill, and for several seconds, I didn't recognize him. My pulse quickened as I wondered whether he was a relative, and the old half-sibling dream doggedly raised its head again. But when I saw his face, my childish hopes were replaced with bewilderment. Clean-shaven and dressed in a nicely tailored suit, Fletcher strode purposely up to the grave site, greeted the minister with a solemn nod, and took a place two paces from my side.

I stared at him, dumbfounded. A few days ago, the same man had essentially accused Sheila of killing his father. Now he was attending her funeral?

I tried to catch his eye for some hint of explanation. But once again he avoided the contact, seemingly intent on the ceremony. Only after the minister had finished his fitting, though necessarily impersonal discourse, did Fletcher's gaze waver toward me.

He offered only a single, mute nod, then averted his eyes again. Reading anything from his expression was next to impossible. His manner, so sophisticated and reverential, was in complete contrast to that of the boorish giant I had previously met. Yet somehow I sensed that this incarnation of Fletcher Black was even further removed from the reality. As perfectly as the suit fit him, as elegant a picture as he made, I couldn't help but notice the rigid set of his shoulders, the tautness of his jaw.

He was uncomfortable in the suit. And it was a fairly good bet that he hated even being here.

The coffin began its descent into the ground, and I tried once more to make myself accept what was happening. Fletcher's presence was just one more incomprehensible incident in a span of days that, for me, continued to feel hopelessly surreal. From the moment I had received the hospital call about Sheila, I had felt like Alice in Wonderland—dropped into a world of nonsense where nothing I saw was what it appeared to be. Sheila had said she loved me; yet she had cast me aside, lied to me, run from me. She and Mitchell had seemed to have genuine feelings for each other, yet they were a wealthy widower and a drifter, eloping without a prenup. Sheila had died trying to warn me of something, but her words had been nothing but gibberish. My heart ached to know that I would never see her again; yet every time I thought of her, my gut twisted with anger.

Fresh dirt lay piled on the grave's edge before my foot, and as I thought again of the severed picture of me as a toddler, of the tumult I must have endured, I felt an impulse to step forward and kick it. I imagined the clods of earth falling down, thudding onto her coffin and covering her, ending once and for all the anguish she had inflicted on my soul.

I would never have done such a thing. It was just a thought. But I must have stepped forward slightly nonetheless, because almost immediately I felt a steadying hand grasp my arm above the elbow. I turned and faced yet another rendition of Fletcher Black.

His eyes were studying mine with concern. His touch was gentle, his expression kind. "Are you all right?" he asked quietly.

I met his gaze, and my heart warmed. This behavior, surely, was genuine. Considerate and caring—at least when caught off guard. I felt a wave of self-satisfaction. I had known from the start that there was good in the man, no matter how hard he'd been working to conceal it.

"I'm fine," I answered with my best smile. "Thank you."

To my surprise, his expression immediately clouded over. He dropped my arm and turned away from me.

The coffin reached its destination, and the whirring of the machinery ceased with a thump. I stared down into the grave, my stomach churning.

Contradictions. They were everywhere. They were all I had left of her.

Staring at that hideous coffin, its one skimpy floral arrangement barely covering a third of its surface, I was nearly overcome. I needed another cry. Not just for the loss of my birth mother, but for everything in her life and mine that had never been—and now would never be—right. And had I been standing above her coffin alone, surrounded only by those I had paid to be here, I might have given in to the urge right then. But I wasn't alone. Sheila's stepson had come too, and as uncertain as I was of his motives in doing so, the mere knowledge that there was a warm body next to mine somehow gave me the strength to stave off my sobs—at least for a little while.

I was only vaguely aware of the minister leaving, and of the funeral director explaining that the remainder of the burial could take place after I was gone. I moved toward my car like a robot. A hand touched my arm.

"Do you need a ride somewhere?" Fletcher inquired, his voice strained. In the sunlight, his eyes seemed a grayish blue, midway between his dark suit and the sky above. They were beautiful eyes, but he was guarding them again, using a thin veil of resentment to mask whatever hid beneath.

"No thank you," I answered, wondering again why he had come. Was he feeling some sort of guilty obligation, given how he had tried to pressure me about the inheritance? Or was this a new plan—an act to win me over? If so, he needn't have shaved his beard and donned such an expensive suit. One civil conversation would suffice.

"I appreciate your coming today," I said evenly. "It was very thoughtful of you. Thank you."

His eyes flashed with the same penetrating sadness I had seen so many times before, but he averted them quickly, nodding his head. "You're welcome," he answered, dropping my arm. "No one should be at a funeral alone."

There was a flash of sensitivity in his words that moved me, but before I could respond to it, his tone turned cool again. "Is there—anything else you need while you're here? Did you get what you wanted from the inn?"

His discomfort in my presence was palpable, and I ached with the frustration of it. I wanted to know what was hurting him—why he felt like he had to keep up this facade with me.

We needed to talk.

"I do still need to pick up Sheila's things," I explained. "Would it be all right if I came by the inn now?"

He nodded. But his attention had become fixed on something over my shoulder.

A car door slammed behind me, and I whirled toward the sound.

A dilapidated station wagon had stopped at the base of the hill next to my own car, and a pale, haggard-looking woman was standing next to it. She appeared to be in her fifties, with short, dark hair and bespectacled eyes that darted back and forth between the grave site and me.

Someone came.

My heart raced. I walked toward her.

"Are you here for Sheila Tresswell's funeral?" I asked before I had even reached her.

The woman shrank back at my approach, but after hearing my words, she relaxed again. She watched me thoughtfully as I neared, and then she smiled. "Yeah, I am," she said in a voice so meek I had to strain to hear it. "Are you her daughter?"

I nodded, a wave of emotion rushing through me like a flood. *Her daughter.* Keeping my tears dammed took every ounce of strength I could muster. "You knew her?" I whispered hoarsely.

The woman smiled again, shyly. "We were friends for a while. But it's been years, now."

I smiled back, even as another pang of disappointment shot through my gut. She was not a relative. But that was okay, I assured myself. She was a friend. I should be grateful that Sheila had had at least one of them.

"I'm so glad you came," I sputtered. "The funeral is over, but—" I paused, uncertain how to phrase my request. *Would you mind hanging around for a moment and telling me absolutely everything you know about my birth mother?* It sounded too ridiculous.

"You look so much like her," the woman offered, sparing me. "Sheila told me once that she had a daughter. She never would say much more, which I thought was sort of strange, but I could tell she missed you." She grinned, revealing crooked teeth and a lifetime of dental neglect.

"She gave me up for adoption," I explained, intent, for whatever reason, on setting the record straight.

The woman's eyes widened. "Oh," she said, her voice turning slightly anxious. "But you two met up again after she got out?"

A coldness began to gnaw at my insides. I cleared my throat again. "I met her for the first time six years ago," I answered. The rest I didn't address. I wasn't sure I could.

"Well," she offered, her voice softening. "Sheila was a good one. Always made me smile. Everybody got down, you know, but Sheila, she had a gift. Always said she wanted to be an actress, and she was pretty enough for it, too. But she took what she was dealt and did the best she could with it. Kept everybody smiling."

The gnawing turned to an ache that moved upward through my chest. "When exactly did you meet?" I asked.

"In '82," she answered. "When I went in. She was still there when I got out in '87; I'm afraid we lost touch after that." She settled back against the car, and her eyes became distant. "I never knew what she was in for—she wouldn't say. I just knew she was one of the good ones. I felt like calling it quits myself a couple times, but Sheila was the kind that could always talk you out of it. *There's always something to live for,* she'd say. *No matter how bad you've screwed up, there's always something. You just have to figure out what.*"

She looked at me and chuckled. "I always figured for her, that was her kid, but then I wondered why nobody ever brought you to visit her. Now I get it. Sheila didn't talk, you know—never would say anything about her life outside. And she never had any visitors. Whole five years I knew her, nobody ever came. Still, she kept her spirits up." She smiled at me maternally. "That's why I say, honey—your mum was a good one."

My whole body seemed frozen.

"That's why I figured I'd come today," she announced, straightening. "I never went back to see her, you know. I said I would, but I just couldn't do it. Couldn't face that place again. I know it's late now, and heck, looks like I even missed the minister, but I'm here." She smiled at me again, sadly. "Sheila's gonna have at least one visitor now—I owe her that."

She gave my upper arm a squeeze. "It's nice to meet you, honey. If you don't mind, I'll just pay my respects and be on my way."

She was three paces away from me before I was able to speak. "I'm sorry," I croaked. "But I didn't get your name."

"Stephie," she answered, turning. "Stephie Linwood. I live in Boswell now."

"And when you met Sheila," I forced out, "you were where, exactly?"

Her eyes turned cautious. "Muncy," she answered.

I nodded immediately, hoping to give the indication that I already knew. "Right," I said. "Thank you for coming."

She nodded back at me, then began her trek the rest of the way up the hill.

I turned and walked to my own car. My hand shook as I extended it toward the door handle.

Muncy. The word seemed to pound against the inside of my skull, ricocheting from side to side. Muncy was the name of a small town near the center of Pennsylvania.

The site of the women's state penitentiary.

Chapter

9

I STUFFED SHEILA'S clothes into a couple of garden-sized trash bags and hauled them to my car. Her clothes, her boots, her knickknacks, and the big shabby suitcase were going to the first charity drop-off center I could find.

As for the smaller suitcase, the one with the quilt and the Bible, I had opened the lid just wide enough to throw in Sheila's purse, then shoved the works into the corner of my trunk. When I got home, the suitcase would go straight into storage, along with what I had saved of my parents' belongings, until I could find a suitable place to rent. Then everything I had of Sheila's would be settled deep into the back of a closet somewhere, and with luck, out of my mind.

I couldn't bring myself to dispose of everything that was hers. Not when someday the keepsakes might mean something to my own children. Family *was* important; I of all people ought to know that. And if I handled things right, maybe the next generation would be able to remember their biological grandmother with fondness—as opposed to with a searing pain in their middle.

Prison. Sheila had been in prison. And not just for five

years. Longer. What sort of crime resulted in a sentence
that long? I doubted simple fraud would suffice.

I returned to the house, opened her medicine cabinet,
and threw everything that looked feminine into the trash
can. When the bedroom seemed clear, I walked out into
the common room to look for more. A ceramic vase
caught my eye, and the impulse to fling it to the tile floor
was strong. But I fought it. This was Mitchell's house, not
Sheila's. And none of this was his fault.

When I could find nothing else that appeared to have
been hers, I allowed myself to slump into the chair by the
rolltop desk, lay my head down on my arm, and give in
to the tears I had suppressed all day. I hadn't cried since
discovering the torn picture of myself as a toddler, and I
hoped not to cry over Sheila ever again.

My birth mother had been a convicted criminal. It was
reality, and somehow or other, I had to learn to live with
it.

The pieces fit all too well. Sheila's rootlessness, her
lack of friends. The fact that she had, at least according to
Estelle, been living out of a car. She had been an ex-con,
with no family and no support system. She would have
had trouble finding employment. She would have had
trouble finding a place to live.

What do you do for a living?

I had asked the question innocently that day at the coffee shop. I had wondered if she shared my interests: writing, acting, children's education. I had thought her
answer vague even at the time, though I had no reason,
then, to be suspicious.

I'm between jobs right now, she had said with a smile.
But I've done a variety of things. What about you?

She had turned the question back onto me, as she had

done on numerous other occasions during that interview. She had seemed interested in everything about me, and I had been happy to oblige. Only afterward did I realize how little I had learned about her.

When the worst of my sobs had subsided, I grabbed a tissue from the desktop and dried my raw cheeks. The Black family portrait caught my eye, and I reached up and pulled it from the wall, touching the glass beside Mitchell's face lightly with my finger.

"I'm sorry," I whispered. "I'm sorry this had to happen." I thought about how differently things might have turned out had he and Sheila never met, and the image of his sunny, open smile haunted me. He looked so sweet. So vulnerable. Sheila had taken away his loneliness for a while. But being with her had cost him everything.

Another round of tears threatened, but the bulk of the pressure had lifted. I replaced the picture and stood up. "What Sheila did to you is not my fault, Mitchell," I whispered, remembering Resolution #2. "But I am sorry that it happened. And there *is* something I can do now to help set it right."

My eyes moved down toward the young images of Fletcher and Tia, and I set my jaw with determination. They had worried about their inheritance long enough. Today had been my deadline. No other potential heirs of Sheila's had come forward, and any stragglers were out of luck. I would not have Sheila's ill-gotten gains on my conscience any longer.

I leaned down, picked up the phone, and called my home number. *Last chance for heirs from the woodwork,* I thought to myself ruefully, listening for the waiting-message tone. My nerves were taut, and I despised the now-familiar feeling. The revelations about Sheila had been bouncing my emotions up and down like a yo-yo, and it was time I steadied myself by gaining some distance. If I didn't, I would never get rid of the crushing fear that another bigger, and even more horrible, bomb was set to drop.

"Meara," the message began, *"it's Alex. I know you're not at the house, but give me a call when you can, okay? I did find out something for you—about land values in the Laurel Mountains. I think you'll want to hear it."*

There were no more messages. Both relieved and disappointed, I hung up the phone. I had asked Alex several days ago why real estate in this area might be valuable. Now that I knew I had no claim to it, I wasn't certain I still wanted the answer.

My fingers dialed his number anyway.

"Meara!" he exclaimed, answering on the second ring. "So glad you got the message. Hey, about what you asked me—I did find something. Word has it that a major developer has been looking into that area for one of those all-inclusive ski resort complexes. The upscale kind, gargantuan, with its own spa and outlet mall. Year-round activities. You get the idea. Meara? You there?"

My heart fell. "I'm here."

"Deals like that are complicated—besides all the zoning issues, they would need a huge tract of land, and that usually means negotiating with multiple sellers. In any event, if the developer is serious, you can bet the agents out there will be tripping over each other for a piece of the pie.

"So tell me," he finished, his voice turning playful. "Why did you ask? Please say there's money in this for me. You know how much I want that PT Cruiser—"

"Thanks, Alex," I interrupted. I glossed over the question of my interest in the topic, diverting him back to the abatement and more mundane issues. Then I thanked him again and hung up.

I glared at the young Fletcher in the picture, my pride in my character-judging abilities temporarily quashed. "Well, that explains that," I muttered. No wonder he had been rushing me—he wanted my signature before I found out how much the land was really worth. "You don't care what happens to this place, do you?" I accused the boy in the photograph. "All you want is to take your money and run. Of all the horrible, selfish, shortsighted . . ."

I bolted out of the chair and paced the common room, my wrath quickly intensifying. Mitchell's body was barely cold, and his children were already plotting to destroy everything he and their mother had worked for? How could anyone grow up in the midst of such natural beauty—such a rare, unspoiled parcel of wilderness as this—and appreciate it so little? How could they sleep at night knowing that for the sake of a few lousy bucks they would be handing a death sentence to this entire area of the ridge?

"I don't care if it *is* your land, Fletcher Black," I hissed, turning on my heels and stomping determinedly toward the door, "I'm not going to let you do this."

This time, I had come prepared. Not only did my car contain everything I would need to survive in a motel during the mold abatement, but I had also included a few extras in case I decided to tarry in the Laurel Mountains. And tarry I would—starting right now. My hiking boots were on, I was decked out in comfortable jeans, and I even had a backpack complete with compass and flashlight. No mountain man was going to evade me now.

I had thought, after the funeral, that Fletcher might accompany me back to the inn. He had not. When I had finished my conversation with Stephie he was nowhere to be seen, and I assumed that he had returned to his cabin. I was assuming now that he would still be there.

I headed off over the meadow, anger fueling my every step. I was not the sort of person who angered either easily or often, but when it came to an issue I felt passionate about, all bets were off. And defending the environment—unfortunately for the Black children—was one of my greatest passions.

I crossed the meadow with resolve, though when I passed in front of the white frame house, the same sense of curiosity that had accosted me the last time I passed it reasserted itself, breaking my focus.

"What?" I said out loud, irritated. I stopped and allowed myself to stare. Architecturally unimpressive, the two-story clapboard house was a mishmash of original farmhouse and amateurish additions, with three different colors of roofing, at least two kinds of siding, and a host of areas in which raw wood appeared to be rotting. It might have been comfortable once upon a time, but at present "uninhabitable" was generous.

And yet it seems so warm. So happy.

I frowned. There was nothing enticing about what I was seeing. Absolutely nothing. If anything, it was downright spooky.

Crawling up into the porch swing . . .

I felt a coldness in the pit of my stomach, and shook myself. *No.* I was not going to play those mind games now. I was on a mission, and I would not allow myself to be distracted. I had to confront Fletcher, and I had to do it before he slunk off to the West Coast again. True—I hadn't a clue where his cabin was. The only directions I had were David Falcon's words: *just over the hill.* But they would have to do.

I headed up the same trail I had taken the other day, but with the proper gear, I moved more quickly. *An outlet mall,* I thought bitterly as I climbed. With the beauty of the forest's mature canopy hitting me square in the face at every step, the very thought of developers flashing their fat wallets at Mitchell's children sickened me.

So why was Fletcher still in Pennsylvania, and why had he come to the funeral? If he was trying to win me over with charm, he was in desperate need of some tutelage. More likely, he was as interested as I was in seeing who else from Sheila's past might turn up. He would love to find out about another burned ex-husband or two, wouldn't he? It would be very helpful in shoring up his case when he contested the inheritance . . .

I reached the clearing where I had talked with him a few days ago and tried to find the path he had taken when he left. But the only visible trails were the one I had come up on and another at the opposite pole, both of which swept back down the hillside.

No trail, eh? I scowled, but my determination only grew. Of course there wouldn't be an obvious trail to his cabin. He was probably the only one who made the trek, and he wouldn't want any old guest of the inn to wander over. "Tough," I grumbled as I climbed.

I kept moving upward for some time, thankful that regular walking outdoors kept my leg muscles in good shape. When at last I reached the summit of the hill, I exhaled with satisfaction. The view was breathtaking. I had no idea how much of the land stretching before me had belonged to Mitchell Black, but owning even a portion of it must feel like having a piece of heaven. My lungs pulled in pure breaths of mountain air while my eyes delighted in the contrast of blue sky and brilliant green. I could see the inn, with its parking lot in front and meadow behind, as well as part of the white house. There didn't appear to be any other buildings on that slope, and while I could see a few other roofs on outlying hills, for the most part, the natural splendor of the view was intact.

I turned and looked out over the hill's far side. Where was Fletcher's cabin? I had not thought, in my angry haze, that a small, one-story structure might be difficult to see amid the leaves. Still, if a vehicle of any sort could manage to reach it, there must be a narrow lane snaking up toward it from somewhere.

I walked back and forth on the hill's crest, but quickly became frustrated. The slope on this side was more gentle and irregular, and large portions of it were blocked from my view.

Think, Meara, I demanded, having no intention of giving up. *If you owned this land, where would* you *put a cabin?*

I looked over what I could see of the terrain with a critical eye. I would want a good view of the mountains, so my cabin would have to be somewhere near the top, in a small clearing. But I wouldn't want it too exposed, either, if I valued my privacy when hikers were about. Perhaps I would set it back into a natural plateau . . .

My eyes fell upon what could be just such a site, almost directly below me, and I smiled. It was certainly worth a try.

I had only walked a few hundred feet before I was stopped short by a sound that first startled, then delighted me. It was the buzzing of some sort of power tool, and it

was fairly close by. I grinned. It was possible that someone else could be up here, collecting firewood. But the
odds were that it was Fletcher himself—giving his location away as surely as with a flare gun.

Shortly after, I spied the cabin. It was exactly where I
had thought it might be, resting atop a small plateau, nestled snugly into the hillside with hardly a tree sacrificed
on either side. But its location was one of the few things
I was right about.

I had been expecting a rustic hunting cabin—a one- or
two-room shanty, perhaps without plumbing. But the
structure I approached was hardly a hovel. Though small,
it was relatively new and smartly built, with thick log
walls and a high-pitched, sturdy roof. Large windows and
skylights ensured a bright interior, and the stone chimney
arising from its center bespoke year-round coziness. A
mud-covered pickup truck was parked on a smaller
plateau below, out of sight of the front windows.

The buzzing sound stopped, and for a moment I
thought my presence had been discovered. But I saw no
one. The noise had been coming from the opposite side of
the cabin, and as I walked around the front porch I could
see a large stone patio, adjacent to a glass-walled sunroom, that served as an outdoor workshop. A four-foot
stretch of log stood up on sawhorses; a chain saw rested
on the ground beside it.

My brow wrinkled. What kind of person dropped good
money on such a spectacular cabin—which I had to admit
showed distinct shades of Frank Lloyd Wright—only to
turn around and sell it, knowing that it would be de-
stroyed? My hackles rose again.

So where was he? My eyes were drawn farther into the
trees, and I noted an outbuilding I couldn't immediately

classify. It was some sort of pavilion, but it hosted logs rather than picnic tables. Row after row of tree trunks of all sizes were stacked from its floor to its ceiling, carefully separated by wooden pallets. Between the rows of timber I could see a flash of red, and in the next moment, Fletcher walked out beside it, a short section of log in hand.

It was several seconds before he saw me standing quietly next to his sawhorses. When he did, the expression of shock on his face could not have been greater had I been wearing pink Spandex and aiming at him with a semiautomatic weapon.

"Meara," he gasped, setting down the log with a thump and narrowly missing his own foot in the process. "How did you get here?"

He was back in his customary getup again—faded red T-shirt, even more faded jeans, and work boots, and the unpretentious ensemble was such a natural fit it seemed impossible that I had just seen the same man in a thousand-dollar suit. Had his face not still been clean-shaven, I might have suspected I hadn't. But he was the same man. The same spoiled rich man who held what must be a very lucrative job in California, yet who came out here, to the wilderness, to get his feet muddy and play with power tools. Did he think of all this as a game?

"I flew," I responded.

He looked back at me sternly. "*Why* are you here?" he inquired, walking forward. He pulled off his work gloves and lay them on top of the log he had been sawing, then faced me squarely, putting himself between me and the cabin. His posture wasn't threatening, but he was not asking me in for a drink, either.

"I'm here," I explained, my voice unmistakably bitter,

"to tell you that I'm on to you now. I know about the development deal. And I'm not going to let you get away with it."

He stared back at me, but his eyes were unreadable, once again obscured by a thick shield of resentment. "Development deal?"

"Don't play dumb," I chastised. "We need to talk about this."

He turned and picked up his work gloves again. "We already did. I have nothing else to say to you." He raised a pair of goggles over his eyes and picked up the chain saw. "Step back, please."

A wave of fury swept over me, and I reached in to wrest the chain saw from his hands. He held on to it, looking at me in astonishment. "Are you crazy? I could have turned this on."

"Why don't you?" I baited, my rare ire in full swing. "Why don't you butcher every tree on this place right now? Or perhaps you'd rather rent a bulldozer and take out the whole hillside yourself? You might as well!"

He pulled the goggles off again, displaying wide eyes. He ripped the chain saw from my hands and set it down on the ground. "What are you talking about?"

"You know very well what I'm talking about!" I shouted. I started to say more, but contained myself. Yelling at him might make me feel better, but it wouldn't change his mind. For that, I would have to get more creative.

On impulse, I reached out and grabbed the sleeve of his shirt. There wasn't much slack around his biceps, but I was too disgusted with him to want to take his hand. "Come with me," I urged, pulling him toward the plateau's edge. He followed, unresisting, as I had learned most men would when dragged by a person half their size. We had only to move a few steps before a magnificent view of the valley presented itself.

"How can you not see what you have here?" I asked, my voice firm, but not quite so shrewish. "You grew up with forests all around you, didn't you? Is that how you can take them for granted?"

A partially rotted tree stump rose up from the ground beside me, and I hopped up onto its uneven surface. I was used to sparring with ten- and eleven-year-olds, and I hated losing my height advantage. "I'll tell you the same thing I tell my students in the suburbs, who don't appreciate nature either, unless they're taught. This tree right here," I instructed, pointing downward, "was probably two hundred years old when it died. Think about that! It could have been a sapling when George Washington marched through here. And there are others like it, all over these mountains. But not very many anymore, because people are cutting them down every day for any number of idiotic reasons. I've hiked all over this ridge, and this place is one of the biggest undeveloped, relatively undisturbed areas I've seen. For all you know, it could be the last one with any virgin timber. Doesn't that mean anything to you?"

I paused to take a breath, and to try to assess his response. But his expression was inscrutable. Outwardly he seemed as perturbed as ever, yet at the same time there was an unfamiliar twinkle in his eyes. Could it possibly be amusement?

"This is *not* funny!" I raged, offended. "Your parents would never have sold this place, would they? And yet the second they're gone you're ready to sell it to the highest bidder! This forest will *die*, Fletcher. They'll clear-cut

the slopes for the ski runs; bulldoze half the mountain—
and for what? So that a bunch of shallow women can get
mud facials while their pampered teens stock up on designer underwear, that's what! You know all those trickling little brooks down there? The ones you probably
searched for crayfish in when you were little? Well,
they'll be nothing but parking lot drainage ditches, haul-
ing off melted snow stained gray from SUV exhaust. Is
that what your parents would have wanted? Your grandparents? Is that what *you* really want?"

The perturbed look on his face was gone now, replaced
by an odd glow of mirth. To my amazement, he reached
up and grabbed me by the waist, lifting me from the
stump as if I were a child. It was an unaccountably brazen
act on his part, but I was too surprised by it to protest.

"Stop jumping around like that," he admonished, setting me gently on the ground. "You're going to twist an
ankle."

I stared at him, flustered. Then I crossed my arms over
my chest, trying to regain some of the dignity I had lost
by being manhandled. I was a teacher, blast it. I was supposed to be the one doing the manhandling.

I took a slow breath. "What I'm trying to say is that
whether you and your sister appreciate it or not, unspoiled land with mature forest like this is *priceless*. And
if you're not going to protect it, then I will. I can easily
drag out this whole inheritance mess for so long that even
if you do finally get everything, your grandchildren will
have to wheel you in to pick up the deed—and by then
your precious ski resort will have long since been located
elsewhere!"

I finished with my best glare, proud of my chutzpah.
What I could afford in attorney's fees couldn't stall a

parking ticket for fifteen minutes, but I was hoping he wouldn't realize that. I was hoping— Well, I wasn't sure what I was hoping. But I certainly did not expect what I got.

His eyes were shining openly now, and his mouth, for one brief, beautiful moment, broke into a fetching, contagious grin. My anger faded as I recognized, finally, the mature version of the happy, carefree youth I had seen in the portrait. But the unguarded smile lasted only a second. He caught himself, and it was gone. "So," he questioned, his voice formal, "you're a teacher, are you? What level?"

"Elementary."

"Then you should know," he lectured, pointing at the tree stump, "that that hickory couldn't possibly have been a sapling when Washington was here. It was only a hundred and forty years old when lightning struck it, and it wasn't in the best of health at the time. And as much as I wish this were a virgin forest, it hardly qualifies. The proper term for the preserved portions is secondary old growth."

I stared. Was the man never short of new personas?

"It's not like I had time to count the rings," I protested. "And why should I take your word on it, anyway? What do you do for a living?"

He stiffened. "I'm a forester."

My brow creased. I didn't know any foresters personally, but I doubted that many of them walked around wearing fancy suits and flashing huge checks for real estate, even if they did work in California. "You left here and went to the West Coast to be a forester?" I asked skeptically, wishing immediately that I hadn't.

The topic had hit a nerve. His expression darkened;

any trace of levity vanished. "That's what I said," he returned gruffly.

Dismay washed over me. I had thought I was getting through to him, that we were finally beginning to connect. The moment had lasted all of five seconds.

I was certain there was a warmth in him. I had sensed it at the funeral and again when he lifted me from the stump—a gentleness, a natural cheerfulness. But it was buried under a dozen sopping-wet, freezing-cold blankets.

I took a breath, then tried to catch and hold his eyes. "I didn't mean to pry," I said quietly. "All I'm trying to do is—"

"I know exactly what you're trying to do," he snapped. "And you're not going to weasel any more information out of me. So save your breath for the hike back down."

He started to walk away. But after a few paces he stopped and looked back at me, his expression waffling—by the second—between determination and remorse. His voice softened. "Do you need help finding your way back to the inn?"

The gentleness of his voice tugged at me, evoking a pleasant sense of satisfaction. My original assessment had been correct. Fletcher Black, whether he wanted me to see it or not, was a good person. I wasn't sure why he was acting so strangely, but I was sure that it had something to do with the fact that he had been hurt. Now he was angry and mistrustful, and he was also afraid. Afraid of something beyond the threat I posed to his inheritance.

I could swear he was afraid of me.

Chapter

~10~

WHEN IT CAME to dealing with men with bizarre issues, I thought I had seen it all. Derrick, the tall, dark, and handsome, had had a thing about staying faithful in a long-distance relationship. Specifically, he claimed that no real man could do it. Kevin, the sweet, cuddly fellow to whom I had devoted a full five of my prime childbearing years, had suffered from a severe case of PIS: Perpetual Immaturity Syndrome. My ex-fiancé, Todd, who I had met in the hospital as we nursed our ailing parents side by side, seemed to have a much better understanding of family. Unfortunately, he proved a little confused as to whether I should be his wife or his mother.

Yet never, in any of my various ill-fated relationships, had I ever encountered a man who was afraid of me. I was not the sort of woman to inspire fear in anything over five feet, much less a rock-solid he-man who looked like he could go several rounds with a grizzly.

Did I need help finding my way back to the inn? Of course not. But if he thought that a little rudeness on his part would be enough to make me turn tail and go home, hire a lawyer and let the paid staff fight it out, he had a good deal more to learn about me. First off, of course, was the fact that I couldn't afford a lawyer. Second was the fact that no self-respecting daughter of Colleen and Patrick O'Rourke could ever countenance turning her back on a soul in need, even if the soul in question didn't realize he needed anything.

Particularly then.

"Now there's a vote of confidence," I said cheerfully.

He was looking anywhere but at me. I smiled at him anyway. "You don't have to worry about my navigational skills. I was a Girl Scout, first class. And though I couldn't commit to it this year because of my mother's health, I usually spend my summers as a camp director. I know my way around a forest."

He didn't answer. For a long time he just stood there. "So are you leaving or not?" he asked finally, studying something in a tree branch far above his head. "I have things to do. My lawyer will be in touch."

I sighed inwardly. The man was a tough nut to crack. Perhaps it would be best to get to the heart of the matter. "Could you just tell me one thing, please?" I asked pointedly. "If you owned all this land free and clear, what would you do with it?"

I wished I could tell him I didn't want my birth mother's inheritance. But that wasn't true anymore. If all he was going to do was sell it to a developer, I did want it. He obviously didn't need the money, and by claiming my share I could at least preserve a part of this forest. To heck with what Sheila did or didn't deserve. Mother Earth rated a higher calling.

His response to my question was to turn around and walk away.

I stewed in silence for a moment, then decided to try

another tack. Settling the inheritance was important, but good citizenship was not the only thing that had driven me up this mountain. Fletcher himself intrigued me, and I wanted to understand him. I wanted to know where the pain came from.

I called after him. "Please don't go, Fletcher," I appealed. "There's something important I still need to ask you, and I promise it has nothing to do with your father's estate. Will you wait a second? Please?"

He stopped walking. His sides heaved as he released a sigh. Then he turned around, crossed his arms over his chest, and looked off into the trees again. "Fine," he said begrudgingly. "What is it?"

I stepped up closer to him, then took a breath. "I understand how you must feel about Sheila. That's why I was wondering, why *did* you come to the funeral?"

I watched his reaction like a hawk, knowing that if I saw guilt, it would confirm he had come for the wrong reasons.

He didn't answer for a long time. His eyes never wavered toward mine, but their gray-green depths showed his thoughts nonetheless. There was no guilt in him, only sadness.

"Because," he said finally, his voice low, "I believe my father would have wanted me to."

A wave of warmth rippled through me, and I smiled. He was telling the truth. He had gone to the funeral out of respect for his father, even though he knew that Sheila had most likely been a gold digger. Perhaps he suspected, as I did, that no matter what her motives were, Mitchell would never have married the woman if he hadn't truly loved her.

And Fletcher would never have shaved, put on a suit,

and gone to his ex-stepmother's awkwardly deserted burial site if he hadn't loved his father.

"Thank you," I whispered, my heart melting even as my mind grew more confused. "That was very kind of you."

He made no response.

"I wish I'd had the chance to meet your father," I said wistfully. "My own died a few years ago, and I still miss him terribly. There's something about having—"

In the middle of my musing, a thought sliced its way into my brain so sharply my body reeled. "Oh, my God," I mumbled weakly, nearly stumbling.

Fletcher stepped forward and caught my arm. "What's wrong?"

"My birth father," I babbled, heart pounding. The thoughts were coming so fast I could barely process them, yet every other one seemed to be spilling from my lips. "Sheila told me he was dead. That he died as a teenager."

But Sheila hadn't been a teenager herself when I was born, I recalled. She had been twenty-one. "Everything she told me about herself was a lie," I cried, moving from shocked to exuberant. "*Of course* she lied about him, too!"

I could remember Sheila's sympathetic tone when I had posed the question in the coffee shop. *Your birth father was killed in a motorcycle accident a year after you were born. He was a nice enough boy, but immature—and very reckless.*

I had asked for details. What did he look like? What were his interests? But she had dodged most of my questions with the finesse of a political mouthpiece. He was average height, with brown hair. He liked motorcycles and girls. *I hate to admit it,* she had explained. *But I'm afraid it's been so long I really don't remember him very well. I thought I loved him at the time, but I was too young to understand the meaning of the word.*

What about his parents? I had asked, still hopeful. Birth grandparents would have delighted me; my adoptive grandparents had never lived nearby, and they had all passed on early in my life.

Sheila's face had grown tight at the question. *His parents were not good people,* she had said stiffly. *They were horrible to both of us. They pressured me to have an abortion.*

My mind raced. Stephie had told me at the funeral that Sheila had always wanted to be an actress. What if she had actually been good at it? The entire story about my deceased birth father and his parents' attitude could have been no more than a ruse—carefully constructed to dissuade me from searching for more information about them. It had worked, hadn't it?

I realized that Fletcher was still holding my arm, and I grabbed on to his other one and pumped them both. "Don't you see what this means?" I practically shouted at him. "My birth father could still be alive! He could even—" I paused another moment, overwhelmed by the thought. "He could even have had other children. I *could* have half siblings!"

I sprang up and threw my arms around Fletcher's neck, squeezing him tight. Since I was affectionate by nature, such a gesture meant no more to me than a handshake, and as Fletcher's arms wrapped reflexively around me, I was certain he understood that. But after only a fraction of a second, I could feel his muscles tense. Too preoccupied to contemplate why, I simply released him and set off around the cabin.

I heard his footsteps behind me. "Meara," he called uncertainly. "Where are you going? What are you going to do?"

"I'm going back to the inn, of course," I answered without stopping. "I'm going to get in my car and I'm going to go find out who my birth father is."

I heard no response from him, but I suppose I wasn't listening. I was too intent on scrambling up the hill I had just come down, and as steep as it was, the going was much tougher this direction.

I had climbed for several minutes before nearing the hill's summit, where I was surprised to encounter a familiar pair of boots dangling at eye level. Fletcher was sitting calmly on an outcropping of rock above, watching me.

My eyebrows rose. I didn't know what his game was, but I didn't have time for it. Not now.

"You don't need to escort me," I insisted, scrambling up. "I told you, I can get back to the inn just fine."

"I'm not worried about that," he corrected, rotating to face me as I passed him. "What worries me is what you'll do after you get there."

My brow furrowed in confusion, and I looked at him over my shoulder. "I do need to make a few long-distance calls before I go, but I promise to reimburse you. I left a ten on the desk for the ones I already made. Didn't you see it?"

He looked at me as if I had sprouted green tentacles. "I don't care if you call Outer Mongolia," he responded, his tone still serious. "I'm just telling you you shouldn't rush into this birth father thing."

I stared at him, trying to remember how much of what was going on in my head I had actually said out loud. Even if he did understand what I was doing, why would he care?

"Please, just take a minute to calm down," he urged. His voice was soothing now- -and entirely unfamiliar. "You should think this thing through before getting your hopes up."

I looked into his earnest eyes and found myself flummoxed. When I was nice to the man, he frosted over like an icicle. Yet here I was tripping over myself to get away from him, and suddenly he was concerned and protective.

He was also giving me the impression that he knew what he was talking about. "Why do you say that?" I asked, turning to face him.

His eyes looked straight into mine. He took a breath. "Because of Tia," he explained. "My sister. She tracked down both her birth parents, and the reunions were a disaster."

I pictured the dark, exotically pretty girl of the portrait, the daughter who looked so little like the rest of the family. Both her parents had had light eyes, hadn't they? I should have guessed that she was adopted.

I stood still a moment. I knew perfectly well that reunions did not always turn out happily; I had lived through one disaster of my own already. But I had no intention of giving up my dream of finding a loving biological relative just because I was afraid of being hurt. Wounds healed. Family was forever.

"I'm sorry things didn't work out well for your sister," I offered. "But surely she gained something positive from the experience."

The look he threw me said clearly that in his opinion,

she had not. "She found her birth mother first, and they met," he explained, his voice laden with remembered anger. "But they had virtually nothing in common, and neither came away with any interest in an ongoing relationship. Tia was disappointed, but she kept insisting she was glad just to have closure. So she went on and contacted her birth father too, even though her birth mother told her she shouldn't—that he had been a one-night stand who wanted nothing to do with a child."

I cringed. Manner of conception was a sensitive issue for an adoptee. Whether you wished for it to or not, it mattered. Rape, incest, or prostitution were the worst possibilities, but meaningless recreation was bad enough. Every child had the right to a father—not a sperm donor in denial.

"But Tia's not the type to take no for an answer," Fletcher continued. "Against my advice and everyone else's, she confronted the man in the middle of his driveway one day as he was coming home from work. She told him who she was, and he proceeded to scream at her about how she wasn't his—that her mother was nothing but a lying whore."

A heavy weight fell upon my stomach. "I'm sorry," I said again, throwing Resolution #2 to the wind. "That must have been awful for her."

"It was," he confirmed. "And I don't—" He stopped the thought and rose, looking uncomfortable. "You can do what you want," he announced. "I'm just throwing in my two cents on Tia's behalf."

I couldn't help but smile. Compassion was in his blood, even though he seemed to wish it weren't. His sister's dreams had been shattered; he didn't want to see even a stranger making the same mistakes.

"So what are you going to do?" he questioned, attempting a disinterested tone. "Do you even know the man's name?"

I straightened and turned away from him, carefully hiding my grin. If he felt the need to be protective of all female adoptees, I wasn't going to stop him. The topic was the only thing so far that had succeeded in bringing his guard down.

"Sheila said his name was Michael Smith," I answered, allowing myself a rueful chuckle at the thought. "I doubt she could have picked a name harder for me to trace, since she'd already taken Johnson for herself."

I headed down the slope toward the clearing, but soon found him ahead of me again. "How do you do that?" I remarked, miffed. "What are you, part Native American?"

"Possibly." His tone turned serious. "If you know for a fact that Sheila didn't want you to find your birth father, shouldn't you wonder why?"

The question bothered me, and I stepped up my pace and passed him. "Sheila didn't want me to find *her* again," I argued. "Maybe she figured he could lead me back to her."

"Or maybe," came a voice even with my side, "she was trying to protect you."

I was protecting you. Rosemary died. Stay—

Sheila's last words flashed through my brain again. But this time, they evoked only anger. The woman had committed some crime so terrible she spent more than five years in prison. Virtually everything she had ever said to me was a lie. Why should I take her dying words any more seriously?

"You have no idea what you're talking about," I protested, suddenly irritated by his interference, well meaning or not. What did he know about my situation with Sheila, anyway?

A cold chill swept over me. What did he know, indeed?

He had lied to me about how he made his living, I was sure of that. Had he lied when he said he had never met Sheila? Had he lied when he claimed he didn't understand her reference to his mother?

"I'm perfectly capable of protecting myself," I insisted. "The question is: who are *you* protecting?" It was a fitting question, but one that would have carried more punch had I not slipped on some leaves and crashed into him while delivering it.

He steadied me with a strong arm, and as I leaned briefly against him I had a flash of thought I knew I should quash immediately. I prided myself on being able to ignore any male packaging when the product enclosed was suspect, and right now, Fletcher Black was suspect. The fact that my heart was beating at twice its normal rate had nothing to do with my willpower. I was ruled by my mind, not my hormones.

He didn't answer the question I had posed, and I straightened myself and clarified. "I asked you point-blank the day we met if you had any idea what Sheila meant in her last words to me, and you said no—that you'd never even met her. You've done your best since then not to talk to me at all. Yet the minute you find out I intend to search for my birth father, you fall all over yourself to stop me. Am I not supposed to find that odd?"

His eyes filled with confusion. A few times he opened his mouth as if to speak, then shut it. Eventually the same distant, guarded look took command again.

"I don't know any more about your birth mother than

you do," he asserted. "But from what I can tell, despite the fact that every warning sign in the book is screaming at you to leave this birth father issue alone, you're running into it headlong with both arms flailing, just like Tia did." He paused a moment; then his voice turned harder. "But you're right—you're not my sister, and you're not my problem. So go ahead, break your own heart. Damned if it matters to me. I'll see you in court."

He pivoted sharply and headed uphill, but not before I caught sight of that same accursed pain—festering behind his eyes more strongly than ever.

I closed my own eyes a moment, then swore. It was no use. Physical attraction I could fight, but that look, I could not. It drew me in like a beacon. The man had his secrets, but he was a soul in need. And even if I didn't think he was hiding something from me, even if I didn't need to reach an agreement with him over the inheritance, I would still have turned around and said what I said. Because a charge was a charge.

The fact that the man was gorgeous was immaterial.

"Fletcher," I called after him, idly reconfirming my preference for tight-fitting male jeans. The baggy carpenter look favored by the younger set was insanity. "Would you mind terribly if I stayed at the inn for a few days? The mold abatement contractors have temporarily barred me from my house, and I'd like to do some research in this area anyway. I promise not to break anything."

He stopped and turned, studying me. For a moment I was certain he would say no—that his defensive instincts would get the better of him. But surprisingly, something else did.

"Stay as long as you like," he said flatly. "Just stay away from me."

Chapter

~11~

I SETTLED MYSELF in front of the computer, my heart thumping violently against my breastbone. The Somerset County Courthouse was still for a Monday morning—so still that as I had strolled through its marble entryway, I could swear that my ragged breathing was creating an echo. I had come in as soon as the doors had opened; I had already been waiting for five minutes before the licensing clerk appeared behind her desk with a bemused expression.

I had explained quickly that I was not here to obtain a marriage license. Rather, I was hoping to find one. I neglected to tell her that there was a good chance no such license even existed. I didn't want to think that way.

Realizing that nothing Sheila had told me six years ago was likely to be true had opened so many doors simultaneously that I was uncertain where to begin. All I really knew was that my biological mother's name was Sheila Tresswell, that she was born in Uniontown, and that she had given birth to me when she was twenty-one years old. But David Falcon's research had filled in more of the puzzle. At the inn last night I had stayed up until the wee hours, poring over the papers he had given me and trolling the Internet with Mitchell's computer. I felt guilty about the latter, but the temptation of having information about my past sitting out there somewhere, waiting to be uncovered, was too powerful to resist.

What the lawyer had discovered, working forward from Sheila's birth certificate, was that she had grown up the only child of a broken home. Her parents had divorced when she was five; her father died a few years later in a mining accident. The public records shed little light on the subsequent actions of the mother and daughter, other than establishing that Margaret Orr never remarried—at least not in Fayette County. But in 1972, when Sheila would have been nineteen, Margaret passed away. Her death certificate indicated that she had died of lung cancer, and that her last known address was a public housing unit in Uniontown. She had received an indigent burial.

Sheila's own paper trail ended there as well. In his notes, David Falcon surmised that she had probably either left the area or married and changed her name. He had found no marriage record for her, but he had checked only in Fayette County. She could have gotten married anywhere.

Like Somerset County, for instance.

The clerk reached down beside me and booted up the computer, then clicked a few times with the mouse. "Here's where you start," she advised. "You searching by name?"

I nodded.

"You shouldn't have any trouble then," she said with a smile. "Printer's to your left. Let me know if you need any help."

She left me, and I took a much-needed deep breath. *Don't be so tense,* I chided. I had no proof that Sheila had ever married at all, much less in this county. But it was a reasonable enough place to search, given that I had been born here.

That fact had been the only valuable information my own birth certificate had offered me. The "amended" version to which I was entitled as an adoptee had my birth parents' names and information blocked out, replaced with those of my adoptive parents. I knew from my Internet search that I could request my original birth certificate from the state, but that it would be released to me only if my birth father consented. If not, I would only have access to nonidentifying information such as my birth parents' medical histories and possibly their occupations or hobbies. Either way, I might not hear anything for weeks.

I wanted to know something today.

I positioned my shaking fingers over the keyboard and typed in the name Sheila Tresswell, backing up three times to correct my errors. I had spent the latter half of last night tossing and turning, and much of my sleeplessness had come from guilt. I knew now that my birth mother had had a tumultuous childhood. She had been left all alone in the world at the age of nineteen, and a year later found herself pregnant. She had no money, no family, and most likely little education. How *could* she have raised me all on her own? No matter what sort of lifestyle she had lived later on, no matter how she had ended up in prison, I had no business judging her for giving me up. Especially not when my life had turned out so well.

I punched the ENTER key, and the hourglass appeared.

Calm down, I ordered myself. Even if, miracle of miracles, Sheila had ever married in this county, there was no guarantee that the information on that record would lead to my birth father. For any ex-husband of hers to be both easy to locate and willing to talk to me was an incredible long shot. And even if I succeeded on those two counts, Sheila might or might not have confided in a husband about a previous pregnancy. I could only hope that she had.

My eyes were fixed on the hourglass; each second seemed like ten. Images spun in my head—Sheila, young and vibrant, wearing a lacy white dress; Sheila, broken and sobbing, living in a boyfriend's dumpy apartment, staring at a picture of me.

The screen flickered. *Your search matches 1 record.*

My heart pounded in double time. I moved the mouse and scrolled down.

Sheila Marie Tresswell.

My gaze leapt immediately to the man's name below hers.

Jacob Martin Kozen. Date of Birth: February 25, 1945. Occupation: Police officer.

Hot tears sprang up behind my eyes, and my breath shuddered. *You did get married,* I thought to myself with a smile, an unaccountable sense of joy spreading through me. *You married a policeman . . . you weren't always alone.*

I drank in the remainder of the screen in a rush. Sheila's occupation was listed as "waitress." Her birth information matched what I already knew. Jacob's parents were probably also divorced; at least, they had different last names.

The couple had married right here in Somerset, in the

middle of winter. The ground would have been snow-covered then, I mused, seeing once again the image of the white dress. But then my eyes rested on something else, and an icy ball slammed straight into my stomach.

Date of Marriage: January 16, 1973.

The year before I was born.

I sat frozen for a moment, my breaths coming quick and shallow. Then after a flurry of furious thought, I rose with a jerk. "Excuse me," I called out to the clerk, "but could I check divorce records on this same computer?"

The clerk stepped over, seemingly oblivious to the distress buffeting my insides. "You just click on this," she explained, pointing. "But print that record first if you want it. Do you want it?"

I nodded. She tapped the mouse, and the printer at my left whirred. Then she clicked onto the second database. I thanked her and dropped back into the chair as she departed. S-H-E-I . . .

My fingers trembled so violently I could barely type. I finished with my right index finger, using my left hand to steady my wrist. K-O-Z-E-N. This time, the hourglass didn't last long. Not nearly long enough.

Record of Divorce. Jacob Martin Kozen. Sheila Tresswell Kozen. Date of Decree: August 14, 1979.

The numbers spun in my head, and I grew suddenly queasy. *Six years.* Sheila and Jacob had been married for six years. They had not divorced before I was born. They had not even been in the middle of a divorce when I was born. They had been married for seventeen months already. They had stayed married for five years after.

I hit the mouse button with a snap, then rose and waited by the printer. As the second sheet ejected I collected both, shoved them into my notebook, and walked

out of the limestone courthouse and onto the sidewalks of
Somerset. I was dimly aware that I had not thanked the
clerk.

I walked for forty-five minutes before driving my car.

Seeing a twenty-some-odd-foot moving van in the
meadow behind the inn probably should have come as a
shock to me. But this morning, I had no shock left to
offer. I simply parked my car in the lot next to Fletcher's
mud-encrusted pickup and walked over to investigate.

The vehicle was pulled up to the door of the old white
frame house, and several men in light blue work clothes
were carrying an assortment of boxes and shabby-looking
pieces of furniture down its front steps and onto the truck.
The men took little notice of me as I approached, and I
stood silently for a while by the van, staring at its California plates and trying to grasp the situation with what
was left of my brain.

No explanation presented itself. I peeked in the back
of the trailer and saw a variety of beat-up furnishings,
broken appliances, and dusty, loosely packed belongings
that would seem more at home in a flea market than a
moving van. The exception was a series of strong, new
boxes that lay along the side wall nearest me. Leaning in
to look at them, I came face-to-face with an upright garment box, the type that contains an integral hanging bar.
The box was clearly labeled "suits," but its top had gotten knocked askew, and with another good shove would
be on the floor. I tried to reach the lid from where I was
standing, but couldn't, and since the movers were not
around, I mindlessly walked up the ramp to replace the
lid myself.

I was in the process of settling it over the top of the

box when the sight of the clothes inside stopped me cold. *Suits.* The box contained six of them. Fine wool suits, all summer weight, all with designer labels. Expensive bespoke suits, like the one Fletcher had worn to Sheila's funeral. But that particular example wasn't among them, bringing his grand total to seven.

"Better get out of the way, ma'am," a voice barked. Two of the movers had returned and were struggling up the narrow ramp with a dingy, immense sectional couch. I moved to the side as they steered it into the center of the van and dropped it with a bang. I apologized and slipped out around them, embarrassed at my nosiness, but not embarrassed enough to resist eavesdropping outside for a moment.

"I'd take this one home if it weren't for all the mouse turds," the older of the two muttered.

The other man merely snorted.

They started back out, and I hastened up the house's steps, anxious to appear as if I were supposed to be there. What was going on? Where was Fletcher? The house's door was standing open, and I didn't bother fighting the urge to walk through it.

Coming from the bright sunshine outdoors, my eyes took a few seconds to adjust to the relative darkness within. At first all I could make out was a hall, connected to an empty living room that smelled strongly of dust and mothballs. I took a tentative step forward, but was quickly pushed to the side by a man carrying a metal headboard down the staircase. I backed down the hall into the next nearest doorway, then turned around.

I was in the kitchen—a kitchen that looked as though it had not been updated since the sixties. The cabinets were white-painted metal, liberally chipped and scratched, and the counters were a glaring shade of red. The built-in stove seemed ancient, as did the ceramic sink. But the refrigerator—an elaborate model complete with ice and water dispensers on the door—looked almost brand-new.

The smell of pies. Wonderful, scrumptious pies.

My eyes narrowed at the misplaced thought. I was an excellent baker, and pies were my specialty. But this would hardly be an ideal kitchen in which to make them. Why would I think about pies now?

"Meara?"

I turned with a start. Fletcher stood behind me in the hallway, holding a large picture frame under one arm.

"Did you need something?" he asked, his voice deadpan.

I looked at him without responding, my mind still in a fog. When it occurred to me how ditzy my speechlessness must seem, I managed to force myself into gear.

"I just wondered what was going on," I explained. "Are you taking this stuff back to California with you?"

He stared at me, and since it took him just as long to answer, I stopped feeling self-conscious. "No," he answered finally. "Everything in the van is going to Goodwill. So if you have anything of Sheila's that you were going to take, just have these guys throw it on. If you want."

"Thank you," I agreed, thinking of the bags that were still in my car. I had carried them all the way to Somerset and back, forgetting them entirely.

"Why don't you come back outside?" he suggested, tilting his head toward the door. The note of tension in his voice was slight, but I caught it. He didn't like my being here. Was there something I wasn't supposed to see? I mulled over the thought. I must have mulled it over for quite a while.

"Come outside," he said again, and this time it was a command rather than a suggestion.

I complied. He led me out of the house and then started across the meadow, looking back occasionally to see if I was following. I fell into step a few paces behind him and stayed there, my mind miles away.

They were a married couple, a voice in my head taunted, just as it had all morning, every second I hadn't succeeded in thinking about something else. *And they gave their child away.*

When we reached the inn, Fletcher opened the French doors to the common room and held one open for me.

They had a little girl, the voice continued to jeer as I walked inside. *But they didn't want her. Neither of them.*

"I suppose you noticed the boxes already," he said, walking down the hallway and turning into the bedroom across from mine.

I continued to follow, having no idea what he was talking about.

"I told the men not to mess with anything in your room. They didn't, did they?" he asked, looking in that direction.

I shook my head, not that I knew. I was too busy staring at the collection of boxes and assorted pieces of furniture that had been haphazardly stacked from floor to ceiling over every square inch of the other bedroom's floor space.

My mind continued to reel. "Would you please tell me what's going on?" I asked, reasonably politely. "Whose stuff is this?"

"Mine," he answered. "You have a problem with its being here?"

"No, of course not," I said quickly, trying to regroup. Evidently, he was clearing out the white house and giving most of its contents to charity. What he put here must be what he wanted to keep—stacked and ready for export to California.

A sound met my ears, and my beleaguered brain snapped to attention. It was the cuckoo. The cuckoo from the Ferris Mountain clock on the landing. In all the time I had spent at the inn thus far, I had not once managed to catch the little creature in the act. Inconsequential as the desire would seem, it was a tiny thrill I was determined to allow myself.

"Excuse me," I blurted, wheeling around and flying up the steps. I reached the landing on cuckoo number nine, with plenty of time to catch the last two. "I knew it!" I exclaimed, watching the tiny, featherless baby bird emerge from its splintered shell, beak open wide. My heart warmed at the simple sight. "It's perfect."

I stood a moment longer, tracing my finger over the delicate lines of the nest, marveling at their intricacy.

"You like the clock?"

I turned toward Fletcher's voice. He was standing at the bottom of the stairs, watching me with an expression only one step removed from a grin.

"Of course," I responded with surprise. "It's extraordinary." My mind returned to the day he had offered to buy me out—how he had so glibly referred to the inn as "broken down." How could he not understand what a treasure this was?

I watched him thoughtfully. "Was this your mother's clock?" I asked.

He paused only a second before answering. "Yes."

"Was it a gift?" I pressed. Judging from the state of the white house, I had begun to doubt that the Blacks, though land rich, would have had the liquid wherewithal for such a purchase. But after seeing the box of suits, I was fairly certain who did.

"Yes," he answered, his tone defensive again. "Any more questions?"

He did have money. He had to, and lots of it. Money he obviously didn't want me to know about.

A thought struck. He had said that everything on the moving van was going to charity, but he couldn't possibly intend to give those suits away. I couldn't stand by and let him make such a costly mistake, even if it did mean confessing my snooping.

"Your suits," I said in a rush. "You left a whole box of them in the van. You'd better get them before they're packed in."

His eyes narrowed. "What were you doing in the van?"

"Nothing," I protested. "I just noticed the lid was off, and I thought I would put it back before whatever was inside got dirty—"

"I'll bet," he said sarcastically. He turned his eyes from me and exhaled. "For your information, I couldn't care less about the suits. They're going to Goodwill."

I stared, unable to squelch the penny-pinching ethics my father had so laboriously drilled into me. "But they're worth a lot of money! If you really don't want them, you could at least take them to a consignment store—"

"Goodwill can sell them," he interrupted. "Some guy will get a great bargain. It'll make his day."

I stared down at him another moment, then closed my

eyes. The man was an enigma, and trying to figure him out was more than enough to drive me batty—even if Sheila's wedding date was not still echoing in my brain, periodically pushing itself to the forefront like the worst moment of a bad dream.

"Fletcher Carlisle!" a scratchy voice screeched suddenly from the hall below. "What in the devil do you think you're doing?"

I opened my eyes to see Fletcher whirl around. From my position on the landing, I couldn't see who was yelling at him.

"How many times have I told you not to wear those damned boots in here? There's mud all the way down the hall and out the back! What are you? Ten years old? If you don't sweep that mess up right now I'll turn you over my knee if it cracks both my leg bones to do it!"

To my amazement, Fletcher grinned from ear to ear. "Now, Estelle," he said warmly, stepping out of my field of vision. "You know you've missed my mud."

I heard a thwack, which I strongly suspected to be dusting cloth on denim. A man's laugh followed, deep and rumbling. The sound resonated through me, cheery and reassuring, and I wished desperately to hear it again. I began to creep down the stairs.

"Missed cleaning up your mud off the tile every damned day? I should say not!" Estelle protested, though her tone was clearly teasing now. "If this is the way it's going to be till you get that house built, I'll just lock the blasted doors myself and throw away the key."

"You couldn't stand it," he answered. "There would still be dust in here. Floating around. Building up. A little more every day—"

"Oh, you!" I heard another thwack. "And how am I

supposed to clean this place now? You've got your stuff all shoved up against the furniture. You promised me I'd have a pathway, and just look at that—I can't get within three feet of that bureau!"

"I'll move it," he assured, his voice all charm. "Just for you."

Estelle scoffed.

I reached the bottom of the stairs, though neither of them seemed to notice me. Estelle reached up a bony hand and tweaked Fletcher's stubble-covered chin. "I have missed you, you lout. I'd tell you I nearly cried when I heard you were back to stay, but then you'd get all full of yourself, wouldn't you? So I won't say a word. Except that if you think your sweet talking is going to make me forget that mud in the hall—"

She stepped around him, saw me, and stopped cold.

"Hello, Estelle," I offered quietly.

She cast a questioning glance at him, then looked back at me. "You still here, honey?" she asked with forced warmth. "What for?"

Fletcher stepped forward. "She's not quite done with Sheila's things," he explained. His voice was stiff and distant again, and my heart fell. The fact that the mere sight of me had soured both their moods was hardly flattering.

"She needs a place to stay for a few more days," he continued. "I told her it was fine. Now if you'll both excuse me, I have some more moving to do." He brushed past us and disappeared down the hall, leaving Estelle and me to stare awkwardly at each other.

I took in her disapproving glare with curiosity, remembering how she had asked me what I knew about Fletcher, then warned me to stay away from him. Given her obvious fondness for the man, I suspected now that the warning had been delivered for his benefit, not mine. Which made sense, given that he had money. Clearly, in Estelle's mind, the apple didn't fall far from the tree.

Either Sheila's tree, or Mitchell's.

"So Fletcher is moving back here," I stated, trying to wrap my mind around the concept. The things stacked at the inn weren't going to California after all—they must have just come from there. He was clearing out the white house; Estelle had alluded to the building of a new one. Could he really be planning to build another house and live here, on his family's estate? For good?

A surge of hope spread through me, and my cheeks grew hot. *If so,* I thought with joy, *it means he has no intention of selling.*

A broad smile erupted on my face, and without a word I left Estelle and headed after him.

Chapter

~12~

"FLETCHER, WAIT!" I held the French doors open and called out to him, but though he ceased his trek across the meadow, he did not turn around.

I said nothing more, but hastened out to meet him.

"I need to talk to you," I explained, circling around to face him. "Can we sit down somewhere?"

He exhaled with displeasure, his eyes looking anywhere but at me. "I'm trying to work here. Can it wait?"

"No!" I demanded. "This conversation is already overdue. You can walk away from me if you want to, but I'm still going to talk."

"I don't doubt that," he muttered, rubbing his nascent beard. His eyes met mine briefly, as if assessing my level of determination. Then he started walking toward the white house again. "Come on," he offered over his shoulder.

I followed him around the side of the dilapidated house to where a collection of flat-topped sandstone boulders rose out of the steep slope. He moved toward the tallest one, then leaned against it with his feet crossed at the ankles and his arms crossed over his chest—his favorite defensive position. I chose a boulder uphill, so that I could sit down without having to look up at him.

"Here's the deal," I began. "All I've ever wanted regarding Sheila's inheritance is two things. To do right by any of her other heirs, which I now don't believe exist, and, if necessary, to keep you from destroying this place."

He made no response.

"And if you had been honest with me when I asked you what your plans were," I continued in an accusing tone, "we could have settled all this yesterday."

He threw me a questioning glance.

"I thought you wanted to sell," I explained. "Everything you said at the meeting led me to believe that—that you wanted nothing to do with this place, that you just wanted to get back to California. But if you really want to keep this land intact and live on it yourself, that changes everything."

His eyes narrowed. "Why should it?"

"Is that what you'd like to do?"

He didn't answer.

"Oh, for heaven's sake!" I groaned, springing off my rock. "Do I *look* like some kind of real estate barracuda?"

Amusement sparkled in his eyes, and for a brief moment I thought I might have gotten through to him—that he was beginning to trust me. Then just as quickly, that abominable distant expression of his returned. But I was not so easily discouraged. I smiled, climbed up on the boulder he was leaning against, and settled myself next to him as if we were old chums. "Just answer me, please?" I encouraged. "What could you possibly stand to lose?"

The second our shoulders grazed, he moved away to face me.

"Plenty," he retorted.

I didn't say anything more. I just looked at him. I was being honest, and I was certain that if he looked into my eyes long enough, he would realize that.

After a few seconds of staring, something inside him did seem to break. He blew out a breath and turned his gaze to the ground. "Fine," he acquiesced. "You heard what Estelle said, anyway. Yes. I want to live here. I've always planned to come back and live here, and I have no intention of selling any part of this property to anyone. But that doesn't matter, because other than my sister, I also have no intention of sharing it with anyone."

His voice softened slightly. "I have nothing against you personally, Meara. But I do have plans. Plans that were in place long before my father died. Construction on the new house was supposed to start next week; now it's on hold indefinitely. I'm not trying to cheat you out of anything else your birth mother might have left you, but I will contest your inheritance of this land. I have to."

I studied him as he spoke, transfixed by the conflicting string of emotions that drifted across his eyes. Compassion. Anger. And as always, hurt. Then a series of images flashed across my own mind. How natural he had seemed hanging about the cabin in his mud-covered clothes. His pride in speaking of forestry. How nimbly he moved over the landscape.

Now I understood. He wasn't interested in the money the land might bring. Nor did he give a hoot about the Sheepsworth Inn, with its elegant—a.k.a. stuffy—milieu. All along, what he had really cared about was the forest. He was a certified, tree-hugging nature lover, just like me, and it was his passion for this place that I had seen in his eyes when he had tried to buy me out.

Of course he hadn't wanted me to know how much

this place meant to him—not when his personal wealth made him a target for extortion. He might have moved to California for a while, but his heart had remained in the Laurel Mountains. He had always wanted to come back here, to raze the aging farmhouse and build a new one, perhaps originally as a gift for his parents. But his mother had died young. And his father—

Oh, Mitchell. No. My stomach twisted, so much so that I put my hand to it. Mitchell must have known how important the land was to his son. No doubt he had intended for him to inherit it all along. Fletcher had purchased adjoining property; they had made plans for the new house together. But that was before Sheila.

After Sheila, Mitchell had lost his mind. He had met her, courted her, and married her, all without telling his children she existed. He hadn't bothered asking his lawyer for advice. He hadn't bothered with a prenuptial agreement that would have protected his children's interests in a divorce. Most importantly, he hadn't bothered to update his will—an oversight that could have permitted the court to draw a line down the middle of the property and award half the Black legacy to a stranger.

Mitchell had forgotten his son altogether. And until the morning Fletcher had found me sleeping at the inn, he had no idea that his father had failed to safeguard his inheritance. When he did find out, his father was already dead. You couldn't yell at a dead person. No matter how betrayed you felt.

I knew all about that one.

"Fletcher," I said softly, a wave of guilt badgering me for being part of such a mess, even involuntarily. "I don't want the estate. I never did. It belongs to you and Tia—not to Sheila, and not to me."

He didn't move for a moment. His gaze met mine, his eyes wide.

"What does that mean?" he asked. "What do you want?"

I smiled at him again. "It means I'll sign whatever you want me to—returning whatever I would have inherited from Sheila. I don't want anything from you."

He stared at me for several seconds, another string of garbled emotions parading across his face. Disbelief, relief, gratitude, and joy all took their turn, but suspicion grabbed the first foothold.

"I offered you a huge sum of money!" he exclaimed. "Why didn't you take it?"

I felt a sudden desire to deliver a playful punch to his perfectly shaped jawbone, but I settled for a chuckle. "My, but you do have a high opinion of me. Is it the hair? Too 'Satan incarnate'?"

He almost laughed. But not quite.

"I don't want your money," I reaffirmed. "But I suppose I do want something. I'd be terribly grateful if— sometime— you would smile at me like you were smiling at Estelle just now. Because as I keep telling you, I don't want to be your enemy. And this distant, scowling thing is getting really old."

Despite himself or otherwise, he did smile then. And the effect was worth the wait. His face lit up with a grin so honest and heartfelt it warmed me to my toes, and as his eyes held mine, I saw a newfound fondness there.

"I don't know what to say to you, Meara. Except thank you."

His deep, gentle voice rumbled through me, bringing with it a subtle, nagging pull that made my own smile widen, even as alarm bells rang. *Whoa,* I ordered myself. *Steady.*

Women with better self-control would think I was overreacting. But I had come to recognize these twinges of mine for exactly what they were: ominous forerunners of the same damnable, incredibly powerful pull that had thrice made me leap headlong into a man's arms—desperate to hold him, desperate to make him happy, and heedless of the consequences to myself. I was *not* going down that road again. It had happened with Derrick, with Kevin, with Todd. In every case, it had started just like this. I saw something in a man that touched me. I saw hurts I felt I could heal. I offered comfort, and he took it. And took, and took, and took.

I fell in love too easily, and always with men who wanted something different from life than I did. I wanted commitment; Derrick had wanted freedom. I wanted children; Kevin had wanted to be one. I wanted excitement and challenge; Todd had wanted his dinner on the table by five. I had vowed on my birthday to never again allow a man to use me, and that meant not letting my heart fall for anyone whom my brain had not thoroughly screened, analyzed, and preapproved. No exceptions allowed.

"No thanks are necessary," I answered, averting my own eyes. "I'm just doing what's right." My heart sank, and I hopped off the rock. Or at least I tried to. But midway down I was surprised to feel Fletcher's hands on my waist, catching me and breaking my fall. My arms rested on his as I landed, and as we stood that way, studying each other, an irrepressible flush of heat swept through me. I was attracted to him, there was no point in denying that. But I could stop myself there. Now that I was on to me, I could control the Florence Nightingale thing. I could, and I would.

His eyes studied me back, and for a few tantalizing seconds I was certain the attraction was mutual. But then the lights in his eyes went out—as abruptly as if doused with water. He released me and stepped away.

"Thank you again, anyway," he repeated awkwardly. "You're welcome to stay at the inn as long as you want. My sister should be back in a few days. Perhaps you'd like to meet her."

"I would," I answered, feeling inexplicably sad. "I'd like that very much."

He clapped his hands together—an uncharacteristic nervous gesture. "All right, then. I'd better get back to supervising these guys. I'll—" He seemed at a loss for words. "I guess I'll see you around."

I nodded. His gaze lingered on mine only briefly, but in it I got another glimpse of the emotion most likely to be my downfall.

Pain. Something was still hurting him. Something beyond his worry over losing this place. Something beyond, even, the sting of his father's disregard.

What could it be? And why did the mere sight of me seem such a catalyst?

"Fletcher," I called after him, before I even realized I was doing it. "Would you mind if I used the kitchen at the inn? I have a hankering for my own cooking tonight. Perhaps you could join me—and bring whatever papers I need to sign."

He stopped and turned, considering the offer for a seemingly endless period. "Sure, Meara," he said finally, his apprehension poorly concealed. "I'd like that."

I stirred the pasta into the boiling water, regretful that the meal preparations were nearing a close. I enjoyed cooking. Having something to do with my hands was always therapeutic, but particularly so when my brain was heavy with thought. This evening, the burden was crushing.

Settling my conscience over Sheila's estate had been a relief, and a big one. But I had no shortage of angst with which to replace it. The revelations of the morning were once again foremost in my mind, and the voice that had taunted me all day seemed only to be getting louder.

They were married when you were born. They still didn't want you.

The scenarios ran through my head in an endless chain, pummeling me in tandem.

Maybe they did want you, but the county took you away.

My stomach churned.

Or maybe they thought they couldn't afford you.

I leaned my face into the rising steam. Lack of funds was no excuse. Welfare was alive and well in the seventies. Besides, he was a cop.

Maybe you weren't his.

I stepped back from the stove. A child of adultery— now there was something to be proud of. And who had my real father been? Her boss? The meter reader?

I looked around for something else to do, but the table was already set. The spaghetti sauce was simmering, the salad was tossed, and the bread was warming in the oven.

A bun in the oven. What a happy surprise.

I exhaled and looked around again. There was nothing else to do. I walked up the hall to the front of the inn and glanced idly through the narrow window beside the door. I had no idea when Fletcher might arrive, but it didn't really matter. If he got here before the pasta was ready, fine.

If he didn't, I would start without him. My offering of food had not been a romantic gesture; it had been a compulsion. Feeding people was what I did.

Or maybe she didn't cheat on him. Maybe she was raped.

I slapped my hands over my ears, knowing that the effort was useless. The thoughts that tortured me—the what-ifs—I had already wrestled with for most of my life. I knew that nothing stopped them, that nothing would ever stop them, except for the truth. I thought I had known the truth once, but now I was back to the guessing. The uncertainty. The fear.

I hated it, and I had to make it stop again. No matter how unpleasant things got in the short term.

I took a deep breath, then turned back toward the kitchen. It had been thirty seconds, hadn't it? At least I could stir the pasta again.

I was walking past the door to the front bedroom when something low to the ground caught my eye. It was the framed picture that Fletcher had carried over from the white house, then placed on the floor with his other boxes. I hadn't seen the canvas side then, but now the image upon it drew me in like a magnet.

I walked into the room and turned on the light, then took the heavy frame in my hands. It was an original painting, and an unusual one. A sea of cheerful faces smiled toward the artist—girls and boys of all ages, some standing, some sitting or kneeling, all flanking the mature couple at the portrait's center. The faces were skillfully detailed, yet each held a distinct, subtle spark of animation that rendered it closer to a caricature than a facsimile. I recognized the principals immediately, and my breath caught.

The man was Mitchell, smiling and affable, his arms open wide to encircle both his wife and his daughter. Rosemary stood close, vibrant and warm, a spitting image of herself as she had looked in the photograph. Tia, however, was younger, an impish-looking girl of eleven or twelve who clutched a paint palette with a fake, cheesy smile. Fletcher sat Indian style at his mother's feet, an adolescent with hair as red as a fire engine and a grin from ear to ear. In his hands, I noted curiously, was a screwdriver.

The background, though abstracted into an interesting pattern of straight lines and swirls, was clearly meant to represent the white house and green hills beyond. What the people represented was far less obvious, since I was fairly certain that Mitchell and Rosemary had had two children and not nineteen.

The sound of the French doors opening met my ears, followed by Fletcher's voice drifting in from the common room. He sounded uptight, as usual. "Hello? Meara?"

"I'm in here," I answered absently, unable to tear my eyes from the portrait. After a few seconds he appeared behind me.

"Tia painted that," he said with pride, the strain in his tone easing. "One of the few times she ever painted people. I've always liked it."

"She's very talented," I praised, looking again at the palette in her hands. All the children, I noticed now, were holding something or other—from goldfish bowls to Frisbees.

"Yes, she is," he agreed. "But she prefers abstracts. Painting things that actually exist doesn't interest her nearly as much as creating something that doesn't."

I turned and looked at him, posing the obvious question. "And this family? Did all these children exist?"

He paused before answering, and his eyes smiled as he studied me. Then he took the portrait from my hands and set it upon a chest of drawers where we could look at it together. "They all existed," he explained. "But they were never all here at the same time. They were foster children that my parents cared for. These, and many more over the years. These are the ones who were here the longest, the ones Tia remembered best. She stylized the portrait to show all of us together at once—one big happy family."

"Foster children," I repeated in a whisper.

Foster children.

A chill swept up my spine. Images stirred my brain. The newel post, the upstairs bedroom, the front of the white house. Just little tricks from a mind already over-burdened with grief and speculation? Or was I remembering something real?

I had been born in Somerset County. The Blacks had served as foster parents in Somerset County.

The leap was not tremendous.

I reached out a hand. My finger pointed to a pretty girl of eight or nine with soft brown eyes and long, straight hair pulled back into a ponytail. She was poised on one knee with her hand on a soccer ball. "Who is she?" I asked, my voice still a whisper.

"That's Katie," he answered, his eyes twinkling as he talked. "She was our soccer star. She's a photographer now—travels all over the world."

Katie. He remembered her.

My eyes scanned carefully through the rest of the children. It did not take long to conclude that my likeness was not among them. But my fascination was unabated.

"And this boy?" I asked, pointing at a jolly-looking

fellow of six or seven, from whose pocket peeked an overlarge calculator. "What was his name?"

"Andy," he answered. "Our math whiz. Sweet kid. Scary smart. He's an engineer now."

I worked my way across the painting, asking after each child. I realized how odd my absorption must seem, and I feared that at any moment Fletcher might cut me off, resenting the intrusion. But surprisingly, he seemed to be enjoying himself. He remembered all the children well, speaking of each with undisguised fondness. Many of the children's lives had turned out less than perfect, but his parents seemed to have made some attempt to keep up with every one of them.

I couldn't help but wonder about me.

"Fletcher," I asked tentatively, as soon as his reminiscence was complete. "How old are you?"

His eyebrows rose slightly at the question, but he did not appear offended. "Thirty-two," he answered. "Why?"

I swallowed. Tia appeared younger than her brother, both in the photograph above the desk and in the portrait. If I had been here before the age of four, neither of them would have been old enough to remember me.

I looked again into the children's shining faces.

"I always wanted brothers and sisters," I said wistfully. "You and Tia were so lucky. I envy you."

He chuckled. "A few days with us would have cured you of that. The Black household was all bedlam, all the time."

I tore my eyes from the picture and faced him. Both my voice, and my hands, were shaky. "I was a foster child in this county myself. From some age until I was four. I thought that some things around here looked familiar, but I didn't take the feelings very seriously, because I do that to myself all the time. But now that I know—"

I broke off. My heart raced.

"Do you think it's possible? Could I have been here, too?"

His brow furrowed. The lights that had danced in his eyes as he spoke of his foster siblings petered, replaced with a queer sort of dread. "How old are you?" he asked.

"Thirty," I answered. "You would only have been six when I left."

He looked at me another moment, then pulled his eyes away. His expression turned stony. "It's possible, I suppose," he said without emotion. "But I wouldn't remember."

He turned his back to me, making a pretense of adjusting some of his packing boxes.

A jab of pain struck through my chest. He seemed to care so much about the children in the picture, I couldn't help but feel slighted. Of course he wouldn't remember me; I wasn't expecting a celebration. But shouldn't the possibility of our twice-crossed paths strike him as mildly intriguing?

"So," he said tonelessly, continuing to fiddle with the boxes. "What are you cooking? Something sure smells good."

The pasta.

My mind shifted quickly back to the mundane. I flew into the kitchen and rescued the pot from the stove, grateful, suddenly, for the diversion. "I *hate* mushy spaghetti," I groused out loud, stirring. "Forty-five more seconds, and I'd have had to start all over."

He joined me with a few long strides. He was back to uptight again, my inquiry having dashed the easy, comfortable mood he had slipped into when speaking of his family. But he was at least making an effort to be pleasant.

"Don't fuss on my account," he said with a smile. "I'm hungry enough to eat it raw." He leaned down and booted up Mitchell's computer, which occupied the counter space nearest the common room, then watched me with a curious expression. "Do you like to cook?"

"I love it," I answered distractedly, attempting to pour the water off the spaghetti. Unfortunately, I was a little too distracted. Unable to find either a colander or a spaghetti strainer, I had resorted to holding the pot over the sink with the lid askew. But true to my clumsy nature I let some of the boiling water slosh onto my hand, and my resulting jerk sent a third of the spaghetti down the drain and a quarter of the water splashing across the counter and onto my shoes.

I dropped the pot into the sink and cursed.

"Are you all right?" he asked, at my side in a flash. "Did you burn yourself?"

"No," I said quickly, embarrassed. I ran cold water over my hand and shifted my feet. "My wrist is just a little singed. That, and I feel like I'm standing in a hot tub."

He took my hands and looked at them, then glanced down over the rest of me. "You go get those shoes off," he suggested. "I'll put the food on the table. No reason you should be doing everything anyway."

I wanted to explain that setting out the meal was one of the most rewarding parts of the process, and that in my book, hijacking it did not constitute a favor. But since I was pretty sure I really had scalded my feet, I bit my lip and limped to my bedroom instead.

When I returned several minutes later, comfortably shod in a thick pair of socks, Fletcher had cleaned up the mess and moved on to slice the bread. I hovered nearby and watched, wishing he would stop and give the knife back.

"I hope you don't mind," he said, tossing his head in the direction of the computer, "but my lawyer is supposed to be E-mailing me a file. I thought I would print it out here, and you could sign it." He cleared his throat. "If you're still willing, that is."

"Of course I am," I answered, staring at the blinking cursor in the Google search box. "This place belongs to your family, not mine."

Not that I have a family.

He made a response, but I didn't hear it. My thoughts were still centered on the children in the painting—the huge, hectic family he'd been fortunate enough to grow up with. He hadn't been a foster—he had been a bona fide, legitimate member of the Black family. He had always felt loved, and wanted. He had no questions about his origins—no lost years to be accounted for. How could he possibly understand how much I craved that kind of rootedness, and how deeply I longed to be part of a family again?

I leaned over the keyboard, and my fingers started typing. *Jacob Kozen. Pennsylvania.*

"Meara?" Fletcher inquired. "Did you hear what I said?"

"No, sorry," I answered, hitting the ENTER key.

He continued to talk, but I didn't catch the words. The only words I caught were the ones that flashed onto the screen, right next to an icon of a telephone. *Jacob Kozen. (814)-555-1221. 245 Birch Street, Connellsville, Pennsylvania.*

"Meara?" Fletcher's voice called again, this time more insistent. "What's wrong?"

It can't be, I thought, my pulse pounding in my ears. It couldn't happen like this. It was too easy. Connellsville was less than half an hour away.

"What is it?" he pressed, moving to look over my shoulder. "Who is he?"

"My birth father," I answered in a whisper. "I think I might have found him."

Chapter

~13~

FLETCHER PUT HIS hands on my upper arms, gently rotating me to face him. "You found your birth father? Already?"

His voice was quiet and deep, rife with concern. The contrast to the standoffish man who couldn't bear to look at me, much less touch me, was striking. It was also more than a little frustrating. But my mind was too flustered to dwell on his motivations, and my shaking limbs were not selective in their appreciation of a sympathetic touch.

"I think so," I whispered.

"But how? Yesterday you didn't even know his name."

I explained about my trip to the courthouse—how knowing the county of my birth had helped me locate Sheila's marriage record. "I don't know for sure that her husband was also my birth father," I admitted. "But if he isn't, he must know who is."

Fletcher said nothing for a moment. Then he released me, fetched the bread, and set it down on the table where the plates of spaghetti already waited. "Sit down and eat," he ordered, sitting himself. "You'll need to think about this on a full stomach."

I picked at my food for the next ten minutes while he

ate his with gusto. We didn't talk; I wasn't sure I could. My head was in the clouds again.

My eyes flickered periodically to the telephone. *Answers*. They could be just a phone call away.

Fletcher polished off two plates of spaghetti, his salad, and half the loaf of bread before propping his elbows on the table and staring at me from behind folded hands. "Well?" he asked. "What are you planning to do?"

I swung my gaze slowly from the telephone back to him. "I'm going to call, of course," I answered. "The truth can't be worse than not knowing."

His eyes narrowed slightly, telling me he disagreed. He seemed to be debating whether or not to give advice, and as I watched the struggle it occurred to me that since he had grown up playing big brother to scores of foster siblings, the role was probably ingrained.

"What about risk versus reward?" he suggested finally. "There is a possible reward: you and your birth father could be reunited and live happily ever after. But you have to know how slim the odds of that are. The odds of your finding out something that's going to hurt you, on the other hand, are sky-high."

I shook my head. "You don't understand. This isn't just about reuniting with my birth father. It's about knowing who I am. Why I was given up. What happened to me before I was adopted. Living with the question marks just isn't acceptable."

I took a breath. "You also underestimate the reward. Knowing the truth could offer me more than just a birth father—I could have other biological relatives out there, too. Siblings, grandparents—alive and well, maybe even wanting a relationship with me. If I gain even one, it would be worth it."

He dipped his chin, but didn't speak.

"When the reward is that great," I continued, "the risks don't matter. I know I might get hurt—in fact, I'm almost certain of it. But I'm willing to pay that price."

He studied me, his expression somber. I thought he would say more, but he appeared to think better of it. He scooted back his chair and rose from the table.

"What?" I prompted.

He didn't answer.

"What were you about to say?" I repeated.

He shook his head. "It's none of my business."

I frowned at the flatness of his tone. These glimpses of the real Fletcher—the warm, compassionate one—were tantalizing in the extreme. No sooner did I think I had reached him than the curtain came crashing down again.

He gathered up his plate and utensils and carried them to the dishwasher, and I collected my own half-full dishes and followed. "I noticed somebody got the mud off the floor," I teased, attempting to lighten the mood. "I suppose poor Estelle gave in and cleaned up after you after all."

I tried to watch his expression, but he kept his face turned away from me. "I swept up. Estelle has a wicked right hook."

I grinned at him, but he didn't notice. He finished loading his dishes, moved straight to the computer, and began to click the keys. The printer hummed, and in a few seconds a copy of my Google search page emerged in the tray. Shortly after, another document joined it. Two and a half pages of legalese.

He removed the paper, laid the Google sheet on the counter, then took the other pages and returned to the table. As he read over them with concentration I made a pretense of tidying up the rest of the kitchen, but my eyes kept straying to the same spot on the counter. *Jacob Kozen. (814)-555-1221.*

Just a phone call away.

After a few minutes Fletcher rose, walked to the desk for a pen, then turned and looked at me. "The papers seem to be in order," he announced. "But if you'd rather wait and have a lawyer look at them first, I understand."

I looked into his eyes, which were a steely gray in the indoor light, and wished that he would put forth an iota of effort into making me trust him. My instincts insisted that I could, yet he seemed almost to be discouraging it. If he would only look me in the eye and tell me the document was fair, I knew I would believe him. I wanted to trust him. I wanted him to trust me.

But he was acting distant again.

I took the pen from his hands with a sigh and sat down to study the papers. The language was dense, as expected, but I could find nothing questionable in it. At least not until I reached the next-to-last paragraph.

"Burial expenses?" I said with a frown. "This says that Mitchell's estate will pay for Sheila's funeral, but I've already paid for it." I proffered an accusatory glance, wondering if he was trying to take advantage of some tax deduction I wasn't aware of. His eyes avoided mine.

"You put up a down payment," he responded. "But I paid the bill in full this afternoon. A refund will be sent to your home address. If you don't get it in a week, you should call them."

My eyes widened. "You didn't have to do that," I protested. "She was my birth mother."

He shrugged. "She was my stepmother."

I studied his tense frame some more, trying to make

sense of his attitude. Was he simply trying to do right by his father? Or was he actually feeling sorry for me? I was fairly certain he had overheard my telling Alex about my financial difficulties. But there were other possibilities. What if he had lied about knowing Sheila?

"Look, Meara," he asserted, breaking the uncomfortable silence, "if my father had survived the accident, don't you think he would have paid for his wife's burial? You've chosen not to inherit anything from either of them—I can't let you go in the hole covering her expenses. Not when—" He cut himself off. "The money isn't a problem. So just accept it. Please."

I caught his eyes at last, and the earnestness I saw there moved me. I knew very well that he was hiding something, but when he looked at me like that I was only too willing to assume that whatever it was didn't matter. He had a good heart; I was certain of it. Whatever private demons he might be fighting, I could not believe that the same man who had instinctively rushed to my side when I scalded myself would deliberately set out to take advantage of me a few minutes later. I laid the papers down flat on the table, read through the last paragraph, and seeing nothing else remarkable, signed them.

I rose, and he stood silently for a moment, staring at my signature as if it were penned in gold. Then he turned to me and extended his hand. "Thank you," he said, his rumbling voice low. "You have no idea what this means to me."

I extended my own hand and shook his. "I think maybe I do," I replied with a smile. As our hands touched, I noticed that the butt of his palm was rough, as if callused. But the shake was brisk, not giving me the time to notice much more.

"Still," he continued, his voice sounding more comfortable again, "I hope you didn't feel pressured. It's just that without these papers, I can't get moving on the construction, and the new house has got to be in livable condition before winter hits."

My brow furrowed slightly. "Why couldn't you stay here over the winter?" I asked, referring to the inn.

He grimaced. "This mausoleum? The doorways are low, the beds are short, and my mud would give Estelle a stroke within a week."

I grinned. "Well, what about your cabin, then? It looked plenty cozy to me."

A sparkle lit up his eyes. "The cabin would be fine," he explained. "But the route up to it is impassable in the snow, and the road can't be redone without damaging the forest on that slope. So for most of the winter, it can only be reached on foot."

Good humor swelled within me as I realized how talk of the cabin—much like talk of the woods and talk of his foster siblings—seemed to disarm him. I would remember that.

"So?" I teased. "You mean you're too soft to scale an icy mountain with a tank of propane and two sacks of groceries on your back?"

His eyes narrowed at me, and he grinned. The effect was heavenly.

A pang of hunger accosted my stomach, reminding me that I had hardly eaten. The inheritance was off my conscience, I was not as badly in debt as I thought I was, and Fletcher and I were making definite progress toward a friendship. Now all the moment needed was dessert.

I snapped my fingers. "I almost forgot!" I walked to the far corner of the kitchen and retrieved my masterpiece from under its covering. "I think a celebration is in order here. Are you still hungry?"

"Always," he said optimistically, watching me.

I grabbed a pie server and two plates. "I've had pies on my mind all afternoon," I explained as I cut into the perfectly browned crust. Cooking was enjoyable, but baking was glorious. "When I was looking for a grocery store earlier, I ran across the most wonderful farmer's market, and these peaches smelled heavenly. Sorry I didn't get any ice cream to go with the pie."

I dished a giant piece onto a plate, added a fork, and handed it to him with a flourish. Then I noticed his face. He looked horrified.

His hands lowered the dish to the counter. "You bake pies?" he asked, almost in a whisper. He was practically pale.

"Of course," I answered. "Are you allergic to peaches or something?" All traces of mirth had disappeared from his expression, leaving it clouded once more by the same wretched cast of pain I thought I had vanquished, at least temporarily. The loss of our newfound camaraderie made me mad enough to scream, and I almost did. It was a piece of pie, for heaven's sake. What was wrong with the man?

He pulled himself together. "I'm just not as hungry as I thought, that's all," he explained with artificial cheer. "It looks good, though. Could I take a rain check?"

I laid down the server that was in my hand and snatched up his dish. "If there's any left," I retorted, picking up the fork. "But don't count on it."

I ate my pie in silence as he paced the common room. He seemed to be brooding about something, but both my sympathy and my curiosity were outranked by my wounded pride. I knew I was being silly, but I couldn't help myself. It was a fabulous pie. Fabulous pies were the only kind I made, and nobody turned them down. *Nobody.*

"There's something I'd like to ask you, Meara," he said as soon as I had set down my empty plate. I took a deep breath and looked up at him, telling myself I was being overly sensitive. So the man didn't like pie. What did it matter?

"You said something the other day about Sheila," he began, his tone serious. He walked toward me, and my mind refocused. "You said that before she died she told you something about my mother. I was hoping you would tell me again what that was."

Surprised, I tried to meet his gaze. But we were truly back to square one. He glanced at me only briefly, then stared over my shoulder. "Why do you want to know?" I questioned.

He exhaled with discomfort. "Because I would like to understand what happened." He backed up a few steps and leaned against the counter. "I know that everyone thinks my father was some gullible sap who got taken for a ride. Whirlwind courtship, secret wedding . . . it all points to gold digging. Except for the fact that my father was visibly cash poor. Without the income from the inn, he could barely pay the taxes on this place. If Sheila wanted big bucks, marrying him would be idiotic."

I averted my own eyes, thinking of Sheila's lengthy incarceration, which Fletcher knew nothing about. If he did, he'd have no doubt of her culpability. Gold diggers who lived out of their cars didn't have to aim high.

"When I first found out what had happened," he continued, "I assumed the worst along with everyone else.

But I would like not to do that anymore. I would like to give my father the benefit of the doubt."

I looked at him incredulously.

"He might have had a trusting nature," Fletcher defended, "but he wasn't stupid. And if there's even a ghost of a chance that the two of them really were in love, I owe it to him to respect that. That's why I went to the funeral." He took a deep breath. "My father would never have sold this land out from under me. Not in a million years. And he wouldn't have taken stupid chances with it, either. Stupid chances like forgetting to revise his will."

"But he didn't revise his will," I pointed out gently. "What are you saying?"

"I'm saying that the only thing that makes sense to me is that he not only loved this woman, but trusted her, too. Trusted that if anything should happen to him, she wouldn't stand in the way of my inheriting the land." He exhaled again. "But that leaves open a big question. If he loved and trusted this woman so much, why would he keep Tia and me in the dark about her?"

I swallowed, a ball of lead forming in my stomach. I wished with all my heart that I could agree with him—that I could believe that Sheila's motives were pure and that his father hadn't been careless. But I knew far too many damaging things about Sheila to buy that. A part of me felt obligated to share the truth, but a larger part of me couldn't bear the task. He was having a hard enough time dealing with his father's sudden death—if he found some measure of peace in believing the man *hadn't* been duped by a career con artist, what purpose would be served by disillusioning him?

"Perhaps," I suggested, hoping no guilt was evident in my voice, "your father was worried that you and Tia would resent his falling in love again so soon."

Fletcher shook his head. "He might have been concerned about my reaction. But he would have told Tia. They were very close—she had even been encouraging him to start dating."

I took a deep breath myself, uncertain what to say. Most likely, Mitchell was embarrassed about his relationship with Sheila because he knew she was not the sort of woman his children would approve of. Or his prim-and-proper lawyer friend. Or anybody else.

"So I'm convinced there's a missing piece somewhere," Fletcher continued. "Some particular reason—related to Sheila rather than my father—why their relationship had to be kept secret. That's why I want to know what she said to you."

He was looking at me again. I stood up to face him. "She told me that she had always loved me," I repeated, disturbed by the still-raw emotion I could hear in my own voice. "Then she said, '*I was protecting you. Rosemary died. Stay*—' something. She couldn't say any more."

He stared off into space, weighing the words. Then he shook his head, his expression frustrated. "I don't get it. My mother's been gone for a year now. Why would her death have anything to do with you?"

A ripple of joy passed through me. Sorry as I was that he couldn't explain the meaning of the words, I couldn't help but be delighted to believe—once and for all—that he wasn't hiding anything about Sheila. He seemed genuinely baffled.

Another silence passed; then he stood up straight and offered a polite smile. "Well, I'll keep thinking about it. In any event, thank you again for signing the papers. And thank you for dinner. You're an excellent cook."

Whether he meant the compliment sincerely or not, I

beamed. "Thank you for letting me stay here and use the kitchen," I returned. "It's much more pleasant than living out of a motel and eating fast food."

Our gazes locked, but just when I thought the sparkle might be returning to his eyes, he looked away again. He offered a hasty good-bye and headed for the French doors, then surprised me by stopping with his hand on the knob.

He turned around. "I almost forgot. The phone number. You're going to call that man as soon as I'm out the door, aren't you?"

My eyebrows rose. He was right—my mind had begun to retrain on my birth father the second he had turned away. I was about to reach for the paper even as he spoke. "Yes," I answered unapologetically. "I couldn't sleep tonight if I didn't."

He sighed, then walked back to the table and sat down, propping his feet on a second chair. "Go ahead then," he said with resignation. "You can take the phone to another room if you want some privacy."

I stared at him. "You're waiting around?"

He leaned his head back and folded his hands over his middle, evidently assuming this answered my question.

I smiled, then picked up the phone. There were many things I didn't understand about Fletcher, but so far, none had overcome my pleasure in his company. I wasn't sure why he was staying, but if he was doing it because he thought I might be in need of moral support afterward, he was very perceptive.

Six years ago, when I had set up the first reunion with Sheila, I had been determined to keep all news of the encounter from my parents. I was terrified of hurting them, yet so great was my guilt in taking the step behind their backs that I was uncomfortable sharing the experience with anyone. I had taken on both the euphoria and the anguish alone, and the scars of that time still remained. I was glad there was no longer any need for secrecy. I was glad Fletcher was here.

Bolstered, I took a deep breath, looked down at the paper, and punched in the numbers. *Jacob Kozen.* Was he the one? Would he even talk to me? The ringing began. I cast a glance at Fletcher. His eyes were closed.

"Yeah?" a male voice barked into my ear. It was strong and demanding—just short of testy.

"Hello," I sputtered, willing my voice to stabilize. "I'm sorry to bother you, but I'm trying to reach a man named Jacob Kozen."

"You got him," the voice responded, softening slightly.

My heart pounded. I took a second deep breath. "My name is Meara O'Rourke, Mr. Kozen. I'm trying to contact the Jacob Kozen who married a woman named Sheila Tresswell back in 1973."

A silence ensued. The phone wobbled in my hand; my arms and shoulders began to tremble.

"Yeah," he repeated, his tone suspicious. "That would be me. Who wants to know about Sheila?"

I breathed in again; my lungs shuddered. "I do. You see, I was born in 1974. She was my biological mother."

An even longer silence followed, broken only by a barely audible gasp, then heavy, ragged breathing. It seemed forever before the voice, now thin and tenuous, spoke a word that made my heart stop.

"Mandy?"

Chapter

~14~

"TAKE A LEFT at the next light. The diner is about a block up on the right."

Fletcher slouched in the passenger seat of my Hyundai, his large frame cramped even with the seat pushed back. He had offered to drive me in his truck, but I liked the control of having my own car, and I was feeling beholden to him enough already. I would never have asked him to make such a trip with me; I had felt obligated, in fact, to turn down his offer. But he hadn't taken no for an answer.

"I'll wait outside," he announced as I made the turn. "Unless you want me to go in with you?"

"That won't be necessary," I responded, my tone tense. My nerves were on a razor edge. I hadn't slept a wink.

My conversation with Jacob Kozen had been short, but since hanging up the phone last evening my mind had replayed every word of it continuously, spinning the phrases in an endless, anxious loop.

I believe Sheila called me Amanda, yes.

Is she with you?

It was an odd question. Occasionally I stopped to think about that. But mostly I heard myself explaining that Sheila was dead, and apologizing for the news like the old Meara apologized for everything, feeling sorry to be the bearer of bad tidings, assuming without question that he would be upset at the death of a woman he had divorced a quarter century before.

He had not sounded upset. It would be more accurate to say that he sounded flabbergasted.

A car accident? Really? That's a shame. Did you two meet before it happened? Did she tell you about me?

I had stumbled over my words. *We met; but only briefly. She didn't tell me anything about you—in fact, she didn't tell me anything, period. That's why I'm calling. I was hoping we—* I had to stop and swallow. *I have a lot of questions about the circumstances surrounding my adoption. I was hoping you might be willing to help me answer some of them.*

He hadn't responded for a long time, and as I stood quivering, phone in hand, my knees threatened to buckle. Fletcher must have seen them shaking, because it was at that point that he had risen from his chair and come to stand beside me.

Sure, the voice had answered, finally. *I'd like to meet you. Are you in the area?*

I had said that I was only a short drive from Connellsville, and Fletcher mouthed a warning for me not to say anything more. He needn't have worried. I dodged the topic of my location, set up a public meeting, and hung up.

Only later did I realize that I had neglected to ask the obvious question. I suspected that was because I was afraid of the answer.

I steered the Hyundai into the cramped lot and tried hard to concentrate on parking—resisting the urge to scan the large, slanted diner windows for a man sitting alone. A man, perhaps, with a face much like mine.

I pulled into a spot, shifted the car into park, and killed the engine. Fletcher unbuckled his seat belt and stretched, and as I attempted to collect myself I wondered again why he had insisted on coming. It was a sweet thing to do for a friend, but for someone he barely knew, the gesture went above and beyond the call of duty. He didn't appear to have any romantic interest in me—rather, his repeated standoffishness seemed designed to discourage the thought. So what was his motivation?

I didn't return the inheritance with strings attached, I had assured him last night. *You don't have to feel obligated to me.*

I don't feel obligated to you because of the inheritance, he had answered, his tone good-natured. *I feel obligated to you because you fed me spaghetti.*

He had been adamant, and I had been too preoccupied to debate. I wanted to believe that he was simply a kind person who, after witnessing how devastating a similar reunion had been for his sister, felt compelled to offer aid. I was aware of the possibility that his interest could be self-serving—I just couldn't imagine how.

I watched him as he squirmed in the seat, trying to find a comfortable position for the wait. He was wearing his standard mountain apparel: formfitting jeans, a cotton T-shirt, and hiking boots. The shadow of stubble that had been growing on his jawline since Sheila's burial seemed to have doubled in mass over the night hours and was nearing a respectable beard. Oddly, it was a dark red one—an appealing contrast to his light brown hair. I had never been a fan of beards, but on him, I rather liked it. Clean-shaven, he was strikingly handsome, but the beard seemed more natural, more honest. And the real Fletcher was the one that intrigued me.

"What is it?" he asked, giving me the idea I had been staring. "Are you having second thoughts?"

His voice was mild; his eyes, concerned. I opened my door. "No," I answered, attempting more confidence than I felt. "I'll be fine."

I stepped out of the car and closed the door, then spoke through the open window. "I appreciate your coming, Fletcher," I admitted. "Even though I told you not to."

"My pleasure," he answered offhandedly, flinging his dirty boots into the space I had just vacated and attempting to recline diagonally. "Just don't tell this guy where you live unless you're okay with the possibility of him bugging you in the future," he suggested. "And for heaven's sake, if you get bad vibes, just leave. I'll be waiting right here."

"I don't know how long I'll be," I acknowledged, regretful now that I hadn't let him drive me in his truck.

He seized my sweat jacket off the dash, rolled it into a pillow, and laid his head back against the passenger window. "Don't worry about it," he responded. His eyes closed.

I smiled, wondering why I should trust a man I had known less than a week to protect me from a man who most likely was a blood relative. There was no logical reason I should and several reasons I shouldn't. Nevertheless, there was something about Fletcher that made me feel safe with him. A gentleness of spirit, perhaps, that shone through even when he hadn't wanted it to.

I straightened, turned toward the diner's entrance, and

started walking. My eyes stared at the ground until I reached the glass door, pulled it open, and stepped inside. Then, heart pounding, I lifted my chin and surveyed the crowd.

Was he here? One man sat alone at the counter, nursing a cup of coffee and reading a newspaper. He was the right age, but he took no notice of me. Two men at a booth near the door noticed me immediately, but they were too young to qualify, and their gaze hardly suggested perusal of a long-lost daughter. Jacob Kozen, according to the marriage record, should be fifty-nine years old now. That was one of the few things I did know about him.

I walked farther into the diner, wondering if I had arrived first. There were only two more men in sight who were roughly the right age: one was with a woman of equal maturity, the other was with an elderly man. Neither bothered to look up.

"Excuse me. Are you Meara?"

I spun around. A man stood directly behind me. He was tall, with a full head of bushy brown hair and dark eyes that surveyed me with a bemused expression. He must have walked in right after I had.

"Y-yes," I stammered, cursing my nervousness. "And you must be Jacob."

"Call me Jake," he said in a smooth, assured tone. "Everyone else does."

For a long moment we stood motionless, studying each other. He was an attractive man—solid and in good shape for his age, with only the slightest hint of a paunch. His skin was weathered and suitably wrinkled, but his face, with its thick eyebrows, square jaw, and wide, easy smile, held an ageless sort of charisma. His bearing exuded self-confidence, as if he were well used to making good first impressions, and his eyes reflected none of the taut apprehension I was certain were in my own. In fact, the look he offered was more that of a satisfied customer—as if I were merchandise ordered sight unseen, and he was tickled pink I had turned out so well.

I grew suddenly uncomfortable. "Maybe we should sit down," I suggested.

He agreed, and we took a booth. A waitress descended upon us, but though he ordered a half-pound cheese-burger and fries, a glass of orange juice was all I felt I could manage. The waitress departed, and as his bold, piercing eyes fixed on me again, I fought a strange urge to call her back.

"I can't believe it," he said with a grin. "You look just like your mother."

"There is a resemblance," I agreed, anxiously scanning his features to compare them with my own. My face was thinner than Sheila's had been . . . had his long, narrow visage contributed to the mix?

"She was a good-looking woman," he reminisced, leaning back in his seat. But before he had finished the thought, his expression clouded slightly. "Back in the beginning, anyway."

A sour feeling rose in my stomach, and I began to fight the conflict I had known such a meeting might bring. I was here because he knew things—things about Sheila, things about me. I was grateful for his help, but at the same time, I could not keep myself from resenting his upper hand. Getting the information I wanted—information I deserved as much as anyone else—required that I put my emotional well-being at his mercy. Whether he was my birth father or not, he could easily bend the truth about my adoption for his own purposes. He could lie to me on a whim. He could refuse to help me entirely. Was I really ready for that?

I sat up, my pulse racing. *There is no need to panic,* I assured myself. *Just slow things down.* "So," I said, attempting lightheartedness. "The marriage license said you were a policeman in the seventies?"

His chest swelled with pride. "The seventies, the eighties, the nineties. I retired last year."

"That's impressive," I responded mindlessly. "Were you with the Somerset force the whole time?"

He shook his head, watching me with a curious expression. "No, I moved around."

Silence descended, during which his eyes continued to drink me in, almost without blinking. Such a reaction was not unexpected; Sheila hadn't been able to keep herself from staring at me either. Yet something about Jake's gaze was different. Whereas I had surveyed Sheila with an equal sense of awe, meeting his eyes now was awkward—almost unnerving.

"I know it must be odd to receive a phone call out of the blue like this," I blurted, suddenly anxious to get on with it. "And I want to assure you that I have no intention of intruding on your life. But I would very much like some closure about my adoption."

He nodded, and his visage once again turned sober. "Of course you would. But I don't understand. You say you met Sheila, but she wouldn't answer any of your questions?"

I took a breath, wishing my explanation didn't have to be so complicated. I didn't want to lie, but where could I begin? And how much did I really want to share with him? I had never laid out for anyone the whole convoluted series of events that had begun the day I met Sheila in the coffee shop. I didn't want to do so now, either.

"She called me to her bedside after the accident," I said, simplifying. "But she wasn't able to speak clearly. And she died shortly afterward."

"I see," he answered, his tone softening. "So how did you find me?"

I explained about the marriage license and the Internet search, and he surprised me with a chuckle. "Well, it's a good thing I'm not trying to hide from anyone, isn't it? Amazing what you can find out on-line." He offered a charming smile, but in the next instant his gaze changed from admiring to appraising, and his voice lowered. "How much *do* you know about Sheila?"

My eyes met his, and we both knew what he was talking about. My heart pounded anew. "I know that she was in prison."

He nodded. "And how did you find out about that?"

"Another woman who'd been at Muncy," I explained. "She came to the funeral."

A trace of nervousness flickered across his features. "Sorry I didn't make it. But I didn't know—I don't read the obits. What did this woman tell you?"

I squirmed in my seat, all too cognizant of what was happening. Jacob Kozen knew more about Sheila than he was inclined to share. He was fishing to see what I had already discovered, all the time being careful not to tip his hand. Resentment swelled within me once more, but I resolved not to hold his reticence against him. If the truth about Sheila was as disturbing as I suspected, he might only be trying to spare my feelings.

"I know that whatever she did, she was in prison for a

long time," I answered. "But it seems she didn't confide in this friend about her personal life."

He nodded again. "Sheila never was a talker," he confirmed. "I'll give her that."

The waitress returned, bringing our drinks. Jake cast a fetching grin at her as she placed his in front of him, and she eagerly smiled back. The flirtation was as unconscious as it was harmless, and I knew I had no business judging him for it. Nevertheless, as I watched him grab two packs of sweetener for his tea and rip them open with a flourish, I found myself fighting back ire. How could the man be so blasé? Right now? How could he even think about food, or sweetener, or buxomy waitresses, when one look at my orange juice was enough to turn my stomach?

I drew myself up straight. I could wait no longer.

"I want to know why she went to prison," I announced. "And I want to know why I was given up for adoption when the two of you were married when I was born." My voice quavered toward the end; my heart beat violently in my chest.

His gaze trained back on mine, his expression at first surprised, then contemplative. Out of the corner of my eye I noted that my arms were trembling again, and I hastened to put them under the table and out of sight.

The silence that followed seemed endless. "I hate to have to tell you this," he began finally, his voice flat. "But your mother was a drug addict. Heroin, to be exact."

My heart stopped in midbeat. I had to force myself to breathe. *In. Out. Calm down. You knew this was a possibility.* "I see," I answered, my voice cracking. "So that's why she went to prison? Drug charges?"

He confirmed my words with a slow nod. His eyes

bore into mine, and though just seconds ago I had been irritated by his nonchalance, the intensity of his gaze now disturbed me more. "She was in deep," he continued. "Real deep. I tried to help her, but I couldn't. I wasn't in the best place myself back then."

A shiver ran up my spine, and its impact rocked my shoulders. *Stop it!* I ordered myself, furious. I didn't want him to see how unsteady I was . . . after all my preparation, after all the truth scenarios I had imagined I could deal with. This wasn't the worst of them, and still I was crumbling. I had to buck up.

"She tried to be a good mother," he went on, his tone more matter-of-fact than soothing. "But you know how it is with drugs. You just can't think about anything besides where your next fix is coming from."

No, I thought angrily, my teeth beginning to chatter in my jaws. *I don't know how it is. I'm not that stupid.* "So I was taken away by the county?"

He took a long, slow breath. I stole another glance at his eyes, wondering if he could see how much his words were hurting me—wondering if he cared. But all I perceived was concentration. Or perhaps calculation.

"Sheila never *wanted* to give you up," he said mildly. "She just couldn't deal with being a mother. There were a lot of problems at home, and later on, you weren't living with us much anyway. When Sheila finally got convicted, it was just the end. I knew she was going away for a long time, and there wasn't anybody else who could take care of you. I was in debt up to my eyeballs thanks to her, and neither of us had any family to count on."

He paused and watched me, his expression suddenly anxious. "I thought you'd be better off adopted."

My blood ran cold; my mind reeled. The information

was coming at me fast and furious, far too quickly to process. He didn't make it sound as though the county had taken me. He made it sound as though Sheila had lost her rights, and he had given his up.

He hadn't thought he could raise me alone. Perhaps he too had had a drug problem. Or perhaps . . .

"I have to ask you," I said, lifting my shaking hands above the table again and folding them together to still them. "I know that you and Sheila were married when I was born. But were you sure—" I broke off, nauseous. "I mean, with her being an addict, I wondered if—"

His facial expression didn't change as I spoke, but his eyes flickered with indignation. "If you want to ask me something," he said coolly, "just ask."

I looked away from him, a fresh wave of resentment surging. Jake had divorced Sheila twenty-five years ago and had probably not laid eyes on her since. Now she was dead. Yet the mere suggestion that his ex-wife might once have been unfaithful to him was enough to threaten his ego? When here I was, trembling all over, practically begging for the truth?

"I want to know if you're my biological father," I snapped, unable to control my frustration. "I'm not judging you—or Sheila. All I want is a straight answer."

Our eyes met once more, and this time, mine held his fast. I studied their brown depths, trying desperately to read the man inside. *Was* he my birth father? Did I even want him to be?

When I had first met Sheila, I expected to sense something immediately—some sort of connection between us. I hadn't, even though the legitimacy of our bond was not in question. What I did feel upon meeting her was a final acceptance, a feeling of wholeness, and of hope. I didn't understand her, but I thought that perhaps I could, some-day.

Could I ever understand Jake Kozen? This smooth, blue-collar Casanova who had felt unable, even at the age of twenty-nine, to raise a daughter alone? I had sworn I wouldn't judge him. But I couldn't deny the fact that if I were meeting him under different circumstances, I would already have run—not walked—the other way. Paternal instinct was one of the qualities I had come to value most in a man. Had he even a drop of it?

His eyes flickered with a range of emotions. My out-burst seemed to have caught him off guard, but its effect was far from negative. I sensed a grudging respect, then something I could describe only as intrigue. His face soft-ened, and his lips curved into a smile.

"Of course you're my daughter," he answered evenly, his eyes glimmering. "I'm sorry I didn't make that clearer. I assumed you already knew."

You're lying.

I gave no indication of the certainty that swelled within me. I merely forced my lips to smile, concealing the clench of my teeth.

You're not my father, and you know it.

The diner spun; my head seemed to wobble.

"Do you want a copy of your birth certificate?" he asked. "I still have it somewhere. And the adoption records, too. I'll—" He paused, studying me again.

Could he sense my mistrust?

"I'll be happy to answer any questions you want," he offered. "I guess the answers aren't exactly what you'd hoped for though, are they?"

I shook my head only slightly, but the diner spun worse. I couldn't move. His expression now was kind, his words, sensitive. But at that moment, in the depths of his eyes, I saw something else. Something that hit my already twisted gut as violently as a fist.

Ice.

His dark pupils couldn't hide it—couldn't match the friendly, casual smile on his face. There was a coldness in him. A core beneath the facade. Hard, callous, unbending.

Unmerciful.

"I'd like to get to know you better, Meara," he continued, the polite words flowing smoothly from his mouth. There was nothing sinister about them. Nothing at all. "Well, what do you say?"

He smiled at me. I looked in his eyes again.

I felt terror.

A cold blackness exploded in my gut. My body reeled with a rush of adrenaline, and I slid from the booth with a jerk.

"I'm sorry," I exclaimed, fighting to keep my voice from screaming and my feet from hustling me away. "It's just that I'm not sure I'm ready for this." I reached into my back pocket, extracted a few dollars, and laid them on the table next to my untouched juice. "Th-thank you for answering my questions," I stammered, avoiding his eyes. "And yes, I would like the adoption records. Could you mail them to me?"

"Of course," he answered, rising with me. "But I don't know your address. Give me your number and I'll call you when I find them."

"I'm listed in the book in Pittsburgh," I replied, thinking quickly as I moved backward toward the exit. There was no point in hiding that fact—my number and the address of my parents' house would show up in any Google search, just as his had. "I'm in the process of moving, but I'll pick up messages at that number."

He started to follow, and I hastened my retreat. "I'm sorry to leave so soon, but I really have to go. Thank you for agreeing to meet with me. Good-bye."

I reached the door and pushed it open with my shoulders.

Fresh air hit my lungs. I took it in with hungry heaves, moving quickly across the parking lot toward my car. I didn't look back. I couldn't look back.

I could feel his eyes still watching me.

Chapter

~15~

FLETCHER SWUNG OPEN the inn's front door. Seconds passed before I realized he was waiting for me to walk in first.

"Thank you again for going with me," I said when we had both entered the foyer. My voice sounded ominously vacant, even to me. "I'm sorry I wasn't better company."

He offered a frustrated look, but said nothing. Silence had been the norm ever since I had rushed across the parking lot and jumped into my Hyundai, waking him from a sound sleep by nearly breaking his kneecaps. He had taken one look at me, limped around the car, and pushed me over into the passenger seat. Ten minutes into the drive home, he had asked me if I wanted to talk. I had said no. We hadn't uttered a word since.

I walked back into the common room and stopped by the French doors. My eyes fixed on the aged house across the meadow, and my focus blurred. It didn't seem to matter what I was looking at. Driving through the Laurel Mountains was lovely this time of year—the leaves were at their freshest green, and overnight rain showers had left miniature waterfalls trickling down the outcroppings of rock along the roadside. But in my mind's eye, all I had seen was Jake Kozen, standing outside the door of the diner with one thumb perched in a front jeans pocket, his other hand shielding his eyes from the sun. He had stood there, watching, as we drove away.

I shivered.

"All right," Fletcher announced. "That's it."

I turned my head toward him. I hadn't even realized he was beside me. "I'm sorry. What did you say?"

He exhaled. "You're shaking again."

I crossed my wrists over my chest and rubbed my upper arms. "Sorry."

With a groan of exasperation, he rotated me to face him and caught my eyes. "Don't apologize," he said firmly. Then his expression softened, and his voice dropped low. "I understand if you don't want to talk to me. But surely there's someone you can talk to. Just give me a number. I'll get them on the phone."

There must be someone. My lower lip trembled, and I felt the familiar, warm welling of tears behind my eyes. Was there someone I could talk to? Certainly I had friends, many of them close. But none of them knew about Sheila. I couldn't possibly convey to anyone over the phone the nightmare of emotions I had experienced in the last seven days—much less explain the horror now gnawing at my bones.

"I'd rather not talk to anyone right now," I said in a whisper, certain that my voice, if I attempted to use it, would crack. "But thank you."

Fletcher released me. He turned his back, rubbing his face with his hands. Then he walked away from me along the windows, staring pensively out over the meadow. He seemed to be deliberating.

"Please don't feel like you have to baby-sit," I urged, finding my voice shaky but functional. "Going with me and driving me home was more than enough. I'll be fine." I wanted to assure him that I was not an emotional wreck—that I would not crumple into a weeping mass the second I was alone. But I had never been a very good liar.

He faced me again, the worry lines on his brow proving that my bravado wasn't fooling him. My knees began to weaken.

"It's not like it was a total disaster," I sputtered, making one last attempt to get a grip on myself. "He was perfectly—" I broke off as words failed me. *What was he?* Jake's steely eyes flashed across my memory, and my lungs failed me, too. I attempted a deep breath, but made only a choking sound. I turned quickly to the side.

It was no use. I was going to cry. Right here, right now. And if the sight of a woman bawling made Fletcher as uncomfortable as it made most men, he would hie himself away at the earliest opportunity and never be seen again. Then I would be alone here, too. Truly alone.

The sobs came fast and furious. I covered my face with my hands and concentrated on standing. I wanted to walk away, but my legs wouldn't respond. Staying upright seemed enough of a challenge. I was miserable and embarrassed, and I cursed my lack of composure. Had I not known perfectly well that learning the truth about my origins could be unsettling? Had I not sat in this very room last night and insisted to Fletcher that the risk was worth it?

Yes, I had. I had told him that I wanted to find my birth family, and that I was willing to suffer through whatever would be required to make that happen. Yet when I finally found the one man who could answer all my questions, what had I done? I had *walked out* on him.

My knees gave way in one motion, and I braced myself for a fall. But miraculously, none came. I stayed right where I was, with my face pressed firmly against Fletcher's chest.

My eyes flew open. He was holding me. When and how this had come about, I didn't know. One of his arms was around my waist, expending some degree of effort to keep me upright. His other hand rested on the small of my back, unmoving. He was holding me like my father used to when I was a child and fell off my bike, or when I was a teenager battling the dramas of adolescence. It was the sort of embrace that gave without taking, comforted without demand. There was no hint of grudging obligation, no overtones of desire. Just support. And empathy.

I had almost forgotten what that felt like.

My legs steadied, and my eyes went dry. I felt a strength flowing through me, and in a moment I raised my head.

Fletcher loosened his hold and, on determining that I was supporting my own weight again, dropped his hands and took a half step back. His eyes surveyed me critically, but the results seemed to please him. "Better?" he asked softly.

I nodded. "Much."

He released me entirely and returned to the window, looking out. "You know," he said pleasantly, as if the last few minutes had never occurred, "it's a gorgeous Tuesday, and as far as I know, neither you nor I have a job to go to." He turned back to me. "How would you like the grand tour? The hike up to my cabin only scratches the surface of this place. I'd love to show you the rest of it—now that I'm not worried about your stealing it, that is."

The last words were tongue-in-cheek. He offered a friendly grin, and I found myself returning it. He was right. It was a beautiful day. And the last thing I needed after the morning's revelations was to wallow inside a gloomy inn. What I needed was warm sunshine. And good company.

"Give me ten minutes," I responded, drawing in the first full breath I'd managed in a while. "And you're on."

Eight minutes later I opened my bedroom door and started down the hall toward the common room. My hiking boots were on, my energy level was climbing, and I found myself inordinately anxious to feel some sun on my shoulders. Wearing a tank top in the mountains in June was risky, even on a day as warm as today, but with my sweat jacket tied securely around my waist, I felt prepared for any chilly stretches. The cold water I had splashed on my face could not entirely remove the redness from my eyes, but it had raised my spirits. That and the joy I felt at the prospect of seeing more of the ridge, not to mention spending more time with its owner. The concern in Fletcher's eyes seemed, at least temporarily, to have eclipsed that damnable look of hurt he always carried, and if comforting me was also therapeutic for him, I was more than willing to cooperate.

I caught sight of him at the table nearest the kitchen, hastily eating something from an aluminum tin. He was so absorbed in the process that he failed to notice me until I was practically beside him. At which point I realized, with a start, what the tin contained.

My pie. The homemade peach pie he had so bizarrely

rejected last night had now, within the span of eight minutes, been reduced to no more than a sliver. If I hadn't come out of my room when I did, I suspect the evidence would have disappeared entirely.

"I thought you didn't like pie," l said smugly, beaming.

Eyes averted, he put down his fork, rose, and carried the tin back into the kitchen. "I never said that," he defended sheepishly. "I just asked for a rain check. Now I've collected. That okay?"

"Perfectly," I responded, still smiling. "Did you like it?"

He walked back out into the common room. "It was—" His words broke off as his eyes swept over me, from head to foot, then up again. It was the sort of glance men had favored me with since puberty, but that the more gentlemanly ones seemed to assume I wouldn't notice. I smiled at the compliment, but the communication went unseen. Fletcher's gaze never reached my face—at its second pass over my shoulders his color went pale, and he whirled around toward the kitchen again.

"It was very good pie," he said over his shoulder, his voice tense. "I, um, left you a little." He rummaged in the cupboards a moment, looking, I was sure, for nothing at all.

"I'm glad you liked it," I offered, watching his machinations with amusement. "Pies are my specialty."

He was in the middle of swinging open a high cabinet when his arms paused in midair, his eyes staring straight ahead. For several seconds, he remained motionless; then he closed the cabinet with a slam and clapped his hands together. "All right then," he announced, leaving the kitchen empty-handed, "let's get going. You'll need a water bottle and maybe a snack. We'll be out for a while."

He moved past me toward the French doors, his gaze missing any part of me by at least three feet.

"I'm ready," I answered, patting the small pack I had fastened around my waist.

The gesture was lost on him. He was already outside.

I followed my guide obediently through the woods, sometimes on barely visible trails, sometimes on no trails at all. He started off moving slowly, but when he realized I had no trouble keeping up he increased his pace, moving over rocks and down cliffs like a deer. I continued to follow without protest, and I could tell that he was impressed.

It was some time before he slowed, informing me that we had reached the oldest, most well-preserved section of the forest. The pride in his voice was plain, and his face shone with the simple joy of being here. His enthusiasm was contagious, but then, my own delight needed no prompting.

The stands of timber arising from the steep slope were magnificent. The mature, high canopy created a forest floor that was almost eerily quiet, dappled with the faintest traces of sunlight and awash with the fresh fragrance of spring-dampened earth. The complete lack of other human sounds or trappings lent the woods an ageless, fairylike aura, giving me a curious desire to skip between the giant gray trunks as if I were a child. I refrained. But as we walked slowly through the centuries-old hardwoods, I did occasionally let my fingers drift across a stretch of bark, spinning fantasies of the history each tree might have witnessed.

Fletcher spoke little on his own, but he was quick to answer my questions, his eyes twinkling at my interest. I no longer had any doubt of his expertise in forestry, though the nature of his work in California—and the source of his personal wealth—remained obscure. I saw no more of the curious nervousness he had displayed in the kitchen. Out here in his chosen element there was a peace about him, a contentment not even my peach pie could ruffle. Here he was relaxed and confident—even though, as I couldn't help noticing, he was still reluctant to look anywhere near my shoulders.

"We're almost to the swimming hole," he informed me much later, after a prolonged jog around another hill brought us to a trail heading sharply downward. "It's only ten minutes from the house, if you go directly."

His news was welcome. I was enjoying myself immensely, but the limits of my endurance were swiftly approaching, and I had no desire to admit it. The wind picked up suddenly as we descended, and though the sound of bending tree boughs and ruffling leaves was pleasant to hear, the gusts were chilling to my bare skin. I was in the process of reaching to untie my jacket when I realized that the trail was opening up before me, leading to the shores of a wide creek bathed with sunlight.

I took my hand off my jacket and moved out into the sun.

The clear, flowing creek was mesmerizing. Upstream it was broad and shallow, trickling no more than a foot or so deep over smooth boulders that broke its surface into small whitecaps and eddies. Just before me a straight line of larger boulders stood guard as the earth dipped, creating a modest waterfall. Downstream the creek narrowed sharply, the water funneling into a circular area whose darker color betrayed an abrupt change in depth.

Fletcher had left the water's edge to climb up a bank

downstream, and when I heard him call out to me, he had reached a ledge eight feet or so above the waterline. No sooner had I glanced up at him than an odd feeling took hold of my senses, and I found myself staring at the rock on which he stood.

"This is it," he shouted cheerfully. "Ye ol' swimming hole. It's only about five feet deep in the middle, but that's all it took to keep the kids happy. There aren't any stiff undercurrents here, so it's reasonably safe, too."

I continued staring until he climbed down and joined me again. He pointed to a huge, smooth-topped boulder above the waterfall. "Now *that* was a boy's paradise. Designed by God specifically for serious games of 'King of the Mountain.' To be played only when no adults were watching, of course. Only caused two broken bones over the years, as far as I know."

"How many of them were yours?"

He grinned. "Well, both. But one was only a hairline fracture."

I wanted to smile, but something was stopping me. Something about the swimming hole. Something about the cliff above it. It was percolating in the foreground of my mind, but I couldn't seem to grasp it.

"I only had real fun when I was little myself," he continued. "Once I got old enough to play lifeguard, I had to be the bad guy. Then it was no more 'King of the Mountain,' and one at a time on the trolley. You see, there used to be—"

He pointed toward the cliff, and a flash of understanding jarred my brain. I could picture a child jumping from the boulders. Sliding down some sort of cable, holding on tight until just the right moment, then letting go and plunging into the water below. It was frightening. Exciting. One of most amazing things I'd ever seen.

"A trolley line," I whispered, staring toward the water. "Stretched from one bank to the other."

"Exactly," he confirmed. "You can see the layout was perfect for it. Fantastic fun. I'd go for it myself right now if it were still here."

The sun was beating down on us soundly now, and a fine sheen of sweat had begun to break on Fletcher's brow. My own skin felt clammy.

Children. I could picture them as if part of a dream. Jumping. Sailing. Splashing. Laughing.

"Meara?" Fletcher's voice turned serious. "Is something wrong?"

I didn't answer him. All I could do was stare at the deep circle of water, listening to the children's laughter in my mind. It was real to me. Too real. I couldn't be making it up.

I barely noticed as Fletcher sat me down on a large, chair-height boulder beside the creek's edge. Without hesitation he untied my jacket, opened it up, and flung it loosely around my quaking shoulders. Then he stretched out beside me and propped himself up with his elbows, basking in the sun.

Minutes passed before either of us said a word.

"Fletcher," I said finally, my voice barely above a whisper.

"Yes," he answered, not moving.

My heart began to race. "Did you ever have so many things going on in your head at the same time, you wondered how much more you could stand?"

He didn't respond right away, and I plowed on.

"I know you must think I'm some sort of lunatic, and

I really don't blame you. I come here out of the blue, threaten to take your land, start claiming I'm a long-lost foster child, and then fall apart in the middle of your inn. It hasn't been a stellar performance."

My voice was self-conscious. None of the men I knew had much patience for weighty conversation—certainly not for emotional topics with no direct relation to themselves. I hated to alienate Fletcher further, but if I didn't talk to someone soon, I feared I would explode.

"I'm sorry to lay all this on you just because you're here," I continued. "But this morning didn't go quite as I expected, and I don't seem to be dealing with it well."

Fletcher sat up. He waited a moment, as if expecting me to say something else. When I didn't, he tried to help. "So, you found out Jacob Kozen is your birth father?"

God, no, I thought. My pulse pounded; I couldn't seem to speak.

"If he wasn't the person you hoped he'd be, I'm sorry," Fletcher offered. "But don't blame yourself for not feeling like you think you should. You may share some DNA, but that doesn't mean you have to like the man."

I turned my head and looked at him, amazed once again by his perceptiveness. I swallowed, gathering the courage to say out loud the words that had been badgering my brain, begging for acknowledgment even as they pummeled my soul with guilt.

"Fletcher," I forced out, the venom in my tone chilling even me, "I despised him."

Chapter

~16~

FLETCHER STIFFENED. WHEN he spoke there was anger in his voice. "What exactly happened at that diner? What did he say to you?"

"It wasn't what he said," I clarified quickly, not to defend Jake so much as to avoid upsetting Fletcher. I hadn't intended to make this his problem. "He was civil. He was polite. Nothing happened. It was just—" The coldness of Jake's eyes flashed through my mind once more, and I shoved the image away with a fury. "Like you said before," I tried to explain, "I just got bad vibes. That's all."

"That's not all," he argued. "You said you despised him; I think you meant it. You don't seem the sort of person who would hate someone without a reason."

I paused, considering. Did I really hate Jake Kozen? I was feeling so many things, it seemed impossible to know where one ended and the next began. I felt disappointment. I felt hurt. I felt an uncanny sense of fear I couldn't bear to contemplate. But at the forefront now was a burning pressure that began in my gut, then radiated painfully upward through my chest and behind my eyes. It had to be hatred, an emotion with which I was wholly unfamiliar, and wholly uncomfortable. It hurt. It was wrong. I wanted to be rid of it.

"Can I ask you a question?" I blurted.

He nodded.

I took a ragged breath. "Imagine that you are twenty-nine years old, stuck in an unhappy marriage with a drug addict. You have no money, no extended family. You have a baby, but your wife is too messed up to take care of it. Then—" I cut myself off sharply, realizing that my listener wasn't completely uninvested in my story. Painting Sheila as a demon would only call Mitchell's judgment further into question, and there was no point in laying that on Fletcher now. "Then suddenly your wife is out of the picture, and you're all that child has," I continued. "You're in debt. You have to work. If you kept the child it would spend long odd hours in day care or with a sitter."

In the back of my mind, I could hear a child crying as I spoke. A small, auburn-haired little girl. I could see her mother crouched in the corner of a cramped apartment, shooting up, oblivious to her daughter's distress. I could see the cop husband coming home after a long day on the beat to find the house filthy, his child miserable, his wife passed out on the floor . . .

"Might you consider giving it up for adoption?" I finished, desperate to quell the horrible images. "Would you consider that, maybe, a home with two parents would be better than what you could provide?"

Fletcher looked away from me, and my heart raced. I wasn't sure what I wanted him to say. I only knew that his answer was important to me. "I mean, might that be considered a selfless thing to do? The thing that was best for the child?"

He stood up and stepped toward the creek. Then he leaned down and grabbed a fistful of stones, wound up his arm, and sent one sailing to the far bank.

He said nothing.

"Please answer me," I pleaded.

He threw another stone. Then another. At last, with a giant exhale, he turned around. His eyes brewed with anger, but I knew that none of it was directed at me. "I'm not the right person to ask that question," he stated. "I can't give you the answer you want."

"I'm not asking you to judge anybody," I insisted, realizing as I spoke that I was lying. "I'm just asking what you would do."

He shook his head. "It doesn't matter."

"It matters to me," I returned, frustrated. "Just tell me the truth. *Please.*"

He threw the last few stones together, creating a star cluster of tiny splashes in the rippling creek. Then he faced me again. "All right," he began, his voice hard. "Here's the truth. If I were ever fortunate enough to have a child of my own, he or she would be the center of my world. And whether I was twenty-nine, eighteen, or seventy-three, I'd move heaven and earth to be the best damn father I could be—no matter how poor we were, or how hard I had to work, or what else I had to give up. Because the child would come first."

He walked over and dropped down beside me on the rock. "I know that's not what you want to hear. But if you're looking for somebody to help you justify that man's actions, you'll have to keep looking. Because I won't."

A numbness crept over me as I digested his response—the sickening confirmation of what I already

knew. Jake Kozen's refusal to raise me might be rational-
ized on some cerebral level. But my heart would never
forgive him.

I had not been some nameless, faceless offspring,
signed away before she had even seemed real. I had been
a cooing, smiling, crawling baby, then a toddler—maybe
even a preschooler. Jake Kozen had known me, lived
with me, cared for me. What sort of man could create a
baby, watch it grow, and not fall hopelessly, completely
in love with it?

A part of me had wanted Fletcher to say that men were
different, that they could love a child from a distance in
some academic way, without that fierce, protective drive
I knew would make me fight tooth and nail to hang on to
a child I loved. Certainly there were circumstances in
which a parent might, for the child's own well-being,
allow it to be raised by others. But Jake's willingness to
give me up completely—to risk never, ever seeing or
hearing from me again—bore no trace of a selfless gesture. What his actions brought to mind was the desire for
personal freedom—a decision based on lifestyle, on con-
venience.

Or maybe on something else.

"Would it matter," I asked tentatively, my voice barely
above a whisper, "if the child weren't yours? I mean, bi-
ologically?"

Fletcher's head whipped toward mine, his eyes blazing
with a passion that took me aback. "Of course not," he
proclaimed.

I breathed in with a shudder. It was no use. Whether
Jake thought I was his daughter or not, whether his ex-
cuses sounded logical or not, there was no avoiding the

cold, hard fact staring me in the face. The man who had been the first to raise me had never really loved me at all.

The knowledge ate my insides like a corrosive.

"I shouldn't have said anything," Fletcher apologized.

I looked at him. The speech he had just delivered began to repeat itself in my head, and as I listened, I felt a surge of warmness in my middle. *Paternal instinct.* Fletcher, at least, had it in spades. There were times I thought the quality had become extinct.

"I needed an honest answer," I explained, offering him a small, appreciative smile. "I have to face all this some-time—I might as well do it now."

He said nothing, but returned a smile before rising once more and stepping toward the water. A strong wind buffeted us both, and I took my sweat jacket from off my shoulders and pulled it on. Heavy nimbus clouds were rolling overhead, and as a large gray one drifted under the sun, the temperature dropped dramatically. I shivered again, this time from real cold.

I stood up and moved forward. I was only a step short of Fletcher when the reality of my intentions hit me, and I stopped.

I had intended to pull his arm around me. In another two seconds I would have settled into the warmth of his side, just like that, as automatic as saying hello.

I shook my head to retrieve my wits. True, I was used to being affectionate with the men in my life. But Fletcher and I were only just becoming friends. He wasn't mine, nor had he given any indication—other than that one involuntary glance in the kitchen—that he cared to be.

I dropped back. The mistake was nothing to beat my-self up about—I just wasn't thinking. In any event, Meara

O'Rourke was perfectly capable of weathering the wind without a man to hold her. No matter how wretched she felt.

"I guess we'd better get back," Fletcher said, looking at the sky.

He offered another small smile, then passed me and headed up the trail. I watched him, a curious wave of melancholy descending over me. Then I fell into step behind him.

His ten-minute estimate proved right on the mark, which, given the path's steep uphill grade, proved fortunate for my now-exhausted legs. The trail to the swimming hole opened up just behind the white house, and as we rounded that structure and reached its front porch, my ego finally gave way to my screaming muscles.

"I think I'll rest here a minute," I said, attempting a matter-of-fact tone as I dropped onto one of the cracked concrete steps.

Fletcher stopped and leaned against the stair rail opposite me with a smirk. "With so little left to go, too."

I glared at him.

He chuckled. "You did great, actually," he praised. "We passed a few shortcuts, but you seemed up to it. Next time we'll see the other section."

My eyebrows rose. "There's more?"

"What I own myself—on the other side of the cabin," he explained. "There's an abandoned campground at the bottom of the far hill, complete with an in-ground swimming pool. It hasn't been used since the seventies, but I think it's salvageable."

I sat up a bit. The camp director in me couldn't help

but think what a paradise this land would be for young nature lovers. "What do you plan to do with it?" I asked.

He considered. "I'm not sure yet," he said unconvincingly.

His tone did not invite further questioning, and I let out a frustrated sigh. He had been wonderful to me today, but the fact that we were becoming closer only made his secretiveness more irritating.

I shifted on the step, my rear end protesting its hard surface. "I wish the porch swing was still here," I muttered, contemplating the distance to the inn, in particular to the soft couches that flanked its fireplace.

Fletcher looked at me oddly.

I hadn't thought about the words as I said them. But from the look on his face, I was certain of their accuracy. There *had* been a porch swing here. I rose and walked up the steps, then stood staring at the place where the swing had been. There were countless holes in the ceiling, right above the expected spot.

Fletcher appeared behind me. "I must have put that thing back up about sixty times. But the rafters finally rotted, and it wasn't safe."

A pregnant pause ensued. I turned and looked at him. "You don't believe I was a foster child here, do you? You think I'm just imagining things."

His eyes widened slightly. "I believe you. Why wouldn't I?"

Embarrassment surged. He hadn't said he didn't believe me, he just hadn't acted surprised by the idea— much less excited. I wanted so badly to feel a connection to this place; I couldn't help but be hurt by his lack of enthusiasm. "I just thought—" I wasn't sure what to say. "Maybe it seemed like too much of a coincidence."

He shrugged. "I can see where it might seem that way to you, being adopted out to Pittsburgh. But most of the fosters went back to their families—families that still live around here. I run into them all the time. Sometimes it seems like half the planet either lived with the Blacks or knows someone who did."

He smiled at me then, and it was a friendly, encouraging smile. But it was not an unguarded one. I could see a hesitancy in his eyes—feel the stiffness of his body as he stood unnecessarily far away.

Was he truly as indifferent as he seemed? Or was he, perhaps, resisting a connection to me as actively as I was encouraging it?

Another wave of melancholy washed over me. I wanted to be a part of this beautiful place, of this once-large, loving family. However peripheral, however far-removed, I wanted my name on that roster. And I knew now that that wasn't all I wanted. I wanted a connection to Fletcher himself. I wanted a place in his heart.

But that wasn't happening. What was happening was that he was humoring me. I had had a perfectly horrifying morning, and he was doing his best to keep me from falling apart. But I was just another foster child. Why should I matter to Fletcher now? I hadn't mattered to my own birth parents then.

My eyes moistened again, and my face flushed with heat. Mortified, I turned away. I couldn't keep doing this—not twice in one day. It wasn't fair to him. I *had* to get a grip.

The floorboards squeaked as he walked around in front of me.

"You know what I think?" he asked calmly.

My hands were over my eyes. I shook my head.

"I think you could take a lesson from my sister," he said. "Because I don't think crying is going to do it for you. I think you're going to have to get angry and yell."

I lowered my hands enough to look at him, then found my voice. "Your sister yells?"

He chuckled. "Only when she's breathing. But at least she gets things out of her system."

He settled himself against the porch railing. It wobbled precariously under his weight, but he seemed to anticipate the movement. "So, go ahead," he offered, crossing his arms over his chest again. "Yell at me."

"I can't yell at you," I protested, feeling silly.

"I don't know why not. You did the other day."

I recalled my rant on the stump. "That was different," I argued. "I thought you deserved it. But I'm not mad at you now."

"Then pretend I'm Jacob Kozen."

All it took was the sound of the name. A quiver of fury shot down my spine, souring my stomach and shooting heat to the ends of my fingertips. Perhaps Fletcher was right. Perhaps crying wasn't enough.

"Go ahead," he insisted. "Tell me what you'd like to tell your birth father."

"He is *not* my birth father!" I snapped, my ire rising.

Fletcher smiled, then prompted me with a nod.

I considered his suggestion.

Why not? The specter of my parents' disapproval loomed, but with a mental heave, I pushed it aside. Neither of them had accepted the therapeutic value of venting, believing that refined individuals swallowed their emotions and moved on. But as much as I cherished their memory, I knew that they had not always been correct.

"I don't care *what* he says, Jake Kozen is *not* my birth

father!" I exclaimed. The volume felt good, and I turned it up a notch. "The man was lying through his teeth! For all I know, he was lying about everything—just like Sheila did! Nothing she told me six years ago was true either, but at least when I met her, I *liked* her! Jake Kozen is nothing but a sleazy, selfish, low-life scumbag who probably became a policeman just so he could push people around! I hated him from the first moment I saw him, and I hate him now! He never loved me, he never cared about me, and I'm not about to give him another chance to hurt me. Ever!"

I took a quick breath, then went on shouting. "All I wanted was to know the truth about why I was given up! Neither of them gave me even that! I still don't know what really happened, I still don't know why no one wanted me, and I still haven't found a single biological relative on the face of this earth!"

My voice cracked. "Then again, if Jake Kozen is any example of what kind of people I did come from, I'm not so sure I even *want* to find them!"

I took a step backward and leaned against the house.

"I wish I could just forget it all," I continued, my voice lower. "Pretend I never met either one of them and move on. But I can't. The same questions that tortured me before are going to keep on torturing me until I know the truth."

I said nothing for a while. Fletcher remained silent, watching me.

"I want to believe that Sheila was a good person," I continued, quieter. "I know that may not be true, but I hope that it is. She had a rough start in life, but both times I met her it seemed like—"

I faltered. "It seemed like she really cared about me. I don't know why she told so many lies—"

I was protecting you.

Sheila's dying words leapt forward in my mind, and my heart flip-flopped. I jerked myself up straight and shouted again. *"That bastard!"*

The porch railing veered backward as Fletcher startled. He caught himself with a hand on the post.

"Sheila knew he was evil!" I bellowed. "That's why she didn't want me to find him! And sure enough, the second I do, he tells me some cock-and-bull story that makes her out to be the villain! Maybe she wasn't a drug addict after all! Maybe she went to prison for something else—"

I stopped myself. But it was too late.

I had forgotten about Fletcher. I had forgotten that his father had married Sheila too, and that he had been trying to believe the best of her. I had forgotten my intentions not to mention her criminal record.

My slip did not go unnoticed.

"Sheila was in prison?" he asked, standing. "When? For what?"

I took a breath. Guilt suffused me. "I'm sorry," I apologized. "I suppose I should have told you, but I didn't want—" I broke off, chagrined. "I don't know what she went to prison for. But I believe that's why I was given up. Her rights were terminated, and Jake didn't want me because I wasn't his."

Fletcher turned away from me. He stared into space.

I came around the side of him and watched anxiously as his eyes brewed with concentration, then clouded with horror.

"What is it?" I choked out.

He didn't answer.

"Fletcher," I repeated, my pulse racing. "What's wrong?"

He turned his head back toward me. "Nothing," he answered. "My mind just wandered." He turned and descended the porch steps at a jog, then looked up at the sky. "We should probably get you back to the inn. It's going to start raining any second, now."

Neither the absence of the sun in the sky, nor the moisture that threatened on the brisk, cool wind, could sap any more warmth from my body. All of it was gone now, replaced by nothing but a gripping, prickling cold.

I ran down the stairs after him and grabbed his arm, turning him to face me. "Don't lie to me," I begged. "You remembered something about Sheila. I could tell. What was it?"

Sporadic water droplets began to strike. He removed my hand from his arm. "I'm sorry," he said gently. "I didn't mean to upset you. I thought for a moment that something about your situation seemed familiar. But I was wrong. I was thinking about something else."

I studied him in confusion. His words were calm; they sounded perfectly reasonable. He thought he had remembered something relevant, but he had been wrong.

I wish I believed him. But I knew that he was lying.

I took a step back.

My insides ached. I owed him so much. His presence had made this otherwise ghastly day tolerable—even pleasant at times. And he had been right, I did need to yell. But he wasn't right now. He wasn't right to lie to me, whether he thought it was in my best interests or not. I had heard enough lies to last a lifetime, and I couldn't take any more. Not now. Not from him. Especially not from him.

"Thank you for the tour, Fletcher," I said, my tone polite, but distant. "Your land is lovely. But there's no need for you to walk me back to the inn. I've taken enough of your time today already."

It took all my resolve. But I walked away from him.

"Meara," he called after me, his deep voice not needing to be raised to be heard, even over the increasing patter of rain striking grass. "I enjoyed your company today. I hope you know you're welcome to stay as long as you want."

I offered a smile and a wave of thanks, but the gestures were stilted. I couldn't look back at him.

It hurt too much.

Chapter

~17~

THE ANTIQUE BED squeaked with my every movement, and since I was tossing and turning more than I was still, the cacophony was almost laughable. But I was a long way from laughing.

It was three o'clock in the morning, maybe four. The light on my digital watch still worked, but since two-fifteen the numbers had started to disappear whenever I pressed the button—a sure sign that the battery was weakening. Not so, my resolve.

Alone in the inn all evening, I had indulged in my fill of both crying and shouting. By nightfall, I had a plan. There would be no more personal interviews—no more phone calls, no more meetings to manipulate my emotions. I would find my truth in the facts—the cold, hard, institutional kind.

At first light I would type up a request to the state for my original birth certificate. Jake Kozen had offered to send me a copy himself, and if his name was on it, he might do that. But his name would mean nothing. A mother could write down whatever name she wanted, and if Sheila had been unfaithful, she probably would have concealed the fact. Hoping for her to have legally acknowledged another man as my birth father was a pitiful long shot—but one I was determined to try.

As for confirming my whereabouts as a preschooler, I knew that my own records from the juvenile court would be sealed. But Sheila's criminal record was part of the public domain —and as soon as the doors of the county courthouse opened, I planned to find out once and for all exactly what my birth mother had been convicted of. Perhaps then I could determine whether her parental rights had been terminated against her will. And when.

I flipped onto my stomach, trying to get comfortable. I had to sleep. I could not endure two sleepless nights in a row—my senses were muddled enough already.

An image of Fletcher wafted across my mind. He was standing by the creek, the sun bouncing off his hair. He was smiling at me, but there was something in his eyes—something that worried me.

My stomach churned. I had vowed to stop thinking about him—to stop wondering what it was that he was hiding. I had to stay focused. I had to protect myself.

I pushed his image aside.

It came back.

I grumbled and flopped over again.

A soft clicking noise echoed through the hallway. I stiffened, instantly alert. The clicks were followed by a low whine—the unmistakable sound of a door swinging on its hinges.

Goose bumps rose along my arms. The whining noise ceased, followed by the return click of a lock. Then quiet footsteps sounded on the common-room floor.

I sat up straight, my heart beating audibly in my chest. I swung my legs out and placed my bare feet onto the rug below. How many people, besides Fletcher and Estelle, had keys to the inn? Probably quite a few. There was nothing to worry about—after all, this was an inn, not a house. None of the guest-room doors had key locks, but mine did have a bolt, and after Fletcher had barged in on me that first morning, I had been careful to use it.

My efforts at calming myself were futile. This might technically be an inn, but it no longer seemed like one. I had cooked in the kitchen, run the dishwasher, used the phone. The whole building seemed mine now, and I could think of no reason for anyone else to be in it, particularly not at this hour of the morning.

Another sound of moving hinges reached me, but I could not discern its source. With a surge of adrenaline I crossed the room and swept a candlestick off the marble mantel that crowned my dormant fireplace. Then I crept silently toward my door.

Could someone be here to steal something? Or was I overreacting? There was one way to tell. Anyone who was here without malice would not be afraid to show themselves.

I leaned my head against the edge of the closed door. "Hello?" I called, loud enough, I thought, for anyone in the common room to hear. "Who's there, please?"

I waited, but there was no response. No voice, no more opening doors, no more footsteps. Only silence.

I took a deep breath. Any number of people could have every right to be at this inn—a caretaker, a relative. It was I who was the visitor here, and it would be foolish of me to panic. Still, coming in the back doors at this hour was odd, and not answering me was even odder. Could the person be hard of hearing?

Had there been a phone in my room, I might have

called the police just to be on the safe side. But the only phone at the inn was in the common room.

I breathed out, moved away from the door, and got back into bed. But after several minutes of lying stiff as a board, I realized that waiting was pointless. I couldn't sleep. I might as well find out who was sharing the inn with me; once I knew, I could relax. Or—in the unlikely event that the person was uninvited—hightail it to my car.

Clenching both the candlestick and my car keys tight to my side, I returned to the doorway, listened carefully, then opened the door just wide enough to look out. "Hello?" I called again. "Who's there?"

Still, I heard no response. But I could see a dim light, shining down the hall from the common room. *Burglars,* I told myself confidently as I stepped out, *do not use keys, and they don't turn on the lights.* I moved steadily, one step at a time, calling out periodically as I went. "Hello?"

I reached the doorway to the common room, and approached it warily. "I know someone's here," I called louder. I passed through it and stepped out into the open space, but still saw no one. What I did see was the light—coming through a door I had formerly paid little attention to, assuming it was a closet. That door was now standing open, and a rustling noise drifted up from below.

I moved to look through the doorway, my breath held. A wooden staircase headed steeply downward to a dank cellar, illuminated by a single lightbulb. For a second I saw nothing else. Then Fletcher's large frame moved into my window of view, his expression startled.

My breath let out with a gush.

"It's just me," he explained hastily. "I didn't mean to wake you." His face filled with remorse. "I didn't mean to scare you, either. Sorry."

I set the candlestick and keys down outside the door frame, out of sight. "It's all right," I insisted, clearing my throat. "I guess you couldn't hear me down here. What are you doing?"

Some part of me heard my mother's voice, patiently indoctrinating me in the ways of polite ladies. *You're the man's guest, dear. You've no business interrogating him about his business.* I forced myself to squelch it. My mother had been a saint among women, but the new Meara had her own protocol.

Not waiting for an answer, I grabbed the rickety handrail and descended the steps myself. It occurred to me as I watched the path of his eyes that the oversized T-shirt I was wearing was on the short side. But I was not going to worry about that now.

I paused on the bottom step, hesitant to move my bare feet onto the cold concrete floor. Looking around, I realized I didn't want the rest of me there, either. The inn's foundation had been crafted of native sandstone, but it was hardly a prime example of the process. In several places the walls seemed to buckle, the mortar between the stones being laced with cracks and sprinkled with mildew. The low beams of the ceiling above bent in the middle like swaybacked horses, and the irregularly sloping floor bore ample evidence of previous floods.

"Nice place," I teased, trying to lighten my own mood. "What do you keep down here, fish?"

Fletcher looked over his shoulder, where a plethora of boxes and household junk was arranged on platforms several inches off the floor. "We've been moving things out of the house for a while now, a little at a time," he explained. "But there's not much good storage space here. You think this is bad, you should see the attic."

"I'll pass," I said quickly, thinking of the upstairs bedroom again. "I repeat, what are you doing here now, in the middle of the night? Walling someone in?"

He grinned a little, but his amusement was fleeting. He watched me thoughtfully for a moment, then tapped the book he had been holding in his hand. "I came for this," he explained.

I gazed at the oversized hardcover book, which appeared to be some sort of ledger. "And that couldn't wait till morning?"

He shook his head slowly. "I couldn't sleep. I wanted to know."

My heart rate increased. "Know what?"

He raised a hand to his beard and rubbed his chin. "Can we go back upstairs?"

It was a stalling tactic, but since my toes were freezing, I decided to permit it. I climbed back up the staircase into the common room and dropped onto one of the couches, folding my legs beneath me for warmth. Fletcher shut the door to the cellar and sat down next to me, dutifully averting his eyes from the thin fabric that clung to my torso.

"This was my mother's record-keeping book for the fosters," he explained, turning the book over in his hands. "It has all the children's names, their ages, when they came, and when they went."

My eyes widened. I stared at the ledger, unable to move.

"I wanted to see if there was a listing for an Amanda Kozen," he continued. "I figured that if you were here, it must have been in the mid-to-late seventies."

I nodded mutely, still staring. My pulse pounded in my ears.

His voice softened. "I've looked all through it, Meara.

There was no Amanda Kozen. There's no Amanda anybody."

My eyes shot up to meet his. That couldn't be. It just couldn't. I knew I had been here. "What about Mandy?" I suggested, my voice a croak.

He shook his head. "I didn't see anything even close." He extended the book in my direction. "But you're welcome to look through it yourself."

I stared at the dusty ledger once more, then held out a wobbly hand. As soon as my fingers closed over it, Fletcher released his hold and rose. "I'm sorry for worrying you," he said quietly. He walked across to the French doors. "I'll head on home now."

I rose and whirled toward him. "Why did you come down here?" I demanded. I had asked the question before, but his answer made little sense. "You were so anxious to know if I was a foster child here that you couldn't sleep? What difference would it make to you?"

He blinked back at me, the alarm in his eyes as frank as that of a wild animal staring into headlights. He collected his thoughts before speaking. "When you asked me if I was remembering something, I was. I was remembering something my parents told me, about another little girl that was here. But she wasn't you."

I walked closer to him, digesting the statement. "What did they tell you?"

He shook his head. "It doesn't matter. You can't be her, because if you were, you would have been in the ledger. My mother was very meticulous about that."

I studied him with concentration. He didn't seem to be lying to me. Not exactly. It seemed more like he was trying to make a case. A case he wanted to believe himself— but didn't.

I took a deep breath and prepared my words. "If you climbed all the way down that mountainside in the middle of the night just to double-check whether I was this girl, they must have told you something very important about her. What was it?"

His eyes brewed with turmoil. "It's confidential information, Meara," he said evenly. "I really can't get into it."

"You don't have to give me any names," I pressed. "Just give me the gist."

He pulled his eyes from mine and opened the French doors. "I can't talk about this right now," he said stiffly. "I'll see you tomorrow."

"Fletcher!" I protested, but my call went unanswered. He closed the doors behind him and stomped off into the night.

For the second time in three days, I received a bemused nod from the civil servant whose job it was to open the doors of the Somerset County Courthouse. He probably assumed I was still badgering someone about a marriage license.

He couldn't be further off.

I meandered in the corridors for some time before locating the district clerk's office and making my request. For the next twenty minutes I sat up straight on a painfully hard bench, feeling like a shell of myself. I had barely slept at all after Fletcher's exit, but I had nevertheless arisen at dawn, typed up the birth certificate request, and mailed it on my way to town. I was determined to proceed with my plan.

Fletcher had told the truth about his mother's ledger—there was no Amanda Kozen listed. During the most probable time period, however, there were two other entries for little girls. One, who had been two at the time, had stayed with the Blacks only a few weeks. But the other girl, listed as Lisa Dobson, had lived with the family for almost a year, starting at the age of three. The comment line by her name said simply "single mother—addict." Why a three-year-old entering foster care might require an alias, I didn't know. But I did know that I had been at the Blacks'. And no one was going to convince me otherwise.

"Ma'am?"

My chin jerked up as the clerk appeared leaning over the counter. "We don't have anything on a Jacob Kozen," he announced. "Only on Sheila Kozen. You want a copy?"

I nodded.

The request for a criminal record on Jacob Kozen had been an impulse. I did not care to analyze why the lack of one was a disappointment.

I waited another five minutes before the clerk returned and handed me a package. It was a thin white envelope with no markings. I thanked him and took it.

I stood still for a moment, staring. I had expected a plain slip of paper, something I would have to look at immediately. Now I had a choice.

I took in a ragged breath. I didn't know what to expect from Sheila's record. I wasn't even sure what I was hoping for. But as my knees wobbled beneath me I realized that whatever it was, I wasn't quite ready for it.

I tucked the envelope beneath my arm and started walking. I had the document; that was the important thing. There was no reason I couldn't treat myself to lunch before opening it, or do some sightseeing, or take a nap. Or all of the above.

Maybe, after all that, the fear in my chest wouldn't feel quite so stifling.

Chapter

~-18-~

B<small>Y THE TIME</small> I returned to the inn, it was late afternoon. I had had an uninspired fast-food lunch, followed by a leisurely walk along my favorite nature trail in nearby Ohiopyle State Park. I had spent close to an hour doing nothing but sitting on a bench, watching the Youghiogheny River churn over giant boulders to form myriad whitecaps and waterfalls. The serenity of the spot had allowed my brain to assume a peaceable blankness, and for a while, I had felt better. But as I was also becoming increasingly drowsy, I had decided to head back while I could still safely drive.

The envelope remained on the Hyundai's passenger seat, unopened.

As I pulled into the inn's parking lot, thinking about nothing other than my impending nap, Fletcher appeared suddenly in my side-view mirror, causing me to start. He seemed to have come from nowhere, and was proceeding straight for my car. As soon as I parked and popped opened the door, he took hold of the handle and swung it open fully, surveying me with a worried expression.

"Are you all right?" he demanded more than asked. "Did you see him?"

I shook my head to help clear some of my confusion, but it didn't help. "Of course I'm all right," I responded, having to push him back a bit to get out. "What are you talking about? See who?"

Clearly relieved, he retreated a few steps. "I thought you might have gone to see Jake Kozen again."

A cold day in hell, I thought, but my words were more polite. "No, I didn't. Why would you think that?"

When he didn't answer, I frowned and turned away toward the inn. Lack of sleep made me cranky, there was no doubt about that. But the aggravation I was feeling toward him this morning had a deeper source.

He had walked out on a discussion last night—a tendency I was all too familiar with, and all too sensitive to. I knew it was unfair of me to punish him for the sins of other men, but I couldn't seem to help myself. Kevin's inability to discuss anything of significance—such as when he thought he might be ready to get married, have children, or even get a real job or take out the garbage—had resulted in the waste of five years of my life, and a good deal of my self-respect. Kevin could never bring himself to tell me anything he thought I didn't want to hear, ostensibly because he was trying to be considerate. The real problem, of course, was that he was a coward.

And so, as far as I was concerned at the moment, was Fletcher.

He was hiding things from me that he had no right to hide, and he had refused to admit that even when asked point-blank. His secrecy had irritated me from the beginning, but after yesterday, it had truly hurt. Because I had finally begun to trust him.

I took only a step or two before he caught my arm. "Wait, Meara. Please?" His deep voice was gentle, and I knew that whether I was mad at him or not, that sound, combined with one look at his face, would bring back emotions I was better off not feeling. I stopped walking, but my eyes stayed on the ground.

"I owe you an apology," he said.

I looked up.

"I shouldn't have walked out on you last night," he continued. "You have legitimate questions, and you deserve answers to them."

I turned to face him, surprised. All memories of Kevin, who had never once admitted he was wrong about anything, vanished.

"I didn't want to tell you what I was thinking of because I wasn't sure it had anything to do with you," he explained. "You were upset enough as it was—I didn't want to lay more on you only to have it be a false alarm. But I didn't intend to keep you in the dark forever." He paused, then breathed out heavily. "I've found out some things, Meara. We need to talk."

My voice seemed gone, so I merely nodded.

He led me across the lot and into a grove of pines, then gestured for me to find a seat amid a group of boulders arranged in a circular pattern. The makeshift "conference room" was clearly man-made; in one place, two flat rocks joined at an angle, almost like a recliner. I sat down there, and he smiled at me. "My favorite spot, too," he remarked. Then his voice sobered.

"When I found your car gone this morning I was afraid you were going to confront Jake Kozen—to ask him whether you were in foster care here, or to ream him out for abandoning you. I'm glad you didn't."

My brow creased. "I have no intention of ever seeing him again, so don't worry."

He studied me, and his gaze seemed approving. But it was obvious he had more to get off his chest. "I hope you don't mind my interfering in your affairs," he began, not sounding at all apologetic. "But I did. I have a friend who's a state trooper, based in Somerset, and when you said that Kozen had been a cop, I figured it wouldn't hurt if I gave Ben a call. You seemed so afraid coming out of the diner yesterday—I thought maybe Ben could find out something about the guy, make sure he was okay. He called me back this morning."

I stared. I had told Fletcher that I hated Jake, yes. But I had never confessed the cold, cryptic fear that had overtaken me at our meeting—I had not fully acknowledged it even to myself. Evidently, I had also not been able to hide it.

"What did he say?" I blurted, not minding Fletcher's interference in the least. Rather, knowing that he had gone out of his way to protect me gave me an almost overwhelming urge to throw my arms around his neck. But looking at him now, sitting, as he always did, intentionally beyond my reach, I was able to resist the impulse. His continued efforts to keep a physical distance between us were not my imagination, and it was time I accepted the fact that he wasn't interested. Quite probably, there was someone else. Someone he was being admirably faithful to.

"Ben didn't recognize Kozen by name," he answered. "But he asked around. Turns out he didn't have to dig too deep. Kozen's been on most every small-town force in the area at one time or another, and he's developed a reputation."

His last words cut through the depressed haze in my mind. I refocused. "A reputation for what?"

"In short, for being a jerk. He's known as a hothead. The reason he's moved around so much is because he kept burning his bridges. Lots of reprimands—insubordination, policy violation, moral indiscretion. Numerous complaints against him for unnecessary use of force, though none were ever substantiated. He was never found guilty of anything serious enough to land him in real trouble, but he was asked to resign from a few departments."

My heart pounded.

He exhaled. "I'm not trying to upset you, or tell you what to do. But you said you wanted the truth, and I think you have the right to know what kind of person Jake is before you make any more decisions based on what he told you."

I nodded mutely.

"I'm afraid there's more," he continued. "One of the officers Ben talked to was a woman who worked with Jake in the early nineties. She said that he was—and I'm quoting this secondhand—a 'stinking, sexist lecher,' and that she had complained about him repeatedly to her superiors but was never taken seriously. In fact, she ultimately switched departments because she couldn't work with him."

My eyes moved to the ground. None of what Fletcher was saying surprised me. But learning that Jake was every bit the slimeball I perceived him to be still hit my gut like a fist.

It doesn't matter, I assured myself, *because he's not your birth father. There must be someone else out there. Someone kind, someone who never even knew they had a biological daughter—or granddaughter, or sister . . .*

Stop dreaming, Meara. There's no one.

Tears welled behind my eyes. The emptiness I felt inside would have been intense, no matter what my physical circumstances. But the frustration of Fletcher's nearness—sympathetic, yet intentionally distanced—served only to compound my torment.

I could accept his lack of interest in me, but I could not be unaffected by it. He was unlike any man I'd ever met, and I would be attracted to him even if he were five-foot-two and bald. Not only was he intelligent, kindhearted, and honest—but he loved the outdoors as much as I did, he seemed to want children, and he wasn't afraid to apologize. He passed all my criteria with flying colors.

True, I was vulnerable emotionally, not to mention theoretically on the rebound from a botched engagement. But none of the above could stop me from wanting him. I'd been in his arms before; I could not forget the feeling. Despite my insistence that I didn't *need* to be held, the fact remained that I wanted to be. I wanted Fletcher—his warmth and his comfort. I wanted him so badly my chest ached.

But he wasn't mine. And whatever he might offer platonically, I had no business taking. Not when my own thoughts were anything but.

"I don't care about Jake Kozen," I said harshly, springing up. I had a mission to accomplish today, and I was going to finish it. "All I want to do is settle the facts about my adoption, and I'm going to do that right now."

I marched to where my Hyundai sat in the lot, retrieved the envelope from the passenger seat, and slammed the door. "This is a copy of Sheila's criminal record," I announced, ripping open the top as Fletcher approached. "We'll see whether Jake told the truth about it."

Fletcher reached forward and put his hands on mine, stopping me. "You got her criminal record?" he asked, his voice cautious.

I averted my gaze and tugged back on the envelope. No way was I looking at those eyes of his again.

"Don't open it, Meara," he said softly.

I looked at his eyes again. They were brimming with empathy. It was obvious he knew something. "Why not?" I practically shouted.

He studied me a moment. Then he withdrew his hands and stepped back. His eyes left mine, and he let out a heavy breath.

I got the feeling he was preparing to say something, but I didn't wait to hear it. I had sworn to go by the facts. I ripped the rest of the way into the envelope and extracted the paper.

My breath came in with a shudder.

Sheila T. Kozen. Date of Conviction: December 17, 1978. My eyes scanned downward. The stated charge seemed to rise off the paper to meet me—bold and glaring.

Attempted Homicide.

I stood with the paper clenched in my hands, unmoving. Fletcher hovered silently nearby.

No. Not Sheila. It couldn't be.

I folded the paper and stuffed it back into the envelope.

A dark weight seemed to be pressing in from all sides, constricting my lungs. "You knew about this, didn't you?" I asked unsteadily, trying to breathe.

He didn't answer right away, and I turned to look at him.

His jaw was set with determination, his shoulders poised and strong. But his eyes were as full of pain as ever, and there was a sadness to him that I had not yet seen. A sadness fully matching my own. "I suspected," he answered, "when you told me Sheila had been in prison. But I didn't know for sure until this morning."

I leaned heavily against the side of my car. No wonder the pain was back in his eyes. He had just found out that his father had married an attempted murderess. I wasn't the only one hurting.

"How did you know about it? Who did she—" I broke off. A thought was percolating in the back of my brain, a thought that demanded nurturing. A thought that brought with it the faintest glimmer of hope.

Fletcher moved to stand in front of me. "I know because it happened here," he said, his deep voice soothing. "At the inn. It happened when you were living with us."

Any other time, the sound of his last words would have warmed me. But now they were no more effective than a spark on the tundra. "Then I *was* here," I confirmed flatly.

"Yes." He continued, speaking every word as slowly and carefully as if I were made of glass. "It happened during a parental visit. My mother usually did those at the inn. Sheila and Jake got into some sort of argument—"

The thought in the back of my brain shot forward. My eyes widened. "She tried to kill *him*," I interrupted. "That's what you're trying to tell me, isn't it? Sheila tried to kill Jake, and that's why she went to prison."

I watched him, breath held.

He nodded.

Thoughts raced in my head. Pieces of logic danced frantically in the air, desperate to grasp their complements.

I always loved you, Meara. I was protecting you.

"Jake was an abuser!" I exclaimed, thinking out loud as the puzzle at last took shape. "He battered Sheila. That's what happened, I know it. He has a violent side to him. I could see it!"

My breaths came quick and shallow. "That's why I was in foster care in the first place. Sheila wanted me away from Jake. She probably wanted herself away, too, but she couldn't manage it. He had her under his thumb—that's what happens with battered women. And she would have been in an even worse predicament with him being a cop. Who could she go to for help?"

The question was rhetorical, and Fletcher didn't answer it.

"The fight they had at the inn," I plowed on, "he could have attacked her, threatened her. Maybe he threatened the both of us, and she had finally had enough. She had a gun and she shot him in self-defense. But it was the seventies; no one understood how battering could affect a woman, and even if they had, he was a cop—the law would have taken his side."

My heart threatened to burst from my rib cage. I thought of my first night at the inn, and how the end room upstairs had filled me with a vague sense of dread. Was the fear real? Had it happened there?

"Meara," Fletcher said evenly, "before you say any more, there's something you should read. Come with me."

He turned and walked toward the inn.

"What?" I asked, following. I did not want to hear, or know, a single other thing. The facts were finally all coming together in a way I could understand. It wasn't pretty, but at least it made sense. At least it allowed me to believe that one of my birth parents was a decent person—that one of them had truly cared for me.

"All I could remember," he explained as we walked, "was that when I was young, the mother of one of our girls had been convicted of shooting her father at the inn. I came back here this morning to search through my mother's papers, thinking she might have kept some newspaper clippings. And eventually I did find one."

We reached the front door of the inn, and he opened it for me. I followed like a zombie as he led me into the common room. Then he stopped by the large table, picked up a small, yellowed rectangle of paper, and handed it to me.

Cold, hard facts, I reminded myself. That's what I had to depend on.

I took a breath and started reading.

Woman arraigned in shooting of police officer.
Sheila T. Kozen, 25, of Somerset pled guilty yesterday to charges of attempted homicide in the shooting of her husband, Somerset police officer Jacob Kozen, at a local motel last Tuesday. A witness to the shooting testified that the couple were arguing when the woman shot her husband at close range, seriously injuring him with a bullet wound in the side. The victim was unarmed. Sentencing has not yet been scheduled.

I flipped the paper over. The back side showed part of an advertisement for jewelry. There was no date.

I laid the clipping and the envelope down on the table, then stared at the floor. "Seems a little skewed," I said, my voice thin. "I don't suppose the judge who sentenced her cared what they were arguing about. Or whether she was being threatened when she pulled the trigger. The witness was probably some crony of Jake's."

"Meara," Fletcher said gently, "the witness was my mother."

My chin snapped up. "Your mother helped put an innocent woman in jail?"

He bristled, but only slightly. "Sheila confessed," he said patiently. "There was no question that she shot the man."

"But it was self-defense!" I railed, whirling away from him. "It had to be!" A queer, uneasy feeling came over me. A heaviness, a pressure in my skull. It had been building for a while, but in the midst of everything, I had barely noticed it. My own voice now hurt my head, every word like a nail strike to the back of my eye. There was no mistaking the signs. I was getting a migraine.

"I'm telling you, Sheila wasn't to blame, no matter what it looks like," I continued, my mind still scrambling. "Your father wouldn't have married her otherwise, would he? He had to have known who she was."

Fletcher didn't respond. Over twenty-five years would have passed between the shooting and Mitchell's marriage to Sheila. Maybe he didn't know who she was.

"It can't be what it seems," I insisted, my voice cracking. "At least one of my birth parents had to be a good person."

Immediately, Fletcher put his hands on my upper arms and turned me to face him. "*You* are a good person," he said with emphasis, holding my eyes. "And so were your real parents—the ones that raised you. That's the only link that matters. You can sympathize with your birth parents or you can hate them, Meara—whatever works for you. But don't ever judge yourself by what they did."

The pull of him was nearly unbearable. He was wearing a worn flannel work shirt, its sleeves rolled up to the elbows, its folds soft. I could imagine the feel of his shoulder beneath my cheek, the comforting pressure of his arms encircling my back. I wanted that safety, that security. I wanted it as much as I had ever wanted anything.

But it was not being offered.

He let go of my arms. He remained standing close, but not close enough to stop the hurting. Either in my head, or my heart.

I raised my hand to my face and rubbed my temples. I might as well have a migraine. Why not?

"Thank you for trying to h-help," I stammered, every syllable reverberating painfully in my skull. "But I'm done thinking. I have a headache, and I need to lie down."

Reluctantly, I pulled myself away from him and took a giant step toward my room. But then I stopped. Splitting head or no, I did not want to be guilty of walking out on a discussion myself. "Is there anything else you wanted to talk to me about?" I asked, my voice barely above a whisper.

"No," he answered, his own voice just as quiet.

I started walking again. If he said anything else, I didn't hear him. I hadn't slept for two nights straight, and the pain in my head was excruciating. I had some heavy-duty painkillers in my travel case that had been prescribed for my mother before she died, and I had been saving them for just such a migraine. I was going to take them, and I was going to fall asleep.

Whether I woke up anytime soon, I didn't really care.

Chapter

~-19-~

THE BEDROOM WAS dark when my eyes opened. I felt heavy-limbed and disoriented, and though my clock informed me it was early morning, I had a hard time believing it. Had I slept all afternoon and through the night?

I pulled up the corner of my shade and peeked out. The sun did seem to be contemplating an appearance—the horizon showed a subtle brightening, and the birds had already begun their morning serenade.

I was still dressed in the clothes I had put on yesterday morning, and I needed a shower. But even more than that, I needed a cup of tea. The migraine was gone, but if I were to go any longer without my regular dose of caffeine, I would soon be courting another one.

I rose from the bed, stretched, and drifted out my door and down the hall toward the kitchen. I was aware of the dark cloud that pervaded my mind, weighting my every movement, but I had no plans to engage it. I had compartmentalized the horror of that feeling; it was with me, but I could keep it at bay. I could continue with the basics: tea, shower. I knew that I could exist on autopilot as long as I had to until the grief subsided and my strength returned. I had done it before.

I stumbled into the kitchen, blinking my eyes to clear the cobwebs. Then I filled the teapot with water, set it on the stove, and collected my tea bag and cup. I was in the process of trying to separate the paper tab from the tea bag packet when a sound immediately to my left sent me leaping into the air.

"Good morning."

It was a female voice, smooth and low, almost musical. I whirled toward it to see a tall, slender woman about my own age dressed comfortably in a blue cotton-knit top and leggings. Her shining black hair hung straight nearly to her waist, and her skin, radiant without makeup, was a soft beige color that could almost be brown. Large, dark eyes gleamed from a face as perfect as that of a china doll; yet her good-natured smile lent it a warm, earthy glow.

I dropped the tea bag.

"I didn't mean to scare you," she said pleasantly, and as I drew in a ragged breath, my wits deigned to return.

"Tia?" I croaked.

She smiled again. "That's right. And you're obviously Meara, the generous one. Fletch told me all about you. Or at least I thought he did." Her grin turned slightly devious. "Seems he left out a few things."

My brow creased. My head was still fuzzy; I was having trouble following her. "Pardon?"

Continuing to grin, she stepped closer, picked up my tea bag, detached the clinging paper packet, and dropped the business end into my cup. "Just a suggestion, but you might want to go for coffee, instead. I've already made a pot. More caffeine—quicker to the veins. What do you say?"

I blinked. Perhaps I had taken one too many painkillers. Tia's movements were lissome, almost surreally so. "No thank you," I managed. "I'm really more of a tea drinker."

She shrugged, placing her own half-full coffee cup on the counter opposite the stove. Then she hopped up next to it, crossed her legs, and watched me thoughtfully. "Fletch told me that you gave up any rights to the estate," she began, her tone friendly, despite the punch of her words. "Frankly, I was amazed. I thought he would have a real fight on his hands. Not that any normal person would want a bunch of trees, but anyone who knew how Fletch felt about this place could certainly stick it to him." She smiled at me again. "You didn't. I appreciate that."

I tried hard to focus, willing the water in the teapot to heat. "Your brother is a good person," I explained, fighting the sensation that I was watching my body from a distance. "I would never take anything from him—or you. And I love trees."

My words reached my ears, and I wondered if I was making any sense.

Tia's smile widened. "You're in worse shape than I thought," she said with a chuckle, her smooth voice tinkling like a bell. "You and Fletch didn't hit Dad's brandy earlier, did you? That would explain why I found him sacked out on the couch."

My brow furrowed again. "He was on the couch?"

Her almond eyes continued to study me, and I sensed she was a woman who didn't miss much. "Until about an hour ago, yes. I woke him up when I came in." She retrieved her coffee and took a sip. "He looked like hell, actually—I could hardly get a word out of him. He just asked if I was going to stay here, then said he was going home to sleep."

A flush of warmth pulsed through me. Fletcher had stayed here. With me. All night. Maybe part of yesterday. What had he been thinking? Had he been worried about me?

The teapot began to hiss, but I stood still, staring into space. It was Tia who leapt down from her perch, picked up the pot, and poured the water. It was a good thing—I probably would have scalded myself again.

"*Ookay . . . ,*" she said slowly, amused. "I'm just going to carry this to the couch for you, and you can sit down and relax until the caffeine hits your brain. I know—I've got you at a disadvantage. I'm already on my third cup. Very rude of me."

I chuckled myself—though not nearly as melodiously—and followed her to the couch. She said nothing more as we drank, but stretched her long legs out in front of her, raising one at a time with her toes pointed, as if performing an exercise. Her expression was contemplative, and as the caffeine at last began to penetrate my fog, I found myself transfixed. Most women with her degree of beauty and poise would use them to intimidate, but Fletcher's sister showed not a drop of pretension. *I am who I am,* her body language proclaimed. You could either like it or you could go to hell—whatever floated your boat.

I wondered how much she knew about me.

"So," I said finally, feeling more like myself. "When was the last time you and Fletcher talked? Other than this morning?"

She stopped her toe pointing and folded her legs beneath her. "Monday night—after you signed the papers."

I nodded. That meant she probably didn't know that I had been a foster child here, much less the rest of it. I wasn't going to think about the rest of it.

"He admitted that he had misjudged you," she continued, "and he advised me not to come out and make bodily threats, which had been my original plan." She grinned at me in a peculiar way, which was both completely amiable and completely serious. I could see a fire behind her eyes, a fierce protectiveness. But I could also see that it wasn't born of malice.

"Fletch needs this place," she explained, her fondness for her brother evident in her voice. "It's what makes him tick. You can take the man from the mountain—a.k.a. to an apartment in San Francisco—but you can't take the mountain from the man." Her expression darkened. "Not that it hasn't been tried."

I threw her a questioning glance, but she shrugged it off, her face brightening again.

"So, I understand you're staying here a few days, taking in the sights?"

I nodded, explaining briefly about my mother's passing and the abatement. It occurred to me that I had not checked in with Alex since the process began, and I made a mental note to call him this morning. The contractors could be done by now. I could go home.

"I'm so sorry," Tia offered. "I had no idea you lost your mother and your birth mother so close together."

Her empathy was open and sincere, and I remembered that she, too, had been adopted. Without warning, my eyes moistened. "And I'm sorry about your father," I said softly. "About both of your parents. I know how you feel. We're too young for this."

Her face showed agreement, and I took a deep breath.

"Fletcher told me about your search for your birth parents," I explained. "He thought the story might be helpful to me. I hope that's all right."

I expected her to look away then, to show some sign of pain at the memory. But her eyes remained on mine, steady and strong. She merely nodded, seeming to anticipate—even to invite—more discussion. Without forethought, I complied.

"What I found out about my birth parents wasn't what I expected. Everything was worse than I expected. I always knew that bad news was a possibility, but . . ." My voice trailed off.

After a few uncomfortable seconds, she finished for me. "But in the back of your mind, you still hoped for the fairy tale. I know."

She rose from the couch and stepped into the kitchen for more coffee, speaking as she went. "So did I," she said casually. "And I had no reason whatsoever to hope. I knew that my birth mother had her rights terminated because of neglect. But even then, I kept wanting to think that somehow it wasn't her fault—that somebody else started her on the drugs, that she was just naive, and then helpless, but that really, inside, she was some kind of saint."

She returned to the couch and sat down, her cup full and steaming. Her eyes met mine once more, confident and comforting. "She wasn't. She wasn't even particularly nice. She came from a wealthy family, and she seemed intelligent—at least in an academic way. But when it came to making life choices, she was an idiot. She had no goals, no conviction, no backbone. She ran off when she was a teenager, then promptly got into drugs, got pregnant, and got disowned. She blamed everyone else for everything. When I met her she was off the drugs—I can't imagine what she was like when she was on them."

I swallowed, my own story temporarily forgotten. "That must have been awful for you."

"It was hell," she acknowledged. "I cried for a week. But I got over it." She offered a smile. "You will too."

I smiled back, feeling stronger. The coldness of yesterday's revelations still chilled me, but I could keep it from dominating. Talking did help.

"I still don't know who my real birth father is," I blurted. "And I'm not so sure I want to know anymore. I mean, why not stick with the fantasy? Do I really *need* to find out that he was just some asshole?"

I cringed. What had I just said? The sentiment was so crude, so unlike me.

To my surprise, Tia chuckled. "For heaven's sake, Meara, don't look so scandalized. If the shoe fits, wear it! Why, some of my best friends' birth fathers are assholes. Mine certainly is. The guy swore up and down that I wasn't his child, never mind the fact that he was the only Korean man my birth mother had ever been with—not to mention the only Asian person for two counties in any direction!"

She laughed again, and this time I found myself laughing with her. It felt amazingly good.

My mirth melted into a sigh, and my eyes moistened. I wiped my eyes on my shirtsleeve. "I must look dreadful," I apologized, remembering my state. "I'm sorry."

She smirked. "I should hope so. God knows I have standards for whom I drink coffee with at dawn."

I broke into laughter again, almost spilling tea on the couch. Then I straightened and looked at her seriously. I had known the woman for only a few minutes; already I adored her. Had I before?

No, I told myself. There was no point in analyzing those years—lamenting what might have been. It was moving-forward time. "You really got over it?" I asked soberly, never doubting that she would understand the question. "You felt . . . .well, *normal* again?"

She smiled. "You never get completely over it. It always hurts, if you dwell on it. But you *will* stop judging yourself by your genes. You can convince yourself that as regrettable as your birth parents' miserable lives are or were, their problems are not yours. Breaking ties was their decision—you've got every right to stick to it."

I exhaled with a curious sense of relief. "Thank you, Tia," I said sincerely. "Can I ask you one more question?"

She nodded.

"Do you regret finding out what you did?"

"No," she responded. "As tough as it was, I could never have tolerated the alternative. I was too restless, too unsatisfied. Do I wish I had found another reality? Of course. But not knowing wasn't an option for me."

I nodded, understanding.

"Now, for Fletch," she continued, "it was a whole different story. He said he didn't want to know, that he didn't want to find her or even know her name. At first, I didn't believe him; I thought he was resisting out of fear. But I finally came to realize that for him, not knowing *is* the best way of managing. All the hurt and the hostility some adoptees carry . . . when it's targeted at a concept, it's diffused. But when you put a name and face to it—a real person—it sharpens. It can take on a life of its own. He didn't need that. He doesn't need that. I didn't tell him half of what I found out, because that was the way he wanted it. And I never will tell him, unless he changes his mind, of course."

Uneasiness swirled in my stomach. "Fletcher was adopted, too," I murmured, restating the obvious. I was taken aback, but I wasn't sure why. He hadn't ever told me he *wasn't* adopted, had he? I was certain I hadn't asked.

Tia sighed dramatically. "He didn't tell you, did he? Typical Fletch. He tells the whole story about me, hoping it will make you feel better, but neglects to mention that he's in exactly the same boat. That's a man for you."

I looked at her questioningly.

"Men react differently to adoption than women do," she attested, taking a long draught of coffee and settling herself more comfortably among the cushions. "At least, that's been my observation. They don't have the same desire to be open about it; it's like a dirty secret. I think it goes back to the rejection thing. All men fear being rejected by a woman, and a male adoptee, right from the start, knows that he's already been rejected by the one woman who should have been more devoted to him than anyone else on the planet. His own mother."

My mind flew to Fletcher—how vehemently he had condemned Jake's decision not to raise me, how passionately he had talked of parents putting their children first. He had suffered through much of the same rejection and self-doubt that I had—and yet he'd said nothing. He hadn't wanted me to know, hadn't wanted my pity. Yet he had been both willing and anxious to help.

"Are you and Fletcher—" I began, but cut myself off. I wasn't sure how to state the question without overstepping.

Tia didn't seem to mind. "We're half siblings," she explained. "He's only twelve months older, but birth mom had a thing about commitment. He was taken away when he was a baby, because she kept leaving him alone. She was pregnant with me at the time, so the county took me too as soon as I was born. We were our parents' first fosters, and we never left. It was years before they could adopt us legally, of course, but we never knew any different. We were very lucky."

"Yes," I agreed. "You were."

There was more I wanted to ask her—a thousand things more I wanted to know. About her. About Fletcher. About their parents and their foster siblings. The loss of my own family had left a vacuum inside me, and my desire to fill it was irrepressible. There was a warmth here, a love of life, that both fascinated and tantalized me. I knew I had no right to leech off anyone else's hearth and home, but still, I couldn't stop the longing. I didn't want just to be a houseguest, or a former step-in-law, or even an ex-foster child. I wanted to be close to both Fletcher and his sister. I wanted to be their friend.

The phone rang. Tia and I stared at it, not moving.

"You expecting a call?" she asked.

I shook my head. "I haven't given the number out, except for an emergency. Maybe it's Fletcher."

She offered a delicate snort. "Fletch would never call here. Wander over in the middle of a hailstorm for a newspaper, yes. Call, no. Besides, I'm sure he's still asleep." She rose and walked to the phone. "Probably just a telemarketer."

She picked up, and I sensed immediately that the call was for me. I also sensed it was not good news.

She covered the receiver with her palm and looked at me. "Alex Witzig? From Pittsburgh? He says it's urgent."

My heart pounded as I rose. I couldn't imagine what the problem was. But I couldn't say I was surprised to be having one.

Chapter
~20~

I TURNED ONTO my parents' street north of Pittsburgh, but found my usual parking spot in front of their house already occupied. I secured a spot a block away, then walked carefully back over the same sidewalks I had traveled in my youth, which had, in the time since, begun to buckle over the rising maple roots. The neighborhood was an old one. Once it had been the height of upper-middle-class living—solid, two-story brick row houses with wide porches and tiny, well-delineated backyards. But by the eighties, the defection of younger families to more spacious, outlying suburbs had given the neighborhood an older demographic, leaving me with few other children to play with. Now, the street consisted almost entirely of the pensioned elderly.

Alex, who was tall, blond, and wiry, met me at the door. As always, he was dapper and dressed for success, though no amount of external decoration could conceal his inherent squirreliness. He was a sweet soul, and I was fond of him, but there had never been any chemistry between us. I needed wholesomeness in a mate; he longed for an equally materialistic woman who wouldn't balk at the cost of his ties.

"Thanks so much for meeting me here," I exclaimed, giving him a quick, grateful hug. "I don't know how I could handle all this without you."

"Expect the personal touch," he teased, quoting his realty company's slogan. But his expression quickly sobered. "I wanted to talk to you for a minute before we go inside."

He put a hand on my elbow and led me a few paces back out into the yard. "I've been talking with the owner of the abatement company, and he seems to be on the up-and-up. They did report the unlocked door themselves. But just to be sure, we've got somebody at my office doing a little fishing about the company's previous jobs and any rumors that might be circulating. In the meantime, it would be better if you didn't give off any paranoid vibes to the workers here today—if you get my drift."

I let out a breath and nodded.

"Isn't there some chance they just forgot to lock up?" I asked hopefully.

Alex shrugged. "Anything's possible. But what the foreman told me was that he locked the doors personally last night—that it was always his job. Then this morning, the back door was open. Not standing open—just unlocked again."

We began walking toward the house. "Have the police been here?" I asked.

"Briefly," he answered. "But until you can say whether or not anything is missing or damaged, there's not much they can do." We reached the front door, and I walked inside. "I looked around myself," he continued, following me. "But I couldn't tell anything. I can't remember what you had in the way of electronics, but your computer seems okay."

I glanced briefly around the small kitchen and combined living and dining room. "Just the television and VCR," I answered, the loss of household luxuries being the least of my concerns. Neither my parents nor I had ever owned anything of monetary consequence: our few electronics were cheap, old, or both; my mother's jewelry, with one exception, all costume. The house's most valuable contents were a few large pieces of antique furniture, none of which could be easily removed. Still, the feeling of violation rankled, and anger brought a red heat to my cheeks.

I hurried toward the staircase, leaping up the steps two at a time with Alex lagging behind. I entered my bedroom, opened the closet door, and looked with relief at the large, fireproof safe on the floor. Squatting down, I determined that it was still locked. I withdrew my keys from my pocket and opened it. "My mother's wedding ring is in here," I explained to Alex when he caught up. "And all my computer backups."

"Good," he commented. "Anything else missing? Moved?"

I relocked the safe and stood. The question was a difficult one to answer, given the chaos caused by the abatement itself. The house seemed foreign, filled with unfamiliar equipment and tools, not to mention a half-dozen meandering construction workers. I walked slowly from room to room, examining everything I could think to examine. But there was relatively little to sort through—I had already been in the process of packing, and none of the boxes that I had carefully labeled and sealed appeared to have been opened.

"I really think everything's fine," I said as we finished downstairs. I allowed myself a smile. Perhaps it was a misunderstanding, after all. Who would break into a house during a mold abatement? Wouldn't they expect, at that time more than any other, that one's valuables would be protected?

"Well, that's a relief," Alex said, wrapping an arm around my shoulders and delivering a quick squeeze. "I would hate for you to lose anything you cared about after the year you've had. *But* . . ." His face broke into a devious grin. "I suppose things are looking up in the romance department now, eh? Or did you not look closely in the kitchen? I must say, O'Rourke, you do move fast. Poor Todd is probably still crying in his formula."

I blinked. I had no idea what he was talking about, but he had given me a welcome thought.

"Todd!" I said, putting more happiness into the word than I had in months. "Of course. He still has my key. I asked him to give it back, but he refused. He probably came over to look for something of his that he thought I had, and then forgot to lock up. It would be just like him not to give a hoot whether I was worried about the house or not."

Alex exhaled. "Good theory. You should call him and see."

"Yes, I should," I agreed, dreading the thought. I knew that the second Todd heard my voice he would assume I wanted him back, and when he realized he was wrong, he would launch into his mortally wounded act all over again. As it stood, my last words to him had been sensitive and civil. But any response to the rudeness of his subsequent phone messages would not be—not coming from the new Meara.

"What were you saying about the kitchen?" I inquired, moving in that direction. When I reached the doorway it occurred to me that I hadn't really examined that room at all, knowing full well it held nothing any competent burglar would want. What it did hold now, I noted with a start, was a colorful bouquet of carnations and roses. I walked curiously toward the counter.

"The foreman says those arrived yesterday," Alex informed. "And I have to confess, I looked at the card already. Don't hate me forever—you know I have your best interests at heart. *So,* care to share? Who is this guy?"

It was a modest arrangement: a spring mix of yellow, pink, and white, flanked with baby's breath. I could smell the roses from a foot away, even through the mustiness of the house's air. I loved roses.

The mere sight of these made my stomach churn.

"Well, open the card!" Alex pushed, unaware.

With an unaccountable revulsion I shuffled my feet forward and extracted the small white envelope. Ordinarily, the card would come last. Ordinarily, I would begin by sweeping a finger along the soft petals and immersing my nose in the nearest rose. Then I would linger a moment, delighting in the vibrancy and symmetry of nature.

Not this time. As I opened the already-opened envelope and plucked out the card, my breath seemed thick in my throat, my pulse palpable in the burning scarlet of my cheeks.

Yellow roses framed the card's corner. The loopy handwriting was clearly a woman's . . . an employee of the florist, not the sender. The message was simple.

Enjoyed meeting you. All my best, Jake.

In my mind, I was back at the diner again. I could see

Jake's smile, charming and bold. I could see his eyes, dark and glinting, piercing through me. I could feel the coldness.

The hate.

The card fluttered to the floor.

"Hey!" Alex protested, stepping forward to retrieve it. "He couldn't have been all that bad, could he? These cost at least twenty-five bucks. Thirty with tax."

I couldn't answer. My limbs were stuck in place, my voice out of commission.

Jake had sent me flowers. Within a day of our meeting, he had gone out, hunted up my home address, and paid for a bouquet of flowers.

"Meara," Alex pressed. "Is something wrong?"

"No," I lied, my heart pounding. It had been pounding all morning, but now it was outdoing itself.

Was I losing my mind? True, Jake had refused to raise me on his own. He was rumored to be a second-rate policeman and a first-class sexist. But at this point, that was all I knew for certain. Hadn't he been polite at our meeting? Helpful and cordial? Wasn't sending flowers a nice thing to do?

My rational mind pled his case, but my gut wasn't buying it. Instinct told me that he had lied about being my birth father; instinct told me that he was violent. Both he and Sheila had lied to me, true, but in a case of he-said/she-said, it was her I would believe.

Jake had done something to her—something so horrible that it had provoked an otherwise decent woman into taking a shot at him. Why else would the mere memory of his eyes make my stomach roll with nausea? The hair on the back of my neck stand? My palms dampen with sweat?

I could not afford to be rational. My first priority had

to be my own safety—and sanity. I would not have anything more to do with Jake Kozen, ever. And if he thought he could manipulate my feelings with a twenty-five-dollar bouquet, he was sorely mistaken.

I grabbed the vase from the counter and dashed it to the trash can.

"Whoa!" Alex exclaimed, turning me to face him. "So I get it. The guy's a creep. Fine. Anything you want to tell me?"

I shook my head firmly, then concentrated on calming myself. Alex was a good confidant, but explaining this situation would take more background information than I cared to give. "Nothing I can't handle," I assured him. "Just a miscommunication."

His eyebrows rose. "You sure? I'm not much good with my fists, personally, but I've got a cousin—"

"Thanks, Alex," I interrupted. "But that won't be necessary."

He studied me a moment, then seemed to decide he could believe me. "Okay, but if you don't mind, can I have the flowers? One of my listings is getting shot for a television spot this afternoon, and these would look great in the breakfast nook—"

"Knock yourself out."

I averted my eyes from the flowers and breathed deeply. I needed to focus. What was important now was determining whether or not my parents' house had had an unwelcome visitor.

I scanned the rest of the kitchen and noted that the drawer beneath the telephone was sitting out an inch, which it had had the tendency to do for years unless jiggled when pushed closed. I always jiggled it. Seeing the front sticking out had been a pet peeve of both mine and

my mother's, though it was a sight we had secretly
missed after my father passed away.

"Did you open this drawer?" I asked Alex.

"No," he answered. "But any of the workers might
have. Maybe looking for a phone book?"

I nodded in agreement, trying to stem my alarm. I did
keep the phone book in that drawer. I also kept my personal
address book there—normally. But I had packed it when I
left, in case I needed to impose on a friend for lodging.

I jiggled the drawer closed. Alex was right—one misplaced drawer was no cause for panic. The explanation
could be as simple as a worker searching for a pen.

"You really should check those messages," he suggested, pointing to the blinking light on my answering
machine. "A couple are mine, but it just occurred to me—
there could be one from Todd. Perhaps a tidy confession?"

Perhaps, I thought, my mind racing. I turned to face
Alex. "This may not be important, but would you mind
asking the foreman if anyone has been in this drawer? It's
not a problem—I'd just like to know."

He looked at me for a moment, then offered a good-
natured salute and retreated. As soon as he left the
kitchen, I lowered the volume on the answering machine
and pressed the PLAY button.

"It's me," Todd's sniveling voice proclaimed. *"It's
Sunday night, another weekend lost, and I'm not calling
you again. Do you understand that? Not ever. This is it.
The end. Finito. We're finished. Through. Good-bye, and
good riddance. You'll never do any better than me, you
know. You're a dreamer, and it's going to cost you. And
when you hit bottom, don't come crying back to me, because I'll be long gone. Hasta la vista, baby."*

I rolled my eyes. And to think that I used to find his clichés endearing. Not very long ago, I couldn't have listened to such a message without feeling guilty—without feeling personally responsible for not following through with the engagement, for failing to make things work. Now I felt nothing but relief to be free of him. The new Meara had accomplished something.

The next message was from Alex, giving me an update on the abatement. The third message was the one I dreaded. Jake's smooth voice boomed from the speaker, and my every muscle went taut.

"Hello, Meara. It's Jake. Just wanted to tell you again how much I enjoyed meeting you yesterday. I also wanted to let you know that I found your birth certificate and some other papers you might be interested in. I'd be happy to drop them in the mail to you, but . . . Well, I've been thinking about our conversation, and I think there are a few more things about your mother that you should know. Could we meet again sometime soon? You name the time and place. I'll be there. Just give me a ring."

I drew in a ragged breath and closed my eyes. There was nothing sinister in the message, I assured myself. Jake even sounded as though he had decided to come clean about why Sheila went to prison—not that his motives for lying about that were any mystery. What cop with half an ego would want to admit that he'd been shot by his own wife?

"Well," Alex announced, returning to the kitchen just as his voice finished up a fourth message. "The foreman assures me that no one's supposed to be opening your drawers. On the other hand, he admits he can't watch all his guys twenty-four/seven."

He looked over my shoulder at the answering machine, which was in the process of rewinding. "Any messages from the ex-fiancé?"

I nodded.

"Was it him?"

I shook my head. "I'm not sure. Maybe." I felt numb.

Alex leaned over my shoulder and picked up the phone. "Tell me his number," he ordered. "I'll call the guy myself. You shouldn't have to deal with him, anyway."

Feeling a rush of gratitude, I delivered Todd's work number. But my relief was short-lived. As soon as Alex was occupied, my mind strayed back to Jake.

Why was he doing this? The flowers, the phone call? If I was right, and he knew he wasn't my birth father, what *did* he want with me? What was the point?

Dark eyes loomed again in my mind. I had sensed something in that diner. Something that frightened me. I hadn't seen just coldness in his eyes, had I? I had seen hatred, too.

Hatred of me.

Alex hung up the phone with a bang. He had been talking, but I hadn't been paying attention. My blood had run cold.

"Simpering momma's boy," he exclaimed, shaking his head in disgust. "God, I'm glad you didn't marry that wuss. What a woman like you needs is a good old-fashioned *man's* man. I should call my cousin—"

"Has Todd been in the house?" I interrupted again, deflecting Alex's well-established matchmaking compulsion.

"He says no," Alex answered, working his jaw with vexation. "I won't tell you what else he said. Unfortunately, I believe him on the first count—I don't think he was here. Do you want to file a complaint with the police about the break-in?"

I shook my head slowly. If I didn't get a grip soon, my limbs would start to shake, and that had been happening far too often lately. I was pretty good at keeping a cheerful face, but covering angst was difficult when one was quivering like a spoonful of jelly.

"I don't like it," I responded, working hard to keep my voice normal. "But I can't see that I have any basis for any charges. The foreman could have just forgotten to lock up. Let's let it go."

Alex nodded, studying me. "All right, then. No problem. You want to get some lunch? They tell me if everything proceeds on schedule, you can move back in the day after tomorrow." Without waiting for an answer, he leaned over and extracted my bouquet from the trash can, repairing its skewed stems with his free hand.

As I watched him, my mind played a different picture. That of a seasoned cop, picking a lock as though it were child's play. Opening my back door. Roaming. Searching. Musing.

All my best, Jake.

A shiver ran down my spine. "No thanks." The quivering was seconds away; there was no point in fighting it. My parents had lived happily in this house for decades; I had lived here myself and had always felt safe.

I didn't anymore.

"I have to get back," I insisted, my voice hollow.

His brow creased. "Get back where?"

I didn't answer immediately. It was a very good question.

Chapter

~21~

THE INN WAS unlocked. I moved down the hall at a good clip, then scanned the common room for signs of life. It was quiet.

"Tia?" I called. "Are you here?"

There was no answer. I peeked into Sheila and Mitchell's room and saw men's clothes strewn on the bed, some already packed into black plastic bags. Evidently it was Tia who had been elected to sort through Mitchell's personal belongings. I did not envy her.

But where was she? Her car was still in the parking lot.

I exhaled in frustration. Two hours of driving, and my pulse had still not slowed. I was unsettled, and I wasn't sure how to fix myself. All I had been able to think, as I said good-bye to Alex with an artificial smile on my face, was that I wanted to be back here. Now that I was here, I seemed to want something else.

"Tia?" I called again. She was not anywhere on the first floor. I moved hesitantly to the bottom of the stairs and looked up. *Had* it happened up there . . . in the end bedroom? Did some part of my mind still know that?

I drew in a breath and raised a foot. Whatever had

happened in the past, it was still the past. It couldn't hurt me now.

I forced myself up the rest of the stairs, once again pausing briefly on the landing to admire the clock. Would Tia take it with her? She should. With no one living here permanently now, it might get stolen. I reached the upstairs hall and began walking, looking through each door in turn.

I glanced into the second bedroom on the right, and relief washed over me. Two plum-colored suitcases lay on the floor, each opened, with various feminine belongings scattered in all directions. Tia herself lay on the canopy bed, fully clothed, snoring softly.

I smiled. She had arrived at the inn in the wee hours of the morning, hadn't she? Of course she was tired. Her car was a rental—perhaps she was jet-lagged. In any event, she was still here. And she was safe.

Safe, I repeated to myself, turning quietly from the door and heading back down the stairs. Why wouldn't she be? Was I becoming paranoid?

I brushed off the thought and headed to the kitchen. But though I busied myself by making and eating a grilled cheese sandwich, then cleaning the range and countertops to obsessive-compulsive standards, I did not feel any better. The uneasiness was still with me.

I wanted something. And despite my mental protestations to the contrary, I knew exactly what it was.

The sight of Fletcher's beat-up truck on the path below his cabin drew my lips into a smile. He would be here. He had to be—unless he had hiked away or hitched a ride with someone else. I moved to the cabin's front porch and rapped on the door. It opened within seconds.

Fletcher stood in the doorway, consuming most of it. He was wearing the most dilapidated clothing I had yet seen: a T-shirt with holes around the pocket and ancient jeans spattered with a combination of deep brown and an odd, shiny substance.

His initial reaction at seeing me was shock, though the sentiment was less severe than the last time I had surprised him here. What delighted me more was the soft smile that followed—and the pleasure that flashed, perhaps not to his knowledge, deep within his eyes.

He was glad to see me.

"Meara," he exclaimed, not moving. "You came back."

I nodded.

"What happened?" he questioned, his expression turning worried. "Tia said you got a call from your real estate agent—that your parents' house was broken into."

I nodded again, feeling awkward. I didn't want to talk about what had happened in Pittsburgh. All I could do was look with yearning at his strong arms—one holding the door open, the other resting at his side. But I continued to stand on the porch, and he continued to keep his distance.

As well he should.

"I'm sorry to barge in," I lied, cursing my slip in language. Resolution #2 was going poorly. Resolution #1, on the other hand, appeared not to be a problem. Fletcher, unlike every other man I had had the misfortune to be attracted to, did not seem interested in using me. He could, if he wanted to. I was upset; I was vulnerable. I had hiked up to his cabin in search of comfort, and even the most clueless of men could pick up on that. It was a weakness of mine—needing somebody. Needing affection. I might as well admit it. It was a part of my personality.

Along with the fact that I was a hypocrite. Aside from one inadvertent, lustful stare, Fletcher had been deliberate in his attempts to discourage me romantically. Yet here I had come anyway, looking for solace. I was trying to use *him*.

"I'm not sure anyone did break into the house," I continued, unable to rid my voice of its melancholy. "The door was unlocked in the morning, but it might have been left that way. In any event, nothing was taken."

Fletcher smiled, though the concern did not leave his eyes. "Well, that's good news."

"Yes," I agreed, now feeling both awkward and melancholy at the same time. Coming here had been a mistake. But could I bring myself to leave?

"Well, come on inside," he offered suddenly, as if the thought had just occurred to him. "You didn't see the cabin before, did you?"

He swung open the door and stepped aside, and as I perceived the note of teasing in his voice, the awkwardness between us eased. "I wasn't invited," I said pointedly, my voice stronger. "In fact, I seem to recall I was threatened with a chain saw."

He grinned. "How odd. I remember it the other way around." His smile broadened, and his gray-green eyes sparkled. Another pang of longing shot through me, but I tried to ignore it.

"It's not much," he said as he led me in. "But I like it."

I looked around. Though plain and sparsely furnished, the cabin was enchanting. Its first floor consisted almost entirely of one great room, through the center of which rose an impressive stone chimney. A small kitchen area protruded to the right, the glass-walled workshop to the left. Doors in the back area of the cabin undoubtedly led to closets and a bathroom. The atmosphere was rustic, with walls, ceiling, and floor made of raw, dark wood, but still it was comfortable and airy. Light poured in from skylights in the cathedral ceiling; open wooden steps led up to a loft bedroom.

"It's wonderful," I said in a whisper. "Can you see the stars from up there?"

I regretted the question as soon as it had left my lips, but if the topic of his bedroom was awkward, he didn't show it.

"More or less," he answered cheerfully. "But the meadow's best place for stargazing. Take a look around—you can go up the ladder if you like."

I didn't question his invitation. I just went. I scurried up the ladder as anxious as a child, no doubt the spitting image of Heidi, delighting over her grandfather's cottage in the Alps. I reached the loft and spun around, entranced. Two floor-to-ceiling picture windows flanked the back wall, looking out into the treetops. In between them rested a plain but striking wooden bed, overlong, of an odd width, and unusually high off the ground. I stared at its uneven, quilted surface for a moment, puzzling. Then I walked to the railing and leaned over it to look into the great room. "Is this a feather bed?" I inquired—as innocently as possible.

He grinned up at me from below. "Yes. I made it myself. I got tired of putting up with too-short mattresses . . . but I guess you wouldn't know about that."

I grinned back. "No, I wouldn't." I climbed down the stairs to join him again. "It's fabulous," I complimented. "No wonder you'd rather stay up here than at the inn. It's so down-to-earth, so inviting. Did you do any of the designing yourself? Or the building?"

He didn't answer immediately, and I noted with distress that his face had darkened. It was the pain—again. What had I done this time?

"I'm glad you like it," he said stiffly, moving to lean against the back of his couch. His eyes avoided mine.

I clenched my teeth, wanting very much to scream. What was it about me that kept making him so miserable? What was I doing wrong? Was I supposed to tell him I *didn't* like the cabin?

"So this is your workshop," I said, desperate to break his mood. I skirted the simple, plain-wood sectional couch and moved toward the sunroom, but I didn't make it all the way. On the far side of the chimney I tripped, nearly falling.

I looked down at the object over which I had stumbled, and my eyes widened. It was an Old English sheepdog. Not a real one, but a wooden statue. The life-sized dog lay in a relaxed position, paws splayed, head up, tongue lolling. As if he had just returned from a good long run and was looking for a treat before his nap. His shaggy hair was intricately—and laboriously—carved, his face so lifelike I was inclined to stoop and pet him. I had begun to do just that when my eyes rested on the tag that dangled from his collar. I read its inscription, and straightened.

Ferris.

My eyes turned to Fletcher. He seemed wary again, almost embarrassed. And yet at the same time, strangely proud. "A dog I used to have," he explained.

The name bounced about in my head, and I said it out loud, "Ferris?"

"It's from a movie. *Ferris Bueller's Day Off.* Do you remember it?"

I nodded. I did remember it. I was also remembering other things. Like the tool that Tia had painted in Fletcher's hands—the tool I had thought was a screwdriver. Like the pavilion outside filled with drying logs, and the stains on his clothes. Like the look on his face when I had rushed up the inn's steps to catch the cuckoo chirping. Like the monster check, the expensive suits, and the mystery job in San Francisco. With Herringtons of San Francisco.

Ferris Mountain.

I whirled and looked into the workshop, seeing a back wall covered with tools. Not screwdrivers but chisels, as well as a plethora of gouges, knives, mallets, and saws. I turned again, intending to walk toward him, but found him standing in front of me.

"I like to carve," he informed, his tone defensive. "It's been a hobby of mine since I was a kid."

I didn't comment, but reached out and took his right hand. I lifted it toward me, palm up, and inspected the crescent-shaped callus on the butt of his palm. He didn't resist.

"I use my hand as a mallet sometimes," he explained.

I dropped his hand and stepped back. My eyes fixed on the stone chimney; my lungs felt tight in my chest.

"What's wrong?" he asked. His tone had softened, as if in defeat, and I was sure he knew very well what was wrong.

I breathed out heavily, and my eyes grew moist. I felt stupid; I felt deceived. I felt hurt, more than I had any right to be, that he had withheld something so important from me. Yet at the same time, I felt an incredible sense of elation—and of pride. I knew that he had a good heart and a sharp mind; I had no idea he was an artistic genius. I was in awe of his talent. I was in awe of him.

"Fletcher," I breathed, my voice low but controlled. "Why wouldn't you tell me?"

His eyes met mine, and the flash of guilt I saw in them inexplicably warmed my heart.

"It wasn't personal," he answered. "But before the inheritance was settled, it would have been stupid of me to let you know who I was. A lesser person would have bled me dry. The truth is, I'd have given every penny I have to keep this land."

"You could have told me after the papers were signed," I pointed out. "You could have told me when I walked in just now." A fresh dose of hurt pounded my insides. "What did you think I would do? Pester you for an autograph?"

He shook his head, exhaling with frustration. "No, of course not. That's not it at all. I wanted to tell you, but—" He broke off the thought.

"But what?" I prompted.

"But people who know treat me differently," he finished. "They see my work and they think they know me—they try to define me by it. I'm tired of all that."

Understanding dawned. My ire began to cool.

"I love carving," he continued. "But I still think of it as a hobby. When I told you I was a forester, it was only a white lie. I may not be employed as one, but I have a degree in forestry from Penn State, and all I've ever wanted to do is maintain as much of this ridge as I can. But keeping up land takes money. And I figured out a long time ago that my 'hobby' was the easiest way to get it."

His eyes left mine. "I moved to California because it was the best way to get myself established. But now I'm at a point where I can work on my own terms—as much as I want to, and from where I want to. And what I want to do is work from here, producing just enough to bring in the money this place needs. I don't want anything to do with celebrity—the image-making, the social obligations, the general lunacy of people who have more money than they know what to do with. I came back because I wanted to get away from all that. And the last thing I want is for it to follow me home."

I digested his words slowly, enjoying the feel of them, the passion in his voice. I had been begging for the merest glimpse inside his head—now, in a few paragraphs, he had told me volumes. So much of what I had questioned made sense now; so much of what I already admired in him seemed magnified.

"I didn't mean to accuse you of anything," he apologized. "I was only trying to explain."

I clenched my fists at my sides, not out of anger, but in a frantic attempt to keep my affectionate impulses in check. The effort was painful. I wanted desperately to fling my arms around him and tell him I didn't care if he worked as a fish-gutter—that he was one of the most genuine, kind, and caring men I'd ever known, and that in these last, hellish days just having him near me had made all the difference. I wanted to tell him that—despite my honorable intentions—there was no longer a doubt in my mind that I was falling in love with him.

But I couldn't do any of that. All it took was one look at him—guarded emotionally, distant physically, to know that I hadn't a chance. Somewhere out there—most likely still in California, packing her things—was the woman who owned his heart. He was being faithful to her, as he had from the beginning. Even though she was thousands of miles away; even though another woman was inches from him, lonely and willing.

A bolt of pain shot through me, harsh and merciless. Whoever she was, she was the luckiest woman alive. I hoped she knew it.

Managing a smile required all my strength. "I understand. And if it'll help, I promise never to bring up Herringtons, the concept of celebrity, or the entire state of California ever again. But, could I just say one thing first? Please?"

His eyes met mine, and he grinned a little. "What's that?"

It hurt me, this time, to grin back. "I just want you to know that I think your work is magnificent, and I always have. In fact, my mother was one of your biggest fans." I told him about the ridiculous clock she had wanted, and he laughed out loud.

"Well," he said softly, his eyes sympathetic. "If I had known you both then, I would have made one for her."

My eyes filled with tears again. This time I didn't bother trying to stop them.

Chapter

~22~

THE CABIN'S BATHROOM was nicer than I thought. Larger than strictly necessary, with both a stall shower and an oversized tub. Cleaner than expected, too, though when it came to bachelor pads, I did not expect much. In any event, when I emerged from the room after a brief cry and a ten-minute recovery session, I felt better.

Fletcher had been sensible enough not to make a big deal out of my hasty exit; he took even less notice of my meek return. He was in his workshop, busily engaged with a gouge and a thin, foot-long block of dense wood. Only after I had pulled over a stool and sat down near him did he look at me.

"Yes, I know," I said lightly. "My eyes are red again. Must be allergies."

He offered a knowing grin.

The sight warmed me considerably, but I tried to curb my response. The safest course of action for me was to start thinking of both him and Tia as newfound friends, and I had no business being depressed at the thought of that.

"Can I ask you what you're making?" I inquired,

somewhat on eggshells. I didn't want him to think I was treating him differently, now that I knew that he was not only wealthy, but a virtual icon in his industry. Thinking back, I realized that I had never seen any personal information about the Ferris Mountain artist in print, much less a picture of him. Fletcher had undoubtedly worked hard to preserve his anonymity, but it sounded as though, at least on his home turf in San Francisco, he had been less than successful. I could empathize with his desire for privacy, but at the same time, my own fascination with his talent was hard to suppress. I wanted to watch him work. I wanted to hear everything about it.

"Candlesticks," he answered without emotion. "It's a custom order."

I wasn't sure if he was discouraging further questions or not. But if he was afraid I wanted to know who ordered the carving, how many square feet their house comprised, and whether or not their nose job had been botched, he was mistaken. My mother might have had a secret fixation for celebrities, but the topic held no interest for me.

"What kind of wood is that?" I asked. "Oak?"

He looked up again, and his light eyes smiled. "It's black cherry. Oak doesn't hold fine detail as well."

"Did it come from here?"

His pleasure at that question was obvious. "Yes."

I smiled back, elated to note that my interest made him happy. Perhaps carving was something we could share— as friends. I *had* always wondered . . .

On impulse, I rose from the stool and looked around, then grabbed a fist-sized scrap of wood from the floor and the closest chisel-type tool I saw. "Would you mind if I tried it?" I asked as I sat down again. "I've never been artistic, but I keep hoping I'll stumble onto some medium

I'm good at someday. I won't break anything—I promise. At least not intentionally."

He smiled as if nursing some secret joke. "Sure. Go ahead."

I positioned the block of wood between my knees and raised the chisel.

"Not like—" he began, but the warning came too late. The scrap of wood sprung from the stool and bounced off one of the glass walls; the chisel narrowly missed my thigh.

I looked up sheepishly. "Did I mention that I was born clumsy?"

He chuckled. "Clumsy or not, you'll never get anywhere doing it like that." He put down his own piece of wood and scouted around the workshop for another, which he handed to me. It was a light yellow block, about five inches square. "Here, try the poplar. It's softer. And for heaven's sake, don't hold the wood like that—you'll puncture an artery. Use a mallet this time."

I looked at the nicely shaped piece of wood. "I don't want to mess up a good piece," I said with concern.

He laughed out loud at that, though I wasn't sure why. Once he had helped me get the wood, the tools, and myself in proper carving position, I lifted the mallet. But before I could strike, he stopped me again. "Wait—" he instructed. "You can't possibly see with all that hair in your face. You've got to keep your eyes on what you're doing."

My unrestrained curls were indeed in fine form. I had washed them during my two-minute shower at dawn and hadn't touched them since. But they were not bothering me in the least, as I was well used to looking through an auburn waterfall whenever I inclined my head. I started to explain that, but as Fletcher's hands swept across my cheeks, my mouth promptly closed.

The strands of hair disappeared from my field of vision. His fingers brushed gently against my face and neck as he gathered and manipulated the unruly tresses, and though I enjoyed the sensations far more than I should have, I could not help but dread their result. If he were tying my hair in any sort of knot, my evening brushing would require anesthesia.

"There," he said a few seconds later, tucking what was left of the bundle under the neck of my shirt. "Now you can see. Go for it."

I should have gone ahead without worrying, but I couldn't. Teeth clenched, I lifted my hand to assess the damage. I took a tentative feel, then lifted the other hand to confirm. My eyes widened. It wasn't a knot—it was a French braid. A loose one, granted, but clean and even— definitely respectable.

"How did you learn to do that?" I questioned sharply, the carving forgotten.

"Do what?"

"French braid!" I insisted. What single man knew how to French braid?

"Oh, that," he said offhandedly. "There was always at least one little girl with long hair running around this place. My mother didn't do mornings; she was always busy fixing breakfast at the inn. School preparation was Dad's beat—and he paid me well to help out."

I envisioned an adolescent Fletcher and his father, braiding hair and packing lunches with the efficiency of an assembly line. I chuckled. "What about Tia?"

He scoffed. "Please. None of the girls ever let Tia do their hair more than once—she pulled too hard. She was much happier cleaning up the dishes."

I was quiet a moment, absorbed in my imagination. So

Mitchell had fixed my hair, once upon a time. I must have provided good training.

"So," Fletcher asked, drawing me back to the present, "are you going to bring that piece to life, or aren't you?"

I focused my attention back on the wood, thinking how wonderful it must be to make good money doing what one loved. My own real passion, if I allowed myself to admit it, was camp directing. I enjoyed the freedom, the opportunity to create my own activities and curriculum, the unfettered joy of living in the midst of nature. School teaching had its rewards, but it was more restrictive. I was contained in a concrete-block building, told what subjects to teach, assigned my textbooks and supplies, and expected to adhere to whatever inane policies the administration currently had a whim for. But it was teaching that paid the bills. My summers were an indulgence.

I struck the chisel with the mallet, and a tiny sliver of wood began to peel, leading me to wonder if I really might have some artistic talent. But after five minutes and a fine sheen of sweat, I determined that if I did, it had nothing to do with wood carving.

"Harder than it looks," I announced, rising and returning the tools. The wood was barely dented.

"Well, naturally, it takes practice," Fletcher encouraged politely.

He picked up the future candlestick again, and as I watched the strokes of his carving settle into a masterful rhythm, I became transfixed. It was pleasant just to sit here—being together, not talking. For almost an hour I indulged in his hospitality, watching him work with only occasional small talk, and for most of that time, my mind was relatively burden-free. But as the sun sank lower in the sky, my anxiety began to increase. A desire for physical comfort wasn't the only reason I had come here.

"There's something I want to ask you," I said at last, breaking another lengthy stretch of silence.

He nodded without looking up.

"I've never considered myself paranoid," I began, cursing my pulse for speeding up already. "But I'm having a little trouble distinguishing paranoia from caution at the moment, and I need a second opinion."

Fletcher stopped carving. He laid down his gouge and looked at me.

"The open door at my parents' house," I continued. "It may have been nothing. But when I got there, I found out that Jake had sent a bouquet of flowers to that address yesterday. He also left a message for me on the answering machine."

Fletcher studied my face. "What did the message say?"

I relayed the contents of the card and recording. "There was nothing inappropriate about either. I understand that. But still, I can't help feeling that maybe the coincidence is a little—" I broke off, embarrassed. "You think I'm overreacting, don't you?"

He studied me some more before answering. "That depends. What exactly did Jake say or do at that diner that scared you so much?"

It was a question he had asked me before, but I hadn't fully answered it. I suppose I was afraid that once I put my worry into words, the threat of it would seem more real. But I couldn't put off facing the issue any longer. Not now.

"He was polite enough," I explained. "But when I looked in his eyes—" I stopped and swallowed, forcing the words out slowly. "I told you I got the impression that he could be violent. But it was more than that. He was looking at me as if he hated me."

Fletcher straightened. "Hated you? Are you sure?"

I nodded. "He got so defensive when I asked if he was my birth father—I was sure he was lying when he said yes. Now I can't help but wonder if he resents me—maybe even blames me."

Fletcher was quiet a moment. Then he rose. "I don't think you're overreacting," he proclaimed. "Given what we know of his background, you have every reason to be cautious."

I rose with him.

"Was there anything at your house that could tie you to the inn?" he asked.

My heart beat wildly at the thought. "I don't think so. I've kept all of David Falcon's paperwork with me, here. No one in Pittsburgh even knows where I am, except Alex, my real estate agent, and he's a friend."

"That's good." Fletcher smiled. There was worry in his eyes, but he was trying not to show it. "I'll give Ben another call and tell him what you told me. I don't think you have enough cause for a restraining order, but it wouldn't hurt to get some advice from a pro."

I let out a pent-up breath. As much relief as I felt at having finally shared my fears, I felt even more guilty at having laid additional angst on the Black family's doorstep. "I'm probably way off base," I suggested, backing off a bit. "I've got nothing to go on, really—just gut instinct. And how accurate is that?"

He looked at me thoughtfully. "Meara, when we first met I was practically hostile to you. What did your gut instincts say then? Were you afraid of me?"

I considered, though I already knew the answer. "No. I was never afraid of you. I knew you were a good person—you were just angry. And hurt."

The answer seemed to be more than he bargained for. He stiffened. "Right," he said finally. "And as we both know, I'm a model citizen. Which means maybe you should trust your instincts."

An awkward silence descended, but he broke it quickly. "Until we're sure there's not a problem, why don't you stay here at the inn? Tia will enjoy your company. She'll be around a few more days at least, sorting through Dad's things. And she could use a friend right now. It's been a tough year for her."

And for you, I added mentally. But the invitation exhilarated me. "I would love to stay a few more days," I said with gratitude. "But you have to let me buy the food and cook for everyone. I insist. Unless Tia would mind my being in her kitchen?"

He laughed out loud.

I took that as a no.

"Meara, my dear," Tia cooed, finishing off the last bite of her Stroganoff with a flourish of her fork. "You are a godsend. This meal is heavenly. Forget teaching—you should be a chef."

I blushed. I knew she was laying it on thick, but I was still proud. Stroganoff and cheesy potatoes wasn't a bad meal to pull off in forty-five minutes with no advanced planning. I only wished I'd had time to make dessert.

"Thanks for the compliment," I responded. "And I did think about culinary school once upon a time, but you don't get much money for making hamburger casseroles, and I prefer real food to gourmet."

"Amen to that," Fletcher added. He had been quiet for most of the meal, immersed in a succession of extra-large helpings. Despite my tendency to cook in volume, I suspected there would be no leftovers.

"Dad was a great cook," Tia said fondly, grinning. The area around her eyes was no longer puffy, as it had been when I had returned to the inn before dinner. I had made no comment then, suspecting that she, like me, preferred to indulge her sorrow in private. Indeed, her mood was now quite upbeat, with talk of her father seeming to cheer rather than sadden her. "He grilled one mean peppercorn burger, didn't he? And his lasagna was to die for. But when it came to teaching us to cook—" She threw her brother a smirk. "Well, let's just say it was hopeless."

He smirked back. "Speak for yourself. I can make pancakes."

"Oh, you can *not*," she snorted. "Dog Frisbees, maybe."

I chuckled. The two of them had been picking at each other all evening, and I had enjoyed every minute of it. Despite every scattered, horrible thought still weighing on my brain, being in this place, cooking for three, and feeling like a part of something had made me feel better—and happier—than I had in a long time.

"You'd better learn to cook, though, and quick," Tia informed him. "Unless you think Estelle's going to haul your dinner up that mountain every night. No personal chefs for you out here, brother dear—you're going to have to rough it."

Fletcher rolled his eyes. "For the eight thousandth time, I never had a personal chef. I just ate out a lot. And you're one to talk—last time I was in a kitchen of yours, I couldn't even find a plate."

"There were paper plates in the bedroom," Tia retorted. "And I do not *need* my own kitchen. That's what friends are for. A fringe benefit of the nomadic lifestyle. Take Meara here, for instance," she teased. "I identify a good cook, and she's a friend for life. By the way, is there a guest room in your house?"

"Don't fall for it, Meara," Fletcher warned. "She's a shameless freeloader."

"I am *not* a freeloader," Tia defended. "I work off my room and board. I'll paint anything she wants. Do you like murals?" she asked me. "I'm great at kid's rooms. I also do wallpapering, when I'm in the mood. Just don't ask me to paint your house trim—I don't do the outdoors."

Fletcher humphed. "Now there's an understatement."

"Most normal people," she fired back with a glare, "recognize that humans evolved to our present state of enlightenment in order to *avoid* living in squalor."

"It's called camping, Tia."

"Whatever."

I laughed heartily, losing a splash of my tea. Tia grinned at me, her gaze turning intent again, as it had been doing periodically all evening.

"I'm sorry to keep staring," she apologized. "But it bugs the heck out of me that I can't remember you."

"That's all right," I said quickly, wishing to get off the topic of me and back to the laughing. "You were only five."

I knew that Fletcher had filled his sister in on my saga at some point earlier in the day, and I wondered with no small amount of guilt whether the news of Sheila's nefarious past had contributed to her puffy eyes. But Tia had said nothing to me about my birth mother. She merely seemed delighted to know that we had met before.

"I wonder if I gave you a nickname?" she mused. "I gave all the kids nicknames back then. I was great at it." Her eyes veered toward Fletcher, and her face turned devilish.

He reddened instantly. "Go ahead," he said heavily. "I dare you. Just remember that two can play at that game."

She twisted her lips in contemplation. "Okay, okay," she announced peevishly. "We'll table that one for now. At least you finally told Meara what you do for a living. And incidentally, if you hadn't, I would have."

"I didn't tell her," Fletcher admitted. "She saw the statue of Ferris and figured it out."

Tia grinned broadly. "Well, well! Not only does she cook, but she's smart enough to get the best of you. I think I'll disable her car."

I laughed out loud. "Tell you what, Tia. You tell me his nickname, and I'll serve you breakfast in bed."

Fletcher growled. "I should have known it was only a matter of time before the two of you ganged up on me." His face bore a scowl, but his eyes shone with merriment. "It's probably not the first time, either," he lamented.

The thought prompted Tia to stare at me again. "I've just *got* to remember you," she insisted. Then a lightbulb seemed to turn on. "Oh, wait, pictures! That's why that album was out, isn't it?"

She leapt up from her seat at the table and crossed over to the wall of bookcases in the common room. "I noticed this this morning," she explained, pulling down a plain brown album from where it lay horizontally over a row of encyclopedias. "But I didn't think much of it. You guys were looking for pictures, weren't you? Did you find any?"

Fletcher and I exchanged glances. "I didn't get an

album out," he corrected. "I didn't even think about them. Last I saw any of the old ones was when we were packing up the attic."

Tia dropped the book on the table with a puzzled expression. "But look," she argued, pointing at the spine. "It's the right time frame, isn't it?" The stretch of blue plastic tape had been embossed with an inexpensive label maker. *1977–1980.*

I nodded.

Tia opened the book and sat down. "Dad must have gotten it out himself, then," she theorized. "Or else Sheila did."

I leaned in closely over her shoulder as she flipped through the pages, my breath held. Fletcher watched from the other side. She stopped short a few times, then moved on. I couldn't process the pictures half as rapidly as she could, and I wished that she would slow down. But the next time she stopped, it was with a squeal of joy.

"Meara!" she cried, turning to me. "There you are, see! There *we* are."

My pulse quickened; my face felt hot. I gazed into the photograph.

It had been taken inside a living room, probably at the white house. Six children, all wearing church clothes, beamed at the camera. A few held baskets. "Easter," I whispered, touching the corner of the paper tentatively with a fingertip. Fletcher was there, looking big for a boy of six, all white teeth and bright red hair. Another boy of eight or nine stood next to him, while a shy-looking, fair-haired girl of three or four stood close in front of them both, hiding her face behind Fletcher's arm. A bald toddler sat on the floor wrestling with a basket as big as he was, but the indisputable hog of the limelight was Tia, who stood poised with one toe in the air, brandishing a chocolate bunny above her head.

Then there was me. I was wearing a frilly white dress, with a straw hat and ribbon to match. My hair was long and loose, but orderly in a way that only a brushing in the previous few seconds could achieve. I stood sideways to the camera, my arms clasping the much-taller Tia tightly around the waist. Her free arm encircled my shoulders; my face was pressed into her side. We were laughing.

"See there," she announced softly. "I knew you had good taste."

My eyes swelled with tears.

She flipped a few pages forward and back, but there were no other posed "family" pictures and no other pictures of me, just casual shots of various children playing outside, and several of adults that had been taken at the inn. She returned to the page with the picture of us, and Fletcher reached forward and removed it.

Tia stood up and looked at me, her own eyes moist. "Don't start," she ordered firmly. "Because if you start, I'll start, and I'm over my quota for the day."

I tried to comply, but a drop escaped my left eye. "Sorry," I whispered, smiling. It was a pleasant change to produce happy tears, even if they were bittersweet. I knew now, from my own little face, that I had been happy here. I had been part of a large family, if only for a short while. I wondered if I had never forgotten that—if my childhood longings had not been daydreams so much as memories. Memories of the playmates I had lost.

More tears threatened, and Tia stepped forward and hugged me tight. "There's no point in getting mushy," she quipped over my shoulder. "You probably just wanted my candy. And knowing me, I didn't give it to you."

I broke into laughter again, and when she released me, we exchanged a red-eyed smile. Realizing suddenly how quiet Fletcher had been, I looked over to see him still holding the photograph. He seemed deeply absorbed by it, although he wasn't looking at the picture itself. He was looking at the back of it.

Tia noticed as well. "Did Mom label it?" she asked him. "Does it say Amanda?"

The question seemed to startle him. He looked up with a puzzled expression. "It says Mandy."

His voice was neutral, but his eyes seemed troubled, and a vague sense of dread crept over me. "What's wrong, then?" I asked.

"Nothing," he assured, forcing a smile. "It's just curious, that's all."

"What's curious?" Tia demanded.

He turned the front of the picture toward us. "This little girl here," he explained, pointing to the fair-haired preschooler. "You remember the listing in my mother's ledger?" he asked me. "The only entry that could possibly fit you, assuming there was some reason why you would be registered under another name?"

I nodded. "Lisa Dobson."

His eyes held mine, and he tapped at the picture again. "This little girl is Lisa."

I tried to digest the fact, but it made little sense.

"But Meara has to be in the ledger somewhere," Tia insisted. "She was obviously here, and Mom kept records on all the foster children."

"Yes," Fletcher agreed thoughtfully, "she did."

Chapter

~23~

TIA CONSIDERED HER brother's words. "But if Meara wasn't here as a foster child," she said speculatively, "why would she be here? I can't see Mom sheltering a child outside the system—she was never one to buck protocol."

Fletcher shook his head. "No, because she would never have let an abusive situation go on without reporting it."

The siblings exchanged a glance.

"Meara must not have been here for sheltering, then," Tia declared.

I looked from one to the other, not sure what they were getting at, and wishing fervently that they would talk about something else.

"Meara," Tia asked. "How old was Sheila when she died?"

"Fifty-one," I answered.

Her eyes met her brother's again, and the two of them transmitted a rapid, nonverbal message. "Did she grow up around here?" Tia asked me.

"I don't think so," I responded, my frustration growing. "She was born in Uniontown, and her mother died there when she was nineteen. But I suppose they could have moved around in between. Why?"

More pregnant glances.

"The *Turkeyoughas*?" Tia asked.

Fletcher nodded.

"I'll go get them," Tia offered. "They're in the attic—and I know exactly where." She turned and darted off toward the stairs.

Only after she was gone did Fletcher take a good look at my face. "I'm sorry," he said quickly, chagrined. "We should have asked if you wanted to pursue this." He turned toward the stairs. "I'll call Tia off."

"No," I insisted dutifully. "This is about your family, too. If you want to understand why I was here, that's fine." I tried to smile at him.

He studied me, unconvinced. "I mean it," he said softly. "If you don't want to know any more, we'll drop it. Just tell me."

The tenderness in his voice sent a shudder through me, but I short-circuited the stirring with a deep breath. "I don't want you to drop it," I insisted, lying. I did want them to drop it. Fletcher and Tia had already accepted me as a friend. I was welcome here, and I was enjoying their company more than I could say. Couldn't well enough be left alone?

"I would like to know what you're thinking," I continued, trying hard to suppress my insecurities. Surely Fletcher and Tia, of all people, would not hold me responsible for either of my birth parents' actions. I had nothing to worry about. "Turkey *what*?"

He grinned, and the sight warmed me. If only I could make him happy more often—truly happy. Lately I had seemed to bring him nothing but grief.

"The *Turkeyougha*," he explained, "is the yearbook for the Turkeyfoot Valley Area High School. My parents graduated from there. So did Tia and I."

My eyebrows rose. "Your high school's mascot was the wild turkey?"

"Of course not," he said with false indignation. "It was the ram. What do you take us for?"

I grinned myself. Even under duress, joking with Fletcher was easy. "My mistake," I responded, besieged with another aggravating pang of attraction.

"What occurred to Tia and me," he explained, "is that you might not have been here for protection so much as baby-sitting. My mother was the same age as Sheila. It's not inconceivable that they were friends."

Friends. The word pierced through me, bringing with it a glimmer of joy I was almost afraid to acknowledge. The idea was too fantastic to be true. "They were the same age?" I asked incredulously. "How old was your mother when she adopted you?"

"Barely twenty-one," he answered. "Yes, I know—she was a brave one. She and Dad were rare in wanting to adopt so young, and in being willing to adopt Tia and me together. But they wanted a family, and they knew from the beginning that they couldn't have biological children."

My head spun, but it was a pleasant confusion. Why *couldn't* Sheila and Rosemary have been friends? Maybe Rosemary knew that Sheila's marriage was rocky and agreed to help keep me out of the fray whenever things got rough. But maybe she hadn't realized how rough. Maybe at the inn that night, she was as surprised as anyone when Sheila pulled the trigger. Maybe she had tried to testify in Sheila's defense. But maybe it hadn't come out that way. Maybe—

"Are you sure you're okay with this?"

My thoughts stopped racing, replaced by a sudden awareness of the present. Fletcher was right in front of me; his hands were on my shoulders.

I looked up at him, and my pulse pounded.

He was close. Much closer than he usually allowed himself to be. I wondered if he had any idea of the effect his nearness had on me, and decided that he did not. Because if he did, he wouldn't be standing where he was standing, or touching me like he was touching me. He certainly wouldn't let those gorgeous eyes of his look at me with such concern.

My teeth clenched, and I felt a flash of annoyance at his carelessness. I had nothing but respect for his devotion to whoever she was, but did he *have* to leave his top three shirt buttons open? Did he *have* to exude such an enticing aroma of wind, sweat, and wood? I might be ethical, but I was not made of steel.

He removed his hands and stepped back.

I let out a breath, wondering if my glare had transmitted my thoughts. I hoped not all of them. But the fact was, if Fletcher expected us to coexist as friends, he would have to stay farther away from me than that.

Like in Siberia.

"I'm fine," I answered.

"Good," he responded. He moved back a few more steps. An awkward silence descended. He studied his feet.

"Found it!" Tia announced, strutting into the common room with a thin blue yearbook. The interruption startled me, but Fletcher was clearly relieved.

I turned back to Tia. The book's cover was adorned with a pattern of white diamonds enclosing an atom; the words TURKEYOUGHA '70 appeared beneath. She opened the book to a page she had marked with a finger, then laid it in my hands. "Check it out."

I hesitated a second, my mind still mired in a vain attempt to read Fletcher's mind. But after noting the excitement on her face, I opened the book in haste.

My eyes scanned over rows of long-haired boys and longer-haired girls before coming to rest on the words Tia was pointing to. *Photograph not available: Sheila Tresswell.*

I stared at the words a moment, unable to take them in. It was true. I had not been randomly assigned here as a foster child. I had been here as a friend of the family.

A friend of the family.

"I can't believe it," I murmured, my cheeks flushing with heat. I felt almost giddy with joy, but was embarrassed to express it. How could Fletcher and Tia possibly understand? How could they know how much it meant to me that my connection to this place—and to them—was based on something real?

"So Sheila was a friend," I repeated incredulously.

No sooner were the words out of my mouth than I realized that, for them, the revelation might not be such a happy one. There could be no question, now, that their father had known exactly who Sheila was when he married her. He would have to have known everything.

I looked at Tia with apprehension, and found her casting a sideways glance at Fletcher. He was gazing pensively into space.

She turned her attention to me. "It doesn't surprise me that my father would have looked up an old friend after

Mom died. He was certainly lonely. It's a bit odd he would reconnect with Sheila after what happened, but—" Her voice trailed off, thought brewing behind her eyes.

"He did have an amazing capacity for forgiveness," she asserted. "He was one of the most loving and non-judgmental people I've ever known, and he did believe that people could change."

She looked meaningfully at her brother, but his eyes were still averted.

"This explains a lot, actually," she continued, turning back to me with a smile. "Why my father kept the relationship a secret. Maybe he was concerned about what we would think, or what his friends would think, given Sheila's history. Or maybe it was Sheila who didn't want anyone to know. Either way, they needn't have worried. If he knew the whole situation behind what happened, and still thought enough of Sheila to marry her, then I accept his judgment. She must have had a good heart."

Her eyes held mine. "The car accident was a terrible tragedy," she said gently. "But it would be wrong for any of us to blame what happened on the fact that he and Sheila got married. If they'd never met, either of them could still have hit a deer any day, anytime—only then they would have died lonely. I think we should just be glad that they were able to make each other happy—at least for a little while."

My heart skipped a beat. A powerful feeling of warmth surged through me, and I lurched forward and hugged her close. "Thank you," I whispered. "You have no idea how much it means to me to hear you say that."

"Sure I do," she answered. "I'm buttering you up so I can get more cheesy potatoes."

I laughed out loud. But as my eyes caught sight of

Fletcher over her shoulder, my glee waned. He was watching us with the most peculiar expression—seeming in one second to be touched; the next, irritated.

Tia's gaze followed mine. "Fletch feels the same," she announced, her voice louder. "Don't you, Fletch?"

He blinked at her as if he had been miles away, then smiled. "Of course."

Before I could begin to contemplate the exchange, Tia took me firmly by the hand and led me toward the couches. "You want to see my parents' pictures?" she asked eagerly. "They're a scream." She sat down, pulling me with her, then took the yearbook from my hands. Fletcher didn't follow, but began clearing away the dinner dishes instead. And though ordinarily the sight of any man cleaning up after a meal would thrill me, I couldn't look at him now without angst. He was preoccupied. Distressed. And the source of his problem, once again, seemed to be me.

"I didn't see Sheila's name in the junior yearbook, so she must have only lived here a little while," Tia began cheerfully, opening the book between us and flipping pages. "But they were all in the same senior class. Mom and Dad were childhood sweethearts since they were, like, ten. They got married after they graduated, when Mom inherited the inn."

My eyebrows rose. "Your mother took over the inn right out of high school?" I asked, amazed. "She was responsible for it all by herself, from then on?"

"Why not?" Fletcher piped up suddenly, clear from the kitchen. "Is there some reason you think she wouldn't want to stay here?"

I stared. Not only was the question bizarre, but his tone bordered on defensive. "Of course not," I answered, flummoxed. "It's just surprising that a girl so young would be willing to take on so much responsibility, that's all."

Fletcher dropped behind the cabinets and out of sight. I cast a glance at Tia, hoping she could shed some light on his behavior, but found hers equally inscrutable. She seemed to be fighting a grin.

"Mom's parents were anxious to retire and move south," she explained, collecting herself. "Besides, Mom was what you'd call a type-A personality. Very driven. Very successful. She loved children, and she had strong opinions about parenting. But she was also a business-woman, and a perfectionist. Luckily, Dad was the easy-going type. Here he is!" she exclaimed, pointing.

I gazed at a black-and-white class photo of Mitchell, looking much younger than his seventeen years. Baby-faced and sweet, with a full head of soft, wavy curls, he could have passed for thirteen or fourteen.

"And here's Mom," she said, tapping a picture on the next row.

I started. Rosemary bore even less resemblance to the family picture I had seen; I doubted I could have recognized her. Her hair was short and unflattering, her dark glasses ponderous. Though her eyes were bright and her smile kind, the glasses tipped the scales toward a severe look.

"Heavens," Tia said, chuckling. "This is even worse than I remembered. Mom looks like a wanna-be librarian."

I reserved comment. We browsed through the activity pages, Tia trying to find particular photos she thought she remembered, including action shots of Mitchell in foot-ball uniform. But the award for greatest number of ap-

pearances went to Rosemary. Not only was she valedic-
torian and editor of the yearbook, but she was a member
of almost every school club and president of several: an
overachiever of the first degree.

My eyes scanned the pictures hungrily, looking for an
image, or even another mention, of my birth mother.
There was nothing.

"I wonder if Sheila transferred in later in the year," Tia
mused, noticing the same lack of representation. "Either
that or she was a nonconformist. Not that there's anything
wrong with that," she clarified.

When we reached the next-to-last page of the book,
Tia let out a gasp. I followed her eyes and found my own
transfixed. It was a picture of Sheila—and a stunningly
beautiful one. Resplendent and smiling, she was dressed
in a formal gown complete with sash and bouquet, her
auburn tresses swooping gracefully around her bare
shoulders. Her eyes sparkled, her face shone with joy.

"Maple Queen?" I asked in a whisper. "What was
that?"

"*Is* that," Tia corrected. "A beauty contest, for the
spring Maple Festival in Meyersdale. Huge tradition—if
you're into that sort of thing. A major coup for a Turkeyfoot girl."

I looked into my birth mother's radiant smile, and felt
a rush of happiness. At least her life had not always been
miserable. I turned to Tia. "Were you ever Maple
Queen?"

She narrowed her eyes playfully. "Now, come on," she
chastised, "can you really see me parading around in a
bridesmaid's dress batting my eyes at the mayor?"

I chuckled. "Um, no. I guess not."

"Damn straight."

She closed the book and launched into a highly dramatized account of her days as the resident hellion of Turkeyfoot Valley Area High, and at times I laughed so hard my eyes began to water. But as joyful as the revelations of the evening had made me, I could not stop casting worried glances at Fletcher. He had finished cleaning the kitchen and had moved to stand by the French doors. There he remained still, staring out.

He hadn't spoken since his earlier outburst, and he didn't speak until Tia had finished her story, at which point he announced his departure. "I'm heading back now," he said with a transparent attempt at lightheartedness. "You girls behave yourselves." He threw his sister a mock menacing glance, and she chortled back.

"Not likely."

His gaze moved to me, and as our eyes met, my heart sank. Not only was he preoccupied, he was sad again. I could feel his sorrow from across the room, and it gnawed at the pit of my own stomach. What was wrong with him?

"Good night, Meara," he offered with a nod.

Don't go, Fletcher. Please. I wanted him to stay. I wanted him to trust me enough to talk to me. There had to be something I could do for him, if nothing more than to put my arms around him, to pull him close—

"Good night," I returned quickly, cutting off the thought.

He opened the door.

"Well, I suppose I should hit the hay, too," Tia announced, rising with a stretch. "I'll need an early start tomorrow if I'm going to tackle that desk. Dad was a top-notch house husband, but his administrative skills were nil. The paperwork's been piling up ever since Mom died."

I glanced back at Fletcher and found him stopped in the open doorway, looking at me. Our eyes connected for only an instant before he turned away, but I could swear I perceived a reluctance to leave—a look of longing equal to my own.

He stepped out and closed the door behind him.

I wondered if I had imagined it.

Chapter
~24~

EVIDENTLY TIA WAS a morning person. I had thought that I would be the first one up, given that I had rolled out of bed with the sun and headed straight for the shower. It had been another long and relatively sleepless night, and I had gotten tired of trying unsuccessfully to turn off my brain. But as I walked down the hall toward the kitchen to put some water on, I heard the teakettle already whistling.

"Do I have great timing or what?" Tia praised herself, turning off the burner. She was dressed in a colorful spring dress, sleeveless, straight, and very flattering to her lithe form. Aside from the fact that her newly washed hair was still damp, she looked as though she had been up for hours. "I heard you in the shower, and I thought you'd be ready for some tea soon."

"Thank you," I said gratefully, collecting my cup and tea bag.

She moved away to the main table, which was covered with stacks of loose papers and piles of envelopes, and sighed. "I loved my father dearly," she muttered. "But if I'd had any idea what a pathetic job he was doing keeping up with the household affairs, I'd have smacked him upside the head." She picked up an envelope and waved it in exasperation. "Look at this! A fourth notice on a septic tank service call—for a lousy sixty dollars he could have paid anytime. I swear, unless something was tacked to the man's forehead, it was as good as forgotten."

I poured my tea and came to lean against the counter near her. "My father was like that, too. Mom always handled the finances."

She returned to her work, and for a few minutes we didn't speak. But as the warm tea began to circulate through my body, the questions I had been formulating all night loomed heavy in my mind.

"Tia," I said finally, unable to wait any longer. "Did you notice how preoccupied Fletcher seemed last night? I mean, after you brought down the yearbook?"

She didn't look up. "Yes, I noticed. But you can't push Fletch when he gets like that. Once he retreats into the proverbial man-cave, you can't follow him with a bulldozer."

Her answer disturbed me. "What do you think was wrong?" I asked fearfully.

Catching my tone, she put down the paper she was holding and studied me.

My pulse quickened. "He just seemed so troubled," I explained before she could answer, "like there was a war going on inside him. I *hate* that."

"You're really worried about him?" she asked softly.

"Of course I am!" I returned, seeing no reason not to be honest. "I can't stand to see that horrible pain in his eyes. I noticed it the day I met him. And even though I knew he'd just lost his father, it seemed like more than that. It was like he'd lost his last friend in the world."

The night's tossing and turning must have worn me down more than I thought, because hot tears threatened as I spoke. "I keep seeing that pain, Tia—and I don't know where it's coming from. But more and more, I'm beginning to think it's me. There's something about me, something he knows. He'll seem to be in a perfectly good mood, and then he'll look at me, and he's miserable again. I thought I could help him somehow, but now I'm beginning to wonder if my presence here isn't making things worse. If maybe the best thing for him would be if I just packed my stuff and moved on."

The last words came out with a choke, no doubt making clear just how horrible the thought was to me. I rose and snatched a tissue off the counter.

Tia's dark eyes bored through me. "You think he doesn't want you here?"

"I don't know what to think," I answered, fighting a sniffle.

She studied me for another moment, and then, to my surprise, she smiled. "Sit down, Meara," she ordered. She pushed her papers to the side.

I sat.

"Fletch is going to kill me for this, but it'll be worth it," she began. "You've got no reason to beat yourself up. I promise that that look you're seeing has nothing to do with anything you've done." She offered a smirk. "Well, at least not on purpose."

My worry lines deepened.

"You see," she began, her voice gentle. "In a way he has lost his last friend in the world—except for me, of course, but I'm poor consolation." She took in a breath, then let it out with a sigh. "It's like this. When our mother died, Fletch was engaged. Her name was Isabella. She was a sculptor; they met in San Francisco and had been dating for a long time."

My heart pounded; unjustified ire swelled in my chest.

"Fletch was madly in love with her, though I'm still not sure why. They were opposites in most ways; all they really had in common was their craft. Isabella was intelligent, beautiful, and charming, but she was also sophisticated, particular, and self-absorbed. I suspect she reminded Fletch of Mom a little bit, because she was so driven and headstrong. But Mom had values; Isabella just had Isabella."

Tia took a sip of coffee, her eyes deep in thought. I dared not interrupt her.

"I never thought she was right for Fletch, and neither did Mom, but she kept her mouth shut. I think she'd been waiting so long for Fletch to get married that she was afraid Isabella might be her only chance for a daughter-in-law, and she desperately wanted grandchildren before she died. But me being me, I couldn't help but tell him what I thought. As soon as he told me he was thinking about marriage, I laid out my suspicions. I told him I didn't think Isabella would ever come back to Pennsylvania."

She paused. Her eyes darkened. "Turns out I was right. The woman was a complete fake, and she knew exactly how to play him. When they first started dating she acted like Suzy homemaker, telling him how wonderful his home in the mountains sounded, how beautiful it must be, how lovely it would be to raise a family in the midst of such natural splendor. Maybe she meant it originally and maybe she didn't. Either way, she didn't have a clue. She was born in Los Angeles; she'd never lived anywhere but in the city. I think she had this romanticized view of the bucolic life—like it was something from the great American novel.

"She visited here exactly once, and she couldn't get away fast enough. She made it up to the cabin finally, but then Fletch had to drive her back down in the truck. She wouldn't even spend the night there. Gave him some song and dance about how charming the inn was, and how much she'd love to sleep in one of the antique beds." Tia shook her head in disgust.

"She wouldn't stay at his cabin with him?" I asked incredulously, unable to restrain myself. "But it's so cozy! With that gorgeous fireplace, and that loft—who on earth wouldn't want to crawl up there and snuggle into that feather—"

I cut myself off, but I was too late. Tia's eyes glinted with amusement.

"Isabella didn't seem to appreciate it," she said tactfully, though still with a grin. "Which should have set off Fletcher's warning bells right then. But he was in love with her, God help him, and he was born loyal. So when she started modifying their plans, bit by bit, he allowed himself to compromise."

"What plans?" I asked, my breath held.

Tia smiled at me again, but this time there was a sadness to it. "All Fletch has ever wanted is to live on the ridge, preserve the forest, and raise a family—a big family, just like he grew up with. The carving has always been secondary; if he couldn't make a living with that, he would have looked for a forestry job somewhere, but he never wanted to run the inn. He'd much rather do something with that old campground, like turn it into some sort of nature center."

My heart leapt. So he did have plans for the campground. Why wouldn't he tell me that?

"At first," Tia continued, "Isabella led him to believe she admired his aspirations—even shared them. But after a while she started talking about keeping an apartment in San Francisco, just for visits. By the time the wedding plans were final, she had him down to summers on the mountain. The rest of the year would be spent in some posh Sausalito town house with a view of the bay."

My jaw dropped. "But—"

Tia smirked again.

"But he would have been miserable!" I finished. "Even I can see that." My face felt hot; my fists clenched under the table. "And what about wanting a family? Was she lying about that, too?"

Tia's face was hidden behind her coffee cup. "That we'll never know," she answered. "Because they never got married. Fletch broke off the engagement."

"Well, thank God," I proclaimed, rising. I needed another cup of tea. "He owes you plenty. How did you finally make him see reason?"

"Oh, I didn't," she confessed. "Not that I didn't try. But he was too far gone." She paused. "In retrospect, of course, I wish I'd tried harder."

There was a disturbing somberness to her voice. I poured more water over my tea bag and sat back down. "What happened?" I asked, almost afraid to hear.

She sighed. "When Mom got sick, Fletch started coming home more often. Dad was a wreck, things were going crazy at the inn—it was a difficult time for everybody. I tried to help out, too, but . . . Well, when it came to making important decisions, Fletch was the one Mom counted on. She had lupus, and she had suffered with it for a while, but in the end it attacked her kidneys, and from then on it was touch and go. As soon as Fletch thought things were under control here, she would take another turn for the worse, and Dad would call him in San Francisco, convinced that she wouldn't survive the night."

"That must have been tough," I said with sympathy.

"It was," Tia answered, a bitter edge creeping into her voice again, "but Isabella managed to make it worse. All this happened right when they were supposed to get married—in fact, they ended up postponing the wedding once. But the whole time Fletch was flying back and forth across the country, trying to keep Dad from losing it, Isabella was giving him grief about not being there for her, not taking their relationship seriously." Tia's voice turned grim. "The wedding was rescheduled for a few months after Mom died. Then, just three days beforehand, Fletch's friend Rob, whom he had worked with at Herringtons for years, had an attack of conscience and decided to tell him everything."

I waited, a sick feeling growing in my stomach.

"Turns out that Isabella got a little lonely when Fletch left town—couldn't take the deprivation. So she decided to share her sorrows with his best man. Turns out that wasn't all she shared with him."

A wave of fury shot through me. My teacup slammed onto the table. *"No,"* I protested. "She couldn't have."

"Oh, but she did," Tia confirmed. "And on a regular basis. Rob was her own personal fan club—the perfect therapy. She would complain about how much Fletch neglected her; he would tell her how gorgeous and desirable she was."

Tia took another sip of her coffee, staring daggers over the cup's rim. "You see, Rob was idiot enough to believe that Isabella had fallen in love with him. He was certain she would break off the engagement herself—that after the dust settled, the two of them could get together and Fletch would never have to know when it started. But Ice-a-bella had no intention of giving up her meal ticket—her free pass into the kind of celebrity circles she couldn't penetrate with her own measly talent. When the wedding date became imminent, and Isabella showed no signs of telling her fiancé anything, Rob finally caught a clue. He told Fletch the truth himself. At least he thought enough of him to keep him from making the worst mistake of his life."

My stomach roiled as everything I had gone through with Derrick came screaming back to me in all-too-vivid detail. The moment of reckoning, the disbelief, the horror. The endless X-rated visuals that had haunted my imagination every waking moment for weeks. The incredible pain I had carried with me everywhere, as heavy and unwieldy as a bowling ball. The inevitable self-doubt. A healing process that was as protracted as it was imperfect.

I had been able to stop caring about Derrick—that much had not been difficult. And within a few months I had reached the point where I could think about and even share the experience without crumbling. But the sting of being betrayed by a man I loved was not so easily overcome. Long after all our emotional ties had been severed, the mere thought of his infidelity could still revive the same nagging, inescapable question. *Was it me?*

I had eventually made my peace with the situation. But even now, eight years later, I could remember the pain of it with a clarity that made my gut twist. And Derrick and I had not been engaged.

I swallowed uncomfortably. "Fletcher told you all this?"

"Of course not," she retorted. "Fletch wouldn't tell me a thing. All I knew was that the wedding was off, and that he was devastated. So unbeknownst to him, I hied myself to California and confronted Isabella. I squeezed enough out of her to know that Rob was involved, and he was only too willing to confess the rest."

I rose from the table with a jerk and paced by the French doors, my face still scarlet. But the pacing didn't help relieve the pressure within me, and my emotions soon burst to the surface. "How *could* she?" I railed, practically stuttering. "How could any woman *do* that to a man like him? To be loved by someone like that—and to hurt him so much!"

I wasn't looking at Tia, but her voice sounded almost as if she were smiling. "You're preaching to the choir, here," she said softly. "I nearly scratched the wench's eyes out. I'm still afraid to go back to California—there may be a warrant out for me."

I kept pacing. I thought about going outside, looking for a rock or two to throw. I thought about scouting the forest for a tree limb and practicing a karate chop. But mostly I thought about flying to California and attacking a woman I'd never met.

"The reason I'm telling you this," Tia continued finally, perhaps after waiting for me to cool down, "is that it all relates to the question you asked me earlier. You were absolutely right about Fletch—he is still carrying around a lot of hurt, over and above the loss of our parents. You were also right that maybe your being here is making it worse."

I stopped pacing and looked at her with alarm. "How's that?"

To my surprise, she smiled again. "Well, that's the second half of the story. You see, as wonderful a guy as Fletch is, he shares one truly obnoxious fault with our mother. He's dogmatic as hell. He makes up his mind about something, and that's the end of it. No more discussion. Cutting down hundred-year-old trees to build a shopping center, for example, is wrong with a capital *W*. Extenuating circumstances? Well, they just don't exist. His mind is made up."

She paused for me to comment. I didn't, and she went on. "When the situation with Isabella hit the fan, he was completely blown away. But instead of recognizing the one bad apple, he extrapolated to the entire female race. He looked back over the other hundred or so women he's dated—not one of which, for obvious reasons, ever shared his excitement at the prospect of raising a litter of children in the middle of nowhere—and decided that the whole love-and-marriage business simply wasn't worth the grief." She took a breath, then let it out with a chuckle. "So like an idiot, he makes this vow. He swears to me that he's done with women—period. That he can be perfectly happy living here all by himself—at least until he can find some agency or other that will let him adopt as a single parent."

She shook her head with derision. "Did I point out the fallacies here? Of course I did. But he wouldn't listen. He doesn't listen. Happily-ever-after is nothing but a myth, he says—romantic love is a sham. Won't he get lonely living out here all alone? Of course not, he claims. He still has plenty of friends around, and there will be kids too, someday. What about affection? He says he just answered that. What about sex? *No comment*."

She turned around in her chair and looked at me, a

smile playing on her lips. "So you see," she finished with a touch of drama. "If it seems like you're making his anguish worse, you absolutely are, my dear. In fact, I'd say you're torturing the man."

I felt suddenly defensive, even as my heart pounded at the thought. "What are you talking about?" I whispered.

She chuckled. "Oh, please! I was here last night, remember? I've seen fewer sparks flying on the Fourth of July." She made a show of examining her arm. "In fact, I think I got singed in the cross fire."

I didn't think it was possible, but my cheeks got redder. "Was I that obvious?"

Tia laughed out loud. "Subtlety isn't your strength. But that's okay. For what it's worth, I think you fooled him. You must have, or he'd be running for the hills by now."

My entire body flushed with heat. My limbs threatened to tremble. Everything she'd told me made perfect sense. How the pain in his eyes had only seemed to worsen whenever things went well between us. Whenever I reminded him of Isabella. Whenever he dared to start thinking of me as more than a friend. He *had* been fighting me. But not because he didn't want me.

"I thought you should know," Tia said softly, "because I didn't want you to blame yourself. It's not like you're doing anything wrong." She grinned again. "But poor Fletch—he must think someone up there's playing some colossal joke on him. No sooner does he swear off women altogether than you fall right into his lap—a beautiful, sexy, sweet schoolteacher who cooks like a wizard and says she likes trees."

I blinked, overtaken by a sudden, inexplicable urge to verify that I really did like trees. But before I could get the words out, Tia was talking again.

"You know," she said with a giggle, "when we were teenagers, we made this deal. I told you how much Mom wanted grandchildren—she demanded no fewer than eight. But as you've probably figured out, I'm not the motherly type. Far too flighty. Though I *would*," she stressed, pointing a finger, "make a fabulous aunt. So I told Fletcher that having the eight kids would be his job—that I'd contribute by popping in for birthdays and delivering extravagant gifts. He said that was fine, but that if I expected him to provide eight nieces and nephews, I had to find him a wife that would still look sexy after having eight kids. And—here was the kicker— she also had to be able to bake pies as good as Mom's."

My eyes widened. *The pie.* I'd offered the man a homemade pie, and he had completely freaked. He really did think I was some sort of cosmic setup.

A heady joy rushed through me at the thought. So I'd been torturing him, had I? Well, *good*. The important thing was—there was no other woman. The only thing holding him back from me was his own stupid vow. He had been hurt badly, and he was afraid of being hurt again. But he would get over that, eventually. I did.

I drifted back to the table and sat down. "Well," I asked lightly, my head now firmly in the clouds. "Did you ever come up with any candidates?"

"Of course not. Nobody bakes homemade pies anymore. Though I have sent a few good cooks his way." Her dark eyes locked on mine then, and her tone turned serious. "A lot of women have fallen for Fletch over the years, Meara. It's an easy thing to do, I know. He's good-looking and he's sweet—at least to women who aren't his sister. But you've got to understand, he's not some city sophisticate who just happens to look good in jeans. It's the other way around. He's an old-fashioned, moralizing, stick-in-the-mud, country-bumpkin Eagle Scout who just *happens* to look sophisticated in a suit."

"He was an Eagle Scout?" I commented, impressed.

She stared at me a moment. "My God, you're frightening," she said finally, letting a shiver rock her shoulders. "The point is, you shouldn't let yourself think that Fletch's wanting to live in these mountains the rest of his life is a pipe dream, because it's not. He got talked out of it by a woman once—it won't happen again."

"Why would I want to talk him out of it?"

Her eyebrows rose.

"*What?*" I pressed, feeling defensive again. "This is a wonderful place to live. It's beautiful, it's quiet, there's a grocery store within half an hour. He's obviously happy here. What's wrong with that?"

Her mouth hung open. "Are you serious?"

I stared back.

She shuddered again, then rubbed her arms. The gesture seemed over-the-top, and I began to get the feeling I was being played. "This place," she insisted, "is like something out of a thesis. *Rural Living Linked to Dogmatism, Obsession with Uninteresting Nature-Related Trivia, and General Brain Deterioration.* This place is *boring*, Meara. There isn't a decent bookstore for miles. Upscale shopping? Forget it. You can't even get cable here. To you, this is a vacation, but living here 365 days a year—and being snowed under for at least a third of them—is different. I was so ready to split this place I barely graduated high school. Couldn't wait to see the real world—never wanted to come back. Just visiting gives me hives. More than three or four days here, and I feel like I can't breathe. You understand what I mean?"

"Actually, no," I said honestly. "But to each his own."

She studied me for another long moment, then stood up. "Well, that tears it," she announced. "Don't move. I'll be back in a second."

She traipsed out the French doors and across the patio, then disappeared around a corner of the inn. In a few moments she reappeared, holding something green. She marched back inside and laid it on the table in front of me.

It was a leaf.

"You said you're into trees," she stated. "But do you just think they're pretty to look at, or do you know all kinds of boring stuff about them, too?"

I suppressed a smile. "There's nothing boring about trees."

Her eyes rolled. "Yeah, right. So what kind is this?"

I picked up the leaf and pretended to study it closely. "I don't know," I said, sounding perplexed.

Her face fell.

"It's either a red oak or a black oak," I continued, "but you can't tell from the leaf. I'd have to take a look at the acorns. You see, the caps on the acorns of red oaks are relatively smaller in proportion to—"

She ripped the leaf from my hands and sank into her chair, laughing hysterically.

"Tia!" I demanded, smiling with her now, "what *is* your problem?"

She couldn't respond. She was laughing too hard. Mercifully, the phone rang, giving me an excuse to reach across the table and smack her on the shoulder. "Stop laughing and answer that!" I ordered. "It's not my phone."

She covered her mouth with her hands and shook her head.

I rolled my own eyes, then rose and headed toward the desk. All of a sudden, I was feeling pretty darn wonderful. Not only was Fletcher *not* in love with someone else, but I was pretty sure that his sister, in her own obnoxious way, had just given me her blessing.

And she didn't even know I baked pies.

Chapter

~25~

"BLACK RESIDENCE," I announced, my voice chipper.

"Meara, is that you?" Alex asked.

My spirits sank. I had promised to call him later in the morning. He wouldn't be calling me first unless something had happened. "Yes," I answered. "What is it? What's wrong?"

"Don't panic," he said smoothly. "The house is fine. Nothing's horribly wrong, but I didn't want to wait around for you to report in, either. It's just this: I got a call first thing this morning from the foreman on the abatement crew, telling me that one of his men noticed a car circling the block the day before the break-in. Apparently, this guy didn't think too much about it until he heard about the door being left open, but then he told the foreman right away. I said that everything was fine and that you weren't pursuing the issue with the police, but then I figured I'd better call you first and make sure that's still the case."

No, I thought bitterly. I had put the incident in Pittsburgh out of my mind, and I wanted it to stay there.

"Meara? Are you there? Don't freak out on me, please. If you're worried, we'll get the police involved."

"I'm not freaking out," I responded, knowing my thin voice was less than convincing. In my mind I saw Jake driving slowly in front of my parents' house, his car window rolled down, his head turning, his eyes watching . . .

"Did the worker say if he got a look at the driver?" I blurted.

"No—go on that. He was working on the roof or the attic or somewhere—watching the street from above. In any event, he must have spent more time than he should have watching the cars go by, because he was certain that this one was a dark blue Ford Taurus, probably about ten years old. He says it must have gone around the block a dozen times over the course of the day."

Chill bumps spread over my arms. I rubbed them with my free hand. "Did he say if the car came back after the break-in?" I asked.

"He wasn't working at the site yesterday," Alex explained. "That's why we're not hearing any of this until now. But he's definitely going to keep an eye out for it today. Do you want me to call the police again? It might be better if you called them directly. I have the name and number of the officer who came out yesterday—he'll know what you're talking about."

I took down the name and number, then realized that Tia was watching over my shoulder. "Thanks, Alex. I appreciate your calling. And I'll handle it myself from here. Thank you."

After I had assured him several more times that I was all right, we hung up.

Tia looked at me worriedly. "News about the break-in?" she asked.

I gave her a summary. When I had finished, she looked even more worried.

"Okay," she queried. "So what is it that you *aren't* telling me? You think you know who's behind it, don't you?"

I let out a breath. I wasn't sure how much Fletcher had told her about Jake, but I knew that he hadn't talked to her since I had shared my fears with him at the cabin. I didn't want to explain again—didn't want to face them. But I knew I couldn't escape them, either.

I proceeded to fill Tia in, beginning with the meeting at the diner, and ending with my theory of Sheila's abuse. My voice wavered every time I was forced to speak Jake's name, and as Tia listened, her worry lines deepened. When I paused, she led me back to the table to sit down.

"Meara," she asked. "Why are you so certain this man isn't your birth father?"

I looked into her shrewd eyes, and found myself unable to answer. The only reason I had for believing that Jake Kozen wasn't my birth father was my impression that he had been lying when he said that he was.

That, and the fact that I couldn't bear the alternative.

"I hope that he's not," she said pointedly. "But you have no business staking your whole well-being on it."

I took in a sharp breath.

"Whether he is or he isn't your birth father shouldn't matter to how you view yourself," she continued, her voice firm.

I said nothing. I looked at my hands.

"Meara O'Rourke!" she thundered, startling me to attention. She was giving a good approximation of my own best intimidation stare, and I wondered if she had ever considered school teaching. "I know what you're thinking, and I'm not having any of that crap in my presence!

You do not *need* to find out that Jake wasn't your birth father in order to feel better, or less guilty, or more deserving, or whatever else it is that you're thinking. The man is an unqualified, grade-A, criminal asshole either way. *You* are a wonderful, warm, sweet, and sensitive woman either way. Finding out the worst, as emotionally upsetting as it would be, will *not* change who you are. You will be strong. You will allow yourself to be a basket case for a suitable period of time, and then you will accept the historical reality and move on. Or else I promise you, you will have to deal with *me. Got it?*"

I blinked at her. Then amazingly, I found myself smiling. Tia really did know what to say.

"Now," she continued, her tone still didactic, "speaking as a woman with considerable expertise in the area of jackass birth fathers, I have to tell you this. I agree with Fletch that you need to get a professional's advice about this stalking thing. Did he hear back from Ben yet?"

I shook my head. "Not that I know of. At least not before he left here last night."

She rose. "Well, you need to tell Fletch what you just told me. I suppose we can try him on his cell phone. Not that there's any chance he'll actually answer it. I swear he just uses the thing to collect messages."

She walked to the desk and extracted Mitchell's address book from the drawer, then dialed the phone. She flipped idly through the listings as she waited for a response, but her eyes soon came to rest on something that interested her, and her gaze remained on the page even after she had removed the receiver from her ear and hung up.

"Well?" I asked. "No answer?"

"No," she responded, closing the book. "But I'm sure

he'll be down soon enough. He was muttering something yesterday about being out of coffee at the cabin, though that was probably just an excuse to see you." She returned to the table and began sifting through one of her stacks of envelopes. Her face wore a puzzled expression.

"What is it?" I asked, my heart leaping a little at her last comment.

"James P. McElron," she stated. "Whoever that is. All I know is that my father paid him a heck of a lot of money."

I watched as she extracted what she sought from the pile.

"Look at these," she explained, laying them out. "Four checks to James P. McElron. From $300 all the way up to $1685, none of them with a thing written in the comment line. The first was dated a week after my mother died; the last one, a little over a month ago. And I just saw his name in the address book, too. No location, just the number. Who the heck *is* this guy?"

"Good morning."

I turned to see Fletcher standing at the French doors. Elation rippled through me at the sight, and my eyes lingered involuntarily over his solid form.

"Good morning," I said with a smile, rising. "You want some coffee?"

He smiled back. His expression was guarded, but for once I didn't worry about his reaction. As of this morning, not only did I know the cause of his hesitancy—I also knew what to do about it.

"Don't mind if I do," he answered, heading to the kitchen to pour it himself. "I ran out."

"Of course you did," Tia commented. The sarcasm

was subtle, but the sideways dart of Fletcher's eyes told me he hadn't missed it.

Wary of Tia's "help," I attempted to divert his attention. "Did you hear back from Ben?"

He nodded as he tasted the coffee, then moved out toward the couches by the fireplace. I followed, and we sat down. Tia remained at the table, but turned her chair around to listen.

"Ben says if you're convinced you've got a problem, you should report it and shoot for a restraining order," he began. "But stalking cases can be tough, particularly in a situation like this, when you made first contact. You'd have to provide some proof of what was happening.

"He suggested you save the card from the flowers and the tapes from your answering machine and make note of the times and dates. You should also check and make sure that the police filed a report on the possible break-in. But what you've got so far isn't enough. Jake lives hours away from you—at the very least you'd have to show that he had been near your house."

I exhaled slowly, then explained Alex's report about the blue car. Fletcher's expression darkened. "Then what we need to do," he said, rising and moving toward the phone, "is find out what kind of car Jake drives."

I rose also, my heart beating faster than I would have liked. I was pleased that he and Tia were taking my concerns so seriously. But a part of me wished they would simply laugh and tell me that I was making a mountain out of a molehill. Maybe I could even believe them.

Fletcher picked up the phone and dialed, and I hovered by Tia at the table. She had begun to wrestle with a particularly mangled stack of papers, but after a few seconds she groaned and banged her forehead on the table. "I'm going blind trying to read Dad's chicken scratches," she complained. "It's time for a break."

"You want some breakfast?" I offered. We were low on food, but I figured I could swing French toast. Then afterward I could make a grocery run . . .

"No thanks," she offered, rising. "I'm glad Fletch is getting Ben on the case for you—you're in good hands, there. I think I'll just go back and finish up the clothes. All that's left are the underwear drawers, and at least I know there won't be any surprises there. Identical white boxers, identical white undershirts, twelve hundred pairs of socks—all black . . ." She continued to mutter as she disappeared down the hall.

I turned my attention back to Fletcher. He was hanging up.

"I couldn't reach Ben," he explained. "But I left a message. He'll call back here if he finds out anything. In the meantime," he continued, his tone serious, "there's something I need to ask you." He looked me straight in the eyes, and as much as I wished to savor the moment, the intensity in his gaze was far from comforting. "Did you ever actually *tell* Jake that you didn't want him to contact you?"

My breath caught in my throat. I felt like an idiot. "No," I admitted, embarrassed. "I haven't said a word to him since our meeting. I didn't ask him to call me, but I did tell him that my number was listed."

"I'm afraid you'll have to set him straight now, then. Because according to Ben, until you communicate your wishes clearly, you have no case at all."

A shiver slipped down my spine, and I averted my eyes. Not only was I an idiot, I was a coward, too. I hadn't told Jake to leave me alone because I couldn't stand the thought of talking to him again. I still couldn't.

"What about a letter?" I suggested, only half joking.

"A registered letter might be good for the case," he answered, taking the question seriously. "But if you want the guy to back off now, you need to tell him now. And according to Ben, you should do it in front of a witness."

"I don't want to see him," I insisted, cursing my timidity even as I spoke. "He may have already stopped calling me, anyway."

I broke eye contact and moved to pick up the phone myself. "He only left one message. I'll call and see if he's left another. If not, no problem. Right?"

My feigned optimism must not have been convincing. "You don't have to see him in person," Fletcher assured me as I dialed my home number. "A phone call will do. But you need to do it, Meara. Whether Jake's behind the break-in or not, it can't hurt to make your position clear."

I nodded in agreement, insincerely, as my phone rang. The machine picked up and delivered its message and beeps, and I punched in the appropriate code. *No messages,* I willed, *no messages.*

But I did have one message. And as it started playing, I sank down onto the chair.

"Hello, Meara, it's your old man again. I wasn't sure you got my first message. And did you get the flowers? I'll assume you didn't. I guess I'd better call the florist and complain, huh? I just wanted you to know how much I enjoyed meeting you. I would really like to see you again. Call me anytime. I'll be waiting. My number's—"

I dropped the phone down onto my lap. Fletcher took it and listened a moment, then hung it up. I stared at the desktop, concentrating hard on not being sick. I couldn't think of the man at all anymore without picturing Sheila, bruised and beaten. Without thinking of a little girl, cowering in a corner somewhere. No matter that it was all just suspicion. The mere sound of his smooth, egotistical voice spurred acid in my stomach like a geyser.

"Any specific threats this time?" Fletcher asked, his voice low.

I shook my head. "More of the same."

He dropped down to my level. "When you get back home, save the tape. But right now," he said gently, "you have to call him back. You can use Tia's cell phone in case he has caller ID—though I don't think he had it the last time you called, or else he would already have called here looking for you. Just keep it short. Tell him who you are and that you don't want him to contact you anymore. Then just hang up."

I took a breath, then blew it out with a shudder. He was right, and I knew it. I had to get hold of myself. If corrective action was needed, corrective action was what I would take. "All right," I answered. "If Tia doesn't mind. His number is still here somewhere . . ."

I found the printout on the desktop. Fletcher disappeared down the hall, then returned a few moments later with Tia's cell phone. He took the printer sheet from my hands and began to dial for me. Whether he was doing so in order to be able to tell a judge later that he knew what number was dialed, or whether he suspected my shaky hands might have trouble with the tiny buttons, I didn't know. Either way, I didn't protest. Instead I sat and steeled myself, determined to deliver my lines while ignoring completely the voice on the other end.

Fletcher handed me the phone, and I put it to my ear. It was already ringing.

Chapter

~26~

THE PHONE RANG for a long time. My heart thudded against my breastbone as I waited, and I made a mental note to avoid a second cup of tea. A stimulant was not advised. But I was beginning to see the appeal in hard liquor.

An answering machine picked up, and I closed my eyes with a sigh of relief. It was a best-case scenario.

"You got Jake—what do you want with me? Just leave a—"

"Yeah, hello?"

My eyes flew open again. The gruff, drowsy voice swore in muffled tones as its owner fumbled to turn off the recording. In a few seconds, the live voice spoke alone.

"Yeah?"

My tongue seemed frozen.

"Anybody there?" the voice asked irritably.

I felt Fletcher's hand on my shoulder, gentle but firm. "Yes," I forced out. "This is Meara O'Rourke. I'm calling to tell you that I would prefer it if you didn't contact me anymore."

There was silence. *Hang up*, my mind told me. *Just hang up now.* But despite the man's repugnance to me, I couldn't. What if he had nothing whatsoever to do with the break-in? What if he could say something, right now, that could convince me my fears were ridiculous?

"I'm sorry," I continued, wincing at yet another failure of Resolution #2. "But I'm not comfortable pursuing this right now."

"Hang up," Fletcher ordered.

I wanted to. But I still couldn't. I needed to know his reaction.

"No," Jake responded finally, his voice crestfallen. "You can't do that to me. You can't butt into my life and then tell me to get lost. It's not fair."

Guilt stabbed at my core, bringing with it the inherent fear of inadequacy I had struggled with my entire life. Once upon a time, I hadn't been a good-enough child to keep. So if I wasn't a good-enough daughter, a good-enough girlfriend, would I be thrown away again? Self-doubt, desperation to please . . . they were common traits among adoptees, and I knew that. But that knowledge couldn't completely curb the feelings when they arose.

What if I *was* wrong about Jake? What if he hadn't abused Sheila? What if I had seen only what I wanted to see, because I wanted to believe her? What if he really was my birth father?

"Hang up," Fletcher repeated sternly.

But I continued to listen. And without warning, Jake's voice changed. "You're just like your mother."

The hairs on the back of my neck pricked.

"She thought she was too good for me, too," he said with a snarl. "But she was nothing but a damn whore.

You're my daughter. You *belong* to me. And nothing you can say's going to change that. You can't—"

Fletcher wrested the phone from my hand and turned it off.

"Dammit," he swore, watching as my whole body began to tremble. "Why did you listen to him?" He squatted down beside my chair, then laid a comforting hand on my arm. "You've got to tune him out, Meara. If he's made a specific threat, we'll pass that on, but if he's just trying to mess with your mind, don't let him. You *haven't done anything wrong.*"

Words slipped from between my quivering lips, and the sound of them, repeated even by me, made my insides churn. "He said I belonged to him."

"That's bullshit!" Fletcher stood up straight, took my hands, and drew me with him. His eyes met mine, irate and determined. "Having sex with a woman thirty years ago entitles him to *nothing*. Do you hear me? You had a real father, and it wasn't him. Jake Kozen had the opportunity—the privilege—of raising you, and he turned that down. You weren't given a choice then, and he doesn't get one now."

I breathed in sharply. I was limp as a noodle. My emotions were drained, my brain was mush. I didn't think. I simply pulled my hands from his and stepped forward, wrapping my arms around his waist and burying my head in his chest. I clasped him tightly, savoring the feel of him. Fletcher Black was *good*. A good brother, a good son. He would be a good husband and a good father. I needed that goodness now . . . I needed him.

His arms closed around me and held me tight, bringing a joy so overpowering I all but forgot the horror that had driven me here. Being close to him felt so peaceful, so right. No matter how short our acquaintance, there was no longer a doubt in my mind that I was falling in love with him. His hands moved gently on my back, and though the movement was still platonic, I was sure I could sense a new earnestness. A yearning. A frustration.

He wanted me, too. He wasn't ready to admit it, but that didn't matter. Given the right encouragement, I could be a very patient woman.

"Thank you," I whispered. "You've made all this so much easier for me."

He didn't answer. His hands stilled, and after another moment, he pulled back. I tried not to feel disappointed as he gently took hold of my arms and detached me, setting me from him with a tolerant smile. I understood why he was doing it. He didn't trust himself.

He cleared his throat. "I'm glad I could help," he said in a casual tone.

I surprised myself with a grin.

He moved farther away. "In any event, you've done what had to be done. Now if there's any more trouble, you'll be prepared to defend yourself." He glanced nervously around the common room. "Where did Tia get to? I wonder."

I almost chuckled, but managed to control myself. The man was so darn cute.

"I'm here," Tia answered, drifting down the hall with an envelope in her hand. Her voice was thin; her expression, unsettled. My brief feeling of mirth evaporated.

"Fletch," she said, walking toward him. "You know the letters Mom wrote us, just a couple days before she died?"

"Of course," he said with concern. "What about them?"

She fiddled with the envelope as she talked, her

fingers bending it in and out like an accordion. "Well, Dad didn't mention it, but apparently she wrote one to him, too. It's the same stationery."

He stared at her, puzzled. "What's so surprising about that?"

She struggled with herself a moment, then breathed out heavily. "I didn't find it with his papers, Fletch. It was in the bottom of his dresser—in his sock drawer. Underneath an unopened package of handkerchiefs—the embroidered ones I gave him a few Christmases ago."

"Well, obviously it was personal."

Tia didn't say anything else, but as she looked at her brother, he seemed to read her mind.

"You opened it?" he accused.

She nodded. "I didn't read it—I didn't intend to. I only wanted to see for sure if that's what it was. But then, a word caught my eye, and—"

She whirled and looked at me. "I still haven't read it, Meara. But I thought you ought to know. It says something about Sheila."

Silence descended. The three of us exchanged guilty glances, each one waiting for the others to speak.

My brow puckered with confusion. Even if the women had been friends when they were young, why would Rosemary mention my birth mother in her last days of life? And why, for that matter, would my birth mother have mentioned her?

I was protecting you. Rosemary died. Stay—
The words remained a jumble.

Fletcher studied my face, then stepped forward. "I'd better look at it," he said, taking the envelope from Tia's hands. "If it could be important to Meara, we can't just ignore it. I don't think Dad would mind."

He walked away a few steps, putting his back to both of us. His sides rose and fell as he took in a deep breath. Then he opened the envelope and pulled out the letter.

My chest ached as I watched, afraid to breathe. Tia and I stood silently, waiting. The letter comprised a single sheet of handwriting, and Fletcher read both front and back twice without stopping. Then he stuffed the letter back into the envelope and turned around.

His eyes were awash with pain again, but this time the hurt was fresh, and sharp. I could feel every bit of it as if it were my own, and in a rush, I moved toward him. But his attention was fixed on his sister, and before I could reach him he stepped over and handed her the envelope. "I'm afraid it brings up more questions than it answers," he said in a low voice. "But maybe you should read it yourselves. I can't make any sense of it."

He turned immediately and strode toward the French doors. "I'm going for a walk," he declared, turning the knob. He opened the door and went through it without looking back.

Tia turned the letter front side up again on the cluttered table, then smoothed its wrinkles with the side of her hand. She let out a long, slow sigh, gazed in the direction her brother had disappeared, then swore. "Why didn't I just read this myself? I never should have shown it to Fletch. I was hoping it might clear up a few things for us, but if I'd known . . ."

My mother's admonition against nosiness once again popped into my head, but I beat it down. My heart felt sick; I had to know what was happening. "Would you mind?" I asked.

Tia slid the paper across the tabletop. I rotated it and began to read.

My Dearest Mitchell,

I'm writing this with a heavy heart, because I know that I have ruined what will be our last days together. I could have waited and put it all in a letter, but I knew that wouldn't be fair. I wanted you to feel free to get angry with me, to tell me how you felt. I still wish you would. Anything would be better than these tortured silences.

I love you. You know that. I've loved you since I was a child. I wasn't always the best wife to you, but I tried to make up for it. We got over the bad times, the infidelity, the insecurity, because we loved each other. I'm sorry I wasn't stronger where Sheila was concerned. I wish I hadn't lied to you. I know I was wrong—I know I should have trusted you. You have every right to be furious with me now.

I've been a coward, and I'm sorry. I've been sorry all along. I know it may take a while for you to forgive me—maybe longer than I'll live. That's my fault, not yours, so please don't feel guilty later. I don't want you to feel guilty about anything, and I mean that. I just want you to be happy. Whatever it takes. And I mean that, too.

Please keep this letter. Let it remind you that I loved you. Let it remind you that I always will.

Your loving wife,
Rosemary

I folded the letter and replaced it in the envelope. "I'm sorry," I offered, apologizing for nothing in particular, yet at the same time, everything. Obviously, Rosemary hadn't been honest with Mitchell about something, and that something had involved Sheila. But the reference was so vague that speculating on the specifics would be fruitless.

In any case, it was not the reference to Sheila that worried me—or Tia. We both knew that while Rosemary's passing mention of infidelity might seem like a footnote to an outsider, to Fletcher, it would be anything but. With the pain of his own betrayal still festering, he was bound to be disturbed by the knowledge that one of the parents he loved and respected had once done the same to the other—no matter how long ago.

My stomach felt like lead.

I rose and walked to the French doors, looking out. "Where do you think he went?" I asked quietly.

Tia didn't answer me. When I looked back at her, she seemed a million miles away. "My father was incredibly out of sorts after my mother died," she said softly, talking more to herself than to me. "We just assumed it was because he had always been so dependent on her. But now—" She paused. "Now I think that some of what we were seeing was resentment."

She reached forward and grabbed a check from the top of one of her piles. "I've got to find out what all this was really about. Otherwise Fletch is just going to . . ." Her voice trailed off. She swooped up her cell phone and rose, then crossed to the desk, opened her father's address book, and dialed. In a moment she reached up and turned off the phone with a stab of her finger, then sank down into the desk chair.

"Tia?" I asked, concerned. "What is it?"

She looked at me, her face deep in thought. "I was right. James P. McElron is a private investigator."

I stared at her a moment, not comprehending. "Why would your father need a private investigator?"

She shook her head. "I don't know. But I'm going to find out." She looked up at me. "Would you mind?"

All I could manage was a shrug. Whatever had tied Sheila to Rosemary didn't seem important at the moment. All I could think about was Fletcher—off by himself somewhere, hurting.

I put my hand on the knob. "I think I'll take a walk, too," I announced. I opened the door and stepped out.

"Meara," Tia called.

I turned toward her, and she smiled at me.

"Try the swimming hole."

Chapter
~27~

I ROUNDED THE corner of the white house and walked toward the trailhead leading to the swimming hole, hoping Tia knew her brother well enough to correctly guess his destination. I walked rapidly down the steep trail, slipping once or twice in my haste. If Fletcher was walking steadily, I would never catch up with him. But if, as his sister had speculated, he had paused to throw stones in the creek, I might have a chance.

The trail began to flatten, and I held my breath. When a bright blue shirt came into view through the green leaves ahead, I exhaled with relief. Sure enough, he was standing near the rock on which we had sat together three days before, throwing stones.

I approached him without speaking. He must already have heard me coming, because he took no notice of me as I emerged from the trail and settled myself on the flat-topped boulder. I could tell from his face that he was not particularly pleased to see me.

I had expected that. After all, he thought he wanted to be alone. He assumed that my presence couldn't possibly help and would only aggravate him. I might indeed aggravate him—if he had a taste for tight jeans and scoop-necked shirts. But he was wrong about my not being able to help. I could, and I was going to.

I sat silently for a while, giving him the opportunity to speak first if he wanted. He didn't, so I took the lead. "I couldn't make much sense of the letter, either," I said casually, as if we were already in the middle of a conversation. "But that's all right. The details of what went on between your mother and Sheila aren't important to me."

Fletcher said nothing. His jaw remained clenched, his face stony. The pebbles he was throwing weren't landing in the creek anymore, but were sailing into the foliage well across the far bank.

"It sounded as though your mother loved your father very much," I offered, prompting.

He looked back at me with a glare, the pain in his eyes intolerable. My own gut ached abominably, but I pressed on. "I know what you're thinking. But you shouldn't jump to conclusions."

He bent down, retrieved a larger hunk of sandstone, and threw it. It hit the giant boulder in the middle of the stream and splintered into pieces.

I took a breath and continued. "Whatever happened between your parents in the past—"

"What happened," he interrupted, his voice hard, "is that my mother cheated on my father. Why don't you just say it? The letter was pretty clear on that point."

I disagreed on the latter statement, but didn't argue. "The letter said that whatever happened, they worked through it," I emphasized. "She was trying to apologize."

"Well, I'm sure that made him feel all better," he said cynically. Another fistful of stones flew across the creek and into the woods.

I sighed. I could hardly blame him for being unable to view his mother's alleged infidelity objectively. What happened with Isabella had shaken him to the core; now, with the mother he idolized crashing posthumously from her pedestal, he was undoubtedly feeling that he couldn't trust any woman.

I couldn't let that happen.

I drew myself up on the rock. "No," I agreed. "You're right. An apology wouldn't have made your father feel any better, at least not right away. But with a sincere apology, over time—"

"Apologizing for stabbing someone in the back," he retorted, interrupting me again, "does nothing but add insult to injury."

I said nothing else for a moment, uncertain how to proceed. I wanted him to know that I understood. I supposed I might as well be straightforward.

"I know," I admitted. "I've been there myself. Derrick even used the cliché: *I never meant to hurt you.* What he really meant, of course, is that he hadn't been thinking about me at all. Perhaps it was his preference that I not get hurt; but it was certainly a risk he was willing to take."

Fletcher stopped throwing rocks. He turned and stared at me.

"That's what I meant by a sincere apology, as opposed to an insincere one," I continued. "He claimed that he still loved me. He claimed that we could stay together if only I were willing to forgive him. But in his mind I was the real problem, not him. Because the truth was that he never really loved me at all."

I hopped off the rock, my reverie eating at my insides a little more than I would have liked. My ill-fated first love might be ancient history, but it was still an unpleasant place to go. I reached down and grabbed a pebble myself.

"But your parents obviously did love each other, Fletcher," I continued, tossing it. The stone hit a nearby boulder and bounced off into the churning water. "You can't fake a lifetime of devotion. That means something. Maybe one or the other was unfaithful once upon a time, but you don't know the circumstances, and it isn't fair to speculate now."

I looked up at him. He was still staring at me, but his expression had changed. He was incredulous. "What *moron*," he asked gruffly, his eyes flashing with anger, "would ever be stupid enough to cheat on you? What— were you still in high school?"

I suppressed a smile at the compliment. "No. I was in my early twenties. We dated all through college, but then went to different graduate schools. The understanding was that as soon as I finished my master's, I would move out to join him. We were young, but I was in love with him; I wanted to marry him as soon as we had jobs. He said he wanted the same thing. We'd been living apart for a little over a year when I found out what was going on.

"He never would have told me. At least not until he decided *he* wanted to break up. He liked having me waiting for him in the wings; he enjoyed my visits. But in between, he couldn't resist sleeping around. He was very good-looking; there was no shortage of willing candidates. He figured that as long as I didn't find out, I'd be fine, and he could have the best of both worlds."

I cursed the churning in my stomach, reminding myself I was telling the story for a reason. "But of course I did find out. One of his exes cornered me on campus during a visit—said she felt it was her duty to inform me what a jerk he was. Of course, she was only trying to get back at him for moving on, but her story was real. He eventually confirmed it."

I cast another glance at Fletcher. His expression remained amazed. "Unbelievable," he whispered roughly.

"Why?" I asked. "People cheat every day."

"Not on women like you, they don't," he said emphatically, his eyes flashing again. "Was the man insane?"

This time, I let myself smile. "No," I answered. "Just stupid. Stupid, thoughtless, and immature. The world is full of people like that. And they're not always easy to spot. I beat myself up over Derrick for a long time. But eventually I got over it. I realized it wasn't me. He would have cheated on anybody. It's just the way he was put together."

I looked Fletcher in the eyes, my voice low. "And I was vulnerable to him because of the way *I'm* put together. I loved him, and I didn't want anyone else. But even if I had, I would never have acted on those feelings, because I could never have hurt him like that. I couldn't bear it—it would be like hurting myself. My mistake was believing that his idea of love was the same as mine."

I stood silently for a moment, remembering against my will the sorrow my naivete had wrought. I had learned from Derrick; I had not made the same mistake again. The next two times, I had made different ones.

Fletcher stepped close in front of me, his eyes filled with a tumultuous mixture of empathy and indignation. In a natural motion he brought his hand to my face, the tips of his fingers lightly brushing my cheekbone. I stood without breathing as his hand moved to my temple, then gently swept a lock of hair behind my ear.

My heart skipped a beat. My face flushed.

"I'm sorry, Meara," he said tenderly. "You deserve better."

I was afraid to move. His hand retraced my cheekbone with a feather touch, then moved down my jawline toward my chin.

"Thank you," I agreed. "So do you."

His expression clouded. His hand fell to his side. He turned away from me and dropped down heavily on the rock.

Oh, no, you don't, I resolved with passion. I was doing the right thing by being honest with him—by getting everything out in the open—and I was not going to let him make me regret it. I walked over and sat down beside him, making sure our shoulders touched. Predictably, he shifted away.

"Tia had no business—" he grumbled.

"Tia loves you," I interrupted, my voice firm. "And don't you dare say a word against her, because you're darned lucky to have her in your life. I'd give anything to have a sister like her."

He growled low in his throat. But when I moved closer again, he stayed put.

"So, I know about Isabella," I challenged, my voice lighter. "So what? Everything I just told you was the truth. You want me to apologize for having the gall to talk about something that might make you feel better?"

He threw me a sideways glare. "Our situations were different."

"How?" I pressed. "Because Derrick and I weren't engaged? Or because he didn't sleep with a friend of mine? None of my friends were anywhere near him at the time, but I'm sure he would have considered them fair game if they had been. And the only reason we weren't engaged is because he didn't ask; if he had, I would have said yes, God help me. Now, as far as *quality* of betrayal—timing, cinematic flair—I agree with you, Isabella wins. But for sheer *quantity*, college boy gets the prize. I'm pretty sure he went through the entire women's tennis team."

He avoided my gaze. But in the corner of his eye, I was certain I caught the faintest glimmer of amusement.

"I can't believe I'm having this conversation with you," he groused.

I grinned. "And why not?"

"Because I don't want to talk about it."

"Who's talking?" I teased. "All I hear is myself."

He growled at me again, and I decided I liked the sound. Distinctly bearlike. Mighty, but sweet.

"You've been so much help to me, Fletcher," I said seriously, trying to catch his eyes, "I only want to return the favor."

He lifted his eyes to mine, and the expression I saw in them suffused me with happiness. It was a difficult look to define—a certain sparkle, a warmth. But I knew what it meant. He was falling for me, too. He was fighting it, but he was losing.

Our faces were inches apart, and I longed to kiss him. I had no qualms about making the first move—despite my mother's etiquette training—and having a man actively resist me was tantalizing uncharted territory. But something else held me back. If Tia's tale was to be believed, Fletcher had been living like a monk for months. Watching him now, I decided I believed her. Though he remained perfectly still beside me, his taut muscles and rapid, shallow breaths showed just how deprived that inane resolution had left him. Strong will or no, he was at the end of his rope. One touch of my lips would finish him.

I didn't move. Whatever idiotic vow he had made to himself, the decision to recant it had to be his own. Physical coercion from me would be a cheap shot. Pleasant as the process of his undoing would be, I didn't want him to succumb purely out of lust. I wanted him to open his heart again—knowingly and willingly. I wanted him to trust me.

The fun part could follow.

I pulled back and stood up. "Now, I don't know about you," I said brightly, wondering if he could sense my own frustration—and hoping that he could. "But I'm starving. I forgot all about breakfast, so the only reasonable course of action now is for me to fix a huge lunch." I looked at my watch. "Why don't you come to the inn around noon? I'll have to make a grocery run first."

He didn't answer immediately. He sat looking at me, a parade of emotions racing across his eyes. Irritation, gratitude, fondness, desire. I took them all in with exhilaration. The pain was not completely gone, but at least it wasn't dominant. That slot, I noted with satisfaction as his gaze rested briefly over my scoop-necked shirt, belonged to the latter.

"That sounds great," he said finally, rising to his feet. "I've got work to do this morning, anyway."

I watched him as he turned and started up the path to his cabin, his eyes once again looking anywhere but at me.

I couldn't wait till lunch.

Chapter

~28~

WHEN I REACHED the French doors at the back of the inn, I was practically skipping. My birth mother had not been a gold digger, much less an attempted murderess. I had stayed here as a child because she had been a friend of Rosemary Black's; whatever had happened between the women later, I really didn't care. The sun was shining, and Fletcher was unattached. All that mattered to me now was the present and the future—and at the moment, both seemed wonderfully bright.

I opened the doors and floated inside. "Tia?" I called, seeing that she was no longer bent over the cluttered table. "Where are you? You want to go out with me for a while?"

I received no response, but noted a single sheet of paper sitting prominently on the kitchen counter, weighted down with the teakettle. I stepped over to read it.

Off to see James P. —T

My heart sank. Not only was I disappointed at the lost prospect of an outing with a new friend, but I was beginning to wish I had discouraged her from her fact hunt. I didn't want to hear any more revelations today. The process would only drag me down, and after having just spent such a promising few moments with Fletcher, I was prepared to fight that current any way I could.

A floorboard squeaked overhead, and my face broke into a smile. She hadn't left yet. I could still catch her.

"Tia!" I flew down the hall and up the stairs, my voice bubbling with excitement. "Forget James P. Whatever! Come with me to—" I stepped into her room and stopped short, disappointed. She wasn't there. Her purse and keys were gone from the dresser. I exhaled sadly.

Had my hopeful imagination run away with me? It must have—though I could have sworn the creak I heard was a footstep. Perhaps Estelle was here? She could have slipped in while I was out and began cleaning the up-stairs—she might not have heard me calling. I turned around toward Tia's door. "Estelle?" I called, louder this time. "Are you—"

My words broke off, mangled. My own breath seemed to choke me.

The figure in the doorway leaned to the side, one broad shoulder and arm falling heavily against the door frame. He crossed his legs casually in front of him, then stretched his free hand across the opening. His dark eyes twinkled. His lips curled into a satisfied smile.

Jake.

My limbs turned to lead. I couldn't move. Jake could *not* be here. Not at this place, not now. But he was. And I was.

We were alone.

"Hello, there, sweetheart," he crooned. His voice was gravelly, and not quite stable. My heart pounded.

He was drunk.

"Thought I'd come to see ya," he continued, staring at me. He made a show of squaring his shoulders, his large frame virtually occluding the undersized doorway. "You weren't too nice to me on the phone, you know, missy. Not too nice to your dear old dad. I didn't like that."

My arms and legs began to tremble. Jake was intoxicated. He was angry. And as his body language was making painfully clear, he also had me trapped. There was only one door, and I could not go through it. This bedroom had no bath. Its lead-soldered windows cranked open only a few inches. There was no other way out.

He had me, and he knew it.

"I didn't mean to be rude," I forced out, finding my voice. My mind was reeling. Whether or not Jake posed a real physical threat to me, I didn't know. But I could not afford careless optimism. He was stronger than I was, and I had no weapon. I had to tread carefully.

"How did you get here?" I asked with as casual a voice as I could muster.

It was a poor effort. Jake's crocodile smile widened. "I followed you here, you silly woman," he patronized. "Just when I thought you'd never show up at your house—you did. Then you led me right back here. Didn't even notice me, did you?"

I didn't answer. Obviously, I had not. I was hardly in the habit of studying cars through my rearview mirror, and yesterday I had been particularly flustered.

"Of course you didn't," he bragged, "because I'm good at following people. No one gets away from me. I always find them. Eventually." His eyes held mine, their dark depths glinting with a sentiment that chilled me. A sentiment I had recognized before.

Hatred.

"Why did you want to see me?" I asked quickly, willing away my urge to panic. Screaming and making a run for the door would accomplish nothing. No one would hear a scream from inside; even if I did reach a window, Fletcher had to be most of the way to his cabin by now. And no matter how tempted I was to try, I knew that I could not forcibly push past Jake. Even though he had been drinking, he could not be falling-down drunk. No driver that far gone could possibly have maneuvered all the twists and turns on the road to the inn.

"Have you been waiting long?" I finished.

He grinned at me again. "I asked you to call me. But you were being a little stubborn. I could have dropped in yesterday, but I wanted to meet with you in private."

Tia's car, I thought miserably. It had been in the lot when I returned to the inn yesterday—it had stayed there all night. Had Jake driven by more than once, checking? He was home when I called him this morning. He must have set out immediately afterward—only to find my car conveniently alone this time. He had probably looked for me inside the inn. Sifted through my stuff. Wandered up here . . .

"What is it you want, then?" I braved, squaring my own shoulders. If Jake got a charge out of intimidating women, I would do my best not to give him the satisfaction.

"What do I want?" he repeated in a singsong, mocking me. "What do you think I want?" He stood up straight in the doorway. His voice dropped. "A little respect wouldn't hurt."

I took in a deep breath and stepped closer to him, figuring that the less defensive I acted, the less alert he would stay. If I could convince him I wasn't afraid, wouldn't bolt—he might let his guard down. And if he would move only a little bit, I might have a chance. All I needed was a head start down the stairs. I could be halfway across the meadow before he made it out of the inn, and he wouldn't have a prayer of catching me on the mountain.

"I'm sorry if you think I've been rude," I said with feigned remorse. "I didn't realize. It's just that this whole thing has been a shock to me. Finding out about Sheila going to prison for drugs—it really threw me for a loop. I didn't think I could handle any more right now."

An idea struck me, and my pulse quickened. I turned my back to him and moved toward the window. "You see, I'm getting married in a couple of weeks, and I thought it would be easier if I could put everything about my birth parents on hold for a while. Todd thought I was getting too stressed about everything, and he was probably right." I pulled back the curtain and gazed out. Jake's blue Ford Taurus was parked high on the hill, the farthest spot from the inn. Perhaps he had rolled in quietly, not wanting to be heard. Or perhaps he envisioned a fast get-away.

I snuffed out the thought, concentrating on my plan. My eyes widened at an imagined sight out the window. "There he is!" I said happily. I turned to Jake. "My fiancé, I mean. Would you like to come down and meet him?"

Jake snorted. "I don't hear any car," he said, suspicious.

I stepped back from the window and beckoned him forward. "It's a Mercedes," I insisted, "Very quiet engine."

Just take a look, I willed, hiding my angst behind an innocent smile. All he had to do was take three paces forward. If I could move back surreptitiously while he did so, then my shot to the door would be clear.

He took a step forward, looking at me. His grin became a smirk as he took another. I put one foot behind me, then began to inch ever so slightly farther from the window.

He whirled in an instant, catching me roughly by the upper arms and lifting me from the ground. "Going somewhere?" he roared. My shocked resistance proved futile as he forced me to the opposite wall and held me there, his hands pinning my shoulders, his hot breath, reeking of booze, inches from my face.

"You think you're so smart," he chided. "And you're *so* damn stupid. Like mother, like daughter. I should have known."

I did my best to stare back at him. But it was hard. Though I barely knew the man, I despised him with every bone in my body. I had hated him from the beginning—hated him without even knowing why.

Or maybe I did.

"Take your hands off me," I said petulantly. His grip was bruising my shoulders. The stench of his breath was sickening.

"You're a little spitfire, aren't you?" he said with a smirk. "Just like your momma. She had a fire in her, Sheila. That's what turned me on."

Without warning, his eyes narrowed. "But she disappointed me. She was a lousy wife. Lousy mother, too. She farmed your ass out to anyone who'd take you. Did you know that?"

He paused a second, but his grip on me did not lessen. "Which reminds me," he drawled. "It's damned creepy you being out here again. Why the hell'd you pick this place? That meddling friend of Sheila's bring you here?"

I forced my breath in and out with intentional, slow movements. So, Jake knew where he was. It was here that he and Sheila had argued—here that she had shot him. But none of that mattered now. All I wanted was to get away. I measured mentally the distance from my knee to his groin. It was possible, but it would have to be a surprise, and it would have to be effective. I would not get a second chance.

"Yes," I answered, not sweating the details. "I hooked up with Sheila's friends at her funeral. Would you like to meet them?"

He laughed out loud. "Yeah," he taunted. "We'll all have tea."

"What do you want?" I asked again, daring to squirm.

He responded by pinning me tighter. "I told you already. I want *respect*."

"And what does that mean exactly?" I pressed. As much as I longed to take action, I knew that striking him was risky. He was playing plenty rough, but there was still some chance he didn't intend further violence. He could just be a blustering drunk who, if I kept my own cool, would chill as he sobered. But if I injured him, then failed to get away, retaliation would be a certainty.

His dark eyes glinted. "What that means, missy, is that you *owe* me. Owe me for raising you all that time. Owe me for buying all that formula—all those stinky diapers. Owe me for everything your miserable existence *screwed up*."

He spat as he talked, spraying my face. My stomach roiled.

"Sheila and I had a good thing going," he continued. "I'd say jump; she'd jump. She was fine-looking, and she was mine. All mine. I told her she'd never get away from me. I told her I'd kill her if she crossed me, and I could've gotten to her, too—anywhere." His lips curled into a sneer. "Anywhere except Muncy. The bitch thought she'd won, then."

I stiffened. To hell with the benefit of the doubt—Jake Kozen was crazy. The first time he dropped his guard, I had to strike.

"I had nothing to do with any of that," I protested vacantly. He would not expect me to make a move in the middle of a sentence, would he? "I was only a child, and I never asked—"

I tried not to give any warning. But the mere act of lifting my foot—of shifting my body weight to muster the necessary force—tipped him off. As I raised my leg upward he swiveled his hips to the side, leaving my knee to crash uselessly against his thigh muscles.

His repercussion was swift.

He body-slammed me against the wall, pinning me with the full force of his weight. Before I realized what was happening both my wrists were caught in his left hand, suspended above my head. His face was within an inch of mine. My heart beat like a jackhammer; his foul breath generated an almost unbearable wave of nausea. A flash of heat shot through me, and my pent-up fury exploded. "I don't owe you anything!" I screamed at him. "You abused Sheila, you made her life hell, and she got back at you by cheating on you! You are not my father, and you know it! She didn't farm me out—she sent me to live with friends because she wanted to keep me safe from *you*!"

He grunted viciously, pinning me even harder. Rationally, I knew that yelling at him was dangerous. But for the first time in my life, I seemed to have lost control of my anger. "Just admit it, you asshole!" I raged. "Admit it! I'm *not* your daughter!"

His shoulder shifted, and his right arm drew back. I flinched, certain that he would strike. But he didn't. His arm stopped at his side, and his voice dropped low.

"So she did tell you," he whispered back, his voice pure venom. "You lied to me."

My heart pounded fiercely. A tiny blip of elation swelled in my chest, but it was far too weak to dampen my ire. I wanted his repugnant carcass off of me.

Faint noises sounded from below. I believed I was hearing the French doors, whining their usual whine, clicking shut. There was a good chance I was hallucinating, but I wanted to believe it. I had to believe it.

"Yes, she told me!" I lied, stalling for time. If anyone else was in the inn, I wanted them to hear me before Jake heard them. I kept my volume high. "She told me you knew all along!"

Another noise sounded from below, and I cast a wary glance at my assailant's eyes. But deep in his drunken reverie, Jake did not seem to have noticed.

"That's bullshit!" he spouted acidly. "Little saint Sheila wanted you to believe she leveled with me, eh? Well, forget it! I didn't know she was whoring, and you can take that to the bank, because I sure as hell wouldn't have raised some bastard kid if I had! You were a pain in the ass from day one! Sick, crying all the time. Nasty yellow thing—jaundiced, they told me." His voice turned snide. "Because Sheila had O blood, and you had B. *Just like me.*"

With a look of disgust, he shifted his weight, moving off me enough to put some space between us. I thought of bolting, but decided against it. It would take only a second for him to crush me again; his grip on my wrists was still numbing. I had to be patient.

"I thought you were mine—I had a little piece of paper that said so," he spat. "But the lying slut couldn't get away with it forever. You know why? Because a buddy of mine got shot in the belly one day. Nearly bled to death right there on the street. Hospital was looking for type B blood, so good old Jake steps up to the plate. 'Take mine,' I said. 'I'm type B.'"

His eyes flashed fire. "But I wasn't a type B, was I? Turns out I was a stinking bloody O!" He stumbled a little, inadvertently stomping on one of my feet, crushing my toes. I clenched my teeth at the pain. "So I did a little checking around," he railed. "And you know what I found out? You *couldn't* be my brat. No way, no how!"

I thought I could hear it. I was sure I could. The faintest squeaking of the steps.

"You ruined *everything*," he continued caustically. "Sheila had a nice body. She was hot. You made her look like an old damned cow." His voice changed to a nasally falsetto. " '*Not now, Jake, what about the baby? I have to go out—we need some crap for the baby. Don't do that—it will upset* the baby.'"

He body-slammed me to the wall again. "I put up with it because I thought you were mine!" he bellowed. "But I don't have to put up with you anymore—and I sure as hell don't have to put up with any woman jerking my chain! I'm the one in charge here, and if I want to, I can finish what I should have finished then. I can finish it right now."

I jerked involuntarily, a biting horror driving me to escape—no matter the cost. But there was nowhere to go. His weight pressed me against the wall. My struggles seemed only to amuse him. He laughed quietly in my ear. "Your momma's not here to help you now, missy. It's just you and me."

I bucked violently against the wall, trying to move him far enough away to kick, but nothing I did seemed enough. He had strength, bulk, and a lifetime of experience at restraining people. I had nothing but outrage, and I reacted with the only weapon at my disposal. I stretched my neck toward the arm that held my wrists and sank my teeth into it.

"Damn you!" he thundered, pulling down the hand and shifting to pin me another way. I had no chance to escape. His hold on my wrists never loosened; he merely brought his forearm up under my chin, hard, to prevent a repeat attack. "You're going to regret that."

His right arm fumbled with something out of sight. In the next second, a piece of metal appeared between my eyes, as close as if it had grown from my nose.

It was a switchblade.

"I don't *like* women who mess with me!" he roared at my face. *"Got it?"*

I said nothing. My heart couldn't beat any more violently than it already was. But as my peripheral vision caught a flash of blue in the hall, it did leap. *Don't look, Meara,* I ordered myself, using every ounce of strength within me to obey. The slightest flicker of my pupils toward the doorway could tip Jake off. There was no telling what he would do.

I willed myself to relax. Jake seemed to sense defeat in me, and smiled. "That's better," he said more softly. He retracted the blade, but kept it in his hand. "You just need to admit it, that's all. I'm in charge of you, just like I was in charge of your cheating bitch mother. You can't just call me up and blow me off—it's not up to you. You understand? From now on, you'll do as I say."

Don't look. Not swinging my eyes to the side was torture. The blue area was gone. Had I seen it at all?

Stall him. "I'm not going to report you to the police, if that's what you mean," I said, forcing a soothing tone. "I don't remember you hurting Sheila, or me. I was too little."

"I never hurt you," he snarled. "Jake Kozen don't beat up kids." He forced his forearm hard against my throat, compressing my windpipe until I coughed. Then he released the pressure with a grin. "Grown women who ought to know better is something else."

There was still no sign of blue.

"You did so try to hurt me!" I argued, my emotions once again overpowering my wits. "That's why Sheila shot you! I know it is!"

His eyes held mine. Their black depths glinted. "You'd better be damn glad she did, too. Because you know what?" He leaned in again, his face practically touching mine. "If she hadn't, I'd have rung your scrawny little neck right then and there."

"Meara? Are you up here?" Fletcher's voice floated to our ears. Jake stiffened and pulled back.

Relief flooded my veins. Fletcher sounded as though he were on the stairs. I could hear the last few steps creaking as he sprang up them. "Meara?" he called again, his voice cheerful.

When his tone penetrated my dazed brain, my emotions reversed to panic. If Fletcher sounded happy, he must have no idea what he was about to walk in on. Had I only imagined seeing his shirt in the hall? I couldn't let him walk into this situation blind. He would take one look at Jake and attack—he wouldn't know about the knife. I had to warn him.

But before I could speak, another sound filled me with hope. Fletcher was opening other doors, the two nearest the stairs. He had no reason to do that, no reason to believe I would be hiding in an empty bedroom. He must know where I was, what was going on. He was only stalling, making sure we had ample warning of his approach.

Jake released my arms and stepped back to an innocent distance. He dropped the hand with the knife back into his pocket. "Keep your mouth shut," he whispered.

Fletcher appeared in the doorway. To a stranger, I suspected his flushed face and wide smile would indicate nothing more than breathless excitement. But I knew him well enough to know better. The flush was from pure ire; the smile masked a keen alertness. "There you are," he said brightly, stepping just inside the doorway. He cast a polite glance from me to Jake. "Sorry, I didn't know you had company."

My head spun. I couldn't seem to move. I was too terrified for Fletcher—terrified that at any moment, Jake would lose what was left of his self-control.

But Fletcher stepped forward toward Jake without hesitation, proffering his hand. "Fletcher Black," he said pleasantly. "I own the inn here. Nice to meet you. Any friend of Meara's is a friend of mine."

Jake stood motionless for a moment, staring. I couldn't breathe. If he had any inkling that Fletcher had witnessed what had just transpired, I was certain he would spring like a cat—switchblade extended. And though Fletcher was bigger, younger, and stronger, Jake was an armed veteran brawler. It would be a dangerous battle, and without some weapon of my own, my assistance would be negligible. Once Jake was set off—the die would be cast. Someone would get hurt.

I took a deep breath, wishing fervently that Fletcher had stayed hidden. He could have called the police and waited. I could have—

"Jake Kozen," my attacker answered with authority. To my amazement, he extended his hand. It was empty.

They shook.

"Nice to meet you," Fletcher responded, all smiles.

I remained immobile, feeling as if I had dropped out of one surreal dimension and into another. The Jake I saw was back to his policeman persona—swaggering, confident, charismatic. The happy-go-lucky, gregarious, and not-necessarily-so-bright incarnation of Fletcher was someone I'd never met before.

"Sorry to intrude," the unfamiliar Fletcher apologized. "I'll get out of your hair in a minute, here. But I just had to come and tell Meara the good news." He turned to me, though he kept one eye on Jake even as he spoke. "I heard back from Ben. He's been promoted! Isn't that great? He's really coming up in the world."

Our eyes met for only a split second, but I read his message loud and clear. *Ben is coming up.* The police are on their way.

The knowledge brought me near to crumbling with elation, but I fought to keep my composure. Fletcher obviously had a ruse in play; I could not screw it up. He must have known that Jake was at the inn when he got here. He must have been intentionally quiet, called the police from the common room, then come up and brainstormed how best to intervene. He had probably accomplished it all in seconds; it was only in my mind that time had stood still. Thank God he'd had the sense not to come flying up the stairs like a maniac.

"That's wonderful," I responded. "Ben seems like a nice guy."

"Oh, he's great," Fletcher continued enthusiastically, turning his full attention back to Jake. "He's a cop," he explained. "Down in West Virginia. Just got made detective. You know anything about police work?"

Jake's ego swelled visibly. I slipped back slightly, just out of his reach. He didn't seem to notice. "Hell, yeah," he bragged. "I was a cop for thirty-five years."

Fletcher appeared impressed. "Really? Well, in that case, why don't you join me for a drink? I've got a bottle of brandy just waiting for a celebration. You can explain to me how they decide who gets detective and who doesn't. I've never really understood all that." He stepped up to Jake and clapped a friendly hand on his shoulder.

I stifled a gasp. Every muscle in my body tensed as I imagined Jake waiting for just the right moment, turning sharply . . .

He didn't. "Little early in the day for brandy, don't you think?" he asked with a touch of derision.

Fletcher merely chuckled. "It's never too early for brandy. Hey, Meara," he called to me offhandedly, almost derogatorily. "Would you run and get that bottle from the house? You know the one. Thanks."

Translation: *Get the hell out of here and don't come back.*

I couldn't move. In my mind all I could see was Jake's arm, antsy, his hand fingering the switchblade in his pocket. Fletcher standing close. Too close. Jake raising the knife with a jerk . . .

No! I was not running. I would not allow Fletcher to get hurt protecting me. It was not going to happen.

"I won't keep you long," Fletcher said cheerfully, guiding an unresisting Jake toward the door. "I've got to head out myself in a minute. But you know what they say about drinking alone. So, thirty-five years on the force, eh? Whereabouts?"

The men walked through the door and out into the hall, and I followed at Jake's heels, steeling myself to grab his arm should it stray anywhere near his pocket. But his voice remained casual as he answered the question, and the two proceeded toward the staircase as amiably as old chums. Only when they reached it did Jake turn his head to catch my gaze.

Just wait, his dark eyes taunted me. *Just you wait.*

Chapter

~29~

A COLD CHILL swept along my spine, but I countered it with the heat of anger. I knew what Jake was doing. He thought he was running a bluff of his own, exiting a tight spot the easy way. Why tangle with a man like Fletcher if he didn't have to? Fletcher claimed he would be leaving soon—Jake obviously believed he could get me alone again afterward. Playing nice with Fletcher now would only make Jake's previous and future encounters with me seem that much more innocuous. Whatever squawking I might do to the contrary would be my word against that of a retired police officer.

How many times had that worked for him before?

We descended the staircase and moved toward the common room, my blood simmering with every step. Jake was counting on me to keep quiet. Counting on me to be so frightened, so intimidated, that I would do whatever he said. He had battered Sheila into submission, and he assumed that he could manipulate her daughter just the same. *You owe me.*

I clenched my teeth. Jake Kozen was not nearly as smart as he thought he was. He didn't know that Fletcher had witnessed his attack, and he didn't know that the police were on the way. He thought the ball was still in his court. He thought he could control me.

He was wrong.

The second we reached the common room, I sidled around the pair and slipped into the kitchen. I located the bottle of brandy I had spied earlier in the week and returned to the men. "Here it is," I announced, holding it up with a flourish. "I brought it over from the house yesterday."

Fletcher swung around to face me. He was furious.

Get out of here! his eyes ordered, and his disapproval hit my gut like a blow. But I forced myself to look away. I knew that he wanted me safely gone, but I also knew that in an area this isolated, it could take ten minutes or more for the police to arrive. If I set out after a bottle of brandy and didn't return, Jake would get suspicious. And I would not put Fletcher at greater risk to save my own hide—no matter what he wanted.

"I'll pour for you," I continued, unable to keep the tremble from my voice. "Why don't the two of you have a seat?"

Fletcher spent another split second trying to catch my eyes, then turned back to Jake. "Yes, have a seat," he agreed, gesturing to a chair at a table in the middle of the room. Jake sat, and Fletcher promptly seated himself opposite Jake, closer to me. I breathed a sigh of relief. At least Fletcher was now out of striking range.

As I poured the brandy and delivered the glasses, Fletcher went to work, besieging Jake with a steady stream of law enforcement questions the latter was only too happy to answer. I returned to the kitchen and watched them from a distance, figuring that the sight of me would only agitate Jake—reminding him of his purpose. My pulse pounded. My eyes and ears strained for signs of the state patrol.

Minutes passed.

"It's all politics," Jake drawled, reaching for the brandy bottle and refilling his own glass. Offering him additional alcohol had been an impulse on my part, an impulse I was beginning to regret. Though the brandy was doubtless dulling his reflexes, it also seemed to be rekindling his ire. Despite Fletcher's repeated attempts to keep the conversation light, Jake had fixated on the subject of injustices in the police department, and as I stepped outside the kitchen for another surreptitious glance down the hall, Jake's dark eyes locked malevolently on mine.

"Shouldn't even have women on the force," he said coldly. "They're not worth a damn thing."

I sensed, rather than saw, Fletcher stiffen.

"Women have never caused me anything but trouble—on or off the job," Jake added caustically. "One bitch actually accused me of rape."

My stomach heaved. I was trying not to watch Jake's face as he talked; I knew that I needed a level head, not more anger. But willpower alone could not block out the loathsome voice, and red heat rose in my cheeks.

"She wanted it, of course," he continued. "They always do. But she pitched a fit afterward. Couldn't press charges because she had no case, but that didn't matter—my ass got fired anyway." He scoffed. "Now you know that's not right."

I stepped closer to Fletcher, and could see that his poker face was finally beginning to fail him. His antipathy for Jake was clearly visible in his eyes.

I felt an acute stab of fear. If Jake were to notice, if he were to realize that Fletcher knew what had happened upstairs . . .

But Jake's gaze was fixed on me.

"I could have made sergeant, even detective, about five times over," he spat, oblivious to the way Fletcher's hands now clutched his glass, his knuckles white with tension. "Instead, they had me writing tickets and sitting at a desk all day. And why?" His eyes narrowed. "Because of a bunch of stupid women, that's why. A bunch of uppity bitches who don't know they're only good for one thing."

Fletcher's chair scooted back on the floor. I shot forward, gripping his shoulders with my hands. His muscles were hard as rock. I could feel the heat rising from his skin, even through his shirt. He'd kept his cool for a long time—I couldn't let him lose it now. Jake would go straight for his knife, and this time I wouldn't be the target.

I massaged Fletcher's shoulders with haste. His muscles didn't relax, but he did cease scooting his chair back.

A car door slammed out front.

My heart skipped a beat. I cast a nervous glance at Jake, but once again, he seemed deaf to the extraneous noise. He was focused on me, watching the movement of my hands with disgust. Fletcher made a loud attempt to change the subject, successfully masking several more similar sounds.

I gave Fletcher's shoulders a final squeeze, hustled to the door, and opened it. Two state patrol cars were parked in the lot; four troopers were making their way toward me. I let out a breath. Hot tears of relief welled behind my eyes.

A pleasant-looking, freckled blond man about my own age approached and introduced himself. "You having trouble here?" he asked.

I nodded, then gave as succinct a description of the situation as I could. The blond man dispatched one trooper around the side of the inn; the other three followed me as I walked back into the common room, my pulse pounding.

Jake and Fletcher remained at their places at the table.

"Fletcher," I called, my voice quavering. "Guess who's here? Your friend Ben decided to come over—now you can congratulate him in person."

"Hey, Fletch!" the blond man said jovially, stepping up and shaking Fletcher's hand. "I hear you're having a drink in my honor."

Jake watched with bleary eyes while the lawmen filed in. I moved close to Fletcher's side, my limbs trembling, poised for Jake to explode. But the sight of other men in uniform seemed to make little impression on the career cop. As he focused calmly on the exchange between Fletcher and Ben, perhaps wondering why a Pennsylvania state trooper would be promoted to detective in West Virginia, the two other troopers stepped neatly to either side of his chair.

"So," Ben continued, looking at Fletcher. "What's up, big guy?"

As soon as the troopers were in position Fletcher flung an arm out toward me, pushing me back and away from the table. His eyes remained trained on Jake, all semblance of geniality gone. "Aggravated assault," he said, his deep voice unmistakably livid. "And be careful. He's got a knife in his pocket."

*   *   *

Jake Kozen put up a valiant struggle. But with a trooper on each arm and two more as backup, his drunken resistance was to no avail. Ben Eversen, who had actually been promoted to detective several years ago, had him subdued, cuffed, and dispatched into a patrol car within seconds.

No one got hurt.

Fletcher and I were immediately separated and questioned, then informed that we would have to go to the barracks later to give an official statement. I had no problem with that. I would give any number of statements, any number of times, to put Jake Kozen in jail where he belonged. But I was relieved when the troopers at last concluded their business and began to leave. I wanted to be with Fletcher alone.

Only Ben remained now, standing with us in the front hall.

My legs were still unsteady; my heart rate, still rapid. But Ben's news had been encouraging. Jake's drunken performance would earn him felony charges, and Fletcher's testimony, which included seeing the knife brandished in my face, promised to make them stick. This time, the snake would not wriggle away.

Preparing for his exit now, Ben offered a courteous good-bye to me, then clapped Fletcher heartily on the back. "Got to say, big guy," he praised. "You did a good job here. If you'd tried to manhandle that sleaze, things would have gotten ugly. Good thing you've got experience talking down drunks."

Ben noticed the puzzled expression on my face. "Didn't Fletch tell you? He used to moonlight as a bouncer. Darned good one, too. It helps if you're the non-violent type."

Fletcher's jaw tensed. "I did have a plan B."

Ben shook his head. "No way, buddy. We can't have you banging up that million-dollar hand. It'd wreck the local tax base." He opened the front door, but then paused and turned. "Oh, and by the way—I noticed girl stuff in two of the rooms. Is Tia back?"

Fletcher shook his head gravely. "Forget it, Ben. She'll only break your heart again."

The trooper grinned. "Love's always a gamble," he replied, stepping out. He cast Fletcher a knowing look, one that held a challenge. "But it's worth it."

Fletcher shoved his friend the rest of the way out the door. "We'll see you at the barracks. Thanks."

The door closed. Fletcher turned around and looked at me.

We were alone.

We stood silently. Awkwardly. His face was troubled. Not, this time, with the self-directed hurt of betrayal, but with empathy for me. "I'm so sorry, Meara," he said quietly. "Are you sure you're really all right?"

I managed only a nod. Though both his expression and his voice showed genuine concern, he remained standing several feet away from me. And to my still-shaky limbs, every inch seemed a mile. Why was he holding himself back? Surely he knew how much I craved an embrace. Had he not offered as much before?

"I saw the blue car from the top of the ridge," he explained, not moving. "I got here as fast as I could. I wish I could have stopped him sooner."

I shook my head, but couldn't speak.

He took a small step forward, but kept his hands at his sides. "What can I do?" he asked softly, miserably. "What do you need?"

Whether he was willing or not, I couldn't stand any more. I flew forward, clasped him about the waist, and pressed myself to him. To my delight, his arms wrapped around me immediately, flooding me with a strong warmth that soothed my raw nerves like a salve. When his grip tightened further, the feeling turned to bliss.

He exhaled loudly, and my heart leapt as he dropped a kiss on the top of my head. "So, this *is* what you need," he confirmed, his tone mild. "I'm sorry, but I wasn't sure. After what happened, I thought maybe you wouldn't want—"

I leaned back just enough to look at him. The memory of Jake's roughness wouldn't be easy to shake, but thanks to my rescuer, I had escaped more grievous injury. I knew that recovering completely from such an assault would take more than a few tender hugs. But I was not so traumatized that my heart could no longer recognize genuine affection. I still needed it. I still wanted it. "It's sweet of you to worry," I whispered back. "But don't. I really will be fine." I buried my face in his shoulder. "In fact, I'm feeling better already."

We stood that way a long time, his strength seeming to flow into me, filling the hollowness that a week's worth of uncertainty and terror had wrought in my soul. And as my sense of security began to re-form, my mind turned involuntarily to the puzzle pieces Jake's rant had thrown into the air.

"Fletcher," I asked in a whisper. "Do you think that— the night Sheila shot Jake—it happened because he had just found out I wasn't his?"

His hold on me tightened, but he didn't answer right away. When he did speak, his voice was mild. "Probably." His hand moved tenderly across my back. It was a chaste motion, but I savored it as more. "My guess is that he battered Sheila for years, and when he found out she'd been unfaithful, he flew completely off the handle. If she hadn't stopped him, he probably would have harmed you both."

I drew back slightly. "But why would Sheila confess to attempted homicide without a fight?" I questioned. "If your mother was a witness, she could have testified that Sheila only shot him to defend herself—and me. Wouldn't they want to put Jake in prison? It doesn't make sense."

"I can't answer that," he replied. "Maybe they were afraid that being a cop, Jake would somehow beat the charges. Sheila might have figured that prison was the safest place for her to be, and that you would be better off adopted—through a closed system where even Jake couldn't find you."

I mulled over his words, and a wave of grief washed over me. I could see again the look in Sheila's eyes as she lay in her hospital bed, dying. *I always loved you,* she had said. Deep in my heart, I had wanted to believe her. But I couldn't. Not when she had lied to me. Not when she had completely fabricated her entire history that day at the coffee shop.

Only now, I understood. Sheila had wanted to meet me, but she hadn't wanted me to know the grim truth about my past. Ever. Her own life was nothing but a source of embarrassment to her, and of guilt. A disastrous marriage, infidelity, a criminal record, terminated parental rights. She had to wonder if I would ever be able to understand. She had to have feared that I would never forgive her.

But more importantly, she must have still been determined to keep me away from Jake. He was the birth father of record, and she knew that if I was persistent, I would eventually find him—or vice versa. So she signed up on the registry, hoping to meet with me. She allowed herself a few final, pleasantly uninformed minutes of bonding with her only daughter. Then she told me a story that she hoped would dissuade me from ever trying to find out more—either about her or my birth father. And then she said good-bye.

My eyes welled up with tears.

"Perhaps it would be best to accept what you know and leave it at that," Fletcher said, giving me a gentle squeeze that signified the hug was ending.

He made an attempt to detach himself, but—after a split second's internal debate—I decided to hold on. I was enjoying his embrace immensely, and I wasn't ready to give it up yet.

The tears in my eyes escaped to my cheeks, but surprisingly, there were no more behind them. Jake's admissions, along with my newfound understanding of Sheila, had lifted a huge burden from my heart. And despite the blow Jake's attack had rendered on my psyche, I felt suddenly free—nearly exuberant. My birth mother wasn't perfect, but she had loved me. Truly loved me. Jake Kozen was no relation whatsoever. What else mattered?

I had an answer to that.

"I can't imagine how I could have gotten through these last two weeks without you and Tia," I told Fletcher sincerely, my head still against his shoulder. "You've been so good to me. Thank you."

He made another attempt to detach himself, and this time I let him succeed. "You're welcome," he said. "But it's nothing. I'm just glad you don't have to be afraid of Jake anymore."

He stepped away from me. I studied him as he stood

there, tense, guarded. He was smiling, and his expression was still friendly. But he hadn't given in yet. He hadn't budged. I could envision quite plainly the wheels turning in his head—the fighting, the resolve. There was nothing between us, he was assuring himself. He had merely been comforting a damsel in distress. He didn't want anything more. He could keep things platonic. *No problem.*

My jaws clenched. If I had vowed patience and understanding, I was officially reneging. I had had enough of his nonsense, and I was going to end it. Now.

"It's no fun being afraid," I said pointedly. "It's much more fun to take a risk now and then. That's what life is all about, don't you think?"

A look of suspicion, laced with no small amount of dread, crossed his features. He took another step back, colliding inadvertently with the newel post. "I suppose."

I smiled and scowled at the same time. I was good at that. "Fletcher Carlisle!" I chastised, using what I presumed, from Estelle's earlier rant, was his middle name. "You are unbelievable. You have no qualms about facing a half-crazed, drunken lunatic with a knife, but when it comes to a five-foot four-inch grade school teacher, you're scared to death!"

He stiffened. "What are you talking about?"

"You heard me," I continued, taking a step closer. I straightened my back, partly because I was feeling wonderfully good about myself again, and partly because I knew what effect it would have on the scoop-necked shirt. "You're afraid of me. You know it and I know it. And we both know why. But I'm telling you right now, I am *not* Isabella. And I'm not Amanda Kozen, either. I'm Meara Kathleen O'Rourke, daughter of Colleen and Patrick O'Rourke, who raised me to be an honest, loving, and loyal person—and considering their late start, did a darn good job of it."

He stood motionless, watching me as warily as if he were an animal in a trap. "Don't be ridiculous, Meara. I'm not *afraid* of you."

"You are too. You want to be even more afraid? Listen to this. I could identify any tree, bird, or animal track on this place. My favorite book in kindergarten was *The Lorax*. I contribute to the Western Pennsylvania Conservancy. My favorite place to sleep is under the stars, and my favorite thing to bake—and eat—is pie. You can thank your mother for that one; I think she must have imprinted me early on."

He said nothing, but alarm mounted in his eyes as I talked, and the words "sleeping under the stars" sparked sheer panic. I resisted the urge to scream.

"Just admit it," I cajoled. "You're afraid of me because you're afraid of falling in love again. You're afraid of getting hurt. I don't blame you—I understand. But you have to get over it sometime. You can't spend the rest of your life living in some emotional cocoon."

He bristled. "Thank you for your concern," he said with an intentional coolness, reminiscent of our first meetings. "But I don't need the two-bit psychoanalysis. I have a sister for that."

I ignored his tone completely. "Well," I answered with cheer, "she's right, too, you know."

He growled.

I smiled at him.

"Look," he said, measuring his words. "You're a wonderful person, and I enjoy your company. You know that. But I am not afraid of you. I'm just not interested, that's all. I consider you a friend."

He tried to look at me while he was talking—he really did. But he couldn't make it past the third sentence. His gray-green eyes flooded with guilt, then transferred their gaze to the doorknob. He wasn't a bad actor. But I wasn't an idiot.

"Oh, you are *so* in denial," I said with a chuckle. "You want to prove you don't have feelings for me? Fine. I'm game."

He threw me an apprehensive look.

"Kiss me," I baited. "Purely a physical thing—no feeling, no depth. Just a quick peck on the lips, but no more. Superficial, meaningless. Go ahead."

His face reddened. "No."

"Why not?"

"Because," he responded, pausing a second to complete the thought, "because I'm not attracted to you."

I laughed out loud. *"Right."*

I closed the distance between us.

He didn't move.

"I know you want to kiss me," I said, leaning close. My voice dropped to a whisper. "You want to do a whole lot more than that."

He growled low in his throat, but his eyes were definitely smiling at me now. "You're impossible," he muttered.

"And you," I responded, putting my hands around his neck, "are a chicken."

His eyes narrowed. "So this is your plan to bring me down? Some childish dare?"

I smiled and fell against him. *"Bwock. Bwock."*

His resolve lasted all of two seconds. His arms swept me up in one vehement motion, pulling me tight against him as he leaned down and pressed his lips to mine. His kiss came with a passion stronger than any I had ever experienced, and his ardor, combined with his physical strength, could easily have been overpowering. Yet every aspect of his touch showed a loving, conscious tenderness. His feelings for me were evident in every movement of his soft lips, every caress of his callused hands on my back, and I drank in his attention as if I were starving—returning his enthusiasm in kind; daring, even, to clamor for more.

But I didn't get it. When he seemed to feel I had been thoroughly kissed, he set me away from him with a thump. "There," he said breathlessly. "I suppose I failed the test."

Being separated so abruptly was agony. But I smiled coyly back at him. "Hmm," I murmured, considering. "No. I'm afraid that was only a D minus. You'd better try again."

He narrowed his eyes playfully and growled at me again. A second later, my feet left the floor.

This time, he failed with flying colors.

Chapter

~30~

"YOU WOULDN'T THINK I'd have to say this in a practically deserted inn," Tia proclaimed with mock irritation as she burst into the hall through the front door, "but for God's sake, *get a room!*"

She brushed roughly past us, her eyes rolling. "Anyone in the parking lot can see right through that window—I've been cooling my heels for five minutes waiting for one of you to come up for air. Sheesh! What are you, professional divers?"

I giggled under my breath and straightened, but Fletcher was reluctant to release me. "Go away, Tia," he ordered gruffly.

"Sorry, brother dear, but I live here, too," she retorted, making her way down the hall and tossing her purse on the counter. "Sort of, anyway."

Reluctantly, I extracted myself from his grasp. I threaded my fingers through his and drew us both into the common room. My heart was beating wildly, and I wanted nothing more than to follow Tia's advice. But there would be plenty of time.

Tia looked us over with a devious sparkle in her eyes. "You owe me money," she informed her brother.

"Oh?" he replied without interest.

"I told you you wouldn't last a year," she said smartly. "Now pay up."

He flashed a wicked grin. "Oh, no, you didn't. You said I wouldn't last six months."

Tia's smirk faded.

"So in fact," he continued, "you owe *me* money. Thanks for the reminder."

She humphed. "Yes, well. About that—"

"Let me guess. The I.O.U.'s in the mail."

She smiled innocently. "We'll negotiate later. Right now, I'd like for both of you to sit down. There are some things I need to tell you."

A pregnant pause followed, and as I looked into Tia's flustered and excited face, I felt a strong urge to flee. She had found out something—something more about the past. And whatever it was, I wanted nothing to do with it. I was happy now, and I wanted to stay that way.

"No!" I protested. The sharpness of my tone surprised me, and I lowered my voice. "No, Tia. Please. You can tell Fletcher whatever it is, but I'm done. All right?"

Fletcher stepped behind me and pulled me to him, crossing his arms over me protectively. "Jake Kozen was here," he explained. "He's safely behind bars now, but it's been a rough morning."

Tia paled. Her eyes filled with dismay. "Oh, Meara," she said in a whisper. "I'm so sorry. I had no idea. Are you all right?"

I nodded.

"Then I absolutely have to tell you," she insisted. "You

don't have to worry about that sonuvabitch anymore. No matter what he says, he is *not* your birth father."

My eyes widened. "He admitted that. But how did you know?"

She studied me for a moment, seeming to debate within herself. "I know you've been hit with a lot lately, Meara," she said delicately. "We all have. But I've been able to fill in most of the missing pieces about what went on between my parents and your birth mother, and I really think the healthiest thing would be for the three of us to just get it out in the open and deal with it—once and for all. So please, will you hear me out?"

I wavered. I was afraid. Afraid that picking apart any more of the unknown could only bring me down from the ethereal plane I had so miraculously just landed on. I didn't want to think about my past anymore. What I wanted was to be alone with Fletcher—reveling in the present.

I opened my mouth to say so, but nothing came out. Tia's dark, caring eyes bored into mine, begging. *Please trust me*, they said. *I wouldn't do this if it weren't important. To all of us.*

My innate desire to please surged on strong, and I let out my breath with a sigh. "All right," I answered.

I sank onto one of the couches by the fireplace, letting the steam from a hot cup of tea rise onto my nose and chin. Fletcher had insisted that Tia wasn't telling me anything until we had all had a drink and something to eat, but it was obvious that his primary intent was to get his sister aside long enough for him to explain what had happened with Jake. I didn't mind the delay—he was correct in assuming that I didn't feel much like telling her myself.

He was standing only ten feet away now, clearing off the meager spread of fruit and crackers we had all just silently indulged in. He had been staying close, watching me with worried eyes. But close wasn't close enough—not now that I'd had a taste of his unfettered affection. Admiring him from a distance was torture.

I watched him as he moved toward me, and the look in my eyes seemed to please him. He dropped onto the couch beside me, enveloped me with an arm, and kissed me softly on the temple. Tia sat down across from us, her expression troubled. She had responded to the tale of Jake's attack with nothing less than horror, but hearing it had not dissuaded her from her mission of enlightening me. If anything, it seemed to have galvanized her.

I took a breath and sat up straighter. Tia had my best interests at heart, I did believe that. But I wanted this over with. "So go ahead," I prompted, resolute. "You went to see the private investigator. Why did your father hire him? Did it have something to do with Sheila?"

Tia exhaled slowly. "I think we should start at the beginning." She looked at her brother. "I talked to Grandma this morning. She said to tell you hello."

Fletcher's eyebrows rose. "You thought Grandma would know something about Meara?"

"No. I realized that they had moved to Altoona before Meara would have come here. But I did think Grandma might remember something about Sheila." She turned her attention back to me. "When we realized you weren't here as a foster child, we all assumed that Mom must have taken you in because she and Sheila were friends. But the more I thought about that, the less sense it made."

My limbs went cold. *No.* One of the things that had made me happiest, amid all the gloom of the past, was thinking that Rosemary and Mitchell had been my birth mother's friends. They had to be. "I really don't think I want to hear this, Tia," I said with apprehension. "Can't I just—"

"It's all right, Meara," she broke in gently, sitting forward. "I promise. Once you see everything in perspective, I'm sure you'll be fine with it. Just bear with me."

I took in a deep breath. Then I nodded.

She turned to her brother. "It was the yearbook that bothered me. I just couldn't see Mom being chummy with a beauty queen—you know how cynical she always was about the whole Maple Queen thing. And then there were the pictures, or lack thereof. Sheila was a pretty senior girl in a very small class—how could she *accidentally* get left out of all the candid shots?"

Fletcher sighed. "Mom was editor of the yearbook."

"Exactly," Tia agreed. "And in the perfect position to make sure a classmate she *didn't* care for got omitted. Except for the Maple Queen coverage, of course. Even the editor in chief couldn't suppress news that big."

I looked from one sibling to the other, a new fear eroding my insides. "But what would your mother have had against Sheila?" I asked. I knew I sounded as insecure as a child, but I couldn't help it. My birth mother had been a good person—I needed to believe that.

Tia's eyes held mine. I looked in their sympathetic depths, and realized she understood. "It wasn't that Sheila did anything wrong," she said softly, smiling a little. "But a feud between her and my mother was inevitable, under the circumstances."

She turned back to her brother. "I asked Grandma if she could remember Dad ever being friends with one of the Maple Queens. That's all I told her. Right away, she chuckled to herself and said yes—that a Turkeyfoot girl he used to date had been Maple Queen. She thought her name was Shelly."

Fletcher blinked. "But I thought Mom and Dad—"

Tia waved a hand dismissively. "Yes, well, we were a little naive about that. Mom and Dad might have been childhood sweethearts, but they weren't together every second. According to Grandma, they broke up and got together again pretty frequently when they were young."

"So," I broke in, feeling better, "your mother was jealous of Sheila because she and your father dated."

Tia nodded. "Actually, it was a bit more involved than that. Grandma thought Dad was really getting serious about 'Shelly'—they were together through most of their senior year. But it turns out she broke his heart. Sheila skipped town right after graduation—she wanted to be an actress so badly she left her mother and ran off to New York by herself, even though she was only eighteen. Mom and Dad got back together again, as per their pattern, and the rest is history."

"But Sheila came back," I pointed out. "And then they all became friends?"

Tia didn't answer, but looked at me with an expression that indicated there was considerably more I didn't know. "I can't say Mom and Sheila were ever buddies," she explained. "But Sheila and Dad did stay friends, even after he got married. That's why, when Sheila started having problems with Jake, she brought you to him for help—not Mom."

I digested the thought. Rosemary had kept me here because Mitchell had asked her to. And she must have been kind to me, despite her feelings about my birth mother. If she hadn't, my flashes of memory from the white house wouldn't all be so wonderfully pleasant.

"So after Mom died," Fletcher stated, "Dad took up with Sheila again." His voice had become strained, and I could feel that his muscles were tensing again. "I suppose they had been keeping in touch."

"No," I said quickly, worried about what Fletcher might be thinking. "The woman who'd been in prison with Sheila said she never had any visitors. At least not in the five years she knew her."

Tia nodded in agreement. "Dad and Sheila had nothing to do with each other after the night she shot Jake, Fletch. Up until this year, Dad had no idea where Sheila even was. That's why he hired the private investigator. To find her."

He stared at his sister pensively a moment, then pulled his arm from around my shoulders and sat up. "But that doesn't sound like Dad at all. If Sheila was any kind of friend to him, he wouldn't have just washed his hands of her. He had to understand why she shot Jake."

Tia looked uncomfortable. "That's just it, Fletch. He didn't understand. Sheila, like many battered women, went out of her way to hide the fact that she was being abused. I don't know what she told Dad to convince him to let Meara live with us, but he had no idea Jake was violent. Mom didn't either. She figured out everything, of course, the night of the shooting, but she didn't tell Dad. She told him the same story she told the judge—that Sheila had shot her husband without provocation, in cold blood."

Fletcher's eyes widened. He rose with a jerk.

"Fletch," Tia said sternly, rising with him. "Please sit down. Let me finish."

"How could she do that?" he protested, his deep voice angry. "She was so jealous of a high school crush that she let Dad think his ex was a trigger-happy maniac? Why couldn't she trust him with the truth?"

"Fletch," Tia said again, her tone even firmer. "Don't judge Mom. *Let me finish.*"

The siblings exchanged a glare. Fletcher exhaled, then dropped back down beside me. Tia watched him another moment, then sat herself. "After I talked to Grandma, I went to see the private investigator at his office. I was hoping he would confirm for me that Dad had hired him to find Sheila. He wouldn't tell me a thing when I first asked him—he said his work was one hundred percent confidential. But after I convinced him that Dad had passed away, as had Sheila, and that they had left their children with a long list of thorny unanswered questions, he seemed to take pity on me." She cleared her throat. "And I suppose the outrageous sum of money I offered him didn't hurt either."

She cast a sheepish glance at her brother. "By the way, Fletch—"

He grumbled. "Fine, fine, I'll cover it. What else did the man say?"

She blew out a breath. "He had a tremendous amount to say, because Dad being Dad, he talked the poor man's ear off every time they met—never mind that he was paying by the hour. As you probably figured out from the letter, Mom didn't tell Dad about any of this until right before she died, and her confession really threw him for a loop. Apparently, he felt there was no one else he could talk to."

"What do you mean?" Fletcher asked. "He had us, didn't he?"

Tia's expression saddened. "Not really. I'm sure you and I were the last people he thought he could face."

Fletcher's brow creased.

Tia sighed. "Fletch," she began heavily, "I know that the letter Mom wrote made it sound as though she'd been unfaithful. But that wasn't the case. She was talking about Dad. She was talking about something that happened ages ago, when they were still teenagers, just a couple months after they got married."

Fletcher paled.

My heart thumped in my chest. "No," I whispered, horrified. "Not Sheila."

"Yes," Tia answered, seeming to make an effort not to sound ashamed. She cast a concerned glance at her brother, but he hadn't moved.

"They were only eighteen years old," she repeated firmly. "And we need to remember that. Furthermore, both of them were in very difficult situations at the time. Sheila had come back from New York disillusioned and penniless, only to find her mother dying of cancer. She had no other family, and she and her mother had moved around so much when she was growing up that she had few friends. She was devastated—desperate for solace. And Dad was the closest thing to a real friend she'd ever had."

Fletcher rose. I watched his feet walk away. Tia looked up at him worriedly.

"Fletch," she said, her voice softer. "I'm not saying that what Dad did was right, but could you at least try to understand what he was going through? No matter what our parents told us, their marriage started out horribly. You know what a perfectionist Mom was. You also know that she was a control freak—no one any less easygoing than Dad could possibly have tolerated her. Getting married so young was her idea—she pressured him into it, but then once she had him, she felt trapped. So she pushed him away on purpose, half hoping he would ask for a divorce. When Dad ran into Sheila, he and Mom were living at opposite ends of the house."

Fletcher was somewhere behind me, and I felt his absence at my side like a vacuum. I wanted to go to him, but I couldn't seem to move.

"But they worked through it," Tia emphasized. "Dad admitted everything; he regretted it deeply. For Mom, the shock of thinking she might lose Dad to someone else made her see how much she really did love him. She took responsibility for her own immature actions, and they both committed themselves to making the marriage work. They matured, their marriage matured, they became parents, and life went on."

She paused. I found the strength to turn around in my seat, to look for Fletcher, and was surprised to find him standing behind me, his eyes mirroring the same sympathetic apprehension that were in my own. I smiled with relief. He was all right. He might be upset about his father—but at the moment, incredibly, he seemed more worried about me.

He returned my smile, and as I leaned back on the couch, he laid his hands supportively on my shoulders.

Tia watched us silently, and I perceived that she, too, was surprised by the mildness of Fletcher's reaction. For a moment her eyes seemed moist, but then she cleared her throat and continued.

"I suspected that there might be something between Dad and Sheila because of something Mom told me once—something about working through disappointments. So I asked Grandma about it this morning, and God bless her, she was honest with me. She told me the story I just told you, except that when Dad told her about it ages ago, he didn't mention who the other woman was."

She blew out a breath. "But he did tell the P.I. about it. Apparently, when on the clock, James P. is one sympathetic listener."

I took a quick inventory of my waffling feelings. I wasn't happy about what had happened between Mitchell and Sheila, but if Tia and Fletcher could accept it without resentment or shame, so should I. Sheila had been a good person, and so had Mitchell. They had been young, and they had made a mistake. But they had stayed friends. That meant something.

"So your mother took me in," I said, the thought just occurring, "even though it meant she was doing a favor for the woman her husband had once had an affair with?"

Tia smiled. "Yes, she did. And if you knew Mom, that wouldn't surprise you. She would never blame a child for a parent's actions—she helped children with some of the most wretched parents imaginable. But her keeping you here was a testament to how much she loved Dad, and to the fact that she had forgiven him." Her face darkened. "Still, she was only human. And her actions after the shooting make plain how threatened she still felt by Sheila—even years afterward."

Fletcher exhaled. "So that's why she let Dad think the worst," he surmised. "She wanted Sheila out of their lives—preferably for good."

Tia nodded. "You have to understand, Fletch. Mom never really got over the fact that she couldn't have biological children. I've always thought that her wanting so many children around, all the time, was a way of over-compensating. But Sheila could and did have children, and the fact that she was blessed with a little girl as adorable as Meara had to hurt Mom. She had to always feel inferior, in the back of her mind, not only because Sheila was beautiful, but because she was capable of giving a man something Mom never could—a biological child."

I sighed softly. I couldn't help it. I knew that none of the problems Tia was describing were my fault. But I still felt bad for them. For all of them.

Fletcher gave my shoulders a soft squeeze. The gesture was intended for comfort, but Jake's assault had left me so tender I winced. Fletcher lifted his hands immediately, realizing his mistake. But my own hands flew up and caught them. Soreness or no, his touch was soothing to me, and I wanted him to know that. I kissed him on the wrist and held his hands in mine.

"Anyway, Meara," Tia continued, attempting to lighten her tone a little. "You should know that Dad told the P.I. that he absolutely adored you. He was horrified by what he thought Sheila had done, but when he found out that Jake had relinquished his rights too, he wanted very much to adopt you. My mother, of course, refused. She had good reason, actually, because she knew at that point exactly what Jake was capable of, and she was afraid that if you were living here, he might come back and try to hurt you again. But I think that, in her heart, she was also worried that she could never look at you without seeing Sheila—that she could never love you unconditionally. And she believed that you deserved better.

"So she told Dad no. And with him already feeling

guilty about his history with Sheila, he didn't feel he could press the issue."

She took a breath. "Mom felt horrible about keeping the truth from Dad. It weighed on her the rest of her life. But still, she was too insecure to face the fallout, and the more time that passed, the more difficult she feared it would be for him to forgive her. She only found the strength at the end."

Fletcher continued to hold my hands, caressing my knuckles gently with his thumbs. "So, after she died, Dad was anxious to find Sheila."

"Yes," Tia said quickly, "but not to rekindle some ancient romance. He just wanted to apologize to her. To say he was sorry for abandoning her at the lowest point in her life—to try and explain what had happened. Apparently, he had promised Sheila before the shooting that he would always watch out for her daughter. It haunted him that he had let Meara go—that he had no idea what became of her."

She looked at me. "It turned out that finding Sheila was no easy task for McElron. It took him months. She was making it hard on purpose, because she was still afraid of Jake. She kept track of him constantly; she knew he was still in the area and, until recently, was still a cop. Apparently, he wrote her a few 'anonymous' letters when she first went to prison, describing what he would do to her when she got out. Whether he ever made any real effort to find her, or had actually long since forgotten her, I don't know. But she wasn't taking any chances. The P.I. had a tough time convincing her who his real client was, and even then, he had a tough time convincing her to meet with Dad herself."

She took a breath. "Meara, I know what happened the

night Sheila shot Jake—or at least what the P.I. knew about it, from what Dad and Sheila told him. It's all second-and thirdhand, of course, but it does make sense, if you want to hear it."

Fletcher walked around the couch and sat down beside me again, pulling me to him. "You don't have to hear any more, you know," he said quietly. "It's up to you."

I looked into his gray-green eyes, so caring, so sincere, and the nearness of him bolstered me. Whatever blasts from the past were still to come, I knew that afterward, he would still be here. Tia would still be here. And I would still be me.

"It's all right," I answered. "Let's hear it."

Chapter

~31~

TIA TOOK A breath. "Well, as you're already aware, Jake was not your birth father. But up until the day of the shooting, he thought that he was. And according to Sheila, so did she.

"But Jake found out, quite by accident apparently, that your blood types didn't match. Sheila suspected something was up when he called her and started coolly asking questions about her and your blood types—supposedly for some insurance forms. By the time he had finished ferreting out the truth, however, she had already called Mom and told her to pack up your things immediately—that she was leaving and taking you with her. But Jake—who had no idea where you even were most of the time, believing that Sheila kept leaving you with some mythical aunt—arrived home just in time to follow her car.

"The inn was empty that night, like it often was midweek in the winter. And since it was late already when Sheila called, Mom brought you here and put you to bed upstairs while she waited for Sheila to arrive. Not understanding that Jake was dangerous, she was furious with Sheila—thinking she was just some flighty, incompetent mother who needed a good talking to. When Sheila arrived packing her husband's gun and insisting on taking you immediately, Mom went ballistic. When Jake arrived, all hell broke loose.

"He started screaming at Sheila, you woke up and started crying, and Mom headed up the stairs to calm you down. Then Jake told Sheila that he was going to take the both of you home—and that she and her bastard daughter were going to pay. Sheila aimed the gun at him and told him to leave. But when he advanced on her anyway, she shot him.

"The bullet hit him in the side. He wasn't critically injured, but it did stop him from climbing the stairs to get you. He just sank to the floor and started shouting about how Sheila was going to jail. That he would tell everyone she was crazy and they would believe him, that it was his word against hers—there were no witnesses.

"Unfortunately, he was right—Mom didn't see what happened, and she hadn't overheard any specific threats. What she did know about the situation to that point could actually have been damaging to Sheila's case, because Sheila had never admitted any abuse to her, and she knew that it was Sheila, and not Jake, who had brought the weapon to the inn.

"Jake then threatened both women—telling them that if he got any grief from the law, that someday, somehow, you would simply 'disappear.'

"That's when Sheila got her idea. She wanted you away from Jake, permanently. And she figured she had two ways to do it. She could tell the truth about why she had shot him and try to get you away by explaining that he was dangerous and insisting he wasn't your biological father anyway. But she knew how risky that was. She had crossed Jake in spades; her next encounter with him might very well be her last. And if the law did take his side over hers, neither she nor the Blacks would have a prayer of keeping you safe from the man who was legally your father.

"But she did have another option. She could confess to having shot him without cause, ensuring that she would be safe from him in the only place he couldn't follow her—a women's prison. She knew she would lose the right to raise you herself, but if it was the only way to ensure that you, too, were safe from Jake, then it was a sacrifice she was willing to make. So she offered to Jake that she would take the rap for the shooting and never tell anyone of his abuse or his threats to you, *if* he would agree to terminate his parental rights—allowing you to be safely—and anonymously—adopted."

I thought of my parents, and tears swelled. Whatever mistakes Sheila might have made in her lifetime, the decision to give me up was not one of them. My adoptive parents had loved me without reservation. They had given me safety, security, and stability. They had given me everything Sheila could have hoped for.

A tear escaped and rolled down my right cheek. In the midst of turmoil, under the threat of violence, and in the face of a long prison term, Sheila had managed to make one incredibly selfless decision. She had let me go.

"At first, Jake just laughed at her," Tia continued. "But then Mom, who finally now had a grasp of the situation, stepped in. She told Jake in no uncertain terms that if he did not terminate his rights to you, she would be perfectly willing to perjure herself on the stand and claim that she had witnessed everything—that Jake had threatened to kill both you and Sheila, and that Sheila had had no choice but to shoot him. That got Jake's attention. He was cocky, but he wasn't stupid; he knew there was a significant chance he would run into trouble with a credible eyewitness testimony against him. He was livid, but in the end he realized that the only thing he had to lose by cooperating was the custody of a child that wasn't his anyway. So he agreed. Sheila pled guilty, and Mom backed up Jake's story about the couple arguing over finances. But if Jake hadn't kept up his end of the bargain, Mom was prepared to recant and give the whole truth."

I let out a long, slow breath. My brain seemed numb. I tried to imagine my four-year-old self at the center of such turbulence, but I couldn't. How could so many horrible, hurtful things have happened—to and around *me*—when I grew up so blissfully oblivious? It was as if my whole life as I knew it had never existed. As if it were some sort of fantasy.

I began to tremble again.

Tia took my hands, making me look her in the eyes.

"Don't you *dare* start feeling guilty about any of this," she ordered. "You had absolutely no control over anything. The adults involved were adults—they were entirely responsible for their own actions. Nothing that came out of this is your fault."

"Still," I said weakly. "It was my coming back here that stirred all this up. You would have been better off thinking your father had just met Sheila—"

"Meara," Fletcher interrupted, his voice gentle but firm. "Would you quit worrying about Tia and me? For heaven's sake, we're not going to fall apart over something that happened between our parents ages ago."

His sister looked up at him then, seeming a little surprised herself.

He caught it. "All right," he confessed. "I can't say I'm thrilled about all their choices, but I do realize they weren't perfect. In fact, the more I think about it, the more in character all this seems.

"The important thing," he continued, his eyes meeting mine again, "is your peace of mind, Meara. Are you all right with this?"

I took another breath. I wasn't sure what he wanted me to say. All I could feel was the same vague, nagging guilt. I felt like I should leave.

When I didn't answer, Tia spoke. "Meara," she said softly. "When the P.I. finally convinced Sheila to meet with Dad face-to-face, one of the first things he did was offer to pay the P.I. to find you. When Sheila said that you had already met, and that you were alive and well and had grown up happy, he was ecstatic. She also told him that she didn't need the P.I. because since she'd learned your adopted name she had always kept tabs on you."

A surge of joy swelled within me, dampening some of my guilt. Mitchell *had* cared about me. My hair hadn't frightened him off forever. He had thought about me all those years, as had Sheila. She had even kept track of where I was.

"When they met again," Tia continued, "something happened that neither of them expected. They reconnected. There was something real between them, something that even a quarter century of separation and misunderstanding hadn't completely dissolved. It could have been friendship, but under the circumstances, it turned to love again."

Her lips curved into a smile. "And if Dad weren't so organizationally challenged, that might be all we'd know now. But of course, he kept forgetting to pay the P.I.'s final bill. McElron called to bug him about it just a month ago, and Dad gave him another earful. He announced that he and Sheila were going to get married."

She studied her brother's face. "According to the P.I., Dad sounded extremely happy about it."

I cast a wary glance at Fletcher myself.

"What?" he protested. His eyes smiled, and both Tia and I breathed out with relief. He really was all right.

Tia grinned back at him. "They were keeping their relationship a secret for several reasons. Sheila had kept a low profile for years because she was still very much afraid of Jake. But also, like we thought, she couldn't bear to have Dad's friends and family know that she had been convicted of shooting her first husband. Plus, Dad was still very ashamed of the infidelity. He wanted to tell us about Sheila, and to explain everything that had happened with Meara. But he knew that he would have trouble explaining Mom's actions without admitting that he had been unfaithful to her, and he was very worried about how we would take that."

Fletcher narrowed his eyes at his sister. "Liar. He was worried about how *I* would take it."

Tia looked at him with fondness. "You said it. I didn't."

They exchanged a grin.

"Anyway," she continued, "the P.I. said Sheila was thinking of having her first name legally changed, that they were thinking of passing the property on to Fletch and moving to another state—anything to escape their past. Apparently, they had lots of ideas, but neither of them was the decisive type."

She looked at me. "But there was one thing they had decided on, according to the P.I. As soon as they got back from their honeymoon, Meara, they were going to contact you."

My heart skipped. "Me?"

She nodded. "Dad convinced Sheila that the best thing for you would be the truth. He was certain that if you were as intelligent and grounded as Sheila said you were, that you would believe your birth mother's version of the story and understand her decisions. He promised to be there, too, to back her up.

"He was concerned that if you ever did proceed with a search for more information, you would be devastated to discover Sheila's criminal record without explanation, and would then almost certainly wind up walking right into Jake's clutches, assuming that he was your birth father."

"Smart man," Fletcher noted.

My feet felt suddenly antsy. I stood up. It wasn't bad news, I told myself. Not really. I was sorry that my birth mother had once been the source of such angst in the Blacks' marriage. But I was no more responsible for her actions than Tia and Fletcher were for Mitchell's, and they understood that.

I walked a few paces away and looked back at them.

"Meara?" Fletcher asked cautiously, rising. "Are you all right?"

A queer fluttering seemed to have attacked my stomach, but it wasn't unpleasant. In fact, it was a lightening. A final lifting of the mental burden I'd been laboring under since the day I received the call from the hospital. No—even before that.

I had spent most of my life living in fear of the unknown. I feared that I had grown up without love, and that those lost years, somehow, had damaged me. It wasn't about finding a blood relative—not really. That desire had been born primarily of loneliness. What I had really wanted, and needed, was a better understanding of myself. Of what had made me the person I was.

Reflecting on everything I knew now, I felt, at last, oddly settled. Mitchell and Rosemary had had a lasting, loving relationship that had not only succeeded in raising two terrific kids, but had nurtured countless others, including me. Mitchell and Sheila had loved each other too, in their own way, and they had been happy at the end. The fact that, if they had lived, they would have found me again meant more than I could say. It was all right. Everything was all right.

A realization struck me, and my eyes widened. "Fletcher," I said brightly. "I figured it out!"

He raised his eyebrows. "Figured what out?"

"What Sheila said! She was having such a difficult time talking—I misunderstood her. She was trying to explain to me about the shooting. She said that she had always loved me. Then what she was trying to say was, 'I was protecting you. Rosemary *lied*. Stay *away from Jake Kozen*.'"

He walked to my side. "That makes sense. I bet you're right."

Tia rose and joined us.

"I feel so much better now," I explained to both of them. "Thank you. I know where I spent the first four years of my life, and why. And I know that at least some of that time, I was happy."

The siblings looked at each other. Fletcher stepped forward and took my hand. "Meara, Tia and I have known a lot of kids who grew up in bad situations. Abused, neglected, unloved. And we can promise you,

you don't have those kinds of scars. I don't know how Sheila managed it, honestly, but she must have shielded you from Jake somehow, all along. She and my parents must have worked together to make sure you always felt loved—and secure. Because you wouldn't be who you are today if they hadn't."

I looked at them both, and my heart felt near to bursting. "Are you two really okay with this?" I asked in a brief moment of panic. "Considering what happened? Is my being here going to bother you? Because if it is, I can just go—"

They stared back at me for a second, flabbergasted. Then to my surprise, Fletcher laughed out loud. "You're unbelievable," he said, stepping close and putting his arms around me. "Frankly, I'm proud of the way my father handled things, considering. And my mother too." He raised a hand to my hair and pushed a lock gently back over my shoulder, his eyes twinkling. "God knows I'm glad she refused to adopt you."

I chuckled, and he leaned in and kissed me. It was a soft, teasing kiss, and the pull I felt toward him was irresistible. I moved closer, but it wasn't close enough. Not nearly close enough. I wanted him. I wanted to feel—

Tia cleared her throat. Loudly. "Um . . . I'm still in the room here, guys."

I started, and Fletcher came up for air. "So what do you want?" he grumbled. "A medal?"

"No!" she protested, whacking him on the shoulder. "I want to give my childhood playmate and newfound friend a hug for myself. Now let go of her before I tell her that nickname of yours."

He released me with a grumble, and Tia hugged me

tight. "I'm glad you're feeling better about everything, Meara," she said over my shoulder. "Very glad."

We pulled back, and I saw that the jocular spark in her eyes was back full force, despite the wetness around her lids. "Now," she said brightly. "I know you two will be really crushed to hear this, but you'll have to manage without me for a while, because I'm starving to death, and I have a craving for buffalo wings. And when I want buffalo wings, no one gets in my way." She grinned at me. "And to think that Dad wanted to adopt you." She picked up her purse from the counter and headed toward the front door, talking to herself—at a very high volume—as she went.

"It's a shame really, because I would have liked a sister. Can't think of how I could acquire any other family members now, though. I mean, what kind of sister might a woman look forward to at my age? I'm pretty sure I can't think of any other kind of sister—"

"Good-bye, Tia," Fletcher called firmly. "Don't forget to lock the door."

We heard an overblown sigh. Then the door closed with a click.

I threw my arms around his neck and held him. So much unexpected joy was inside me, it seemed as though the feeling couldn't possibly hold up, couldn't possibly be legitimate. We would all continue to feel sorrow over Sheila's and Mitchell's deaths, but the questions, the hovering blackness, seemed finally to have been vanquished—both for me, and for Fletcher.

I had always considered myself lucky to have been adopted by two people as wonderful as the O'Rourkes. Now I knew that I was lucky enough to have a loving birth mother, too. And for that I was truly thankful.

A thought assaulted my brain, and my hold on Fletcher slackened.

"What is it?" he said, noticing.

I drew back enough to look at him. "I just realized," I said weakly. "I have no idea who my real birth father was."

His eyes flickered with alarm. "No," he said softly. "I don't suppose you do."

I stiffened. I had been so happy to learn that Jake Kozen was no relation, I had given no thought whatsoever to an alternative.

"Meara," Fletcher said pointedly, catching my eyes. "I'm not sure if you're aware of this, but I don't know who my own birth father was. Tia found out, but all she told me was that he wasn't from the area. And I only asked her that," he said with a sly smile, "because I wanted to make sure the local girls were fair game. I don't know anything else about him. And the truth is—I really don't give a damn."

I looked into his light, beautiful eyes, and understood. It wasn't a question of biology anymore. Not for me. I had wanted to know how I came into the world, how I spent my early years, and why I was given up. I knew that now. I also knew that my birth mother had loved me, and that she had made an incredible sacrifice to keep me safe and whole.

The man who had gotten her pregnant wasn't part of that story. He hadn't known me, hadn't raised me, hadn't been there for Sheila, or for me, when we so desperately needed help. True, he might not have been told he had a child, but he had to have known that pregnancy was a possibility. A possibility he had chosen not to follow up on.

Did I really even care who he was?

I envisioned Sheila as a twenty-year-old girl, broke, motherless, and alone. When she met Jake, she must have seen a handsome, charismatic older man with a steady job—someone who could offer her stability. But he had offered her only misery. It wasn't surprising that she would have reached out to someone else. Perhaps anyone else—any man who would listen with a sympathetic ear, offer a comforting touch.

It wasn't difficult to picture. But whoever the man had been, Sheila had chosen, for whatever reason, not to seek his help, even after Jake discovered the truth. She could have told him about me; he could have staked a claim when I was put up for adoption. But either she hadn't wanted him to raise me, or he had declined.

For now, that was all I needed to know.

"I can't believe I'm saying this," I responded. "But at the moment, I don't give a damn either."

Fletcher's smile warmed me like sunlight. "You don't have to decide now," he said softly. "If you think later that you want to find out more, I'll help you, and so will Tia. But if you're happy leaving well enough alone—"

"Well enough," I interrupted, "seems pretty darn wonderful to me."

His eyes were dancing with happiness, and I knew mine looked the same. Here, on this ridge, in Fletcher's arms, was exactly where I wanted to be. It was where I was supposed to be. It was where I wanted to stay.

He leaned in to kiss me again, but this time I drew back. I had resolved to build my own happiness, and I was going to do it right. It was happening fast, but I knew that my feelings for Fletcher were already stronger than anything I had ever felt for my ex-fiancé. With Todd, I had been trying too hard. But loving Fletcher was effortless. He was *good,* and I trusted him. We had the same values; we wanted the same things out of life. But there was still a piece missing. I had sworn I wouldn't lure him into anything his damaged heart wasn't ready for. And I had to hold myself to that. Anything else would be unfair to both of us.

"Fletcher," I asked solemnly, watching his eyes, "tell me the truth. Do you trust me?"

He hesitated. It wasn't a long pause, but even a split second was enough to send a pang of anxiety through my chest. His eyes looked back into mine with a gaze that was unflinchingly honest.

"Almost," he answered.

I drew in a ragged breath, anxiety surging. I pulled myself in closer and caught his eyes. "I would never hurt you," I said softly. "You have to know that."

He let his own breath out with a shudder. "It isn't that."

I dropped back. "Then what is it?" I asked, frustrated. "What can I do?"

His eyes held mine. "Don't go back to Pittsburgh," he answered, his deep voice beseeching. "Stay here with me. I mean—at the inn."

I remembered the question that had puzzled me so last night—how he had asked me if I was surprised that Rosemary would want to commit herself to living and working here. He was afraid I wouldn't want to stay. Afraid that I, like every other woman he'd fallen for, would eventually ask him to choose between this place and me.

Before I could answer, he pulled away.

"I didn't tell you before," he began, his words rapid

and nervous. "But—I do have plans to fix up the old campground, hopefully by next spring. I want to operate my own camp in the summers. I've always wanted to teach kids about forestry—give them an appreciation of trees so they won't go back to the suburbs and hack down oaks just to avoid raking leaves. But I can't get a decent camp up and running by myself. I wouldn't know where to begin, and even if I did, I don't have the time. I need someone with experience at that sort of thing to take the idea and run with it—to brainstorm the development, handle the planning, and hire a really wonderful staff so that all I'll have to do is walk in and work with the kids." He paused. "You wouldn't know anyone who'd be interested in something like that, would you?"

My eyebrows rose. Whether he knew that he had just described my dream job, practically to the letter, I didn't know. I couldn't remember mentioning it. I had told him I was a camp director, but I hadn't told him how much I had always longed to make my living doing something completely creative—like writing children's curricula, or doing educational theater, or both. I had gone into classroom teaching because it was my mother's dream. She had wanted me to have a respectable job with a steady paycheck; I had wanted to make her happy.

Now it was time to make me happy.

"You could incorporate drama as a teaching tool," I suggested, the wheels in my head spinning. "All you'd need is a barn, or an amphitheater. Wildlife, forestry, survival skills, natural history . . . it wouldn't have to be just a summer camp. You could set yourself up to host school field trips in the spring and fall. Weekend workshops. Overnights. And if you're willing, a wood-carving workshop could be a big draw . . ."

His face broke into a smile. "So," he said, his eyes shining. "You're interested?"

I wrapped my arms around his neck again. "Fletcher," I said sincerely, "I would be happy with you anywhere. But as for this mountain spread of yours—"

I broke off with a grin. "I promise you, there's no place on earth I'd rather be. You haven't gotten me off of it yet, have you?"

His face beamed with pleasure, and he swept me in for a kiss. But once again—and with considerable effort—I held back.

I had not completely forgotten my resolutions. I might be on the verge of getting everything I'd ever wanted, but I would not let my soft heart get the best of me, even now. I had vowed that the new Meara would be nobody's doormat. And I meant nobody's.

"Mr. Black," I said formally, "are you offering me a full-time position, with a salary and benefits comparable to what I'm earning now?"

He blinked, then smiled at me. "Of course."

My heart leapt. I leaned into him, so close our noses touched.

"Is that *all* you're offering?" I whispered.

His eyes gave a devious flicker. "No."

"In that case," I replied, moving closer still, "I accept."

Epilogue

～

Eighteen Months Later

I STARED DOWN at the soft cotton blanket, watching its
folds rise and fall with the movement of the tiny chest
swaddled beneath. She was perfect. I couldn't stop looking
at her.

Anna Elizabeth Black lay sleeping peacefully, nestled
deep within the safe confines of the O'Rourke family
bassinet. I knew my mother and father would be happy
about that, since I had never actually slept in it myself. Its
aged wicker was frayed here and there, but the linens
were fresh, and it was beautiful.

Even more beautiful was the walnut crib that stood
waiting nearby—a crib which, if auctioned on the open
market, could probably pay for her college education. It
was an extraordinary sleigh-style crib, hand-carved from
top to bottom with a parade of forest animals to watch
over and delight her. Chipmunks, squirrels, raccoons,
rabbits, possums, and mice played peekaboo through the
bars. Birds lighted on the headboard and rails; two fawns

converged at the foot. From below, one could just spy a skunk hiding beneath the mattress.

I stretched out a tentative hand, daring to stroke her satiny temple with the back of my finger. She had a fine down of hair—auburn, like mine. Her eyes were blue, but I knew that could change. She was only two days old.

Footsteps sounded behind me. I didn't move as Fletcher's arms wrapped around my waist, then pulled me gingerly against him. He leaned down and rested his cheek against mine. "You should be in bed," he whispered. "She'll wake up soon enough."

"I know," I replied. "But I can't help watching her. I still can't believe she's real."

He chuckled. "She's real all right, and she's healthy as a horse. But you won't be if you don't get some sleep."

I relaxed against him further, having no desire to move. The moment was perfect, and I wanted to freeze it. I was happier than I had ever dreamed—more in love than I ever knew a person could be. I was able to give Fletcher everything I wanted and needed to give him, because he not only took, he gave back as well. And gave, and gave.

Anna startled, her little limbs jerking suddenly outward, straining against the blankets. I jumped.

Fletcher chuckled again, tightening his hold. "Will you relax? Newborns always do that. It's perfectly normal. See? She's already asleep again."

He was right. She was.

"Maybe I'm too nervous to be a mother," I said, only half joking. I had barely slept a wink since she'd been born—I couldn't go five minutes without making sure she was still breathing.

"You're going to be a wonderful mother," he assured

me patiently. "You already are. Besides, you have to be. I owe Tia seven more, remember?"

I rolled my eyes. There had been much discussion between siblings over the relative attributes of my pies versus Rosemary's, as well as over the question of whether Tia had played an instrumental role in our union. In the end, Fletcher had relented, insisting that there were far worse fates in the world than raising eight children with a woman he was certain would remain sexy well into her nineties. Of course, I had assumed he wasn't serious.

"Seven?" I repeated dubiously. "I'm thirty-one years old now. I've only got one good decade left, you know."

"Don't underestimate yourself," he said lightly, kissing me on the cheek. Then he released me, leaned over the bassinet, and caressed his daughter's temple himself. "Grandma and Aunt Susan are coming down next week," he whispered. "They can't wait to see her."

I smiled. Marrying Fletcher had been reward enough in itself, but becoming a certified member of the extended Black family was glorious. My Irish grandmother-in-law, in particular, had been spoiling me quite rotten, delighted to find someone who not only took an interest in her family recipes, but also enjoyed the retelling of her parents' immigration tales.

A slightly censored version of my story had been shared with the family's neighbors and friends, and all had received me warmly, including David Falcon, who made a point of insisting how delighted Mitchell would have been with the way things turned out. Only Estelle had greeted my moving into the inn with suspicion. But after a few months of seeing how clean I kept the kitchen, and probably also noting how incredibly happy her precious Fletcher had become, she had deigned to pronounce me worthy.

Tia, as promised, was ecstatic to have me as a sister-in-law. Though she still flitted about the country showing her work at art galleries and doing whatever it was she did with her large pool of equally jet-set friends, it appeared to both Fletcher and me that her time at the inn was steadily increasing. Not only had she painted every interior room in the new house, as well as the theater and other outbuildings at our developing camp, but she had outdone herself with the murals in Anna's room—creating a fanciful forest scene in shades of baby pink.

When she showed up the week that Anna was due with eight suitcases and a kitten, we began to wonder if her maternal side had finally caught up with her. A state patrol car had taken to appearing in the inn's parking lot whenever Tia was in town, and though Ben would admit to nothing, Fletcher was of the opinion that there was a new spring in his friend's step.

Only rarely anymore did my thoughts stray to Jake Kozen, who had been convicted on multiple felony charges and was now safely incarcerated. We had learned during the course of the trial that several area prosecutors had been champing at the bit for another shot at the man—apparently, he had escaped charges on more than one previous complaint of assault, due to lack of evidence. The prosecutor in my case tore into him like a pit bull, and the sentence rendered was harsh. Jake would not be in prison for life, but the prosecutor assured us that when he did get out, he would more likely be toting oxygen than a switchblade.

I still had no idea as to the identity of my birth father. And to my surprise, I still didn't care. I couldn't say that I would never get curious—that I would never again feel a yearning to know whose genes my body carried. Maybe

I would, someday. But for now, I was content. I was at peace with my past, and I was happy.

Fletcher adjusted Anna's blankets slightly, and she began to stir.

I grinned. "And you tell me to leave her alone," I scolded. "You're worse than I am."

He grinned back, then bent over to drop a soft kiss on his daughter's head.

"I'm glad at least one of us has experience with babies," I said warmly. Then my tone turned teasing. *"Momma Bear."*

He glowered. "You promised you were going to forget about that."

I chuckled. "I know I did. But it's so darned cute."

"Someday," he said with a growl, "I'm going to get that pesky sister of mine." He stepped behind me again, cradling me in his arms. *"But,* a promise is a promise. Seven kids in ten years is doable. So, how long do you need to recover in between pregnancies? A couple of weeks?"

I elbowed him in the ribs.

He groaned in mock agony. "Okay, okay. I'll settle for two more the fun way. We can become foster parents—maybe adopt some older siblings down the road. What do you say?"

"The *fun* way?" I protested. "Did *you* just go through nine months of pregnancy and eighteen hours of labor?"

He didn't answer. He just turned me around and kissed me, the way he always did, the way he was so blasted good at.

I leaned into him, relishing the face-to-face contact my pregnant belly had prevented for the last few months.

"You know I'd love to be a foster mother, and to adopt. But as for having two more children the fun way—"

I broke off and kissed him softly.

"I'd rather shoot for four."

ABOUT THE AUTHOR

Edie Claire worked as a veterinarian, a freelance medical writer/editor, and finally as a corporate technical writer before devoting herself to fiction. *Meant to Be* is her seventh novel—her second work of women's fiction. She lives in Pennsylvania with her husband, three children, and a menagerie of pets. You can visit her website at www.edieclaire.com; she also enjoys hearing from readers at *edieclaire@juno.com*.

THE EDITOR'S DIARY

~~~~~~

Dear Reader,

Everyone has a few dusty skeletons in their closet. But what happens when your past collides right into your present? Brush off those cobwebs and jump into THE CAJUN COWBOY and MEANT TO BE, our two Warner Forever titles this June.

Romantic Times declared "humor and **Sandra Hill** are a winning team" and they couldn't be more right in her newest book, **THE CAJUN COWBOY**. So bust out your tissues—you'll laugh so hard you'll cry! Louisiana beauty salon owner Charmaine Le Deux isn't having a great day. She's got a loan shark on her tail and she just discovered that Raoul Lanier, the man she thought she divorced years ago, is still her husband! The only good news: they've inherited a cattle ranch together, giving her the perfect place to lie low. But living with this hunk is anything but easy, especially for a born-again virgin who can't stop tingling whenever he enters a room. So between the Dixie Mafia on hot pursuit, her belly-dancing great-aunt, and St. Jude, patron saint of lost causes, will Charmaine resist his charms? Or can this Cajun cowboy sweet-talk his way back into his wife's arms before she unties the knot for good?

Journeying from the hot Louisiana sun and even hotter southern nights to the beauty and peace of Pennsylvania's Laurel Mountains, we present **Edie Claire**. *The Road to Romance* honored her previous book with their *Road* *to Romance Reviewer's Choice Award*, calling it "emotionally gripping, suspenseful, and superb" and her latest, **MEANT TO BE**, is even better. With just a phone call, Meara O'Rourke's life changes. Her birth mother has died, leaving her half of an historic inn. Unfortunately, the inn also belongs to Fletcher Black. Furious that Meara is intruding into his family home and determined to protect the land that means everything to him, Fletcher doesn't want her there. But Meara can't let go of the sadness—and the passion—in his eyes. As lies unravel and stunning new truths come to light, Meara must risk everything to learn about her past and take the most frightening—and exhilarating—step of all: to claim a love that was meant to be.

To find out more about Warner Forever, these June titles, and the authors, visit us at www.warnerforever.com.

With warmest wishes,

Karen Kosztolnyik

Karen Kosztolnyik, Senior Editor

P.S. Independence Day is right around the corner so declare your freedom by indulging in our two reasons to celebrate—fireworks guaranteed: **Pamela Britton** pens a witty Regency tale about an earl who must live for a month without any help to earn his inheritance and the woman who offers him love instead in **SCANDAL**; and **Lori Wilde** delivers the wickedly funny and steamy story of an FBI agent who's hot on the trail of an art thief, and the woman who's following him in **CHARMED AND DANGEROUS**.